Black Coal and White Lies

Geri Monaghan

abbott press®
A DIVISION OF WRITER'S DIGEST

Black Coal and White Lies

ISBN: 978-1-4582-0230-7 (sc)
ISBN: 978-1-4582-0229-1 (e)
ISBN: 978-1-4582-0231-4 (hc)

Abbott Press books may be ordered through booksellers or by contacting:

Abbott Press
1663 Liberty Drive
Bloomington, IN 47403
www.abbottpress.com
Phone: 1-866-697-5310

Library of Congress Control Number: 2012903335

Printed in the United States of America

Abbott Press rev. date:2/23/2012

In Loving Memory

Irene and Emil Greybeck

Salvatore M. Perella, Jr.

The magic of first love is our ignorance that it can never end.

—Benjamin Disraeli, British Prime Minister and Novelist

To my four daughters, Susan Perella, Cindy Perella, Beth Zullo, and Judy Zirkle. They have always been there for me while keeping me laughing and a part of their lives.

To my brother-in-law and sister-in-law who are very close friends, Carol and Bob DeBiase in Pennsylvania, who chauffeured me around their town, to the libraries, and to the museums to do research. For a while, their home was my home.

To my good friend Carol MacDonald in Vermont, who is always upbeat while encouraging me.

To the Central Intelligence Agency in Washington, DC for responding to my questions.

To Bob Page, Area Director of Sales & Marketing at Omni Hotels, Pittsburgh, for his photos and information regarding the William Penn Hotel.

And last, but definitely not least, to my husband, Art. Besides being a good cook, his love, patience, and understanding helped me immensely throughout the writing of this book.

Chapter 1

Ah, the wonderful summer of 1955—when it all started.

I love hearing the fantastic voice of Johnnie Ray singing "Such a Night." The music can be heard flowing from the living room into the street, filtered through the wooden screen door on the front porch. I play the last verse of the song, which relates the story of how his girl is gone, and then comes the dawn, with the night, heart, and love all gone. The song continues with a lot of *oo oo oo oo*s. I play this verse over and over, again and again.

As I accompany Johnnie with my soprano voice, I know it probably doesn't glorify the song in the least, but who cares? I don't, as singing makes me feel good just like it did in church this morning. Still wearing my blue taffeta dress trimmed daintily in black velvet with crinoline slips underneath, I pretend I'm standing in front of a microphone, and I feel like a star. Something about this song appeals to me, and I can't stop playing the last verse.

Eight or ten times after the night, heart, and love disappear, a man's voice is heard shouting above the redundant words, "Anna, shut that damn thing off before you drive the neighbors and me crazy. If I told you once, I've told you a million times, that's not music. It sounds like someone's in a lot of pain and needs a doctor."

I grimace and arrogantly say, "Believe it or not, Dad, this guy *is* in pain, as his girl has left him and taken her love too. He doesn't need a doctor. He needs her and her love."

He shakes his head while running his big coal miner's hand across his crew cut. My reply has placed a tiny grin on his face that I certainly would have missed had I not turned to give him a dirty look, as "Such a Night" is probably one of the greatest songs ever.

When Dad yells, I know he is disturbed, as few things upset him. The *oo oo oo oo*s have really pushed him to the point where he is compelled to say something or become utterly senseless. Deep down inside, I already knew it was bothering him, but I guess I was pushing him to see how long I could get away with it.

Up until this outburst, he had been enjoying the lovely Sunday afternoon by relaxing comfortably in his favorite brown leather chair, tucked in the corner of the dining room where the blue-and-beige–striped wallpaper-covered chimney juts out from the wall. His small wooden humidor with its bowed legs and curly design carved on the door is lined with tin inside and stands next to his chair, with a jar for a spittoon, and there's no more room for anything else.

In the humidor he stores his Half & Half tobacco, cigarette papers, and Copenhagen snuff. On the top of his smoking stand, a small lamp and ashtray sit on a starched white, lacy doily. This is my dad's corner, even though we all like to sit in his chair, as it's so cozy; you can smell him here, including the sweet smell of his tobacco. We all know to automatically relinquish the chair to him when he appears, even though no words are ever spoken.

His corner is situated across from the stairs leading to our second-floor bedrooms and bathroom. Now that I think about it, from that point he has the advantage of seeing everyone coming and going up and down the stairs or through the house to the front or back doors.

He enjoys reading the *Pittsburgh Press* on Sundays, which he had been doing while listening to my sad love song. Two of Dad's favorite things are reading the newspaper and listening to the Walter Winchell program on the radio. I really don't care for Mr. Winchell, as he talks fast, mixing entertainment gossip with world news, punctuated with the tapping of a telegraph key.

When Dad's doing these two things, I know I shouldn't bother him and try not to, but I can't just sit around and do nothing. Today I feel quite bored, so I'm searching for something, but I don't quite know what that something is.

Dad definitely isn't interested in today's music. "Listen to some jazz, the blues, or the big bands if you want to hear good music. Your idea of music is loud and noisy, and half the time the words don't make sense."

With a little sarcasm I reply, "Loud? Noisy? Gosh, Dad, maybe you can write a blues song using those words. I never say anything when you sit down at the piano and start playing 'Wish I Were Single Again,' even though it upsets Mom quite a bit." Of course we both know that is when he's had a few too many whiskeys.

He shakes his head again, mumbling something about teenagers and how he'll never understand them, as he sits in his chair to continue reading the Sunday paper.

Dad actually loves music and is a great piano player. He can't read musical notes but can hear a song once, sit down at the piano, and play it perfectly. I heard Aunt Ida say once that he's really good even though he plays by ear. I was little at the time when I heard it, and I told Aunt Ida, "He plays the piano with his fingers, not his ear." Everyone laughed at me and had to explain what they meant.

He plays the old songs that he loves so much on our old Chauncey grand piano, which devours our small living room. He can easily play the songs I like, but he always tells me they don't make any sense. I disagree with him, as they certainly make a lot of sense to me. They appeal to my emotions, and sometimes the words are so true that I feel like many of the songs were written just for me.

Even though I love listening to Johnnie Ray, I realize the time has come to get on with another song. Actually, I'm surprised I got away with playing it over and over this long. I'd have continued listening to Johnnie Ray all afternoon if Dad hadn't yelled at me.

Maybe if I played one more song, Dad might begin to enjoy my kind of music. Playing "Cross Over the Bridge" by Patti Page is just not the same. After listening to it twice, I shut it off and close the door so the entire turntable folds into the Philco radio and phonograph console.

I push open the creaky wooden screen door to the front porch and let it slam shut, thus allowing Dad to know I wasn't very happy giving up Johnnie Ray.

Deciding not to sit on the glider, I slide my hand down the back of my dress to smooth it out and sit on the front steps of the wooden porch, being careful of splinters.

I'm underneath a green canvas awning that extends outward from the porch roof and can be rolled up when not in use. A wide scalloped edge trimmed in white hangs from the awning and not only keeps the sun off the porch but also helps to hide anyone sitting on the glider. People walking down the front brick sidewalk would actually have to stick their heads under the awning to see who's sitting on the glider. That's why I sit on the steps—so I don't miss anybody or anything.

With my elbows resting on my knees and palms upward, I rest my chin in my hands and listen to the sounds around me. I can hear Janet, Susan, and Connie, the three little neighbor girls, giggling next door in the other half of our double house; Matt and his twin brother, Mark, who live in the next double house, arguing; a screen door slamming shut; and a dog barking in the distance.

The odors of the Polish, Slovak, Russian, Hungarian, Irish, German, and English Sunday dinners cooking in the various houses mingle together, creating a chef's symphony and permeating the air. After all, it is Sunday, and everyone, no matter what nationality, always has a huge meal on Sundays to share with their family.

Sighing, I wonder what could be wrong with me today and why I enjoy hearing Johnnie Ray sing the last part of that song over and over. It really doesn't matter; they're only words.

All my life, I have been surrounded by laughter, tears, and noise created by my four sisters and parents. If my sisters weren't arguing about clothes and who gets the bathroom first, then my mom and dad were arguing about money or my dad having a drink or two of whiskey.

My two oldest sisters, Edna and Liz, are married and live in the same town, but it's just not the same as living in the same house. Martha's in college and decided to stay there for the summer. For that, I'm elated, as she didn't get along with any of us. Jo just graduated from high school and moved to another state, where she had a job offer. I remember how Mom wasn't very happy about it, but Jo knew throughout all her high school years that she would be leaving the day after she graduated, as she and Mom never did hit it off.

For two months now, I have lived alone with Mom and Dad, and it's not only quiet but also lonesome; I don't have anyone to confide in except my girlfriends. It's not quite the same since they don't live with me. I only wish Mom and Dad could express more physical love, such as hugging and kissing, toward me.

Maybe next week when I turn sweet sixteen I'll start having fun. I wish I could fall in love, but everyone always tells me to be careful of what I wish for. If I only knew at that time how true that saying was and how there is love that can almost destroy you.

Chapter 2

Sweet sixteen and never really been kissed is true for me. I twirl my hair around my finger, feeling the silkiness of it. My thick, dark hair is shoulder length, and I love twirling it.

So far my kisses have emerged from playing spin the bottle at my friend's ninth birthday party—one kiss partially missed when I turned my head and received saliva on my cheek instead, and a nice one that occurred this past spring.

This last kiss was after the junior/senior prom that I attended this past April with Jack Borski.

Jack's a great guy, polite and good-looking, and I like him more than I've ever liked anyone. His brown curly hair and glasses make him look intelligent. He's a wrestler and an honor student. A lot of girls are really crazy over him, but I have the privilege of knowing him, since we share an algebra class.

It all happened this past spring on a Tuesday as I was walking through the hall to my next class. Everyone was moving slowly, yapping away, and small groups were forming. I guess they must have had spring fever.

Out of nowhere I heard my name being called. I turned and Jack caught up to me. "Anna, do you mind if I walk you home from school today?"

Hiding my astonishment, since I only knew Jack from algebra and the drama club, I calmly said, "You do know I live on Fifth Street, which is about eighteen blocks away, don't you?"

He answered with a cute smile that gave birth to dimples. "Yes, I know, but I want to ask you something."

Curiosity overcame me, but, of course, I couldn't let him know. "Okay, meet me in front of the school at the end of the front sidewalk."

I had doubts he'd show, but true to his word, he met me in the front of the school. He carried my books, and all I could think of was how nice, polite, and handsome he was, with that curly hair and glasses.

We talked about friends and school, and when we finally reached Fifth Street, he asked me, "Anna, would you go to the junior/senior prom with me?"

I couldn't contain my excitement and, without thinking, blurted out, "I'd love to, Jack."

Me, a lowly sophomore, and Jack, a mighty junior. Wow, what a thrill for me to be asked to the junior/senior prom!

Smiling, he said, "Great! We'll double-date with my brother and his girl, since he'll be driving my dad's car. Mom will probably be calling you to find out the color of your gown."

"Okay. By the way, how are you getting home now?" I only asked because he lived at Mine 37, five miles away. Our town, Kolfield, is surrounded by mines that are like little towns with rows of double houses and a company store. By walking me home he missed his bus.

He handed my books back. "I'll walk, but maybe one of my friends will drive by and give me a ride. See you in school tomorrow."

Knowing my mother wouldn't be happy because he's Polish and Catholic bothered me a little, but I didn't care. It was time for me to choose my dates. So far she hasn't allowed me to date, and if she did, it would have to be someone she approves.

When I told Mom, she was a little upset at first, but then my older sister Liz talked to her later that evening. Liz emphasized the fact that it was a prom, not a wedding. Mom then consented.

Jack's mother called me the following week, and her voice was mellow and friendly, as if she already knew me.

Mom had answered the phone and handed it to me, moving her eyebrows inquisitively, creating a furrow between them.

After saying hello, a melodious voice came out of the earpiece. "Hi, Anna. I'm Jack's mother."

"Oh, hi. Jack said you'd be calling me."

"I'm calling to find out the color of your gown so we can order flowers to match it."

"My gown is yellow trimmed in white."

"That's a lovely color. I know you're going to enjoy the prom and have fun. I'm looking forward to meeting you. Jack has told me so much about you."

"Thank you. I'm looking forward to meeting you too," I replied, clutching the big black phone receiver with both hands, wondering what Jack had told her.

"Great. I'll see you then. Bye."

"Bye."

The night of the prom, his brother, Bob, parked their dad's Ford in front of our house. He waited there with his date, who was sitting as close as she could to him without wrinkling her gown.

Mom answered the front door, and when I walked into the living room, Jack's face lit up. My strapless yellow gown had a formfitting bodice and then became full, made possible by crinoline slips underneath. My elbow-length white gloves accented the gown, making me feel like an actress in a movie.

My eyes must have lit up too, as he looked so cool in his navy-blue suit, white shirt, and light-blue tie. As I walked toward him, a scent became noticeable and reminded me of walking through the woods.

Jack handed me a rectangular-shaped white box. When I opened it, I smiled and whispered, "They're beautiful."

The wrist corsage consisted of white roses, yellow tea roses, baby's breath, green leaves, and ferns. Jack placed the corsage on my wrist as we smiled at each other, and I hoped he didn't notice my nervousness.

Mom was polite, smiling but not overly friendly, and took only one picture. She had done this so much over the years with my older sisters that it must have been getting boring for her.

Dad entered the front room to meet Jack and shake his hand. Jack's dad was a coal miner too, and Dad knew him. After they exchanged a few words, we walked out the front door with all the neighborhood kids hanging around to see my gown and my date. The girls, with their eyes and smiles so big, made little sighs of excitement while the boys watched and waited nearby so they could finish playing baseball.

Jack and Bob promised their mother they would return with us to their house so she could take a few pictures.

We rode down their street with rows of identical houses facing each other. As we pulled in front of his house, I realized how much it looked like our double house.

Jack got out and ran around to open the door for me. He was so sweet.

Bob and his date took the lead as we climbed the wooden steps to the front porch. Jack held my elbow for support so I didn't trip and fall.

As we entered the house, freshly cooked kielbasa lingered in the air. We were invited into a clean and tidy living room with a large brown sofa and matching armchair. The chair was definitely someone's favorite chair, as the armrests were quite worn. A maple rocking chair adorned with flowered cushions sat in a corner and, of course, a television sat waiting to be turned on.

Family pictures hung on one wall, showing the brothers in their uniforms for various sports events, and a wedding picture of their mother and father. A picture of Christ adorned in a red robe with a blue shroud and a red heart glowing on his chest was on the other wall.

Their mother, Kathryn, was a kind, gentle, loving person, just as I had imagined, while their father liked to laugh and joke around. She reminded me of the mother in the story of Dick and Jane, who had the perfect family, which I learned to read in first grade.

Kathryn just couldn't take enough pictures until finally her boys told her in unison, "Stop." Their father agreed with them while we all laughed. She gave all of us a big hug and ordered us to have a great time.

As we drove away, their father's arm encircled their mother's back as they stood together on the front porch waving while the neighbors sat on their porches smiling. Remembering that scene, I envy Jack and Bob because of the way their mother loves them.

After arriving at the high school and parking the car, we walked up the long sidewalk to the main entrance. A lot of the underclassmen lined up and were leaning and half-sitting on the black metal railings running parallel with the walk to the front door. They wanted to see the exquisite couples and their colorful outfits.

At the prom we danced on the stage in the auditorium and had a good time. Couples, when not dancing, sat in the auditorium seats facing the stage. The smell of flowers, shampoos, aftershave lotions, and powders surrounded all of us. It was unbelievable that these were the same kids we saw day after day in school. Tonight they were all beautiful and handsome, dressed up like movie stars.

At intermission we gathered in the music room, down the hall from the auditorium, for refreshments. Candid pictures of us mingling and eating were taken for the yearbook.

Several long tables had been set up and covered with tablecloths. They contained quite an assortment of food, from pierogi, a variety of sandwiches, sausages, and meatballs to teacakes, nut rolls, and cookies. We moved in a line around the tables so we could have access to everything.

Smelling the foods made me hungry, as I was too nervous to eat my supper. Seeing the variety of food the parents had volunteered to make for us made me think of all of the nationalities involved in our school.

Of course I sampled very little of the food, just like most of the girls. I didn't want to drop anything on my gown or look like a starved animal pouncing on the food. It didn't seem to matter to the guys as they filled their plates with everything.

I did enjoy myself, but somehow I felt like I didn't fit in with all of the other kids—probably because they were juniors and seniors and were Jack's friends, not mine, even though I knew them from school. Maybe it was because I felt the other girls looked more enchanting with their self-confidence and makeup, which I didn't wear.

Afterward, Bob and his date waited in the car while Jack walked me to my front door.

"I hope you had a nice time," Jack said as he placed his hands on my upper arms. His hands felt warm and moist.

"Yes, I did. Thanks for inviting me."

With that he leaned forward and kissed me on my mouth. It was a nice kiss, but there were no shooting stars or fireworks. What was missing, I don't know. Maybe I was going overboard with anticipation and making too much of it, or maybe it was me. Maybe I just didn't know how to kiss.

After that night we saw each other during the day in school, but before you knew it, school was out and summer's now here.

We're still friends, and he told me he has to work all summer but will call me when he can. I'm looking forward to his calls, and on the last day of school he walked me outside and gave me a big hug and a quick kiss.

After all, we live too far from each other to be able to see one another all the time.

The problem is, I haven't heard from Jack at all, not even a telephone call. It hurts a little, but I suppose he's really busy or maybe he just needed a date for the prom and that's why he asked me. We'll see what happens when we go back to school in September.

Never in the world did I dream that an event would take place in a couple of weeks that would determine there was no hope for a real relationship between Jack and me.

Chapter 3

***

As I sit on the front porch steps, I recall there was another time or two I had a kiss but none that really made an impression on me. Up until this time in my life, kisses to me were just a way of shaking hands, but you just touched lips instead. Besides, they were usually with your relatives when you saw them, saying good-bye or having to thank them for something.

A couple of my girlfriends go crazy over their boyfriend's kisses and rave about it, but I don't understand all the hullabaloo. You'd think it was greater than going to the movie theater.

Thinking of the movie theater reminds me of James Dean. Now he's one good-looking guy, and I wouldn't mind trying a kiss with him.

The movie theater used to be the most important thing to me. I remember Jo dragging me along to the Saturday afternoon matinees, as she had no choice if she wanted to go. Dad would give us each a dime. Nine cents was our admission, and the extra penny was to buy a long, thick pretzel stick.

It wasn't fair, as he gave Martha and Liz, our older sisters, twenty cents to go to the movies.

Dad used to laugh and say, "Yes, but it costs them fifteen cents to get in, as they're older and they go at night. When the two of you are older, then it will cost you more and I'll give you more."

We could never win that argument, no matter how much we nagged. Living in a small town has its advantages, such as being able to walk to many places and not needing to drive.

I do love my hometown of Kolfield, nestled among the black coal-filled mountains in Western Pennsylvania. It may be a small town, but it is full of hardworking, friendly people with big hearts.

Once a robust mining town overflowing with football parents, Kolfield is still overflowing with them. Some parents never finished high school but are determined their kids will graduate and get a job, but not in the coal mines. The parents are disciplined, hardworking, and not preoccupied with obtaining a lot of material things. These are qualities needed to start your life over in a foreign country.

My friends are a mixture of rich and poor. Guess I'm in between—not rich and, yet, not poor. Maybe that's what it means when people say the middle-class people. My friends' fathers are a mixture of doctors, dentists, miners, store clerks, bartenders, steel mill workers, and store or restaurant owners.

It is interesting that the doctors, lawyers, and more affluent people live above Main Avenue. The higher the avenue on which families reside, usually the richer they are. The farther down you live, the poorer you are; if you live below the "railroad tracks," that is really poor. It's slowly changing though.

Our house is located on the corner of Fifth Street and an alley. We can peer out the upstairs windows overlooking the alley and the roofs of other houses, as they form a row down the street to the railroad tracks.

The houses below the alley but above the railroad tracks are privately owned. This is easy to tell by the different colorful paints adorning the houses and trim. Neatly pruned shade trees, manicured lawns, and colorful flowers and bushes surround these houses with some type of vegetable garden in the backyard. The porches are in great shape, with privacy panels and decorated with built-in flower boxes that hold bright multicolored flowers.

The bluish-gray houses we live in are rental houses once owned by the mining company but now owned by Mrs. Zakowski, an elderly widow, who comes around each month to collect the rental fees.

Mrs. Zakowski is an amazing woman, and no one knows her exact age, but many think she is somewhere in her late seventies or early eighties.

When she comes around to collect the rent, musty air and an odor of mothballs surround her. She wears heavy cotton stockings that are an ugly tan color. They're rolled up and held in place with garters just below her knees. She wears plain black shoes with a thick heel and a rubber band around each shoe. The rubber bands must keep the shoes on her feet—or else why would you wear them? Her wrinkled dark dresses contain no color whatsoever, and no one knows whether she has several dresses or wears the same one continuously, as they are so dark and dull.

There's always a small black hat perched on the top of her head that looks like it's been dumped there unintentionally and forgotten. She carries a small leather purse held together by rubber bands into which she stuffs the rent money after rolling it up.

This little elderly lady with white hair and wrinkles presents quite a picture, and the children are intrigued as they watch her unwind the rubber bands and insert the money. Being very cautious, she never fails to rewrap the rubber bands around the purse, lest the money might fall out.

Her possessions also include a receipt book with a rubber band holding the receipts in place. Children dubbed her the "rubber band lady." The giggles of the children are always stifled by stern looks from the parents.

Mrs. Zakowski collects our monthly rental fee, which has increased over the years from seven dollars to eighteen dollars a month.

I'm happy with our house although I know Mom and Dad would love to buy their own house. Maybe they can, once I graduate and can help them.

Lately I've been feeling as though I might explode. I stand and stretch a little before walking over and dropping myself on the green metal glider adorned with canvas-covered cushions—green, of course, to match the awnings.

The glider makes a comforting squeaking sound as I move back and forth. My thoughts are calmed, and I doze off slightly but not into a deep sleep as the telephone rings twice. It's too expensive for each home to have its own telephone line so we have a four party line. Each party has a different set of rings and can pick up the phone and listen to the other's conversation. Two rings mean someone is calling us.

Dad yells out the front door from his easy chair in the dining room, "You might as well answer it, Anna. It's probably for you anyway." Dad has realized over the years that the telephone is practically always for one of his daughters and feels he shouldn't have to get up and answer it. Now no one is rushing to get to the telephone, as there are only my parents and me living here.

Jumping up I move swiftly from the glider through the front screen door, through the living room, and around the dining room table, where the phone is located on its own little table. Dad always says we can move like lightning when the telephone rings.

When I pick up the receiver, the familiar and friendly voice of Sonya, one of my best friends, says, "Hey, Anna, what are you doing?"

"Nothing really. Just sitting on the front porch thinking about things. What are you up to?"

"Nothing much. I was playing a game of cards with my younger brother until my sister came home and I just had to call you and tell you. She saw a poster downtown in the Main Line Drugstore window advertising the carnival. It's coming to Kolfield in a few weeks. In fact, it will start setting up two weeks from tomorrow. I wanted to make sure you knew it was coming so we could plan on going."

"Sounds great to me. I need some fun. Mom isn't home right now, and you know I've got to get permission. I don't think it'll be a problem, but I'll let you know tomorrow definitely."

"Hey, maybe we can sneak to the other side, where those weird shows are, and see what they're really like. I heard they had a bearded lady in the show last year."

Laughing, I reply, "I don't know if that is possible, but if they advertise a bearded lady and you have to pay to see it, I guess it has to be true. We can check it out even though I'm not allowed on that side of the carnival."

"Did you hear about Beverly getting grounded for a week?"

"No, what happened?"

"She was sitting in the back in the last booth at Trumbull's Drugstore. Thinking no one could see her, she lit up a cigarette, and who walks in but her dad. He grabbed her by her arm and pulled her out of the drugstore after putting the cigarette out in the ashtray. She was crying and saying she'd never do it again."

"Wow, how embarrassing. I guess she won't try smoking again, will she?"

"You know Bev. We'll see. Thank goodness she's only grounded for a week. Otherwise she'd miss the carnival."

"We have to ask Connie too. Anyway, I'll call you tomorrow about the carnival."

"Okay, see you later, alligator."

"After 'while, crocodile," I say as I hang up the black telephone receiver.

After hanging up the phone, I go back to the glider to continue my daydreams.

Never in my wildest dreams did I imagine that my going to the carnival in a few weeks would affect me for the rest of my life.

Chapter 4

⟡

Continuing my daydreams while sitting on the glider, I think about my mother and father. I'm not judging my mother or father, but I don't understand either of them. They really had no role models while growing up and are learning as they go along—probably like everyone else does when they become parents. But you'd think that since I'm their fifth and last child, they would have learned something about showing their love by now.

Granted, I get away with a lot more than my sisters, but I just think my parents are tired and want to enjoy life a little more instead of having me hanging around. After all, Mom is forty-nine years old, and Dad is sixty-one.

My mother and father are not the parents portrayed in *Fun with Dick and Jane*. How I loved those books in first grade, as everything was so perfect. I still love the book *Little Women* and can lose myself in the story, pretending the March family is our family and that we are always happy and loving.

Come to think of it, I notice that almost all newspaper and magazine advertisements, ranging from kitchen appliances to Schlitz Beer, show the woman wearing a nice dress, which is covered by an apron, and high heels while cooking for the family or serving the man his beer. The husband is usually dressed up in a suit and tie. It leads you to think that the husband comes home and kisses his wife hello and they all sit down and have a nice dinner while they talk about the day's events. Imagine all men wearing a suit and tie to work. Heck, they'd never last in a coal mine.

At least, that is what it makes me believe. "Believe" is a strong word, and I have known that in my life I need to believe in perfect families. Maybe that is why I love to read so much and get lost in the fairy tales; real life isn't like that—at least it hasn't been in my world.

We have adequate clean clothes (even though most of mine are hand-me-downs from my older sisters), meals on the table, and a car, and we live in a rented half double house, so the material things are not lacking. I feel it's the love that's missing—the hugs, the touches, and the kisses. Those are the things I wish I had more of from my parents.

Dad showed us more love than Mom by talking nicely to us, giving us piggyback rides when we were little, and giving us an extra nickel once in a while. He probably spent more time with us than Mom did even though he worked a lot. She was always busy with housework.

Dad has big hands, and his nose is a little flat and out of shape but doesn't take away from his handsome features. In fact, the shape of his nose gives his face character along with his blue eyes that are always twinkling and a mouth that is always smiling. He is tall, very muscular, and strong. He loves to laugh and loves people regardless of whether their name ends in the letters *ski* or a vowel. Some of his best friends live below the railroad tracks, where he joins them on occasion for whiskey and nut rolls or poppy seed rolls. Of course, Mom doesn't approve and gets angry with him.

Dad always wears his light-brown hair cut short in a crew cut, as he says it is easier to take care of (probably easier to get the coal dust out of it too).

He often relates the story to us that when he was a boy he roller-skated with his hands stuck inside his front pockets. He was skating on the sidewalk in front of Nelson's Store on the corner of Ninth Street and Main Avenue when he tripped on a crack in the sidewalk. Since he couldn't get his hands out of his pockets in time, he fell flat on his face and broke his nose. He said he never roller-skated again with his hands in his pockets.

Funny how you remember a story like that and the lesson it carries. That story made me keep my hands free and out of my pockets when I roller-skated, but it also left me with the fear of falling on my face and breaking my nose, so I was never a good roller skater.

Dad is very smart even though he had to quit school after eighth grade and work in the coal mines at the age of sixteen. He had no choice, as he had to go to work and help support his family. He joined the army as soon as he reached the age of twenty-one, and he was honorably discharged seven years later and then went back to the coal mines.

Mom always tells us not to gossip or let anyone know what goes on in our house. Wow, would she be upset if she knew that Jo and I know her deepest secret. We haven't told anyone, not even our other sisters, as we don't want a beating. Mom would want to know how we found out, and we can't tell her. I'm always afraid Jo will blurt it out when she and Mom argue but so far, so good. Maybe someday Mom will tell us.

Chapter 5

⁓⁓

As I continue to glide back and forth, I'm glad that Dad retired last September. He worked very hard in the coal mines for over forty years. He was a motorman, and when he retired was an assistant motor boss. Motormen operate the motors used in the transportation of loaded cars from switches or sidings in the mines to the shaft and of empty cars from the shaft to the switches or sidings.

Dad would come home filthy, covered with coal dust from head to toe. Most of the time he'd shower in the coal mine showers, but when they were crowded he came home to bathe.

Not only was it a filthy job, it wasn't healthy, as he was constantly breathing in the coal dust, which in turn created the black lung disease that so many miners developed, including him. He kept his work clothes in the basement and, therefore, entered and left through the basement doors. That way he didn't track the coal dust through the house.

We have a dark, old basement, and Dad always hung up his mining clothes on long, thick nails sticking out of a long slender board on the wall at the bottom of the stairs. My mother would wash them separately and then hang them back up on the nails for him to wear.

Shelves situated at the bottom of the steps are where we keep canned food. Sometimes I have to go down and get a can or jar off the shelf for my mother. When I do, I love touching the mining clothes, before they are washed (only with my pointer finger though), amazed at how black the coal dust is.

To enter the cellar from the outside, we have to walk down four cement steps under the back porch, as our back porch is situated about eight feet off the ground on high wooden posts overlooking the alley.

The foundation of the house, consisting of the cellar walls, was built with large rocks cemented together. At the entrance to the cellar, one-sixth of the basement, a corner, is elevated two feet from the ground by a stone wall, where "stuff" is stored. The "stuff" consisted of toys, an outgrown crib, curtain rods—things not needed anymore but which are still usable.

Since we just came out of World War II, everyone is still in the habit of saving everything, as there was a shortage of goods during that time. The war was a difficult time for all, and people had to do without many things, including gas, food, clothes, shoes, and many other things that could have made their lives more comfortable. Ten years later everyone is still saving everything, either from habit or fear of another world war.

Directly across the room are the nails that hold my father's work clothes. These are near the bottom of the stairs going up to the kitchen. The coal furnace is in the middle and separates that area from the area where Mom's wringer washer and tubs are located. We can actually walk or run around the furnace (as I have had to do when my sister Jo was chasing me), ducking our heads only under the pipe leading to the chimney.

Our coal storage bin is located under the front porch. The coal is delivered through a small window that has a wooden door on it and is located on the side by the alley. The coal truck pulls up and sticks the chute into the window and the coal slides down the chute into that room.

Then Dad opens the little door inside the cellar leading to the coal bin and takes it out, shovelful by shovelful, to throw in the furnace when needed. He always goes down and stokes the furnace many times during the winter months. No wonder he's so strong and muscular.

We are blessed that we can afford to have coal delivered to us. Some of my poorer friends, when we were younger, used to walk along the railroad tracks carrying a bucket. They would fill it with coal chunks that had fallen off the railroad cars. Sometimes I'd help them, being very careful not to get too dirty, as I wasn't allowed to be near the railroad tracks.

A lump of coal's beauty never ceases to amaze me. It might look like a piece of glass on one side, shiny and smooth, while the other side can be rough. Streaks of color appear in it if you look hard enough. When the sun hits the coal dust laying along the railroad tracks the right way, it actually sparkles and twinkles like little stars or tiny diamonds.

We're fortunate because our cellar floor is cement, and most of the other houses have dirt floors so their washing machines are in the kitchen. That means on washday their entire kitchen is utilized for washing clothes, which creates a lot of confusion.

After taking off his dirty clothes, Dad would come up the old wooden, linoleum-covered stairs to the kitchen. The basement area also gives him privacy from all of the women of the house. Of course, we're all afraid of spiders and mice so we have never been apt to venture down there—at least no farther than the shelves to get something off of them or to give Mom the sheets on washday.

Going down there has never bothered me if someone else is with me or if Mom is washing clothes. Otherwise, I always hope Mom sends one of my older sisters down, as I am plain scared that maybe a rat will jump on me.

Jo always laughed at me and called me a scaredy-cat and other names to taunt me. She wanted me to be brave like her, but I couldn't help the way I felt.

Rocking back and forth on the glider, I laugh to myself as I think about Jo and how much I miss her, even though she picked on me a lot. I still have Liz and Edna to visit, and Martha is in college, but Jo and I had a bond; she was the leader and I was the follower, and now I'm not sure if I know how to lead myself.

Most of the time she never allowed me to go with her and her friends, as she said I was too young. I could never understand her thinking, as we're only eighteen months apart. Maybe that was her way of trying to toughen me up. Yes, I definitely miss her, and I'm sure she misses me, but I know she doesn't miss living here because now she's her own boss.

Someday I'll be my own boss and be independent. If only I could've seen the future, but it was good I couldn't because I'd never have believed that society could be so cruel.

Chapter 6

My thoughts are interrupted as a car turns the corner into the alley by our street, but it isn't anyone I know, and the car keeps on going.

Returning my thoughts to Dad, I wonder what it was like when he was growing up. Since his retirement last year, he sits in his favorite chair in his corner of the dining room with his little smoking cabinet readily available if he wants a cigarette.

Located in the ceiling above his chair, which is also the floor of the upstairs bathroom, there is a small circular vent with a diameter of ten to twelve inches. This is where hot air escapes to the bathroom upstairs, as we have no actual heat piped or pushed upstairs. It has a black iron grill lid designed with a lot of open areas on it for the heat to rise through. Placing your fingers in these open areas and pulling upward can remove this grill.

Laughing to myself, I recall one of the things my sister Jo and I did when we were younger. Joan was often called Chee Chee, Jobug, or Jo. The nickname Chee Chee is a monkey's name. Everyone thought she was active like a monkey. She got the name Jobug because she was forever catching bugs and looking at them, cutting the big black ants in half with scissors or just playing with the different varieties of insects. I always call her Jo.

Jo is the next to the youngest, being eighteen months older than me. She's beautiful with bright blue eyes and our mother's flawless skin. She has light-brown hair that has a reddish shine to it, and she always wears makeup. Jo is not only pretty and very popular but tough, streetwise, and a tomboy, forever tagging along with Dad in his projects and going everywhere with him.

When Dad was reading the newspaper in his favorite chair and we wanted his undivided attention, Jo and I would go upstairs to the bathroom, remove the vent, and play this game we made up. We'd start to spit through the vent, but just before the saliva would drop, we'd suck it back up. We had to see who could let it go the longest without falling. Of course, if it dropped, you were the loser. When it did drop, it would land on Dad's newspaper that he was reading. Dad knew right away who it was and would say, "Damn you, Jo and Anna, stop that." We can joke with Dad, as he's a pretty good sport about everything, and Jo and I do love to laugh.

Jo also loved playing that same game with me after she didn't like something I said or did. I would lie flat on my back, and she would sit on my stomach, holding my hands back above my head to the floor. She'd stick her face right above my face and start to spit, but before the saliva dropped, she'd suck it back up. I'd be twisting my head from left to right, trying to avoid it. If the saliva fell, she'd take off before I could catch her, as I had to wipe my face and get up before going after her. Of course, I couldn't hurt her, as she was stronger than me, and besides, she ran faster. Thank goodness we outgrew that game.

The realization of how much I miss her surfaces as I think about all of the things we did together while growing up. Even though she bullied and teased me continuously, I love her a lot and especially miss our laughter together.

We always walked to church together no matter how bad it was snowing or how cold it was outside. Granted, our church is only five blocks away, but walking in temperatures in the teens made it quite uncomfortable.

Once it was so cold outside that our boogers froze together in our noses and the snow crackled under our feet as we walked. That's when we knew it was close to zero degrees. We were trying to walk up our icy street to go to church and would go three steps forward and slide two steps back, three steps forward and two steps back. We'd laugh because it was taking us so long to walk up the hill, and yet our laughter seemed to slow us down all the more. We were late for church but were still chuckling as we entered the vestibule. In fact, when I think about it, we seemed to giggle at everything.

Sometimes while singing in the choir at church we would start. The choir was in front of the congregation, and since we weren't supposed to giggle, any little thing that happened made us do it all the more. Our shoulders would be shaking as we tried to keep our heads down into our hymnals. If we were taking communion and someone farted or burped, these outbursts would start. When we laughed we had to be careful not to spill some of the grape juice out of the communion glass. We didn't dare look at the choir director, as we knew she was giving us the evil eye.

In our church we were baptized at the age of eleven or twelve. I don't know why, but Jo and I were baptized on the same Sunday even though we were eighteen months apart.

Being very serious, we took our places, facing the altar with our backs toward the entire congregation. When the minister placed his hand on Jo's head and mine at the same time, it started. Why? I don't know, except when we had to be serious, there was no way to contain our laughter. The minister felt our heads shaking and never said a word to us but did press down on our heads a little harder. He didn't know, but that made it worse.

We just couldn't help getting the giggles, and no matter who started, it was contagious for the other one. Even though we always got into trouble for doing it at the wrong times, it didn't stop us. It seemed we had no control over it.

When I was ten years old, we walked through the alleys to our sister's house. There was snow on the ground, and the air was quite chilly. By the time some of the hand-me-down underwear got to me, they were kind of worn and the elastic was loose. As we were walking, my underpants began to move downward, and I tugged on my dress to pull them up and walked slowly and carefully.

Jo said, "Come on, Anna, what's the matter with you? You're so slow today."

I replied cautiously, "Nothing."

After all, I didn't want her making fun of me. Suddenly, my underpants fell down, landing right around my ankles. Jo practically rolled in the alley with laughter. At the sight of her laughing, I started laughing so hard even though I knew she would make fun of me later and I'd never hear the end of it.

Making sure no one was watching, I pulled them up and bunched them together at the top to hold them in place until I ran back home and exchanged them for a better pair. That pair of underwear went into the trash, as I never wanted to be embarrassed again.

I miss that laughter. That incident would be nothing compared to the humiliation that would center on me later in life.

Chapter 7

⁓⁓⁓

Shifting my position on the glider, I think about Dad and how hard he worked to make sure we had food on the table and clothes on our backs.

In my mind I see the miners sitting in the open rail cars, with their hard hats with carbide lamps attached and metal lunch buckets on their laps. I have seen them. What I can't even imagine is the darkness or dangers that await them when they enter that black hole.

Dad always carried a metal lunch pail with a lid so the rats wouldn't eat his lunch, he said. He bought a lock to hold the lid on the pail because the rats were so big that they could lift up the cover on the pails if they weren't locked on tight. I don't know if he was teasing us or if it was really true, but I know there was a lock on his metal lunch pail.

The carbide lamp that attached to his miner's helmet always interested me. Once in a while he would light it for us so we could see how it worked. It had a bluish flame and an awful smell. The miners needed every light they could get once they reached the bowels of the earth. A blackness enveloped you once the entrance diminished and vanished from sight.

Dad would fold a newspaper and stuff it in his pocket or tear sheets out of a Sears catalog. I always thought he took them to read, but when I became older Jo told me it was in case he had to go to the bathroom while walking to or from work. It was during and right after World War II, so I suppose newspaper and catalog pages were cheaper than a roll of toilet paper, and something's better than nothing.

Living with so many women in the house—let alone being a coal miner—had to be difficult for Dad. He was definitely outnumbered.

Chuckling to myself, I think of the Friday nights when he had to let go and party a little. He'd go to the local bar downtown and come home as a happy drunk, singing in his deep baritone voice.

A lot of the miners enjoy going to the Kolfield Hotel that is situated right next to the Fire Hall on Fifteenth Street between Main Avenue and Sunshine Avenue. Cement steps and a railing led from the front sidewalk down to the basement, where a miner can enter with his work clothes on.

Several showers and a room are available to the miners so they can shower and change their clothes before going upstairs to the bar.

Dad always came home first and bathed before going downtown—that is, if he didn't bathe in the large community showers at the mine.

Another favorite place for the miners to hang out is the Palace Hotel on the corner of Fourteenth Street and Main Avenue. It's a known fact that a lot of brass spittoons sit on the floor around the bar. Everyone spits in them while chewing that horrible brown snuff. I wonder who in the world empties those spittoons.

Never being permitted to go in there allows me to use my imagination, which consists of old smelly men smoking and chewing away while throwing shots of whiskey in their mouths.

Every time I walk by the Palace Hotel I try to glance in the open door, making sure no one sees me doing it. The odors coming through the door consist of a mixture of tobacco, sweat, and whiskey. It's always dark inside. Now I crinkle up my nose, as it makes me sick when I think about it.

Strange, I think to myself, that Dad would want to frequent one of those places, and yet he always seems to enjoy it. I know he chews snuff, so maybe that has something to do with it, or maybe he likes to laugh and joke with the other men.

Since I'm the only one on the front porch, I decide to lie down on my stomach on the glider, placing my head on my left hand and using my right hand to push the glider so I can continue the relaxing sound. Warm breezes caress me and I feel so sleepy, but my thoughts go back to Dad.

After an adventurous Friday night, we'd hear Dad singing when he walked home through the dark alley. As soon as we heard his singing, Jo and I would act as lookouts, searching for the first sight of him.

We'd kneel on our bed and watch from our upstairs bedroom window. The bottom of our window was level with the top of our mattress, as our bed was pushed against the wall. We could lie in bed and look straight out the window. It was a little scary when I sat up and looked out the window and down into the alley, especially since I was afraid of heights. There was nothing but a window separating the alley and me. That's probably why Jo was given that side of the bed and why she always called me a scaredy-cat.

Most of the time I thought of the window as my private space. Not only could I look at the sky and the stars and wish upon them, but also it was absolutely beautiful and breathtaking when it was snowing. I would watch the snowflakes swirl and dance around, the wind jostling them before they disappear while lying so nice and warm in bed. Sometimes the wind would add some music by rattling the window or blowing through a crack and sounding like a musical instrument.

There was a crack in the window, and Jo swore that snow came through it and landed on her. I don't know how it could have and told her that. She smacked me on the arm and said, "The snow came in and I felt it. Now shut up." It was probably the cold wind or it was a day she wanted to complain about something or was upset with me.

Jo insisted our bed be divided equally and did not want me on her side of it. Mom had painted our brass bed pink. Jo scratched a mark on the brass headboard with her front teeth, scraping the pink off and showing a line of shiny brass. She'd take her hand, as if she was going to do a salute, and slide it from the teeth marks down the middle of the bed, warning me not to venture over that imaginary line. If I so much as laid an arm or a leg on her side, she would keep hitting it until I removed it.

Once I told her I wasn't going to allow her to climb over on my side of the bed to get to her side of the bed, and her only reply was "Try and stop me." I never tried to stop her since I didn't want to have her start using me as a punching bag or a spittoon. She definitely loves me, but sometimes she has a crazy way of showing it.

Anyway, returning to Dad. After we heard him singing in the alley, we'd watch out for him so he didn't fall into our neighbor's hedges. At that point we'd run down the stairs, through the kitchen, and down the back porch steps. We were so scared that he might hurt himself but, of course, he never did. We must have been a sight, the two of us in our pajamas helping him out of the hedges and hoping Mom didn't hear us. We knew she would scream at him and call him all kinds of names, and they would probably end up in a fight.

That is why we tried to be his guardian angels by watching for him to come home singing, hoping this was a day when Mom's hearing was not too good, so as to avoid conflicts between them.

There will be no yelling when I have my own house. I forbid it.

Chapter 8

Still listening to the soothing sound of the glider, I recall that I don't ever remember Mom and Dad hugging or kissing or saying "I love you" to each other. Only one time I remember they hugged, and that memory has always remained with me.

It happened one night when Dad was getting ready to go to work, and it was snowing outside. He always walked to work, which was several miles away, yet he never complained. He was standing at the bottom of the cellar stairs and had just put on his overcoat. Mom was standing one step up, buttoning his top button on the coat and singing, "Baby, it's cold outside . . ."

After she finished the song, she leaned toward him, put her arms around his neck, and gave him a long kiss. They didn't know I was watching from the top of the stairs, but I can't forget their kiss, as it made me feel so good inside. I don't know exactly how old I was, but I was very young, maybe four or five years old, and yet it has always stayed with me.

When I ask myself why Dad gets drunk once in a while, I can only believe it is a type of release for him. It helps him forget about the coal mines and the hard times.

I've heard that after drinking hard whiskey, you have a hangover that makes you feel so sick the next day. I still don't understand, if drinking makes you feel that bad, why people drink. Maybe that's why Dad doesn't overdo it anymore. Personally, I think whiskey has a horrible odor and don't know why anyone would want to drink it.

But Dad does like his little nip of whiskey once in a while at home. A bottle of whiskey is hidden in the rafters in the cellar. He thinks we don't know about it. Kids see a lot of things when they are little, and adults don't think of children as being observant enough to take seriously.

I laugh to myself. Jo and I always knew about the bottle but never said a word. His main purpose was to keep it hidden from Mom, making sure she never smelled it on him. She would search for the bottle and destroy it with a vengeance. She's totally against drinking liquor in any form or even having it in the house.

I can understand why she feels that way, and the sad times flash through my mind. Those times would start when Dad came home drunk and my mother started yelling at him and accusing him of, as she said, "whoring around." Come to think of it, I really don't know if he did or not.

The dishes had an abbreviated scream of their own when they were thrown and shattered. With smashed dishes on the floor and the crunch of the pieces underneath their feet mingled with our screams, he began to choke her.

Thank goodness for my oldest sister, Edna. She had the courage to pick up the phone to ask for help from the operator.

Jo grabbed me by my arm, pulled me outside, and said, "Don't cry, Anna." We were both crying, but Jo put her arm around me as we huddled under the back porch until the police came.

In such a small town, the police know everyone. They calmed my father down and took him to his brother's house to sleep it off. The next day when we woke up, it was like nothing had ever happened. Everything had been cleaned up, and everyone was happy.

Not me. I was still sad, afraid they would start fighting again. I can still see in my mind pieces of the beautiful pink-flowered china dishes that were laying on the floor while my father choked my mother.

Oh, yes, I think to myself, I can still hear the shouting. My mother always knows how to push my father over the edge so he gets angry, and after that she seems to be satisfied or realizes she pushed him too far.

I recall another bad time when we were sitting at the table having our Sunday dinner. That day our house was filled with tantalizing food smells. I was so hungry and those food odors didn't help; they just made me hungrier. Our dinner consisted of pot roast, mashed potatoes, gravy, and vegetables. I thought I was going to die of starvation when finally we were called to eat. Of course, I love pot roast and mashed potatoes and didn't have to be called twice.

As soon as we were all seated at the table, Mom started on Dad.

"Fritz, why don't you help me more around here? Last night you spent the evening down below the tracks at Mike Kalinski's house. You couldn't stay home with me, could you? No, you have to go play that damn music with them."

Dad just shook his head, not saying a word as he reached for the roast.

"When you came home the smell of whiskey was on your breath. I know you go down there to drink."

When Dad didn't reply, it made her angrier. His silence made the rage and anger surface as she yelled, "I know you're whoring around with Mike's sister, Felicia. She's nothing but a fat bitch, and the next time she walks by our porch, I'm going to tell her off."

At this point she pushed him over the edge. Suddenly Dad shouted, "You don't know how nice these people are. I invite you to go with me, but you never want to go." He lifted the end of the table, and everything slid to the floor.

It happened so fast, and yet it was like slow motion, everything sliding down toward Mom, including that bowl of fluffy white mashed potatoes. Mom jumped backward, and finally the tablecloth moved from Dad's side down toward Mom.

We all scrambled to our rooms or outside so we didn't get in the middle, but we couldn't get away from the yelling and screaming that followed our Sunday dinner crash landing on the floor. I was so hungry that night when I went to bed but was more scared than anything.

Now that I think about it, I believe that was the turning point in my mom and dad's relationship. The next day he left my mother and all of us kids. He made sure we were taken care of and would send money with his brother, Ted, to my mother.

I was seven years old, peeking from the dining room into the kitchen, when Uncle Ted arrived.

"Daisy, Fritz said to give you this money," said Uncle Ted as he laid some dollars on the kitchen table.

"Where is he?" Mom asked with tears in her eyes.

"I can't tell you that. He just wanted to make sure you had money for food and the kids."

"Please, Ted, tell me. I just want him to come home."

"I'm sorry but I promised him I wouldn't tell. You'll just have to wait and see when he makes up his mind as to what he wants to do," said Uncle Ted as he walked out the kitchen door.

"Please tell him I love him," cried Mom as the screen door closed.

I remember the emotions I had at that time, as I missed Dad so much, but I was scared that if he came back he might hurt Mom. Yet, I felt so bad for Mom because she missed him so much and it made her sad.

Dad finally came home after a few weeks, but after that whenever she screamed at him or made life miserable for him, he'd just walk away and ignore her. I feel Dad became invisible after that day, probably resigning to the fact that nothing would ever change, and arguing back only made it worse.

Chapter 9

Dad loved to have a good time, and maybe Mom was too busy cooking and cleaning, or maybe she didn't know how to relax and just let go.

Dad's greatest gift is playing the piano, and sometimes he plays the harmonica. It's amazing how he makes the music flow from them.

When Dad wanted to upset Mom, he'd sit down at the piano in our living room and sing while playing "I Wish I Was Single Again." I enjoyed the part about his pockets jingling, but I didn't like the part about his wife dying. When it finally did get to Mom, she'd yell at him to stop.

Sometimes he'd just play it when she wasn't around. I always thought maybe being single again was one of his secret wishes. I wondered if maybe he felt sad that he had kids and a wife to support, forcing him to work in the coal mines.

I loved hearing him sing "Froggie Went A-Courtin'." There are many versions of the ballad, but I loved the deepness of his voice and how happy it made me feel. It was like a story to me, and I enjoyed listening to him tell it in his musical way.

In this song, Frog rides to ask Miss Mouse to marry him. Some versions end with a cat or other creature devouring the participants. I wonder if he felt like he was the frog in his marriage and was devoured after he got married and had so many children.

When he played "Over the Rainbow," he was oblivious to any of us being around. He'd get a faraway look in his eyes and seem like he was very sad and longed to be somewhere else. No matter when or where I hear that song, I think of Dad and know that he had been like a wild stallion until my mother captured him. I believe that she may have caught him and tamed him, but he still has a longing to be wild.

Getting back to reality, I realize this will be the first time I go to the carnival at night without any sisters, just my friends. I hope Mom will let me go since it will be with a bunch of girls.

I've always loved Mom in my own way. Even though she never gave me a lot of kisses or hugs, I still love her. She has short black hair, permed with little curls all over her head, surrounding her beautiful face. Her milky-white complexion accents her flawless skin. A small and perfectly shaped nose adds to the perfection of her face. She has beautiful green eyes, and when I look in them I can tell if she is tired, happy, or sad.

Her shapely legs, especially in high heels, are very noticeable, with seams in her nylons forming a straight line up under her dress. She's absolutely beautiful, like a movie star. Being a large-breasted woman, she's always tugging her bra straps to pull the breasts up or make the straps more comfortable. I'm never sure which reason.

Never will you see her in a pair of slacks, as she is always in a dress around the house or a suit when she goes out to a meeting, leaving a trail of flowery smells and the scent of Coty powder.

One of the disadvantages of being the youngest is that my parents became tired and stopped taking pictures, since they had been through all of that with the older ones. There are baby pictures of all of my sisters, but the first picture of me is when I was two years old, and that was taken in a photo booth with my mother. That's why I could easily imagine I was adopted instead of Martha, but Dad just laughs and says, "No, we just couldn't afford the film and developing at that time."

Mom is also active in our church, helping with the church suppers, bake sales, and rummage sales. She's a hard worker and a fantastic cook. Too bad she never discovered a recipe for showing love.

Every Sunday Mom and all of us girls go to church. Dad never goes to church. I asked him one time why he didn't go to church with us and pray to God. I'll never forget his answer. He said, "Anna, I don't have to go to church to pray to God. I can pray to Him from anywhere, including the chair I'm sitting in. In fact, I pray all the time; you just don't know it." It made a lot of sense to me.

My name being called in a very familiar voice startles me out of my daydreams. I lift my head and see Donnie standing in the front yard with his baseball bat. Donnie has on his baseball cap and his favorite baseball shirt and is leaning on the bat like it's a cane.

He's taller than me and chubby. His hair is combed straight to the side, and his eyes are shaped differently than mine. Donnie is about six years older than me, but no matter how old I get or how grown up I think I am, Donnie will never get that way. Donnie's mental ability will never go beyond a nine- or ten-year-old boy. He lives on the corner of our street and Main Avenue in one of the gray double houses.

He always comes down to our house and hollers, "Jo, Anna, can you come out and play ball with me?"

When I was younger I'd rush through my supper so I could run outside in the alley to play baseball. We enjoyed playing ball with him, as he wasn't mean to us and would always let us bat.

Of course, Jo always wanted to bat, and Donnie and I had to chase the balls no matter how many kids were playing. We never realized anything was wrong with him until we became older.

Without getting up, I say, "Not today, Donnie. I feel tired."

Giggling, he replies, "Maybe you ought to go to bed."

"No, Donnie, I guess I'm more bored than tired."

"You mean like this board?" he asks with a large grin on his face as he hits the porch. Donnie always smiles. I guess that is one of the things that I always liked about him, his smile and ability to be happy all of the time.

"No, like wanting something fun to do."

"We can play ball because that's fun," he says while sitting down on the front porch steps and tapping the brick sidewalk with his bat.

"No, Donnie, I really don't want to play ball. I think Johnny's at home. Why don't you go and ask him?" Johnny's our neighbor who lives across the alley from us.

"Okay, but I don't like you anymore," he replies while getting up and trying to maintain his balance. "I'm never coming back and playing ball with you again."

He walks away like he's angry at me, but I know tomorrow he'll be back to ask me again even though I've stopped playing ball with him for several years now.

Amazing, I think to myself as I lay my head back down. Donnie is six years older than me and yet he will always be a child. I used to hear adults talking and wondering what is going to happen to him when his mother and father die. It makes me feel sad, and I realize how fortunate I am.

Gosh, I wish Mom would get home. She should be here anytime, as it's almost three o'clock and I want to know definitely if I can go to the carnival. The anticipation of going to a carnival without any of my sisters overwhelms me and yet excites me.

Chapter 10

After Donnie leaves the yard, I go back to my daydreaming. I wonder why Jo didn't go to Hollywood instead of New Jersey. She was always into that beauty stuff.

Mom received an offer to go to Hollywood, but she had to stay home and help her mother with all of her younger sisters and brothers. She had to start helping as soon as she finished the sixth grade. Maybe that's why she's angry most of the time—because she had to give up her dreams and was unable to make her own choices in life.

It seems to me that women don't have as many choices as men. I've heard many women say it's a man's world. Men are always telling them what to do, bossing them around—all except my dad.

Edna was from Mom's first marriage, but somehow Mom met Dad and they fell in love. After her divorce she gave Dad four more daughters. I think of the secret they have and would love to talk to them about it, but I don't dare. Maybe, someday I'll ask Mom about it.

I learned a lot from seeing Mom interact with my sisters, and I don't want that trouble. "Interact" isn't exactly the right word, as Mom's more the ruler with the black leather belt, and our family is her monarchy.

A thick, three-inch-wide, black leather belt hangs on a nail in the kitchen next to the doorway leading to the dining room. It used to hang by its buckle, but thank goodness the buckle fell off. It was my dad's old belt and now hangs as a reminder to be good. When the belt hit our skin, we felt a long, burning sting that left red marks. It hurt more on the back than it did on our behinds. If the buckle hit, a huge welt would instantly appear. It was a glorious day when the buckle fell off, and we secretly rejoiced.

My mother is determined that we're all going to be good girls and not go astray. I believe though that most of the beatings we did receive were a way of releasing my mother's frustration with us. Why she has so much anger is a mystery to me—too many kids, unfaithful husband perhaps, too much housework, budgeting the money, cooking dinners, painful ear problems, and on and on and on. Maybe she's afraid of getting pregnant again or is going through that thing they call "change of life."

Thinking of everything Mom does, I realize how hard she works to make things so nice for us.

Mondays are washdays, with the smell of bleach and soap powders everywhere, even floating up the stairs to the kitchen. Washing clothes with a wringer washer and two rinse tubs isn't exactly fun. I do enjoy watching Mom hold the clothes as they go through the wringer, amazed at the water coming out of them. They go in plump with water and come out flat. Sometimes a bubble forms in the clothes, but the wringer takes care of that. You always have to be careful your fingers don't get caught in the rollers with the clothes. It's not only painful but your finger bones could be broken and permanently damaged. We're never allowed near the wringer when the rollers are moving.

The heavy baskets of wet clothes are carried outside, one at a time, through the cellar entrance to the backyard, with Dad helping when he's home.

Three of the neighboring backyards join ours creating one huge yard. Each yard contains four wire clotheslines attached at the wooden T-shaped posts inserted at each end of the yard. On sunny Mondays, the four backyards running horizontal to each other often look like a huge colorful square of flying clothes flapping in the breeze, sometimes with a snapping sound.

The large clothes are hung on the outside lines, with the underwear on the inside lines so no one can see them. After all, that would be embarrassing if other people, especially the boys, saw your underwear.

On rainy days or snowy days, the clothes are hung in the basement on a rope that is strung across the ceiling rafters. A big folding wooden rack containing many wooden rungs is also set up near the furnace so clothes can be laid over each of the rungs.

Sometimes the clothes are laid on the two-foot metal vent that consists of a big circle in the wooden floor between the living and dining rooms in the open doorway. This vent comes from the furnace in the cellar, and that's the only place the heat enters our first floor to heat the entire house.

Jo and I used to sit on the opposite sides of the vent with our legs folded up so our chins could rest on our knees. We would make up stories while our legs turned red from the heat. Then we would get up to cool off and then go back for more. Our older sisters were always complaining that we were hogging the heat, but we didn't care, as it felt so good. We both hated to be cold.

A joy I had was taking my crayons and sliding them over the black metal strips of the vent while tracing the pattern that composed the little squares for the heat to come through. The crayons melted and disappeared, leaving a liquid color on the metal as I moved each of them along, never realizing an odor was broadcasting what I was doing.

"I smell something burning," yelled Mom as she sprinted into the dining room from the kitchen.

"I'm coloring the heating vent," I answered, so proud of my art.

"Stop that right now. Just look at your crayons. You won't be having any crayons pretty soon. You're making a mess."

"But it's so pretty."

"Anna, what am I going to do with you? Stop it right now or I'll get the strap."

I stopped and immediately stood up, as I didn't want the strap.

Sighing, she said, " You could get burned."

It didn't stop me. I just made sure Mom wasn't home, being very careful not to burn myself and cleaning the crayon off of the grill when I finished. I'll never forget how pretty a scene the colors created and how the crayons disappeared so fast. It's amazing how quickly we grow up and leave some of our childish ways behind.

Going to school is important to Mom, probably because it is something she was never able to accomplish. Most mothers want more for their children than what they are able to obtain for themselves. They don't want their daughters to have to work as hard as they did. Mom preaches to us all the time that having an education will give us an easier and better life.

She never lets me help in any great way. I guess she feels she can do everything faster by herself. Oh, sure, I do little things, such as take the clothes off the clothesline when they're dry or if it starts to rain, and I scrub the coal dust off of the cellar steps every Saturday morning.

Tuesday is ironing day. Mom sprinkles the clean clothes with water by utilizing a used, clean Pepsi-Cola or an RC Cola bottle to which she attaches a small plastic sprinkler head with a cork on it. After sprinkling the clothes, she rolls them up and packs them in the clothes basket so they stay damp and are ready to be ironed.

All our clothes are ironed except for underwear and socks. That means a lot of clothes to iron with a family of seven.

I decide to turn over on my back on the glider and get more comfortable. Maybe I can nap a little. I just feel so restless.

Staring at the old, gray roof boards above my head, I know I can't close my eyes and sleep. Instead I watch as a fly is caught in a spiderweb, and I hope the spider isn't near. No one and nothing should be trapped like that.

Chapter 11

⁓

As I am thinking about all of these things and pacifying myself on the front porch glider, Mom comes driving down Fifth Street in our 1949 black DeSoto. She turns into the alley and I know she is parking her car like the name of my dad's tobacco, Half & Half. She always pulls alongside of our yard and parks one-half of the car in the backyard and the other half in the alley.

Listening to her get out of the car and close the door, I know she has high heels on. I never could understand how she can walk in the alley with them on, but she has no problem with it.

The back door slams after the thumping of her heels ascends the seven wooden porch steps. I'm aware of all of these sounds, always alert when my mother is around. It's amazing how these sounds drift through the house and also around the house, meeting with me on the front porch.

"Boy, that was some meeting. I'm glad to be home. Where's Anna?" she asks my dad as she slides her feet out of her high heels and kicks them over to the upstairs steps. They hit the wood of the bottom step with that familiar sound. She does this every time she wears high heels, and I know the sound so well. She kicks them off to that area so she won't forget to take them upstairs with her.

Looking over his newspaper, Dad replies, "She's on the front porch and isn't very happy because I told her to stop playing that awful music."

"Remember what we talked about last night? I'm going to ask her now how she feels about it."

"That might make her feel better. I don't know what's wrong with her anymore," Dad says as I hear him opening the door on his tobacco cabinet. This means he's going to get his tobacco and paper out to roll up a cigarette. His cigarettes always come out with twisted flat ends, not nice and round with ends that look like they have been sliced with a sharp knife like the Lucky Strikes he sometimes can afford to buy. He says he saves money by rolling his own cigarettes.

Now what have they got planned for me? I wonder as I hear Mom coming to the front screen door. Without coming out she says through the screen door in her usual loud voice, "Anna, sit up. I want to talk to you. Your dad and I want to know if you want a birthday party for your sixteenth birthday. We can hold it at the lot."

The "lot" is what we call two acres of land that Dad had purchased with money he saved working his part-time job. Four years before Dad retired from the coal mine he opened a small bait store on this land situated on the outskirts of Kolfield. In addition to the various worms, he also sells fishing equipment, like fishing poles, tackle, hooks, and many other items. It's his very own domain, since he bought it with his money, and he enjoys every minute he spends there.

That took me by surprise and got my attention fast. After all, it was only last year that Jo and I found out about Mom and Dad's secret after going through our mother's cedar chest.

My mother always kept her cedar chest locked, and Jo was determined to see why. I can't understand it, but every time I'm with Jo she does something like this. We're the duo—Jo the leader and Anna the follower.

One day Mom and Dad informed us they would be gone for the entire day. We were told to stay home and not go anywhere. Boredom set in by early afternoon. I was sitting on the front porch reading, and Jo was upstairs.

"Hey, Anna, come here a minute," she hollered down the stairs.

"What do you want? I'm busy."

"You better come up here and see what I found."

"You're just saying that," I said as I got up and went through the front door.

Curiosity always gets the best of me, and Jo knows it. I ran upstairs and looked down the hall to see Jo in Mom and Dad's room.

"What are you doing in there? You know we're not allowed to go in there."

"No one will ever know. Aren't you the least bit curious what's so important that it needs to be locked in the cedar chest?"

"No!"

I just knew this was leading to trouble since we were not allowed to be in their bedroom, let alone the cedar chest.

Peeking into the room, I noticed how neat the white chenille bedspread looked on the bed. I would have loved to lie down on it and take a nap. The bed was situated between the two front windows that looked down on Fifth Street. The scents of Mom's powders and creams dominated the room. This was my favorite room in the house.

A bedside table with a small white porcelain lamp with roses painted on it sat on another starched doily by Dad's side of the bed. Since there was only one closet in the house and it was located in the back bedroom, a wardrobe was in the corner, where they hung their clothes inside and stored hatboxes on the top of it. A matching vanity and bench seat were located near Mom's side of the bed, in the other corner between the front windows and the side window that overlooked the alley.

The cedar chest was at the foot of their bed and was made of light wood and dark wood, looking as if it was a completed puzzle. The lid was rounded in the front, and a lock was situated in the middle under the lid.

Jo looked the situation over and, after struggling with a butter knife and a letter opener in the lock, realized she couldn't open it. Her blue plaid shirt was hanging out over her jeans, and her hair was hanging down in her eyes.

Stomping her foot and waving the butter knife, she said, "There has to be a way."

Looking at her, I wanted to laugh but knew to keep my mouth shut.

After some serious thought, she smiled and said, "I know. I'll try a bobby pin."

Taking one from Mom's vanity, she straightened it and moved it round in the lock. Nothing happened.

"No matter what, Jo. You do understand Mom will know we've been in this room. Are you sure there isn't a key around here?"

"I looked everywhere. She probably has it with her in her purse."

Suddenly Jo got this look in her eyes. "I know what we can do. Help me move this thing."

"Move it where? There's no place to move it to."

"We just want to pull it out enough so I can see the back of it."

"What do you want to see the back of it for?" I asked, moving toward her.

"I'll tell you after I see it."

The two of us inched it out slowly, as it was heavy.

Jo examined the back and said, "I know how we can get in there."

While I stood there and kept looking out the window for Mom and Dad, she ran out of the room and downstairs, returning in a few minutes with a screwdriver.

"See, we can remove the hinges from the back and lift it up from there."

After removing the screws from the hinges, she pulled the back of the top up.

"Be careful, we don't want to break the lock. Now hold this side up while I take some things out and look at them."

I knelt there on my knees, holding the lid open while Jo removed Mom and Dad's secret.

Chapter 12

That was the day we found a bunch of important-looking papers that turned out to be Dad's divorce papers. Dad had been married and divorced four times before he met Mom, and it wasn't until my sixth birthday that they became married. On that day of discovery I realized that my sixth birthday party was really to celebrate them getting married and was not for me. That was the only birthday party I ever had.

What we never could understand was why he named one of his daughters after one of his wives and Mom allowed it. The name was Martha.

Martha Daisy is the middle child, named after two of Dad's wives, as Mom's name is Daisy.

Maybe it's true when they say the middle child is the one with the problems. To me, Martha is so artificial. She always wants you to think she's better than everyone else and, at times, can be a real teaser, always trying to get someone to argue with her. She loves to stir up controversy. I guess every family has to have one. Martha is in a class of her own.

Martha's nickname was Fee Fee at one time, but she sort of outgrew it. I don't know why that was her nickname or how she got it, but I did know a dog named Fee Fee. We never let her live that down.

Martha and Jo never did get along with each other. They always make snide remarks to each other, and sometimes their remarks and outlandish faces turn into yelling and slapping fights.

Martha has long bright-red hair and used to be a little chunky, but not fat or obese. Then suddenly she wanted to lose weight and became slim and shapely. Her green eyes hover above a small nose that reminds me of a miniature ski slope, and she has a thin upper lip that practically disappears when she smiles. Cute little dimples appear on each side of her face when she smiles, so it helps to make up for her robot smile. A lot of freckles dot her cheeks and nose, and she really is pretty if she isn't putting on airs.

She always walks around with her nose stuck in the air and a silly fake smile on her face. When she smiles, it is a "try as hard as you can" smile, like she is straining all of the muscles in her neck because you can see them popping out the sides of her neck.

Finally, having held the secret for several years, I revealed it. Last month I confronted Dad about his wives because I was angry with Mom, as she wouldn't let me sleep over at my girlfriend's house. Dad knew I was angry—but not with him—and listened intently as I spilled the beans.

With my hands on my hips, I defiantly said, "Dad, I know all about your divorces. You didn't get married until my sixth birthday. I can remember Aunt Hazel going somewhere with you and Mom that morning. Is that when you got married?"

He looked at me but was not surprised. "How did you find out I was married before?"

"Jo and I found your divorce papers in Mom's cedar chest. Is that why I had a birthday party when I was six years old? It wasn't for me, was it? It was for you and Mom because you got married, wasn't it?"

He just looked at me, shaking his head. "Anna, Anna, you really shouldn't have nosed around in your mother's cedar chest."

"Just tell me, Dad, was the party for your marriage or for me?"

"It was for you. You received presents and had a birthday cake, didn't you?"

After calming down, I said, "How come you named one of your children after one of your ex-wives and Mom. Wasn't Mom angry about that?"

"No, she wasn't angry, as she liked the name Martha. We did include Daisy as her middle name though. Martha was my first wife and my first real love. I was in the army and was being shipped out. A reporter was there and even took a picture of me in my army uniform as I hung out the train window, waving good-bye for the newspaper. She was on the train platform, throwing me a kiss. After I left, she wrote me a Dear John letter, and I think that's all you need to know."

"Okay, but do I have any other brothers or sisters that I should know about?"

He laughed and shook his head. "No, that's why I settled down with your mother, because I love her and she's a good woman." Then he refused to discuss it anymore.

Of course, I never approached Mom for answers, because she'd want to know how I found out. Breaking into her cedar chest with all of her private and personal papers loaded with memories wasn't right, and I know that now.

Gee, I think to myself, my sixteenth birthday is their tenth wedding anniversary. Maybe I'll get them an anniversary card and surprise Mom. I want Mom to know that I'm aware of this because it doesn't matter to me and I'm sure no one else cares. Heck, what's the big deal?

At least I hope it doesn't matter to anyone else. Society has its rules, and one is you better be married if you're living with a man and have children. I guess I'm not smart enough to quite understand all of these silent rules and don't even know half of them since they're not discussed. Yet, everyone seems to know them, and having a child and not being married is definitely a no-no. If it's a no-no, why do they do it? I wonder.

"Anna, what's your answer? Do you want a birthday party or not?" asks Mom impatiently as she opens the screen door but doesn't step outside. Without her shoes on, she doesn't want to get a runner in her nylons. She has on a pretty black-and-white dress, and I notice her black onyx ring sparkles, looking nice with her outfit.

After coming back to reality and sitting up, I ask with a serious look on my face, "And just how would everyone get there?"

"Your dad said he'll drive them out in the back of his pickup truck. We can have a hot dog roast. There's only one problem, and that is you can only invite five or six of your girlfriends and no boys."

Whirling in my head I know that won't be a problem, as there are only five or six of my friends who really know my mom and dad and what they are like. They are my best friends, and since they know Mom, she can't embarrass me.

Heck, I bet we can really relax and have fun at a hot dog roast since there will be no boys allowed. That means my girlfriends are able to let loose and be themselves.

"Okay, the party sounds good. Also, Mom, can I go to the carnival with Sonya and Beverly? It's going to be in Kolfield the week after my birthday. Please?" I ask with my fingers crossed and hidden so she doesn't see them.

"I suppose so. Just stay away from those sideshows, and you have to be home by ten o'clock, but we'll talk about it later," she says as she allows the screen door to slam shut.

Chapter 13

Sitting on the glider and keeping a nice rhythm back and forth, I recall Dad's extra money was earned by helping Aunt Hazel with her tombstone business. Aunt Hazel asked Dad for his help after my Uncle Charlie died. Selling the tombstones gave her extra money, but she definitely couldn't install them, so she was the bookkeeper and Dad was the installer.

Dad would pour a cement footer that had to be perfectly level at the head of the grave, and he would place the base of the tombstone on it. After the cement dried, he placed the actual tombstone on top of it. Sometimes if the tombstones were too heavy he summoned Reds, my brother-in-law, to help him. Dad is really good at making sure everything is perfect when he installs a tombstone.

When asked why it takes him so long, he'd say, "The tombstone is like our good-bye to the world, and hopefully when people pass by they'll look at our tombstone and say our name. Now if it's crooked and falling down, they won't pay it much attention, will they? It'll look like that person was never loved and has been forgotten."

Sometimes Jo and I would tag along to the cemetery with him. Walking among the graves, I'd study the pictures on the tombstones, especially the ones of the children, wondering about their lives, how they died, and why they had to die. I never stepped on the actual graves, as I felt it wasn't right.

Dad's trips to the granite shed were always an adventure for us in the summer. We'd hop in his old truck, carrying a bag of sandwiches for lunch, and the three of us would sing songs as we traveled down the road.

The granite shed consisted of three walls and a roof. The harsh sounds of the saws and hammers inside these walls sometimes made it impossible to hear each other talking, so Dad and the granite man would stand outside talking. The men cutting the stones wore glasses and masks so they didn't breathe in the dust.

Jo and I roamed around inside. So many small chunks of gray granite were strewed about on the ground, reminding me of the lumps of black coal along the railroad tracks. The amazing thing was how they could take an ugly rough piece of granite and, with those noisy machines, make it so smooth and shiny. We were allowed to take as many little pieces as we wanted, stuffing our pockets.

This tombstone business formed the "fund" for my dad's whiskey, Copenhagen snuff, Lucky Strikes, Half & Half tobacco and cigarette papers, gasoline, and the "lot" he purchased.

He bought the land, originally thinking Kolfield would extend its businesses in that direction on the way to Bedford, but instead the development went the other direction toward Pittsburgh.

This "lot" consists of approximately two acres of land bought by Dad so he could have some kind of business to keep his "fund" alive. After he discarded many of his ideas on what to do to make money, his business establishment turned out to be a worm farm.

Actually, the worm farm consists of a shack with a tar paper roof that Dad built by himself with a little help from my brother-in-law, Reds.

Since Dad created the worm farm, he gets permission to go on the golf courses at night to gather worms. Jo always loved going out with Dad to catch night crawlers. Sometimes some of her friends would go so they could make some money. For every worm she caught, Dad paid her and then sold them at his bait store.

Trying to catch worms was difficult for me with my rubber gloves on, as I can't stand to touch them. I just couldn't grab them the right way, as the gloves were too thick and bulky.

At night and after a rain was the best time, as that's when the night crawlers like to mate. On my knees and careful not to kneel on any worms, I'd look for two of them stretched across the grass—the top half of their bodies clinging together while their bottom halves were still in their holes in the ground, a couple inches apart.

I'd grab each one right below their heads or tops, as they don't look like heads to me, and pull them so hard they snapped in half. I guess that's why it's best not to wear gloves—so you can actually feel them stretching. When they stretch, you are supposed to ease up a little, but I just wanted to get them out of those holes and out of my hands without them touching my skin.

Finally, after two time-outs and complaints from Jo that I was killing too many worms and she was losing money because I was killing them, Dad told me it would be better for me to stay home. I was glad even though I wanted to make money. I wished I was fearless like Jo.

A lot of fishermen drive by the "lot" as they head for the lakes over near

Bedford and Shawnee Lake. It's perfect for them to stop and buy their bait for their fishing trips. Dad sells night crawlers, California red worms, and grub worms—or grubbies, as we called them.

Later when Mom became involved with the business, they started selling tackle, fishing line, and other fishing gear. Oh, yes, she also managed to include saltshakers and pepper shakers in the inventory, which Dad wasn't very happy about, as he felt his poor worm farm was being corrupted.

Dad built the worm farm from scratch, and Reds helped when he could. Reds is married to my oldest sister, Edna. His real name is Rudy, but we call him Reds, as he came into our family with that nickname, probably because of his red hair. He is great to us kids and loves Edna very much. He is always laughing and never raising his voice. He never complains that we're at their house so much and is always teasing us with jokes and riddles.

He'd say, "Why did the chicken cross the road?"

I'd say, "To get to the other side."

"Boy, Anna Banana, you are so smart. I'll bet you don't know why firemen wear red suspenders, do you?"

"Yes, to keep their pants up."

"No, to match the fire truck," he'd say with a big grin.

"That's not true. My answer is right," I'd laughingly say, knowing that next time he'd probably have a different answer.

They are silly riddles but he never stops with them. He makes everything a lot of fun. He's always so calm about everything, even if we spill our drink or drop a dish. He just says, "Accidents happen, don't worry about it."

Reds is tall with red hair and the most vivid blue eyes. He has this gigantic smile that makes his whole face light up. Edna told us that his mother is a wonderful person and raised him to respect women and treat them well. Reds has seven brothers and sisters. He not only loves Edna but respects her family too.

Edna is Mom's child from her first marriage and was eight years old when Mom and Dad met. She is beautiful, with long black hair, a fair complexion, bright hazel eyes that always twinkle, all of which are accented by beautiful red lips. She is tall but takes after our mother, with the bosom and a small waist and hips. We always think of Edna as our full-blooded sister, and I'm sure she feels the same way about us. She's a big help to Mom, and they're like sisters, as Mom was eighteen years old when Edna was born.

When Edna was living at home, one evening she was getting ready to go on a date with Reds. He showed up in his army uniform to pick her up, as it was the end of World War II and he just got back from overseas a few days before.

My mother yelled from the bottom of the stairs, "Edna, Reds is here. Hurry up and come on down."

"I'll be down in a minute," she yelled as she fussed with her hair while looking in the mirror.

I was six years old, jumping up and down on Edna's bed as she was getting dressed. Edna had on this beautiful white dress, a big white hat, and gorgeous bright-red lipstick placed carefully on her lips. She looked so beautiful.

While continuing to jump on her bed as she looked in the mirror, I giggled and said, "Edna, you look just like a bride."

She turned to me with her pointer finger to her lips and said in an angry voice, "Shhhh, Anna, be quiet. You mustn't say that." With those parting words, she walked out of the room and down the stairs.

Little did I know that she and Reds were eloping that very evening. They were married in Reds's church fifteen miles away, with his mother and sister present. Edna came home after being married and told Mom, who didn't even get upset. Mom served them cookies and coffee, and they went back to Reds's house to spend the night.

As I became older, Edna told me the story many times and we always laughed about it—how children say such innocent things and how they perceive all brides are beautiful and wear white dresses.

Edna is a very generous and warmhearted person. She works as a draftsman, making blueprints at the Kolfield Coal Mining Company. She resigned last year, as she was lifting heavy rolls of blueprints and had a miscarriage. Reds loves her very much and told her to quit. He has a good job at the steel mills and feels she doesn't have to work anymore.

Edna is more like a mother than a sister to me. When working, she treated me to lunches at the Kolfield Company Store located on the corner of Fifteenth Street and Sunshine Avenue. It is located kitty-corner from her old office building.

Two stories high, the store has a rectangular area in the middle of the first floor with tall silver pedestals topped with red round seats, surrounding a matching countertop that acts like a barrier for the waitresses. The women move about, taking orders or making lunch.

Naturally I just happened to be at the store or in front of her office at lunchtime in the summer, when I was sure she wasn't going home. I always knew she would offer to buy me lunch or maybe just a peanut butter sundae. If I wanted an egg salad sandwich, the waitress in the rectangle would hurry up and boil an egg. Not only fresh, the egg salad sandwiches were also always warm.

During the summer my sister Jo and I tried to be at her downstairs apartment on Seventh Street at least three times a week, so when she came home for lunch we could eat with her. She always had good lunch meat, like chipped ham or Lebanon bologna, along with American cheese and fresh bread. After making a sandwich and propping her feet on a footstool, she'd watch her soap opera on TV before heading back to work.

Walking into her apartment is like walking into a candy store. Upon entering the hall from the front door and bypassing the living room on the left, it's difficult to ignore the candy-filled dishes. But we did, as we knew by going straight into the kitchen we would find the best cookies, pies, and cakes waiting for us, as she was always baking.

Almost every Sunday evening Dad, Mom, Jo, and I went to Edna's apartment to watch TV. Jo and I sat on the floor while everyone else sat on the sofa and chairs. We couldn't afford a television set at our house, but two blocks wasn't far to walk and visit Edna and Reds.

The Texaco Star Theater, also known as the Milton Berle Show, on Sunday evenings was my favorite. At first I didn't like Uncle Milty because he acted so weird, but then I realized he was doing the silly stuff to make everyone laugh. Everyone laughed, but sometimes I didn't quite understand his jokes.

Our first black-and-white television set arrived when I was in sixth grade. There was so much excitement in the air that morning. We all knew our television set was being delivered that day.

After school, we ran all the way home and there it was. A huge piece of furniture with a small screen in the middle of it sat next to the living room window. That day I fell in love with *The Howdy Doody Show*, always singing the theme song.

Last year, on my fifteenth birthday, Edna told me she remembered the day I was born because she was fifteen at that time. It was late Thursday afternoon around five o'clock. Mom was on her knees scrubbing the upstairs steps with a scrub brush and bucket of hot soapy water.

Our stairs are such that you go up three steps and then there is a small square landing where we have a coat tree full of coats and jackets. We have to make a right to go up the rest of the stairs to our bedrooms.

Mom was at the small landing that divided the last three steps, having scrubbed the stairs from the top down, when her water broke. I didn't know what Edna meant by water breaking, but I wasn't going to interrupt her story.

Dad told the operator on the phone to call the doctor. After getting Mom settled in bed upstairs, he continued the preparation of the evening meal of pork chops. Dad liked to cook and had started making supper that evening.

Edna told me the doctor arrived in a short time and delivered me in Mom and Dad's bedroom upstairs. Edna, of course, was the babysitter for my other three sisters.

That's the only thing anyone can tell me about my being a baby, other than the time Jo toddled over while I was lying on the couch. She must have wanted the blanket I was lying on, as she pulled the blanket, with me on it, off the couch and onto the floor. I laugh as I think about it—seems to me she started early in life, showing me that she was my boss.

It doesn't seem strange to me that I was actually born and raised in this house. I have never lived anywhere else, so this is my home. I love it, but I'd like to live in another city somewhere to experience what it's like.

As I continue my movement with the glider, I'm sure that Reds would take Edna to the carnival if she wants to go. How lucky they are to be all grown up; they can go anywhere they please without someone's permission.

Chapter 14

My birthday party will be held on our "lot." Our "lot" is an open piece of land surrounded by woods, where Dad's worm farm is located. Since Dad retired he's at the worm farm practically every day, whereas he used to go there only on his days off from the coal mine.

Inside the shack he erected, he built a wooden counter to divide the room. Part of the counter is hinged and lifts up so you can get to the other side. Under this counter he keeps his cash box and the stacks of white cardboard containers with wire handles for the worms. There's a wood stove for the very cold days with its vent pipe going through the roof, allowing the dark, smelly smoke from the logs to escape into the fresh, crisp air.

If we walk out the back door of the shack, there are pits, approximately eight feet by ten feet, on each side; we have to be careful not to step in them. A wooden board about ten inches wide is separating them, and we must walk carefully over the board to get past the pits. There's another board that we move over the area where the worms are plentiful so we can reach them without a lot of stretching. This way we can fulfill a customer's order without falling in. We crawl across this board on our hands and knees, balancing ourselves, looking for the worms. No one is allowed to step in these pits, as that would disturb the worms and, no doubt, kill them. Plus, you can end up with some dirty clothes and shoes.

Dad experimented with clay pits for the California red worms, as there's a demand for this type of worm. After many experiments, Dad is convinced the clay is what makes this species of worms more lively and wiggly. He reads about the worms and researches them as much as possible. He even visited another man who was raising them several hundred miles away. Building the clay pits was not in vain, as the worms seem to be healthier in the clay than just living in plain soil, but they are harder to pull out of the clay. Again, I always have to be very careful not to stretch them too hard and snap them in half.

The fishermen are always happy to see these worms squirming around as we hold them in the air to show them how lively they are. We pick them out of the clay pits and place them in the containers, counting each one, as we sell them by the dozen.

Frankly, as much as the fishermen rave about the worms, I just can't get into it like Jo does. I still hate to touch them and continue to wear rubber gloves. I envy Jo as I watch her count them out or let them crawl around in the palm of her hand.

Sometimes if it wasn't busy, Jo and I would walk across the highway to the truck stop. They have the most delicious corn beef sandwiches with dill pickles on them served on fresh homemade bread. Often, I would end up watching Jo play the shooting game machine, as there was only one machine, and she hogged it all the time. When you tried to shoot the bear and you hit it, it would stand up and growl.

Dad told us we cost him more than he was making selling worms when we went over to the truck stop. Boy, those were the good old days.

Dad is good to people, feeling sorry for the ones who are down and out. He has a big, loving heart.

A couple of gypsies were living in an old shack on the ground next to our lot. They weren't supposed to be there, but Dad never told on them.

In fact, Dad told us one Saturday there was a new tiny baby boy next door. He asked if we wanted to see him. Dad had chopped some wood to take over to them, so we pushed the wheelbarrow over the field and into the woods with him to see the baby. They had stopped there so she could give birth and keep the baby warm until she was able to travel again.

When we walked into the shack, a small fire in a broken-down wood stove was keeping them warm. The whole room reeked of wood smoke, and Dad told them they should be careful. Smoke could be very dangerous, especially to the new baby. The baby was crying so loud even though he was in his mother's arms.

The mother had long dark hair pulled back and large circular earrings in her ears. She pulled back a corner of the blue-striped blanket so we could see him. He was so tiny with a scrunched-up and wrinkled red face, a lot of black hair, a tiny mouth, and tiny clenched fists that seemed to be punching the air.

Looking up and seeing a huge man with a big earring in his one ear amazed and scared me. I never saw a man with an earring in his ear. I backed up and clung to Dad's side like a magnet. Jo wasn't afraid of the man though as she touched the baby's hand and stood her ground.

Dad reached in his pocket and gave them some money for food, making them smile. On the way back across the field, Dad said it might be better to not mention these people to our mother, as she might not like strangers living in that old shed.

Somehow a few weeks later my favorite war saying, "Loose lips sink ships," occurred in front of my mother about the little baby. I was still excited about it because I'd never seen a real baby that tiny. Questions galore were thrown at me that I had to answer.

I was very upset with myself for telling my mom, and Jo was really upset with me. After grabbing my arm and giving me a couple of Indian burns, she said with her eyes blazing and her lips looking like they were like a stretched rubber band ready to sting, "You are so stupid. You can never keep a secret. You're nothing but a big baby. Now go ahead and cry and tell your mommy."

I'd never lie to my mother, as I swear she had some kind of inner power that buzzed her when I told a lie. Mom was angrier with Dad for allowing us to go over and be around complete strangers than the fact that Dad gave them money.

After several days, Mom went over to tell them they shouldn't be there, but I think she really wanted to check on the baby. They had vanished as suddenly as they had appeared. I often wonder where they are now and how big the baby is, as it has been over six years. The baby is probably starting school somewhere.

Sitting on the glider, I wonder what it would be like to travel from place to place and not have a home. You'd see a lot of things, but surely you'd get tired after a while. I only know what it is to live here at my home, where I was born.

If I had only realized this home would eventually instill some sad and painful memories for me in the future …

Chapter 15

Storm clouds roll in with thunder in the distance. Mom yells at me to roll up the awning because a storm is coming. I crank it up so it's rolled up against the edge of the roof and maneuver the green canvas cover over the glider.

I love thunderstorms. Since we're so high in the mountains, it sounds like the thunder is right above our heads when a storm hits. I've spent an entire afternoon doing nothing but reminiscing, so I guess it's a good time to go upstairs to my bedroom and find a book to read.

It sounds so nice to say "my bedroom," as all my life I've shared a room with my sister Jo, not by choice but out of necessity. Even though I now have my own big bedroom, I still miss Jo.

I'm so bored. If Jo was here, she'd find something for us to do. Flopping on my bed I start to cry. I never thought I'd miss her this much, but I do.

I'll never forget when, two months ago, Jo took off to be free as a bird. She graduated from high school in the third week of May and left on the Greyhound bus the very next day to Glasstown, New Jersey, to work at the Clear Glass Company.

The company had advertised in the *Johnstown Tribune Democrat*, and she and her best friend, Lily, were interviewed in Johnstown and offered a job in their New Jersey plant.

Two days before Jo left, she went to Penn Traffic in Johnstown and charged some bath towels to Mom's charge account. I thought, *Oh, great, I'll be left to take the heat for that one,* as I was with her when she did it, but Mom never said a word about it.

Jo packed her suitcase a couple days before graduation, making sure it was hidden under the bed and hoping no one would see it. The next morning after graduation, Jo sneaked her suitcase out the back door when Mom wasn't around. She hid it at Lily's house, and the two of them left that evening. Jo always said that as soon as she graduated she was leaving town, but I just never thought that day would come.

Her bus was leaving at eight o'clock that evening, so I met her at Main Line Drugstore, which is also the Greyhound bus stop. She and Lily purchased their tickets earlier in the day at the little window located at the back of the store.

It was a chilly evening, and the sky was salted with bright stars. Once in a while a whiff of smoke from a fireplace would enter my nose as I walked downtown.

Jo's ex-boyfriend—John Bunkoski, nicknamed Bunky—was there to see her off along with several of their other friends. Jo wanted nothing to do with him, as he cheated on her with another girl a few weeks before graduation. She even went to the senior prom with another boy. Bunky threw her corsage onto the back porch as he drove by, all dressed up for the prom, not believing she would actually go with someone else.

Bunky's blond hair was neatly combed with a nice wave in the front, and the blue in his eyes was more pronounced by the blue shirt he was wearing with his jeans. His eyes looked sad that night, although his full lips were smiling. A small, thin scar was positioned over his right eye like another eyebrow.

Jo did talk to him for a couple of minutes and then looked over at me. She came over and hugged me, but she wasn't crying. She was happy to finally realize her dream of leaving this little coal town was coming true.

"Don't cry, Anna. You're the only thing I regret leaving. As soon as I get a paycheck, I'll send you something. Now stop crying," she said as tears started to gather in her eyes.

"Write to me, Jo, and I'll write to you," I said while sobbing.

I had never felt so sad as my tears continued to flow, and I waved good-bye as the bus pulled away from the curb.

I was crying so hard and didn't want anyone to see me, so I walked home through the alleys. Five blocks later, Bunky jumped out of the shadows, scaring me half to death. He didn't mean to scare me, but I was deep in thought and crying so I didn't hear him.

I didn't want him to know I was crying. "Leave me alone, Bunky."

"Don't cry. I'm sad too. I love Jo so much and she still won't go back with me because I made a stupid mistake. Anyway, it doesn't matter. I'm going to visit her as soon as she gets settled. I'll surprise her."

"But you're going to college, aren't you?"

"Yes, but I have the whole summer to visit her. I'll just hitchhike to New Jersey and try to get her to forgive me, and maybe she'll go steady with me again."

Arriving at my backyard, he stood there with his arms upright and his hands clutching the wire clothesline, moving it back and forth. We talked, and I knew Jo would never take him back, but he was determined to show her how wrong he had been and would do anything in the world to make it up to her. I felt sorry for him, as he really loved her. But he should never have crossed headstrong Jo, as she isn't the forgiving type, especially with love.

"How are you doing in school? Any boyfriends?"

"No, but there is a boy who I have liked for two years. He doesn't know I like him."

I couldn't tell Bunky his name, as I didn't want anyone to know, and the best way to keep a secret is to not tell anyone. I discovered that growing up with all of my sisters.

Actually I had liked this particular boy since seventh grade, and we had been really good friends, but not girlfriend/boyfriend. Of course, he didn't know I liked him. If he did, we couldn't be friends, as he was always asking me for advice about other girls.

"Eventually this guy will notice you since you're a very pretty girl. I know a couple of guys that like you, but I told them to stay away."

"You shouldn't do that. I'm old enough to know who I want to see."

"Look, it's for your own good. They're nothing but trouble. Jo asked me to keep an eye on you for her since she can't do it."

"No one has to keep an eye on me or watch out for me. Jo should know that by now."

"Just smile and be happy. Well, I have to get going, as I have a long walk to Mine Forty."

"Okay, but be careful walking home and don't worry, I'll be happy. I hope you and Jo get back together," I said, clutching my cardigan sweater tighter, as the air felt cooler. Then I gave him a fast kiss on his cheek and ran up the back porch steps.

Mom never said anything about Jo leaving and seemed to be a little more content that she didn't have to worry about her as much. Jo had already told Dad that afternoon she was leaving, and he was happy for her, giving her some money. I believe he knew just how she felt—ready to move on and see and do exciting things, as he once did.

Last week Jo sent a brown suede jacket, a turquoise bracelet, and a picture of Elvis Presley to me, as she felt bad that she had to leave me alone to fend for myself. When she called to see if I got the package, I asked her about Elvis Presley, and she couldn't believe I had never heard of him. I told her I didn't think he was that good-looking in his picture. She thought he was so handsome and talented. How in the heck did she know all of this stuff?

With Jo gone, it's like a big chunk of my life is missing. Now I am the only one left in a house that was once overflowing with voices and footsteps running through it. I feel something I need in my life is missing. Since I don't know what it is, how can I find it?

Chapter 16

A bolt of lightning lights up the room, and the thunder booms. Since it's already eight thirty, I guess I'll get ready for bed.

I'd always been chubby, with the nickname of Porky in grade school, but this past year something amazing happened and my body developed a shape. I have shoulder-length dark hair that I sometimes wear in a ponytail. I have that perfect nose of my mother's and those hazel eyes that, depending upon the color of my shirt, can be green or blue. My girlfriends tell me I have a nice figure but, of course, I don't believe it.

I'm not used to all of these emotions, but I guess it's all part of growing up. Hurriedly I run my bath water and take a fast bath, as Mom says it's dangerous for us to be in the tub when there's lightning.

After my quick bath, I put on my pink chenille bathrobe and close my bedroom door. Standing in front of the full-length mirror on the back of the door, I open my bathrobe and stare at my body. Wiggling my hips, I do a little dance, amazed at the changes in my body but not sure what I'm seeing and what the next change in my body will be. Now I have a small waist, larger breasts, and a flat stomach, and I never even noticed when all of this happened.

After getting my pajamas on, I tie my robe and look for the book I was reading earlier that I had laid on my desk. Not only do I now have my own scratched-up desk, but a white vanity with soft pink material hanging around it and a stool to match, a double bed for only me, and two dressers. This furniture had been used by my older sisters, but I don't care, as I'm used to hand-me-downs and I'm very fond of my privacy and big bedroom.

Before reading, I sit at my desk and write down the names of my girlfriends who I am inviting to my birthday party. Let's see, the first one for sure is Bonnie Lathe. We have been friends for as long as I can remember.

Bonnie lives on the corner of Main Avenue and Fifth Street, so Bonnie and I grew up together, playing hide-and-seek, kick the can, and baseball in the alley until darkness descended and the streetlights came on. She has four older brothers and is quite a tomboy.

She's tall and slim with short brown hair, brown eyes, and a small turned-up nose. Her cute little face is always smiling, and she's a good friend. She's a lot of fun too. Her caring mother and quiet father are easygoing, but she has to contend with a lot of teasing from her older brothers. I always tell her she's so lucky to have so many brothers, but she insists I'm the lucky one to have so many sisters. Gee, I wonder, are we ever satisfied, or do we always want what we don't have?

With the thunder and lightning continuing on the other side of my window, I add Sonya's name to my party list. Out of all of my friends, Sonya seems to be so knowledgeable about boys. She lives below the tracks on Tenth Street with her parents and brother and sister. She has happily married parents, and you can tell it rubbed off on Sonya. She amazes me with her knowledge about boys and sex. If there's something she doesn't know, all she has to do is ask her older sister.

She's tall and thin with wavy blonde hair that looks almost like a boy's haircut, except for the length, clinging to the back of her neck down to her collar. She reminds me of a daisy. She is a leader, while I'm still a follower, since Jo ingrained that in me.

Three years ago, after dark, Sonya walked with me to a quiet street near her house. She stopped walking and looked at me with a serious face before saying, "When I open a car door, you have to push in the light button so the interior light will go off."

"What for? These aren't our cars."

"People keep money in their glove compartments, and there's a bracelet that I just adore and want to buy."

"No, I can't do that. That's stealing."

"Nobody cares. It's just loose change."

"No," I said as I walked away.

My refusal did not stop her, so I started for home. Stealing frightens me, as I have learned a couple of lessons in stealing when I was younger. The consequences aren't worth it.

My first lesson occurred when my mother and I were shopping in the local W. T. Grant store in downtown Kolfield. Mom had an appointment with the dentist on another floor in the same building. After the appointment she decided she wanted to do a little shopping, so we entered the store and went to the second floor. She was holding my hand and let go of it to hold up a blue towel.

I looked farther down the counter, and colorful doll clothes caught my eye. I slowly moved down to the area of little tiny shoes and clothes for baby dolls.

The shoes were piled high in an area surrounded by clear glass boundaries. More glass boundaries surrounded each area of underwear, dresses, and sweaters for dolls in case after case.

Temptation overcame me when a pair of beautiful white shoes trimmed in pink caught my eye. Knowing they would fit my baby doll, I stood on my tippy-toes and snatched them up. I stuck them in my coat pocket. No one was going to miss that one little pair of shoes, as there were so many of them.

After arriving home with my secret treasure, I ran upstairs to our bedroom, where my doll, Sweet Sue, was waiting. The shoes were a perfect fit.

Jo came running up the stairs after school and, seeing the shoes, quickly said, "Wow, where did you get those pretty shoes?"

"Mommy bought them for me."

"Where are the shoes for my doll, or did she buy me something else?" she asked, looking around the room.

"You didn't get anything."

"How come Mom bought you something and didn't buy me anything?"

After sticking my tongue out really fast I said, "Because she loves me more."

Never in the world did the thought occur to me that Jo would tell Mom. Armed for battle, Jo, the first grader, went stomping downstairs and confronted Mom about why Mom didn't buy her something.

"Anna, come here," Mom yelled up the stairs.

After facing my mother in the kitchen, she wiped her hands on her apron and asked me, "What do you have that I supposedly bought for you?"

"Shoes for my doll."

"I want to see them," she said with her hands on her hips and that look in her eyes.

I ran upstairs and brought them down. The whole time I was thinking she wouldn't be angry with me. She would let me keep them. After all, it was just a pair of tiny shoes.

"Here they are," I said excitedly, holding out my hands with the shoes.

"That's stealing. A thief is a very bad person, and you don't want to be one. No one will ever like you," she shouted as she grabbed the shoes.

"Tomorrow we will take them back to the store," she said as she placed the shoes on the kitchen table.

She turned and jerked the belt off the nail and smacked me twice on my behind. I knew Jo felt bad when she saw I got the belt, but she felt worse when I told her Mom loved me more, so we were probably even.

The very next day Mom took the shoes and me back to the W. T. Grant store.

I wanted to put them back where I found them, but she said, "No, it's not that easy."

We went straight to the manager's office, and I had to give them back to Mr. Whyte, the manager.

"What do you say?" asked Mom while pushing me toward Mr. Whyte.

Sobbing and stuttering, I managed to say, "I'm sorry and I'll never steal from your store again."

The fear of being spanked hung over me, ready to suffocate me.

But he said, without even raising his voice, "I'm sure you learned a lesson and will never do that again. You must never steal." With those words, he patted me on my head.

He accompanied me up the stairs to the second floor and watched while I put them back with all the other shoes. My heart was broken, as I loved that pair of shoes. They were a perfect fit!

That was my first lesson in stealing; my second was the one that really made me realize it wasn't worth it. As I brush my hair, I think about how good Edna and Reds are to us, and yet we did them wrong.

When I was eleven years old and Jo was twelve, we walked in on Edna and Reds in their bedroom. We just marched in, and they were lying on the bed kissing, and Edna's hand was on the front of Reds below his belt. We startled them, as they didn't hear us come in the house.

Edna jumped up and was angry, yelling, "Don't you kids know you should knock before coming in?"

I was a little confused, because we never had to knock before. If we encountered a locked door, we just went home; if it was unlocked, we just walked in.

Reds wasn't angry though and said, "Edna, don't yell at them. It's okay, they didn't know we were in the bedroom."

With a big smile on his face, he gave her a kiss and said, "We'll catch up with each other later, okay?"

On this very day Jo and I saw Edna put money in the inside pocket of Reds's army jacket, which was hanging in their bedroom closet. After all of the good things Edna and Reds did for us, you'd think we would never want to hurt them in any way.

A week later, Jo and I walked over to Edna's. No one was home, as the door was locked.

"Anna, let's check out their bedroom window and see if it's open."

"No, Jo, they're not home. Besides, we shouldn't do that. They're probably in there napping on the bed."

"Come on, Anna, don't be such a baby. I'll peek in first to make sure."

A side porch runs along the entire side of the house, where their bedroom window is located. After peeking in the window, Jo took the screen out and pushed the window up, as it wasn't locked. She crawled through the window and said, "Anna, just watch out, and if Edna and Reds come home, call me."

"What are you going to do?"

"Just shut up and do as I say."

I was a nervous wreck, standing on the porch, looking for I don't know what, and just wanting to go home. Jo finally came out and closed the window, putting the screen back on. She grabbed my arm and blurted out, "Come on, let's get out of here."

We ran up the street and through the alley to home. We slowed down half a block from home, and Jo confessed, "I got some of the money that was in Reds' uniform jacket. I'm going to use it for a new pair of jeans."

"Oh, no, Jo, they're going to hate us. We can't take their money."

"Don't worry. How are they going to know we took the money? Don't be such a baby."

Now I felt really sick, as I hated it when I got caught up in these things with Jo. Yet, I never had the courage to say no to her, so actually it was my fault I was in this mess. I really hated myself at that point.

Well, lo and behold, that evening Edna and Reds paid us a visit. Upstairs I heard their voices, and I became terrified. What if they discovered the money missing? What were we going to do? They were talking softly to Mom and Dad in the kitchen. After a while Mom yelled upstairs for Jo and I to come down to the kitchen.

"Anna, don't say anything. Just deny everything. They don't know we did it," Jo whispered, grabbing my arm as I started down the stairs.

Walking into the kitchen felt like walking into a lion's den. Edna and Reds were standing together with their backs to the sink. Mom and Dad were sitting at the table, and Dad had his hands folded in front of him. Mom was pushing her hair back and repositioning her bobby pins. We stood facing them, as if facing a shooting squad.

Edna had her arms crossed, and I'll never forget the fury and darkness in her eyes when she looked at us and said, "I want the money back you stole from us. You two little thieves took money from our house."

Reds didn't say anything, and when I looked at him I felt really bad and started to cry.

"We didn't take your money," Jo yelled.

"You are nothing but little thieves, and you will never come to my house again. Where's our money?"

Jo screamed at Edna, "I said we didn't take your money. If you think we took it, prove it."

"If you don't give our money back, we're going to call the police. They'll take fingerprints and know it was you, and then you'll go to jail."

"Go ahead, I don't care. Call the police," Jo said as she hit the top of the chair with her fist.

I was scared to death and still crying, not saying any words, just sobbing.

Mom and Dad never said a word, as evidently Edna and Reds wanted to handle it their own way.

At this point Reds said quietly, "Now, now, Edna, you don't want to call the police. Jo, we know you and Anna went in through our bedroom window because as soon as we got home, the neighbor next door came over and told us. She saw you climb in the bedroom window while Anna waited on the porch. We checked around and decided to check the money in my army jacket. That's when we discovered ten dollars was missing. Now, we know you did it. We just want to know why you did it, and we want you to return our money."

With that I really started sobbing, knowing we were going to go to jail. I yelled, "Give him the money, Jo. Don't lie. We're sorry, honestly."

Jo gave me the dirtiest look ever, and if no one had been around she would have killed me, no matter how much she loved me. She took the ten dollars out of her pocket and threw it at them. She ran out of the room and upstairs. Mom took down the belt and was about to chase us, but Reds stopped her. "Don't, Daisy. I think they learned their lesson."

Still sobbing, I nodded my head yes and ran upstairs. That was a big lesson I learned in life, and I realized that I had to start thinking for myself and stop being led around by other people, including my older sister.

Even after that horrible experience, Edna and Reds still loved us and would have us over to their house to do all kinds of fun things. We'd make our own root beer and bottle it; make taffy and pull it and stretch it until it was just right; pick cherries off the tree in her backyard and then pit them, one at a time, for cherry pies. Maybe that's why I love cherries so much—they allow good memories to flood my mind.

The rain pours down outside, and the lightning continues to flash in my room while the thunder rolls through the heavens.

Still brushing my hair, I realize I've had two experiences in stealing, but the last one was when I really knew that you just couldn't take things when you want them, as people get hurt and dislike you. You need to earn money to buy things, or it has to be given to you as a loan or gift.

It's embarrassing and humiliating when you get caught, and it seems I always get caught, no matter what I do.

So I guess that's why I can't steal from cars with Sonya. It didn't bother her, and I wasn't her guardian, so I never said anything. I suppose maybe it was just as bad not saying anything. If Mom had said nothing about me stealing, I might have thought it was all right and kept doing it, and I could be in prison now.

Chapter 17

———

I'm not ready for bed, and after another crack of lightning, my thoughts drift back to that humiliating summer before I entered eighth grade. That was the summer I almost lost my friendship with Sonya—the summer I learned the most astounding, mind-blowing information of my life.

While sitting on the corner of the four-foot-high wall built of big rocks, in front of the church on Main Avenue, Sonya nonchalantly told me about boys in general and how different they are from girls. I was astonished at what she was saying. She started laughing.

"Anna, what's wrong with you? You have such a funny look on your face."

The expression on my face must have been shocking. I had never thought about boys and girls being different. I had no brothers and didn't hang around any boys, so I didn't know. At home we never saw our mother naked, let alone our father, not even in his underwear. I just assumed we were all built the same. Why in the world would I have thought any differently?

Then I realized she was just pulling my leg. Laughing, I say, "You almost got me on that one. Jeepers, how dumb do you think I am?"

"You really don't know boys are different from girls, do you?" She had such a serious look on her face.

"Stop making stuff up," I said as I jumped off the rock wall and started walking.

"Wait, Anna. Did you know that the 'thing' boys have in their private area grows?"

Covering my ears, I looked at her. "Stop, Sonya, I'm not stupid. I know better than to believe everything you tell me." With that I walked away.

"Anna, wait, I saw it happen. It grows and gets big and hard! My sister told me they call it a penis."

I stopped and turned to look at her. She had a serious look on her face and wasn't laughing at all, not even smiling.

"I never heard of such a thing, and it grows, like a plant or a flower?

What do you mean you saw it happen? I never see a plant grow while I watch it."

"My sister told me to watch when she danced with her boyfriend, Carl. She was dancing and moving her hips, and she rubbed up against him and you could actually see it growing in his pants. There was a bulge like a big fist in his pants."

At that moment I was very upset with Sonya for telling me this stuff. I pointed my finger at her face and said, "If I find out this is all a lie, I'll never talk to you again. I'm going to the library right now to see if I can look it up."

"It's true, Anna. If you want, I'll go to the library with you."

"Okay, let's go." I grabbed her arm, pulling her along with me.

I was more upset because I felt so stupid. If this was all true, why didn't anyone tell me boys were different? And why did I never even notice?

We walked to the public library located in the West End School on Twelfth Street. The library was located downstairs, and we made our way down to the library door. Before opening the door, I looked at Sonya. "Just remember, if you're teasing me, I'll never talk to you again."

She nodded her head in agreement as the door opened.

The musty book scent that I love so much hit me when we entered the library. Knowing all of these shelves of books were overflowing with information filled me with awe every time I entered. There were shelves and shelves of books surrounding tables and chairs where you could sit and read in peace and quiet. Browsing through the books and touching them always made me feel good inside. It was my escape from the world.

I knew it couldn't be true and soon enough would discover it was all a joke that Sonya was playing on me. We looked up the word "penis," and I was shocked to see there was such a thing.

"Oh, gosh. This can't be true. How come no one ever told me?" I exclaimed.

Sonya brought me a couple more books explaining our bodies so I could read through them. There were illustrations that actually showed the penis, and it was so unbelievable. We spent two hours reading the articles and looking at the pictures. The book stated the penis was also used to make babies.

The librarian walked by several times as we tried hiding the books with our shoulders, arms, and hands. She finally stopped and asked, "May I help you girls with something?"

"No, we're okay. Thank you," I said with some embarrassment and a red face. I didn't want her to know how dumb I was.

After thorough research of the subject, we left the library. I felt absurd for not knowing about this uncanny revelation. Never once did I notice any difference. I never even had a single thought that boys were different. How could this possibly be? How could I have been so stupid?

"Sonya, if you ever tell anyone I didn't know this, I'll never be your friend again."

"It's okay. I won't tell," Sonya said as she gave me a sympathetic hug.

Hopefully, I wouldn't be looking at the boys, trying to see if I could actually see it. For goodness sakes, everyone in the whole world must have known about this difference except me.

Lying in bed that night, I realized something that I had never told anyone. When I was about six years old, my mother took me with her to visit some lady and her son, Paul, who was seven years old. Mom sat at their kitchen table, talking with the other lady, while I played with Paul and some of his toys.

"I have a pony. Do you want to see him?" asked Paul.

"A real honest-to-goodness pony?"

"Yes, he's in the backyard. Come on."

I went over to my mother and said, "Mommy, can I go see Paul's pony? It's in the backyard. Please?"

She looked at the other lady, who shook her head yes, and said, "Okay, but come right back here then."

Paul took my hand, and we went down the steps into the basement, which was actually another kitchen. Walking down the stairs, I noticed a white stove and refrigerator on one side. Then there were doors that opened up into the fenced-in backyard where the pony was allowed to roam.

"Before you can see and touch the pony, you have to come under the kitchen table with me," said Paul.

I remember it was a gray-topped table with shiny chrome legs. We bent down and crawled under the table, and he said, "Now lie down and pull your panties down."

"No, I don't want to."

"You have to or you won't see the pony, and I'll tell your mother you wouldn't do it. We're going to play like my Mommy and Daddy play."

I was really scared and didn't know what was worse, pulling my pants down or having my mother angry with me.

Lying down I pushed my panties down to my knees.

Paul did the same with his pants and lay on top of me. I didn't like that feeling. There was something soft touching me that didn't seem right.

I remember my mother calling down the stairs and saying, "Anna, where are you?"

Paul glared at me and whispered, "Don't tell your mother about this or I'll tell her you wanted to do this."

"I'm coming, Mommy," I yelled as Paul got off of me, and I quickly pulled up my panties.

I flew up the stairs faster than Paul and hugged Mom. She said, "What's the matter? Were you afraid of the pony?"

"Yes."

My mother continued talking with Paul's mother, and I stayed by her side.

"Do you want to go to see my pony again," Paul asked.

"No," I replied.

"Go ahead, Anna. It's okay. The pony won't hurt you," said Paul's mother.

"No, I don't want to go."

"Well, why don't we all go down and I'll show you the pony won't hurt you," she said with a smile on her face.

"That's a good idea," said Mom.

We all went down, and I did get to see the real pony in the backyard.

It suddenly dawns on me the weird soft thing I felt was his penis. Evidently, even though Paul was my age, he thought more of showing his penis instead of his pony. I wonder if all boys feel that way.

Chapter 18

After adding Sonya's name to my birthday party list, I wonder how I ever survived those two years of junior high school. Being self-conscious and chubby, I knew that was why the boys liked the other girls and not me. It seems the other girls all matured faster than me.

The first year was the most difficult, when the West End School and East End School came together. We were all shoved in classes with kids from the other end of town who we didn't even know. When it came to boys, I never acted silly or talked about liking them, for fear of being rejected. It was also the first time we had different teachers for different subjects and changed to many different rooms. It was a lot to digest, but after two months it seemed like everyone knew everyone, including the teachers. We all made new friends.

Seventh grade started out difficult for me, as one of my teachers, Mr. Lowry, thought I could do better. He gave me my first and last D. Mr. Lowry kept a wooden paddle hanging in his room and made me stand in front of the class while he whacked me on my behind once. The paddle didn't hurt, but the embarrassment did. He felt I didn't participate in class discussion like I should, but I was always afraid I'd give the wrong answer even though I was right 95 percent of the time in my mind. He told me that next time he would take me across his lap and really paddle me. I never got any more of those Ds.

Before getting back to my birthday list, I recall that things started happening for me in ninth grade, when I started my period.

That was quite an experience even though I had been patiently awaiting it. They showed us a film about it in eighth grade, so I knew it was coming but took its darn old time.

All I knew from overhearing my sisters talk was I was going to start having periods, I would get them every month, and I would have to wear a Kotex belt that attached to a pad of some kind in my underwear. Hopefully, if I was lucky, they told me, I wouldn't have to wear the worn-out, bleached-white bobby socks that they had to use sometimes.

It was very expensive having all of those females in the house and buying boxes of Kotex. And after all, it was one way of getting rid of the old white bobby socks.

All of my girlfriends had started their periods except for me. They called me a "late bloomer." When I did start getting the signs, I asked one of my older girlfriends from Seventh Street.

Not wanting anyone else to hear, I asked Phyllis to walk with me to the front of the Slovak Catholic Church, which was on the corner of Sixth Street and Main Avenue. I asked Phyllis because she was an only child, seemed more mature, and never laughed at me when I asked her something.

My sisters would tease me terribly if I asked them. I told Phyllis what was happening to me, and she told me what to do and what to expect next.

When my mother did the wash the following Monday, she saw my underwear and said, "Anna, I see you started menstruating." She actually said "minstrating," as she got through only sixth grade.

I remember holding up my hand like a patrol guard and saying, "I don't want to talk about it," and then I walked away.

That was the only time my mother tried to talk to me about any of this. All of a sudden the thought of her discussing periods with me made me embarrassed. After all, mothers didn't know anything, and I could handle this on my own. This was so personal, so private, and yet I could talk to any of my girlfriends about it—but not my mother. My mother never shared this information with me before, so why start now?

After starting my periods, my baby fat melted away, and curves and breasts appeared. Tenth grade was a turning point in my life. Even though I was smart in school and got good grades, I didn't really like to socialize. I preferred reading a good book in the corner of our couch to hanging out with the kids at Trumbull's Drugstore.

Why do I keep thinking about all of these things, and why do I feel so restless? I wish I could change my life so I don't feel this way.

Then I remember being told on several occasions, "Be careful of what you wish for or you may receive it."

Little did I know that I shouldn't have wished for anything different in my life. Change is good but not always.

Chapter 19

━━━

The next name to be added to my birthday list is Connie, who's my very best friend. Even though the majority of our friendship has only been in the school, we tell each other everything.

She has natural light-brown hair that is soft and shiny and curls on its own. The shorter her hair, the tighter her curls, and that's why she wears it almost to her shoulders. Her mouth is the most outstanding feature on her face, as her lips are nice and full. Her top lip is so full that it seems to float, allowing her beautiful white teeth to be seen unless she intentionally closes her lips. She has beautiful green eyes with long eyelashes, rosy cheeks, and an hourglass figure. She wears her sister's hand-me-downs, like me. We're so compatible and enjoy each other so much that we know we'll be friends for life, no matter what.

Connie lives in a company house at Mine Thirty-Five on the other side of Kolfield. Her house is just like ours.

Connie and I rarely see each other outside of school since we live so far apart, but we do enjoy having our lunches together at school. We also share all of our classes, as we signed up for the commercial courses with typing and shorthand and business math. We're going to be the best secretaries in the whole world.

We laugh and giggle and walk the halls to our classes together. Once in a while we talk on the phone when we're home but only if we have a question that can't wait until school. We can't tie up the party lines or someone will interrupt the conversation and demand we hang up and free the line.

We share all of our secrets, including what we know about all of our teachers. There is a rumor that one of our male teachers lives with another man, as they love each other. That doesn't matter to us, as he's one of our favorite teachers.

Last year one of our teachers was murdered. Huge headlines covered the front page of the newspaper, and we were shocked that this happened to someone we knew. She was a happy and considerate teacher, always smiling—at least she was while she was around us. Connie and I knew she could never be replaced, but somehow life continues.

Connie lives with her mother and sister and never complains that she can't go anywhere. She helps her mother with the housework, as she doesn't have a father and her mother has to work full-time. She never mentions her father, and I never ask. She only told me once that he had to go away. The one thing I love about her is she is always so positive and smiling.

I can't wait to tell her about the birthday party, as she's so much fun to be around.

With the rain pouring down, I continue my birthday list. The next name I add is Beverly, another fun person to be with. She always makes me laugh. She lives two blocks away, below the tracks. It's convenient for us to do things together since we live so close. Bev is short and chubby with red hair. She is very pretty, and her smile lights up the entire room. Her gray eyes have a sparkle to them, as she's always laughing. Bev loves excitement and can't wait until we all get our driver's licenses so we can see more things and travel to more places. She said there's so much happening in the world outside of Kolfield, and we need to explore these areas.

Hearing the downstairs cuckoo clock do eleven cuckoos, I yawn and realize how tired I am—too tired to read tonight. I crawl into my bed, and the smell of the outdoors on the clean sheets makes me feel good. The summer breeze has dried the sheets while hanging on the clothesline, and that luxurious scent clings to the sheets.

As I lie in my bed I think about how much fun I had this past year in school. I was even an attendant to the queen of hearts at the Valentine Dance. My partner was Billy Yonovich, a short, dark-haired, good-looking guy with a square face and an olive complexion. It was fun walking together up the stairs and onto the stage through the huge colorful heart to dance. Our class members voted for the king and queen of hearts and their attendants, so I felt honored to have been voted by my friends to be part of this occasion.

Little did I realize how much fun I was really having. I wish someone would have forewarned me about how things were going to change my life forever.

Chapter 20

The sun shining through the bedroom window wakens me, as I forgot to pull the window shade down last night. Turning away I lie there, smelling the coffee my mother and father perk every single morning. The kitchen is directly below my bedroom. Having a small register in each room to let the hot air rise from downstairs up into the bedrooms helps, as sound travels the same way. Sometimes you hear conversations even when you don't want to hear them.

Mom's voice drifts upward. "Liz is coming over this morning, so Anna can watch Louis for an hour, as she has some errands to do. What time are you opening the bait store today?"

"I'm going out as soon as I have my coffee," Dad replies in his soft, deep voice.

Oh, good, I get to watch Louis this morning. I love that little guy so much, and he's so much fun to watch. Maybe it's because I love my sister Liz so much. Liz is next to the oldest, and she and her husband, Pep, are great people.

They have a cute little blond-haired boy named Louis, and sometimes I call him Louie. Liz's husband's real name is Louis too, but everyone in high school called him Pep, as it's short for his last name, Peparsoni. He was a good high school football player, and I suppose that's where the name Pep originated and stuck, from the other football players.

I smile when I think about Elizabeth, as she's such a warm, compassionate person, full of love for everyone. She not only enjoys telling stories but also writing stories and poems, and she loves to laugh. She has blonde hair, blue eyes, and full lips on her tiny face. She's very thin but very shapely and looks more like my father than my mother.

Sometimes I believe she got the most beatings when we were young because she did look like my father. Liz always thought that too and even mentioned it to me.

Lying in the sun and getting brown is one of Liz's favorite things. She always remarks how she loves the warmth of the sun on her body.

One summer, in her shorts and halter, she was lying on a blanket in our backyard. Across the alley lives our neighbor, Donna. She called Liz over to give her some comic books that she had finished reading.

Donna is a tiny, plain woman and is very generous and loving to her children and husband. She isn't the greatest housekeeper but probably because it's not as important to her. She loves to read comic books and is always trading comic books with all of the kids in the neighborhood.

Donna and her husband, Ted, have three children, Teddy, Gwynn, and Johnny. They must all read comic books, as they have stacks of them piled everywhere. We loved trading the different comics with her, as she always had the latest and the best.

Donna noticed welts on Liz's back and was shocked.

"What happened to your back, Liz?" Donna asked as she touched one of the welts.

"Nothing."

"Did your mother beat you with that strap?"

"No, no, she didn't."

"You don't have to lie to me, Liz. I know these welts are from a belt. I'm going to talk to your mother about it."

"Please don't. I don't want any trouble."

"It's my duty to confront your mother. It's just not right."

With that she stormed up the back porch steps and knocked on the back door.

When Mom came out, Donna lashed into her. "Daisy, you can't beat your kids like that. Liz has welts all over her back. If you keep doing that, she'll have scars all over her back."

"Don't tell me how to raise my kids. I'll punish my kids any way I see fit. Mind your own damn business," she yelled as she walked back into the house, slamming the screen door.

"I'm so sorry, Liz. She won't listen to me. If she does that again, you come to my house and I'll call the police," Donna said loud enough for Mom to hear and then walked back across the alley to her house.

Donna still reads comic books, but I don't, so we aren't in contact with each other as much. Strange how people drift into your life and then drift out. It's almost as if you outgrow certain people. They remain the same, but you change.

Sitting up on the edge of the bed, I realize it's time to get dressed so I'll be ready when Louis gets here.

Liz is so lucky to be such a very creative person and, depending on her mood, can sit down and write a short story or a poem and think nothing of it. She loves children and reading to them. She even enjoys telling stories to them that she makes up as she goes along.

Liz could have really done a lot if she hadn't become ill. At the age of sixteen, she sprained her ankle and developed rheumatic fever and then rheumatoid arthritis. I vaguely remember her ankle was hurting and the doctor wrapped it tightly in a bandage and taped it with white tape. She was hospitalized for a while, and then it seemed everything went wrong. It has been a slow process over the years, but the rheumatoid arthritis has been spreading throughout her entire body into every joint. She has a lot of pain most of the time, and that's why she enjoys the warmth of the sun on her joints.

Liz and Pep were high school sweethearts. But he was an Italian Catholic and she a Protestant, so both families were against them dating each other. Pep is about five foot eleven and has sandy hair with brown eyes. He is good-looking with lots of hair and wears eyeglasses. He has an Italian nose and nicely shaped full lips. He has a mole on his upper lip and one on his cheek, but it doesn't take away from his looks.

Pep is a very kind person and would help anyone in the world. If you ask him to do something for you, he never refuses. He never talks about people in a bad way or puts them down and is always doing favors for everyone.

During high school, Liz and Pep would sneak around to see each other. Catholics and Protestants aren't allowed to be seen dating because of the prejudices of my family and many other families. After a high school dance, Pep would walk Liz two blocks away from our house, where our sister Martha would be waiting for them. Martha would then walk home with Liz those last two blocks. No one was the wiser, as the two sisters went together and came home together.

Mom would sometimes walk near the Sixth Street corner and stand in the dark, watching to see who walked them home. She never realized that they separated on Seventh Street. Eventually, when they became seniors, Pep started coming to the house.

Mom loves to watch wrestling on the television, and that smoothed the way for Pep, as he was a wrestler in high school. They would sit there and say nothing, their eyes glued to the loud TV until Liz came downstairs.

Immediately after graduation, Pep got a job at the Bethlehem Steel Mills. Early one morning voices in the kitchen woke me up. I tiptoed down the stairs in my robe to see what was happening; the only unusual thing was Pep was there. Everybody hushed up when they saw me. Then the hugging and kissing started.

After shaking Dad's hand and kissing Liz, Pep walked out the back door without his lunch bucket. I tried to call after him that he forgot it, but everyone told me to be quiet. That didn't make sense to me. Why should he go without his lunch?

When Pep was gone, they told me he had signed up to go in the army but didn't tell his family. He and Liz had become engaged the week before, and this way his family couldn't discourage their relationship. The pretense was he was going to work but was actually leaving for basic training. One of his friends was waiting to take him to the bus station.

After basic training, Pep was sent to Korea, and Liz wrote to him every single night after she came home from work. She worked at Bausch & Lomb, where they made eyeglasses and sunglasses in Johnstown, riding the bus back and forth each day. Mom always saved dinner for her, but she usually didn't want anything to eat. She'd stay in her bedroom, eating snacks and writing letters to Pep. Then she'd read the letters from him over and over.

Liz is skilled in getting someone to do something for her. I can attest to that. She wore socks to work every day, which needed to be washed by hand every couple of days in order to not run out of clean socks.

"Anna, can you do me a big favor and wash out my white socks for me?"

"Don't you have any clean ones?"

"No, and you're the only one that does it right. I don't think anyone can do a better job than you. Would you please?"

"I don't know, Liz. Can't Jo or Martha do it?"

"I don't want to ask them. You're the only one that can get them clean. They aren't as good as you. You know just how to scrub them together with your knuckles, and they don't," she said, smiling at me and giving me a big hug.

So every couple of nights I'd scrub the socks for her and hang them in the bathroom to dry. Sometimes she'd send me to the Sixth Street store to buy potato chips and sodas. I had to be careful Mom didn't know, as she didn't want Liz eating junk food.

Actually, I felt honored to do any chores for Liz, because that's how she made me feel. She encouraged me to feel good about myself.

Pep's two older sisters came to our house to try to talk Liz out of her engagement. They had called first and asked if they could come over to the house to talk to Liz.

My mother (who surprised me that evening by being such an understanding person) made them cookies and served them tea in her good china cups. They all sat and talked while Jo and I listened from the other room, trying to understand everything; a lot of the talk was concerning religion.

Pep's sisters love him very much and were upset that he joined the army. They wanted him to be happy, but they wanted to know Liz better. They knew he loved Liz very much to join the army. It ended happily, because after they got to know Liz, they loved her more than they could have imagined.

Once you meet Liz, you can't help but love her, and when she hugs you, you know she means it. Something in her hugs always makes me feel good. Maybe it's because my mother never took the time to hug me or pat me or kiss me on the cheek or praise me. Liz is the opposite, as she seems to radiate a loving and warm aura all the time.

When Pep came home from Korea, Liz had been attending the Catholic religious classes while he was away but hadn't quite finished. They wanted to get married as soon as possible, as Pep was still in the army and they wanted to be together.

A big wedding was held at the Catholic Church even though she wasn't a full-fledged Catholic yet. They weren't married inside the actual church; instead they were married in the church vestibule.

She wore a beautiful white gown with long sleeves that came to a point on the back of her hands, a scalloped neckline made of lace and adorned with pearls, and a beautiful lace veil. She was absolutely beautiful.

Pep was assigned to Washington, DC, where they found an apartment. Their first child, Louis, was born in Washington, DC, in September, ten months after they were married. Now Pep is out of the service, and they're living back home here in Kolfield.

I have to laugh to myself as I pull my shorts up over my rear, remembering the fun we had the summer before Louis was born. There was never a dull moment when Jo was living at home. I wish I had known how much fun I was having, but sometimes you have to grow up in a hurry and then it's too late when the realization hits you.

Mom hollers up the stairs, "Anna, you better get up. Louis will be here any minute."

"I'm already up and dressed. I'll be down in a few minutes."

Chapter 21

Mom knows I'm up, as she can hear my footsteps and the floorboards squeaking, but I guess she just wanted to hear my voice.

Jo and I know every squeaky board on the house steps leading upstairs. Knowing the creaky steps has saved us more than once when we would crawl cautiously down the stairs, through the dining room, and into the kitchen to steal a snack. Crawling on our bellies wasn't an easy feat, but we were good at it.

As I brush my hair, I realize that I'm so lucky to have a nephew who I can babysit. He is the most adorable little boy, with his blond hair and blue eyes. I love it when he puts his arms around me and gives me a big hug, or I ask him how much he loves me and he holds out his arms as wide as possible.

He walks a little now and says quite a few words. I know he's going to be a very successful person when he grows up, maybe a doctor or a lawyer or a movie star. He'll be so handsome, and all of the girls will swoon over him.

I do a last-minute check in the mirror and then run down the stairs and almost collide with Dad at the bottom.

"Jeez, Anna, do you have to run down the stairs like that? You almost knocked me over."

"What would you rather I do, Dad, slide down the stairs on my rump? You know Mom doesn't like us to do that."

"Did you ever think you could just put one foot in front of the other and walk down slowly?" he says as he shakes his head.

He does that a lot lately when he tells me something I'm doing wrong or something he doesn't like. Maybe he doesn't like teenagers. I know he likes little kids because he adores Louis, or is it because he's a boy? Hmm, I wonder.

Dad makes a pot of oatmeal every morning for us. He says it is good for us. Today I just want toast with jam even though I love oatmeal.

As I finish my toast I hear Liz pull up in her 1954 black Buick. It's not pure black, as it is accented by a peach color, a lot of chrome, and four chrome holes on each side. I like it because it's so new.

Looking out the window facing the backyard and alley, I see Louis standing on the front seat. Running out the door onto the back porch I holler, "Hi, Liz. Hi, Louis."

Louis is trying to get out of the car, but Liz tells him to wait a minute until she can get to the other side. When out, he does a wobbly walk toward me, with Liz holding one of his hands. I pick him up and swing him around, which he loves for me to do.

Louis hollers, "Mo, mo."

I laugh and tell him, "Later, Louie baby, right now you have to see Mom Mom and Pap Pap."

With Louis in my arms, I give Liz a big hug and ask her how she's feeling.

"I'm having a good day today, probably because the sun is shining. I might do some sunbathing later if you care to spend some time with me."

"Sounds good to me. It gets pretty boring around here."

Just then Mom and Dad come down the back porch steps, and Dad takes Louis from my arms. Louis gives him a big hug and a kiss and then leans over and kisses Mom while clinging to Dad's shirt.

"You don't mind watching him, do you, Anna?" Liz asks with complete honesty.

"Heavens, no, I love to watch him. We're going to do some coloring, and I'll probably read him a book. Besides, Dad will probably have him for a little while until he leaves to go to the lot."

"Okay, I'll only be gone for about two hours. If you want to go back to my house with me, be ready when I come back, and don't let Louis sleep, as he can do that while we lay in the sun."

Dad sings a song to Louis while carrying him on his back, and we all go into the house while Liz and Mom stay outside to continue their conversation. It amazes me that Liz and Mom get along so well now that Liz is married and has a baby. I wonder if Liz ever thinks about the beatings that Mom used to give her.

As I watch Mom and Liz through the kitchen window, I realize that older sisters are a lot of fun, and they give you a lot of things for which to be thankful. All of my girlfriends tell me they envy me, as I have so many older sisters and now brother-in-laws and a nephew. I guess I'm very fortunate but still feel there is something missing in my life, a loneliness and emptiness inside of me.

Chapter 22

After I spend the afternoon at Liz's house, she brings me home and I sit on the front porch for a few minutes, enjoying the warm weather.

"Anna, did you call your girlfriends about your birthday party?" Mom asks through the front screen door.

"No, but I'll do it tonight and definitely by tomorrow."

"Martha called, and she'll be coming home this weekend."

Holding my breath I say, "Does that mean I have to go back to the little room?"

"No, you can sleep with her if you like. I don't think she'd mind."

"No, thanks, I'll sleep in the little room until she leaves."

Oh, well, I think to myself, *I'll just have to suffer one weekend while Martha the teaser is home.*

Martha is the third child and hates to be teased even though she is the biggest teaser in the family. At mealtimes when Mom and Dad weren't looking, she'd scoop a spoonful of mashed potatoes into her mouth and then squish them through her teeth at us. Sometimes she'd chew her food and then, making sure it was on her tongue, stick her tongue out at us.

Martha's best way of teasing or trying to hurt us is with words. She'll make a snide remark that someone stinks and wrinkle up her nose or brag about where she's going with her friends. She tries to make us feel inferior to her, but we just laugh and say, "Sticks and stones will break our bones but names and faces will never hurt us," which makes her all the more angry and, believe me, she has quite a temper. Everyone says her temper is because she has red hair, but I think it's because she doesn't always get her way.

Jo and I used to tease Martha that she was pigeon-toed. She really wasn't, but she loved to wear this one pair of ugly maroon leather shoes that had thick rubber tractor soles and heels, and they tied in the front with black laces. Since she loved the shoes so much, we told her she walked with her toes pointed slightly inward; therefore, she was pigeon-toed. One day the shoes just disappeared. Of course she denies ever owning a pair of shoes like that.

Martha's thoughts of being perfect became her Achilles' heel, and that makes us tease her all the more. She also has this fantasy that our dad isn't her father. She feels her father is, as she said, "some rich big shot in Kolfield," and someday he is going to recognize her as his daughter and she'll be rich. Of course, she knows that would be great, as she'd never have to bother with any of us again.

When I think about her, maybe she's right; maybe she isn't related to us. But then again, there is a resemblance among all of us.

Martha's fantasies worsened when she became somewhat like an adopted daughter to Alice and Frank Smith, who are a childless couple. Alice is a short, chubby woman of about four foot ten with gray hair. She is heavyset with a round face offset by a piggish-looking nose. She not only gives piano lessons but is also a great singer.

Her husband, Frank, is taller with thin brown hair that is combed from the left side to the right side across the top of his head. It isn't thick enough to cover his scalp and gives the appearance of someone trying to hide the fact that he is going bald. He's also a volunteer fireman, and I'm sure he also has a full-time job somewhere, but I don't know what it is. His face is tough-looking, as if he is a member of Al Capone's elite group, and yet, after you get to know him, he's a very nice, helpful, and compassionate man.

Alice and Frank drive Martha and her girlfriends everywhere and buy her everything. Of course, all of that only reinforces Martha's opinion that she's better than any of us.

Once I used to have long pigtails that went down my back below my waist. I had never had a haircut until eighth grade. Then Mom, either trying to impress Alice and Frank or granting them the honor of their request, allowed Alice to cut my hair.

Yes, the Alice who was like a mother to Martha and was a singer and piano teacher. She wasn't a hairdresser, but she wanted to cut my hair.

So one summer morning we arrived at their home. We walked up one step onto her porch and past the white swing hanging from the porch ceiling. Not only were red geraniums lining the front of the porch, but they were also on a small table situated on the porch with a chair on each side. As we walked in the front door, Alice greeted us with a smile and a hug, scissors and towel.

She took us through her living room, where she gave piano lessons, and into their sitting room, where the big deed was to be done.

The sitting room was like a big dining room without the table and chairs. A leather easy chair sat on one end of the room under a floor lamp. Nearby was a bookcase with shelves filled with books, many of which were music books. The rest of the room was full of shelves and knickknacks, as she was a collector of figurines and animals. The smell of grilled cheese sandwiches and tomato soup lingered in the air, giving me hunger pangs.

Frank hollered from another room, "I'll be out in a minute. I'm loading my camera."

I was hoping this worked out all right and that I wouldn't have regrets, because once the pigtails were off, they were gone forever. I had no say in this matter, as Mom had made up her mind.

Two pigtails, tied at both ends, were thick and not easily chopped off with the scissors, but perseverance won, allowing them to be kept intact. They were wrapped in tissue paper and placed in a box to be saved for me. Actually, I believed Mom wanted them more than me, because what could I possibly do with my pigtails in a box?

"Shocked" was not the word when I looked in the mirror. I didn't want to cry, but I looked like Prince Valiant, the comic strip character.

Carefully folding the towel to keep some of the hairs in it, Alice asked, "Do you like it? Do you want more cut off?"

No answer came from me, as I was about to burst into tears.

"No, I think that's enough," Mom said as she petted my head.

After arriving home I stood on the back porch and, while holding onto the wooden banister, turned my head from left to right, right to left, back and forth, back and forth.

Jo came out and asked, "What the heck are you doing?"

"I'm turning my head because it feels so light and funny."

"You're so weird. I hope you're not going to keep your hair looking like that. It's really ugly. All you need is a sword and shield."

I knew she was referring to Prince Valiant. Her words didn't bother me, as I wasn't into hair anyway, and besides, it was true. I guessed no one else could even imagine or have any idea how I felt without my pigtails. It was like losing a big weight from my head.

Jo's hair was so shiny and pretty, with a lot of bounce in it, and I envied her a little. She wore mascara, eye color, and lipstick. Of course she spent a lot of time doing all of this, making sure she looked beautiful. I was not jealous, as I admired her and how good she always looked. I didn't want to take the time to do all of this. Besides, Mom said I was too young for that stuff.

By this time in life, all of my girlfriends knew how to put curlers in their hair or had permanents, could flip their hair or pull it back and make it all look gorgeous—all except me, of course. They knew all the tricks and the various things you could do to hair.

Having no idea how to fix my hair, it became quite a problem for me. It took two years to get it to a length that I liked and could work with it, allowing me to experiment with it. My girlfriends tried to show me different things, such as putting Scotch tape over my bangs when I dried my hair to keep them flat or how to sleep with my head full of hard rollers that hurt. At times like those I yearned for my pigtails.

It was a relief though that my mother didn't have to plat my hair every day and yank my hair if I dared move. Now she can even sleep late in the mornings if she wants to. For a long time without those pigtails though I felt like a part of me was missing.

After losing my pigtails, we then lost Martha, who went away to college. Jo and I never missed her, but I'm sure Liz missed her, as they were close growing up, like Jo and me. I think it's sad that I don't miss Martha; after all, she is my sister even if she doesn't think so.

The good thing that came out of Martha going to college was that Jo got the big bedroom all to herself, and I was the recipient of the little room. Of course, whenever Martha came home in the summer, she had to stay with Jo in the big bedroom, but at night Jo slept with me. They avoided each other as much as possible.

With my arms clasped around my knees I lean back while holding up my knees and recall a New Year's Eve two years ago. Martha and Jo were fighting over who was going to use the bathroom first, as they were both going out that night. We had one bathroom for all of us to use, and sometimes it presented a problem, especially if one took too long, intentionally or unintentionally.

I felt fortunate to have a bathroom indoors, as a couple of my girlfriends did not. One time Sonya showed me the pee can that she kept under her bed in case she had to pee during the night. This way she wouldn't have to go outdoors in the darkness. They'd just pee in it, empty each one from every bedroom into a bucket, and take it outdoors the next morning. That made me realize how lucky I was to at least have an indoor bathroom.

Our bathroom is very small and contains a toilet, a tub, and a sink. It usually smells like bubble bath, powder, and soap, except when someone does number two in the toilet.

There's absolutely no room, except for a small area of about two feet wide by five feet long in the middle. At the end of the bathroom on the outer wall is a small window that is closer to the ceiling than to the floor. It's usually open except when it's raining. Beneath the window stands a white porcelain toilet.

Approximately ten inches away from the toilet, a huge mirror in a gilded gold frame hangs on the wall above the white porcelain tub with claw feet. The mirror is almost the same width as the length of the tub.

On the opposite wall hangs a small medicine cabinet above a small sink with two faucets. The front door of the medicine cabinet is a mirror that is about twelve inches high and ten inches wide with a small light above it. This is the mirror into which everyone looks to comb their hair and put on their makeup. It's the only mirror with an overhead light, and you can also look at the back of your hair, since the large mirror is directly across from it.

When a towel is over the bathroom window, you can be sure Jo is using the bathroom to put on her makeup. She covers the window if it's light outside, as she prefers only the light above the mirror.

That New Year's Eve, Jo and Martha were both in high school. They were in their panties, bras, and crinoline slips, trying to get ready for their evening engagements. Jo was in the bathroom, and Martha yelled at her, "Get out of the bathroom, you've been in there too long."

"I have not. I haven't been in here but five minutes."

"No, you haven't, it's more like half an hour. Besides, you're so ugly, you can't make yourself pretty no matter how long you're in the bathroom."

"Who are you calling ugly, you pigeon-toed fat cow?" Jo yelled as she came out of the bathroom and shoved her face into Martha's face.

"Don't ever call me pigeon-toed or I'll slap your face," Martha said, clenching her fists at her sides.

"Pigeon-toed, pigeon-toed, pigeon-toed." Jo laughed in her face.

With that Martha raised her hand and slapped Jo in the face, and then everything happened so fast I couldn't believe my eyes.

The two of them looked like one as they fell to the floor. As they rolled in the hallway, their elbows and legs were hitting the banister and the wall. It was an actual knockdown fight and wrestling match all in one. All I could see were their arms and legs flailing about, as they could hardly move around in the narrow hall.

A coward, I stood at the end of the hall and rooted for Jo. I definitely wasn't going to get drawn into the actual battle. Jo was tough but so was Martha when her temper flared.

My father heard the yelling and the banging of arms, legs, and heads against the banister and floor. He came running upstairs, as my mother wasn't home. Thank goodness he was strong enough to pull them apart.

He yelled, "What the hell's wrong with you two? Don't you know how to share? Get your clothes on. Neither one of you are going anywhere tonight."

I chuckled, as the expression on Dad's face was priceless as he came running up the stairs when he heard the ruckus. Poor Dad was really angry, and then he lost a few seconds, not knowing how to pull them apart. He finally caught an arm of each and yanked them up to a standing position. Naturally they simmered down with him there but continued yelling at each other.

"You ugly witch," screamed Jo, getting in the last words.

Dad yelled, "Shut up, both of you."

Later when Mom walked in the door, Dad said, "Daisy, Jo and Martha aren't going out tonight."

"What happened?"

"They were fighting over the bathroom again. This time they were on the floor, hitting each other. You'd think they'd know how to share by now."

"Tonight is New Year's Eve. They have plans made. We can't just stop them from going out this late. I'll talk to them and make sure it never happens again," Mom said as I watched with a surprised look on my face.

Chapter 23

Martha arrived home last night. I think she intentionally made sure she made enough noise to awaken me. Alice and Frank had driven up to her college and brought her back. They ate dinner near the college and then took one of Martha's girlfriends home to Philadelphia before coming back to Kolfield.

One time last year Pep was driving Liz, Martha, and me to her college. While riding in the car Pep said, "Hey, Martha, I understand that in order to get to your college, you have to go through Intercourse before entering Paradise."

She'd say, "Yes, that's right, Pep, want to come along?"

Surprised and confused when he said that, I asked, "What do you mean by that?"

Liz turned her head toward me in the back of the car and explained, "Those, my dear Anna, are the actual names of two towns that you have to drive through to get to Martha's college."

"Oh, okay. I get it."

"Such a baby," Martha said while shaking her head.

Well, maybe now that Martha is home things will settle down. Mom has been running around for several days, baking and cleaning the big bedroom so her majesty will have a place to sleep. I told Mom to make sure Martha knows that I've got to go into the big bedroom to get my clothes every day, so she better not complain or yell at me.

Mom doesn't believe that Martha can tease or be nasty. Yeah, good old Martha does a good job of hiding her evil witch side and temper in front of Mom and Dad.

The sun is shining through the kitchen window and I know it's going to be a great day. I look over at the sink and notice Mom put a new cloth curtain around the bottom. It's yellow with pretty flowers and brightens the kitchen.

As I'm eating my oatmeal, lo and behold, Her Majesty walks into the kitchen, saying, "Can't you be a little more quiet in the mornings, Anna? I do need my sleep."

At that point I could say, *Yeah, you do need your beauty sleep, as ugly as you are.* Instead I am nice and say, "I didn't realize I made any noise."

"Maybe someday you'll grow up and not be so clumsy. I have to remember you're still a baby," she says as she gives me this fake grin with the veins, muscles, tendons, or whatever those bulges are in her neck that are so obvious as she strains them to make a smile.

At that point I silently count to ten and ignore her. Sometimes I think she's jealous that I'm the baby of the family, but I'm not going to let her upset me. After all, that's what she's trying to do. She's so predictable.

"Have you heard from your sister Jo lately?" Martha asks. "Is she working hard in that factory, or is she unemployed?"

Just then smiling Dad walks into the kitchen and says, "Good morning, Martha." Having already talked to Dad when he was making the pot of oatmeal, I feel I don't have to hang around. This gives me opportunity to scoot out the back door without giving her any answer at all.

I run down the back porch steps and the length of the yard, at the end of which is partially buried a rock about three feet long, two feet wide, and a foot high. When I was growing up, my imagination always led me to believe that it emerged in someone else's backyard on the other side of the world.

Since it's so solid, I know nothing can happen to me when I sit on that rock, as I'm sitting on top of the world. It's my thinking rock, and when I'm not sitting on the front porch, I sit here and do my thinking.

Hunching over and looking for four-leaf clovers in the grass around the rock, I think about my conversation with Mom this morning.

"Mom, do you know how long Martha will be home?"

"Yes, I was going to tell you. Martha got a waitress job near the college for the summer. She starts this week, so she will be going back in a few days."

That means she won't be here for my birthday party, and she definitely won't be here when the carnival comes to town. That's why I'm determined not to let her get my goat this morning. Happiness floods through me.

Chapter 24

Finally, Wednesday arrives, the day of my party and Mom and Dad's tenth wedding anniversary—an anniversary I can never share with my friends.

It's a beautiful warm day with blue skies and big, white fluffy clouds. I'd love to lie in the grass and look at the clouds, figuring out shapes of animals or people or faces. Not today though.

Instead I remove my shoes and wiggle my toes. I love to feel the breeze on my feet and rub them in the soft grass. The time flies by, and I have to get ready. After all, I don't want to be late for my own party.

All of my girlfriends arrive promptly at four o'clock, dressed in their blue jeans rolled to their knees and shirts hanging out. They carry presents wrapped in all colors of wrapping paper with ribbon and bows to match. Everyone places my presents inside the truck on the passenger's side.

I try to guess in my mind what the presents could be, as they're different shapes and sizes, but I guess I'll just have to wait. Over the years I have learned that anticipation is part of the excitement, because it's all over quickly and you have nothing to look forward to.

Standing in the alley by Dad's old green 1941 Chevy pickup truck, we joke around and wait for Dad.

"Okay, let's get going," Dad hollers as he smiles and walks down the back porch steps.

"Get in, but remember to keep your arms inside and don't stand up. We don't want to lose anyone on the way."

We laugh, climbing up and helping the one in front of us by pushing their rear up so they can tumble into the back of the truck. With our knees up to our chins, we sit facing each other. We are excited as we ride through town, waving at everyone.

Riding along, a soft, cool breeze touches my face and I realize that summer is nearly over. Soon the beauty of autumn will appear and captivate us with various colors of gold, red, brown, and yellow. Trees will surround us with these colors as the green disappears. Then the colors will fade. After the leaves have been raked and jumped into many times, they are bagged or burned. Then Old Man Winter appears.

The white snow descends out of the sky, landing silently. The first snowfall creates a cold, white landscape that looks so pure, but it doesn't last. Many snowfalls later, the white snow turns to gray, black, and brown and begins to melt, running down the mountain into the creek.

Suddenly, colors peek through the ground, confirming that spring is arriving. Eventually, the coats and boots are discarded as the sun stays in the sky longer, bringing warmer temperatures. Then summer. I'm thrilled, as that will be my last summer at home before graduating.

My thoughts are interrupted as we arrive at the lot and jump out of the truck, laughing and joking around with each other. The lot is an acre of ground surrounded by woods in the back and Dad's worm farm shed sitting near the front. Dad had planted a weeping willow tree to the right of the shed, and I have to admit it's beautiful. It actually looks like it's weeping, with its branches and leaves hanging downward.

Earlier today Dad and Reds brought over Edna's redwood picnic table and benches so we would have a place to sit and eat. Edna and Reds moved into a new house to the left of our lot, so this makes things very convenient for us. We can use their bathroom or we can pee in the woods. That's not a difficult decision for any of us, as we all prefer bathrooms except for Sonya. She said she doesn't care where she goes, as long as no one sees her.

Mom arrives about twenty minutes later in the DeSoto with hot dogs, buns, marshmallows, and candles. She baked a birthday cake and trimmed it with pink and white icing flowers with *Happy Birthday Anna* on it in darker pink. Mom looks pretty in her blue-and-white–flowered housedress accenting her nice figure that I can't help but notice as she places a tablecloth over the picnic table.

It isn't long after we arrive that Edna and Reds walk through the clover and daisy-infested field, carrying homemade potato salad, macaroni and cheese, and pickled eggs and beets.

"Hope everyone is hungry," Reds says as he places the hot macaroni-and-cheese dish on the picnic table.

I smile at Reds, and he gives me one of his big smiles and a wink. As usual, he brought over a pot of coffee earlier so it would be perked and ready to drink when he arrived on the scene.

"I know, Anna banana, you're sweet sixteen and never been kissed, right?"

"Yeah, right," I say out loud but think of Jack and the kiss he gave me after the prom.

"Hey, Sonya, why does the fireman wear red suspenders?"

She squints her eyes as she looks at Reds. "To keep his pants up?"

"Nope, wrong, to match the fire truck."

We all groan and start laughing. No matter what answer you give, he has a different answer for it.

He smiles at all of us and goes into the shed to get his cup of coffee.

"Hey, let's do the Kolfield cheer," yells Bev as she stands up and brushes off her jeans, as she was sitting on the ground.

We all join our arms, kicking our legs out and chanting, "We are the Kolfield girls. We wear our hair in curls. We wear our lipstick thick so when we kiss, it sticks. We wear our dungarees way down below our knees. We are the Kolfield girls, rah, rah, rah, rah."

Laughing, Dad starts a fire in a circle of big rocks that he placed in position earlier. With the fire blazing, he sits down on a big rock nearby and opens his penknife. He shaves several long sticks and carves two sharp prongs on one end of the sticks so we can stab our hot dogs in the middle and roast them over the open fire.

Next, he brings out the little green GE radio that he keeps in the worm farm shack, plugging it in with a long extension cord running through the shack's door. It's for him and Reds so they can listen to the Pirates baseball game this evening.

The smell of smoke encircles us as we sit there, roasting hot dogs and giggling over everything and nothing. After eating, the sixteen candles are lit on the cake while everyone sings "Happy Birthday" to me. When I blow out the candles on my cake, my only wish is that everyone in the world is as happy as I am at this moment.

We laugh, sing, and tell scary stories, but when darkness surrounds us, we know the day is over and so is my party.

My presents include body lotion, talcum powder, lavender-scented toilet water, writing paper, and a lipstick holder with a mirror on it. These things mean so much to me. In fact, I know I'll always keep the box that holds the writing paper, since it's blue, my favorite color, and has buttons and bows printed all over it. When I look at it I think of Dinah Shore singing "Buttons and Bows."

My friends have no idea how much this party means to me. I'm full of happiness because they shared my birthday.

The ride back home is more fun, as it's dark and we can't stop giggling. Dad takes each and every one of the girls to their house, and we all shout our good-byes and see you later, alligators.

In bed that night, I listen to the train whistle and to the clickety-clack of the train on the rails as it snakes its way to the mines. As I listen to these sounds, I think about the train being loaded with coal to be taken to faraway places—places that maybe someday I'll visit.

Chapter 25

My party is over, Martha is back at college, and, finally, it's time for the carnival. I know Connie is as excited as I am about tonight. It's not only the carnival; we haven't seen each other all summer.

Sonya and Bev have been keeping me informed about the rides being set up and the rumors about how gross the sideshows are going to be this year. Sonya's younger brother and his friends ride their bicycles to the field and watch them assembling the rides each day. They are excited about one ride in particular that almost turns you upside down. All of that enthusiasm spills over to Sonya, who in turn broadcasts this information to everyone via the telephone.

Our plans include walking to the carnival. But first I'll meet Sonya and Bev at Tenth Street, and the three of us will walk downtown to Main Line Drugstore, where Connie will be waiting for us out front.

After getting dressed in my white blouse, green-checked skirt, and penny loafers, I run down the stairs, practically flying.

Dad is sitting in his easy chair with his eyeglasses perched on his nose, looking out above the newspaper. As he pulls the newspaper against his chest, he says, "Heard you coming, Anna. I think you set a record that time. Sometime you're going to fall down those steps and break an arm or leg at that speed. Where are you going?"

"To the carnival with Connie, Beverly, Sonya, and we'll meet some of our other friends there."

He stretches out his right leg and reaches into his front pants pocket. "You better stay away from the sideshows. Sometimes those men can be nasty. Here's an extra dollar for you in case you need it."

"Thanks, Dad. I really appreciate it," I say as I give him a big hug, crumpling his newspaper.

"Go on, get out of here. Have fun, but remember to be home when your mother says to be home."

Entering the kitchen, Mom reminds me, "Remember, stay away from the sideshows at the carnival, and make sure you're home by ten o'clock, Anna, or I'll come looking for you. And remember, no boys!"

"You don't have to worry about a boy walking me home." And then under my breath I add, "As everyone's afraid of you," while making my exit to the back porch. Also, I'm hoping she doesn't hear the last remark because of her hearing problem.

The evening is perfect, with the right temperature and blue skies. Walking up the street to Main Avenue, we see people relaxing after supper on the front porches, sitting on their gliders and swings. They all wave and say hello, and some ask if I am going to the carnival.

Mrs. Jakowski delays me a few minutes, asking about school and family. She's an elderly widow who lives on Main Avenue with her sister. I always enjoy talking to them. They both have beautiful white hair pulled back into buns. They offer cookies, but I politely refuse, telling them I have to meet friends at the carnival.

I know I have to get going or Sonya and Bev will be out looking for me, and I'm right. They have started walking toward me, wanting to make sure I don't waste any time talking.

Reminding me of twins, both are wearing their black poodle skirts with white blouses and saddle oxfords.

Sonya's money is stuffed into a leather change purse, which she insists her mother forced her to use. She prefers to carry her money in her shoe, but her mother explained this is more convenient, as the purse can be kept in her skirt pocket and she doesn't have to bend over to take her shoe off.

"I really think she's afraid someone is going to see my underwear if I bend over." Sonya laughs.

Bev and I start laughing.

"What's so funny?"

"Well, don't you think it would be kind of difficult for someone to see your underwear? With your long legs, you'd have to lift your skirt and crinoline up when you bend down," says Bev, laughing so hard.

Stifling my laugh, I say, "Okay, that's enough. Let's get moving. Connie's waiting for us."

Sonya starts chattering away about the carnival and all of the stories she has heard. As I step up on the curb after we cross Ninth Street, I notice Marcia sitting on the front steps of the apartment house where she lives.

"Hi, Marcia, how are you? Are you going to the carnival?"

Marcia is a new girl who moved to town this summer. I introduced myself to her once when walking downtown, and she seems very nice. Soft-spoken with short dark hair, brown eyes, with small lips positioned on an oval-shaped face, she's short and a little chunky, but I know how that feels.

"No, I have to babysit my younger brother and sister."

"That's a shame. You could have gone with us."

Sonya squeezes my arm, and as I turn to look at her, Sonya's eyes are glaring at me with her eyebrows crumpled together, causing wrinkles in her forehead. I think she's upset at me for talking to Marcia.

"Come on, Anna, let's go or we'll be late," Sonya says.

"Bye, Marcia. I'll see you in school soon."

"Bye, Anna."

Sonya doesn't say a word but pulls me away. When we get out of hearing distance, I ask, "What's wrong with you, Sonya? I just wanted to say hello and be friendly. She doesn't know anyone, and it must be hard moving to a strange town and having no friends."

"Haven't you heard she puts out for the guys? She will go out with any guy as long as they can make out. That's why they left their other town, because of her reputation."

"Don't be silly. Who told you this stuff? I don't believe it."

"It's true. Louise knows someone that has an aunt that lives in the last town she lived in, and that's how she found out."

"For real?" pipes in Bev.

"Stop it, both of you. Louise is jealous that a new girl is in town. I don't believe it, and I'm not going to stop talking to her. Now let's change the subject and think about the fun we are going to have."

The three of us joke and laugh and join Connie in front of Main Line Drugstore. With arms linked, we continue our journey to the carnival. Connie and I hang together while Bev and Sonya do their thing.

A beautiful evening with my friends and laughter everywhere makes everything perfect. Everyone is ready to enjoy the captivating and mysterious carnival, where it all begins.

Chapter 26

When we enter the carnival through a brightly colored arch decorated with animals and rides, everything involving my senses envelops me and makes me giddy with delight.

Brightly colored red, blue, green, and yellow food and game booths stand out among the shouts of whatever they're selling—whether it is food or a ball with which to hit the milk bottles and win a brightly colored chalk Kewpie doll. Shouting and talking voices are mixed with loud music along with the sound of the rides going around.

Right away I notice the octopus ride, the tilt-a-whirl, the caterpillar, and the Ferris wheel. There are also small rides for the little kids, along with a merry-go-round.

The familiar but rare aroma of cotton candy along with hot dogs, french fries, and popcorn seem to be calling to me.

"I'm getting cotton candy. Anyone want to share?"

"I will," Connie says while getting her money out of her pocket.

As we pick off fluffy pieces of our pink cotton candy, it disappears and nothing is left but the paper roll. Walking around, we discover we lost Sonya and Bev. Knowing them, they probably stopped to talk to someone, so we aren't concerned. They'll catch up to us.

Now it's our time to be daring. We sneak over to the side of the carnival where you pay to see weird things. We have to see why we're not allowed there.

A colorful arch decorated and painted with scantily dressed women, bearded ladies, and snakes separates this side from the rides and concession stands. This part of the carnival is colorful and noisy like the other side but a different world. There aren't any little kids on this side.

A barker in a white straw hat with a red band around it and a red-and-white–striped coat with long tails is yelling, "Ten cents, ten cents, just one little dime. Come in and see the two-headed baby."

Connie and I look at each other, grinning. "Let's go and see. This can't be real."

After paying our dimes, we walk into the musty-smelling brown tent. Walking on straw and through another flap we see a wooden box on a small platform. We peek in and there appear to be two heads on a real baby, but the man rushes us out so fast we can't tell if one head is real or not.

"Jeez, Connie, that's just a doll's head laying next to a real baby. It's all a big fake. These guys sure know how to take your money."

"Go on, keep moving, sister. You've seen the two-headed baby."

"It isn't real."

"I said keep moving," he says as he gives us both a shove toward the exit.

Not wanting any trouble, Connie yanks my hand and we run through the tent flap, very disappointed.

Directly across from that show is another tent. A woman stands in front of it on top of a small wooden stage. She's practically naked but has plenty of long, dark hair that falls in soft shiny waves that bob like ocean waves with her movements. Her cheeks are rosy, and her lips are a bright red, almost as if an artist painted them.

A soft see-through red scarf is draped over her shoulders, giving the appearance of a shawl. Actually all she's wearing is a red halter overflowing with breasts and red shorts that are so short they look like underwear. There's bare skin everywhere else. She doesn't allow the red high heels to hinder the movement of her body. Her hips sway in motion to the music blaring from the speakers while a large group of men watch her intently. It's so fascinating to me, and I can't take my eyes off of her. The spell of the moment is broken when a couple of the men start shouting to her.

One old man, at least forty years old, shouts, "Okay, red lady, let's see some more movements before we pay our quarter."

"Yeah, move those hips, baby," yells another one.

"Twenty-five cents to see what this lovely lady in red can do. Come on in and you won't be sorry. She'll give you enough memories to last you a lifetime."

Then he turns and looks at us and says, "Hey there, you two pretty girls, why don't you come in and see what a real woman is. Just one quarter and you'll learn a lot."

Connie and I look at each other and bust out laughing.

Just then, Matt, one of my neighbors, comes over and taps me on my shoulder. I almost jump out of my skin.

"Anna, what are you doing over here? I bet your mom doesn't know you're on this side."

"We're leaving. We were curious about what was here, that's all. You won't tell her, will you?" I ask while scrunching my eyebrows together and pleading with my eyes.

"No, but someone else might, so you better get out of here. This isn't a place for young girls."

I thank him and, laughing so hard, Connie and I walk fast toward the rides.

As we enter the ride area, we see Sonya and Beverly, who magically disappeared earlier, talking to four guys in front of the caterpillar ride. One of the guys has on a black hat with a pink feather stuck in the side of it. He's noticeable because of the hat even though I think the hat looks a little dorky. They all turn to look at us as we approach.

As soon as we get within hearing distance, I yell, "Hey, Sonya, we're going on a ride. Are you and Bev coming with us or what?"

"We're coming, we're coming."

We keep walking, and Sonya and Bev catch up to us, out of breath.

"Did you see those guys we were talking to?" asks Sonya. "The one with the hat wants to meet you, Anna."

"I don't even know him. Who is he? What did he say?"

"He said he thinks you're really pretty and has seen you around town. I told him I'd tell you. His name is Ben Arno, and he even has his own car."

"Forget about him. Let's go have some fun," says Connie as she tugs my hand and starts walking.

"What'll I tell him?"

"Don't tell him anything. I'm just not interested. Come on with us," I say as Connie jerks me forward.

"We'll catch up with you later."

She and Bev turn to go back to the group of guys.

"What I really think is that Sonya or Bev likes one of those guys."

"I thought so too." Connie laughs.

Chapter 27

‒‒‒‒‒

We get on the caterpillar ride, which is exciting when the canvas roof rolls over us and it's dark inside, creating a lot of screams. Many of the boys like to take the girls on this ride so they can kiss them when the cover rolls over. From outside the ride it looks like a giant caterpillar crawling around in a circle when the green roof hides all of the seats.

Next we go on the octopus ride, which has seats attached to a long arm, and they move up and down while going round and round. We talk to more of our friends and sample more food. Sonya and Bev catch up with us later, but nothing more is said about the guys they met.

It starts to drizzle at about nine thirty. At that point it's time to start walking home anyway. As we're getting ready to leave, Zudie and Roy come over to talk to us. They remind me of the comic strip characters, Mutt and Jeff. Roy is short, and Zudie is tall. They are from our biology class this past year and want to walk us home. We're all aware of Bev's big crush on Zudie, so we agree to let them join us.

While we walk home, a few drops of rain spit out of the sky, but there isn't enough to wet us. It does start raining harder after Connie leaves us at Fifteenth Street, and we duck under the theater entrance so we won't get too wet.

A 1948 gray Pontiac creeps by with whistles and hoots drifting out of the windows. It's the guy from the carnival wearing the dorky black hat, and he's driving by very slowly. His face sports a big smile as he drives by.

Curious, I ask, "Does anyone know these guys?"

Holding Zudie's hand now, Bev says, "Anna, that's the guy that wants to date you."

"Are you crazy? Why would he want to date me? I don't even know him."

"All I know is that his friends cornered me at the carnival twice tonight and wanted to know if you'd go out with him. I told them that he'd have to ask you, not me."

Zudie and Roy aren't happy that we are talking about other guys. My friends mentioned earlier that Roy likes me, but I said it wasn't true. Roy is tall with blond hair and blue eyes—a nice guy, but I feel no attraction to him except as a friend. He continues to walk beside me with Sonya on my other side.

The next time the gray Pontiac comes around, Bev and Sonya wave back. The third time the car comes around, it pulls over to the sidewalk across the street from where we are being protected from the rain under a store's overhang. They ask us if we want a ride home.

In unison we all say, "No!"

Two of the guys get out and run toward us. They only want to confirm what Bev said, that the driver wants to talk to me.

"Talk to me about what?"

Bev and Sonya gently push me forward and say, "Go on, Anna. See what he wants. We'll be right here."

Roy's upset. "Don't go over there, Anna."

It's all right, Roy, I'm not going to get in the car with him."

By this time the rain has stopped so I walk across the street, as I'm very curious about him.

With his arms folded over each other, resting where the window is hidden after being cranked down, he observes me. His head is stretched halfway out the opening, and he is watching me walk across the street. The black hat with the pink feather is still on his head. As I get closer, he doesn't look as dorky as the hat. In fact, he looks kind of cute.

He has this mischievous grin on his face. "Hi. I saw you at the carnival. I'm Ben."

I feel such an attraction to him, making me a little tongue-tied, but I manage to say, in case he didn't already know, "Yes, that's what I hear. My name is Anna."

"I've seen you around town and was wondering if I could take you out on a date."

As I look at him now that I'm closer, it's difficult to see all of his face, as shadows from the hat cover it. His nose is large, but his eyes are hidden. His lips are full, and when I look at them, I really want to kiss them.

All in all, he's good-looking and seems like a nice guy—or man, should I say. He excites me and, yet, I'm not sure if I should say yes. He does seem polite and mannerly.

"We could go to the movies Saturday night."

After pausing for several seconds, I say, "Sure, I'll go." While answering him I realize I'm creating a huge problem for myself.

"Where do you live exactly, and what time should I pick you up?"

While he's saying this, I'm thinking to myself, *How am I going to do this?* A million thoughts run through my mind like a speeding train. My mother will never allow me to go out with him. I clutch my elbows tighter as the dampness of the rain is chilling me.

First of all, he's Italian. Second, he's Catholic (because aren't all Italians Catholic?). And third, he has a driver's license. I know he must be a lot older than me. I'll never be allowed to go out with him, and to go out with him in his car would be forbidden.

These thoughts are racing through my head, and I know I'd have to sneak out to be able to see him. Maybe it won't be a great date after all, so why should I go through all that aggravation with my mother? Then again, I don't want to deceive my mother, but what does she know? I might not even like him, and I won't know until I go out with him. Will it be worth the punishment if I'm caught? I know the answer deep inside of me.

"I'm not allowed to date," I say cautiously, looking downward at the wet road.

"You're old enough, aren't you? How old are you?"

"I'm sixteen, but my mother is very strict with me and would never allow me to go out with you in your car."

"Okay, not a problem. Maybe you could meet me on the corner of Main Avenue and Sixth Street at six thirty," he says, smiling.

Even though I love his smile and want to go, I look at him and say, "No, someone might see us, and I'd be in a lot of trouble."

"How about Seventh Street?"

For once in my life I want to do something daring on my own. I want to make my own decision, and that fast I make it.

"I guess Seventh Street would be okay," I say, all the while thinking, *It worked for Liz and Martha. Why not me?* Also, there's a church on the corner and it's farther from my house.

"Sounds great. I'll see you Saturday evening."

"Okay." I turn and walk away from the car.

When I get back across the street, Zudie and Roy have decided they want to go back to the carnival, as the rain has stopped. They're tired of hearing us talk about other boys, and I don't blame them.

Walking home, I let Sonya and Bev know about my date and swear them to secrecy. They're excited for me. I'm excited but scared. They start asking me questions about him.

"I don't really know him, so I can't answer your questions."

"Well, how are you going to get your mother to let you go?" asks Sonya.

"I don't know that either."

"Well, you can always say you're going out with us," Bev chirps in.

"I'll see. Maybe I won't show up at all."

"Don't be silly. We'll figure it out," Sonya says with a grin on her face.

Then the "what if" thoughts start rolling through my mind: *What if Mom finds out? What if she embarrasses me in front of everyone? What if someone sees us? What if I go through all of this and he really is a jerk? Oh, my, what am I going to do, and how am I going to get through the next couple of days without Mom finding out?*

Now it starts to drizzle more and we walk faster, clinging to the fronts of the stores and buildings downtown so we'll be under their protective roof ledges and awnings.

After leaving Bev at Twelfth Street and Sonya at Tenth Street, I still have five blocks to go. Just one more block and I'll be protected from rain by all of the maple trees lining Main Avenue from Ninth Street to Sixth Street.

No one's sitting on the front porches now.

The maple trees are gigantic with a lot of leaves. They shade and hover over the sidewalks in an even row, protecting all walkers not only from the sun but also during a light rain.

I think of all the things that could happen to me because I'm going to go out with this guy. *Why did I say yes? Why didn't I just keep walking? Why did I have to go to the carnival?* Just too many whys.

Something about him attracts me, or is it because I'm feeling lonely and vulnerable at this time? I really don't have anyone to confide in and have never done something like this before. Maybe I won't even show up for the date. Then I thought, *Why not? There's no harm in dating a boy. Or is he a man? I'm not doing anything wrong except telling a white lie.*

Jo is gone, and I can't ask her what I should do. She'd have helped me, just like Liz and Martha helped each other.

When I reach my street, the rain stops. I love the smell of fresh rain. The rain cleans the air, but later I'll be able to smell the worms as they come out of the ground. I'll never forget that strange odor.

I'm excited but I don't want it to show when I walk in the house, so I think of something else. As usual Mom has waited for me, and the cuckoo clock signals us it is ten o'clock.

"Did you have a good time?"

"Oh, yes, we really enjoyed the rides and the food."

"I'm glad you enjoyed yourself, but remember we have a long day tomorrow. You have to help me with the carpets."

"Not a problem," I say as I turn to go upstairs.

"You didn't go to the other side of the carnival by any chance, did you?"

With no hesitation or turning around, I reply, "No, Mom, I'd never do that."

Chapter 28

⎯⎯⎯⎯⎯

𝐼 wake up Thursday morning, wondering what I've committed myself to with this secret date. Still in bed, I wish there is someone available that I could talk to about Ben.

Darn it, Jo, why can't you be here now so I could talk to you about him? She'd probably know all about him. After all, Jo might know him from school. Funny how Jo is glad to be out of school and, yet, I've always loved school, except for one time.

I was in fourth grade and really loved my teacher, Miss Genzi, until one unforgettable day.

Miss Genzi was short and thin with the blackest hair I ever saw, like coal. She was single and had a problem with her left arm. She could never open it straight out, so she always held it to her chest, as if it was in an invisible sling. Having a poor left arm probably made her right arm so strong, as I found out one day.

It was an ordinary school day. Even though there was snow outside, the sun was shining. Miss Genzi was trying to teach us the difference between the verbs "lie" and "lay." Frustration was setting in because no one in the class seemed to understand this verb. She wrote LAY and LIE in big letters on the blackboard on the wall in front of the room. After asking three other kids, who gave the wrong answer, she then pointed to me. Fear rippled through me.

She asked me a question regarding fish and a fishbowl, and would I use "lay" or "lie" as the verb. My heart was pounding—as I didn't understand if she meant did the fish lay or lie, or did the fish bowl lay or lie—and I gave my answer.

Evidently, it was the wrong answer, as she was very upset and ordered me to the front of the classroom. I thought to myself maybe now she could explain it better, as it seemed all of us were confused.

She placed her chalk on the ledge of the chalkboard, and her right hand suddenly grabbed me by the back of my neck and started erasing the two words, "lie" and "lay," with, of all things, my nose. I was so humiliated that I don't even remember if it hurt.

The silence of my classmates was overwhelming, and I tried to be brave and not cry, but the tears came flowing down my cheeks.

When I got back to my desk, my friend Pete, a thin boy with eyeglasses who sat behind me every year from first grade, tried to console me. He never yanked my pigtails like some of the other boys, but he did tease me by pretending to put them in the inkwell on his desk. He liked taking his sharp pencil and ever so lightly tickling the back of my neck and upper arms. It felt so good and made me feel so relaxed.

Pete whispered, "Don't cry, Anna. That was mean of her to do that," as he patted me lightly on the back of my shoulder.

Miss Genzi then said, "Anna, go to the lavatory and wash your face. I hope all of you have learned a lesson from this."

Oh, yes, I learned a lesson, all right. That incident taught me to never raise my hand and always look away, even if I think I know the correct answer. I'm afraid that if the answer is incorrect, the teacher will humiliate me, and I never want to endure that again. I could never tell my parents what happened, as they would probably side with the teacher.

Getting back to my problem, I wonder how this white lie of meeting Ben is going to work out.

The idea of truth and lies reminds me of when Mom took me to visit Aunt Alice in Johnstown. Aunt Alice is Mom's sister and is not fat but a little chubby with reddish brown hair pulled back into a barrette. She's very mouthy and swears a lot. She drives a streetcar in Johnstown, wearing a uniform and hat, looking like she is in the military.

I wanted to wear my good dress, but Mom told me I had to wear my old white dress that was decorated with strawberries.

"Keep that old dress on. We're only going to visit Aunt Alice."

After removing my coat and leggings at Aunt Alice's house, she remarked, "You look very pretty today, Anna. Your dress is so cute with those strawberries on it."

"I wanted to wear my prettier dress, the good one, but Mommy said we were only going to visit you so I should wear my old one."

At that point Mom slapped me across the face and told me to shut up.

"Don't do that, Daisy, she didn't mean anything by it."

I could never understand why she slapped me for telling the truth.

So, really, why should I feel guilty if I lie to Mom about dating Ben? After all, when I did tell the truth, I was punished anyway. I'm glad I remember these things because now I don't feel as bad if I lie to Mom.

With those thoughts in mind, I figure I better get up and get busy, because Saturday isn't far away and I can't act suspicious or Mom will know something is up.

Chapter 29

Sunny Thursday drags as I hang around the house and help Mom beat the rugs that she and Dad threw over the clotheslines. Using a wire beater shaped like a number eight, I whack the rugs as hard as possible. The dust flies from the rugs with each smack and naturally hits my face, but I figure this is a sacrifice, guaranteeing Saturday night out. Besides, I feel better after I beat the rugs.

Friday arrives. Even though the day goes by slowly, I know the evening will go faster, since I work at the bingo hall for the firemen, selling the various colored paper specials.

In the bingo hall, the gray folding tables and chairs are all lined up in long rows. Each of us girls who work here walk up and down the rows, selling the colorful paper specials. The firemen pay us several dollars, and sometimes we receive tips from the various players, especially if they are winners. This is all due to Frank, who hired me and my sisters before me to work for the firemen, as it enables us to make some money.

After walking to the fire hall at Fifteenth Street and to the bingo hall in back of it, I prepare myself for a busy evening. Tying the carpenter's apron around my waist, I fill the pockets with change and specials.

Most of the people arrive early, as they have "lucky" seats and don't want anyone else to take them. Also, they have lucky numbers and like to pick out their bingo cards that are stacked high on one of the tables.

Everyone is busy lining up their bingo cards and getting their red or green plastic chips ready to place on the numbers when the numbers are called. They talk to each other about any and all subjects, and you can tell they enjoy bingo and a night out but also winning some money.

The evening waltzes by, and I keep pretty busy, not having much time to think about anything except selling the specials and running errands to buy the bingo players coffee or a hot dog or soda.

Once in awhile I get a whiff of hot dogs and hamburgers cooking, but the cigarette smoke is surrounding everyone. Practically everyone smokes.

Finally, the next specials are the last set of specials to be sold tonight. I have to help clean everything up when it's all over, and then I'm out of here.

Having a few minutes before selling the last set, I wander outside for fresh air, as sometimes the smoke can be overwhelming. I grasp the top rail of the black double iron railing running parallel with the creek and look down at the water flowing by. There are just enough outside lights from the fire hall that I can see reflections in the water, but I also hear the gurgling as the water swirls between the rocks into the total darkness. It's scary looking down there, and I'm afraid of heights, but tonight I have too many things on my mind to be afraid.

As I look down, I wonder how everything is going to turn out tomorrow night with my big date. I don't know why this is such a big deal—maybe because Ben seems more mature than the other guys I know. I have to ask him his age, and I need to know more about him, since I never heard of him before the carnival. My thoughts are cut short by the words of the announcer saying the last special is about to be sold. That is my cue to get back inside.

When I go back inside, there's only half an hour left before bingo is over. One of my regular customers, Arlene, who always sits at my table, is a plump gray-haired widow. She's cheerful all the time, always smiling. Arlene calls me over to buy some specials.

"I want you to meet my son, Greg. He's been pestering me for weeks to introduce you to him."

I remember seeing him come in every week and sit by his mother toward the end of bingo but never thought anything of it.

He does resemble James Dean, who stars in *Rebel Without a Cause* with his sandy hair, blue eyes, jeans, and that captivating smile. I can tell he cares about his mother, as he comes to take her home every Friday night. You can tell by the way Greg and his mother joke around that they are very close, and I envy their relationship.

"When Greg has to take me home from bingo, he brings the car. Usually though you'll see him riding his motorcycle around town," Arlene says with pride in her voice.

"Nice to meet you," I say and smile at him, extending my hand.

He leans forward to shake my hand and, not letting it go, asks with the darndest, cutest grin, "May I give you a ride home?"

"No, not tonight, I have to clean the tables."

Still holding my hand, he says, "Maybe the next time I have to take my mom home, you'll say yes. I can take her home and come back and get you, since you stay later."

Disengaging my hand, I nod my head. "Maybe, we'll see." And I smile as I walk away. Another bingo player is calling to me that she needs some lucky specials, and she thinks I have them.

Wow, I don't need any further complications in my life. Why, all of a sudden, were these guys taking such an interest in me? They never did before. Now I know what it's like to live in a fishbowl with everyone looking at me. I wonder if it's the way I am fixing my hair, my clothes, or is it because no older sisters are standing in my way?

I'm elated when bingo is finally over and the tables are cleared of all the paper specials, leftover food, and sodas. After telling everyone good night, I start walking home.

Secretly, I hope Ben will drive by so I can get another look at him. In the past I thought a certain boy was good-looking, but after seeing him a second time, I realized it was all my vivid imagination looking for a handsome Prince Charming.

After crossing Fifteenth Street and Main Avenue, I wonder once more if I'm doing the right thing. *Why,* I ask myself, *do I feel so attracted to Ben?* Maybe I won't like him at all once I get to know him, but right now it's creating a stressful situation for me.

Walking by the Palace Hotel on Main Avenue and Fourteenth Street, I hear laughter surrounded by the darkness of the bar. A strong whiskey odor along with cigarette smoke enter my nose. How can anyone have a good time in such a dark, smoky place? I walk faster, as the noise and the voices scare me. I don't know why but they do.

After practically running past the closed Five & Dime store, I slow down and continue my thoughts of tomorrow evening.

A horn beeps and jerks me back to reality. I realize it's Liz's neighbor, Janet. She pulls over and asks me if I want a ride home, but I say, "No, thanks. I want to walk tonight."

As Janet pulls away, I realize that in this town practically everyone knows everyone, so how am I supposed to meet Ben without being seen together? This is a real problem, and maybe I shouldn't see him. I can stand him up, but I really don't want to do that.

So many thoughts race through my mind as I walk the ten blocks home. It's a beautiful night, and the air is fresh and clean. The moon and stars hang over me as I walk home and dream of tomorrow night.

Finally reaching my street, I turn and walk slowly down the brick sidewalk toward my darkened house. I know Mom is sitting inside waiting for me even though it's dark. The back door is unlocked, as we never lock our doors, and as I enter the kitchen, Mom turns on the light.

I want to ask her if she ever goes to bed, but I know better. With a half smile on her face, she says, "I'm glad you're home. Now I can go to bed."

"Good night, Mom," I mumble as I walk past her and up the stairs to my room. I shut the door and put my pajamas on, listening for Mom to go to her bedroom, where Dad is sound asleep. I can hear him snoring. When I hear her bedroom door close, I quietly go to the bathroom and brush my teeth and wash my face and hands.

I crawl into bed and lie there, thinking of what will happen tomorrow evening.

After my silent prayer, I wonder if God gets tired of hearing me every night.

Smiling, I think of all the people's prayers going up to heaven and can imagine the sound of their voices filling the air. It would be like an orchestra composed of voices—men, women, and children—filling the universe and beyond. Why would He single out my prayer to listen to out of all of those voices? After all, there are millions of people praying. But He is God, and there is nothing He can't do. I'm sure a lot of the angels help him. I try not to think too deeply about it, as I'm afraid God may think I doubt Him, and I have to have Him on my side, as He is the only one I can really talk to.

The last train of the evening goes by, and the train whistle makes me feel sad again. I love hearing it, but it seems to be telling me something and I don't know what. Wondering if I should keep that date tomorrow evening is bothering me a lot. If only I could see the future to see if it's all worth this small white lie.

Little did I realize that once in a while a small white lie can grow so large that it's out of control and changes the rest of your life.

Chapter 30

Hallelujah! Finally it's Saturday evening. After washing my hair and taking my bath, I have to make a decision on what to wear so Mom doesn't get suspicious. I decide to wear my dark-blue skirt with my light-blue short-sleeved sweater that has two white angora stripes going down the center and my penny loafers. After informing Mom I'm going to the movies with Sonya and Beverly, she repeats for the umpteenth time that I have to be home by ten o'clock. They're watching the evening news on the TV as Hurricane Diane is ready to come up the East Coast.

Come on, I am sixteen, Dad's sixty-one, and Mom's forty-nine. They're ancient and are probably tired of raising kids by now. They probably think I can't possibly do anything that my sisters haven't done. Also, since I've always been good, why would they think I'd lie?

I'm really nervous. As I walk up Sixth Street, a neighbor boy on his bike scares me as he charges past, yelling, "Hi, Anna."

Composing myself, I answer back, "Hi, Danny."

Sixth Street is quiet, as there are no houses on it facing the street from the alley up to Main Avenue. On the right side of the street is one of many Catholic churches and schools. On the left side are a lot of tall green hedges dotted with white flowers. The hedges are thick, and the flowery smell emanating from them follows me up the street.

Kozak's Store is on the corner of Sixth Street and Main Avenue, where all the kids in our neighborhood usually hang out. Willie and Bev are standing in front of the store deep in conversation. I'm fifteen minutes early, so after waving a quick hi to them, I walk inside to buy a Coke.

Today Mrs. Oliver is working behind the wooden counter. She's a short, older lady with gray hair, a round nose, and puffy pink cheeks. Wearing a full apron over her dress, she continually wipes her hands on it. More of a habit, I think, than anything else.

The store is loaded with all kind of items, some hanging on the walls or racks. A big red Coca-Cola cooler is sitting on the right side, and that's where I'm headed.

"Hi, Anna. How are you today? I haven't seen you around lately."

"I've been here, but I guess you weren't working at the time," I say while lifting the cooler lid and pulling out a cold Coke. The bottle goes from my right hand to my left hand so I can uncap it in the built-in bottle opener. This allows me to shake the water off my other hand and reach in my pocket for a nickel.

"Well, make sure and tell your family I said hi."

"Okay, I will," I say as I hand her the nickel and turn to walk out of the store.

I walk toward Willie and Bev and talk to them. Willie, with his curly hair and big ears, lives on Sixth Street and is a year younger than me but acts like a twelve-year-old sometimes. They're discussing the actor James Dean.

"Don't you think he's soooo handsome, Anna?" Bev asks while I take a sip of my Coke.

"Yes, and he's also a good actor but, believe it or not, there's a guy in Kolfield who looks a lot like him," I reply while rubbing the moisture from the outside of the Coke bottle. In actuality I was hoping a genie would pop out and grant me some wishes or at least a command to turn my feet around and go home.

"And who, pray tell, could that possibly be?"

"His name is Greg, and his mother comes to bingo every Friday. Come down some Friday evening and I'll introduce you."

"I better not. Zudie might get upset."

"Are you walking downtown to meet someone?" Willie asks as he leans backward against the wooden frame on the side of the store window. If we lean on the glass we won't be allowed to hang out there.

"What do you mean by that?" I ask sharply with a touch of surprise in my voice, but it's probably guilt.

"Whoa, I just thought maybe you're meeting Sonya or Connie downtown. What's wrong with you?" he asks, extending his left hand outward with palm facing upward and with a quizzical look on his face.

"Yeah," said Bev, "he's just asking a question."

Bev knows I'm meeting Ben but is sworn to secrecy.

"I'm sorry. I didn't mean to sound like that, but I just have a lot on my mind, especially since Jo moved away. I miss her a lot."

They both nod in agreement, as they know Jo and I are very close.

After that I can't drink any more of the Coke and ask Willie if he wants it, knowing how much he loves Coca-Cola. He grabs the green bottle without hesitation. "Don't mind if I do. Thanks, Anna."

"Well, I got to go. See you later, alligator," I say as I turn to cross over Sixth Street.

"Yeah, when your legs grow straighter," Willie and Bev reply in unison, laughing.

As I walk away I think maybe Ben won't show up, but I am also hoping no one will see me get into his car if he does. I decide to start walking faster, and about two blocks away Ben pulls up to the curb, leans over, and opens the door from the inside.

He smiles at me. "Hi."

My legs are wobbly, as if I'm going to melt into a puddle like a snowman on a sunny day and cease to exist. With fear embedded in me that I may disappear or run the other way, I jump into the car as fast as I can.

The smell of pine trees lingers in the car. I'm not sure if it's his aftershave or the little green tree hanging from the mirror. The cloth seats are gray, and Ben is wearing black pants with a pink shirt. *He must really love pink,* I think to myself, remembering the pink feather in his hat the other night.

As soon as I close the door I tell him, "I'd rather not go downtown to the theater. I'm afraid someone might see us and tell my mother."

He nods his head in approval. "That's okay with me. Do you want to go to Johnstown to the movies, or do you want to just ride around?"

"It's okay to just ride around, if you don't mind. I doubt if we'd make it back in time from the movies in Johnstown."

"Okay. I know your mother is strict, but I thought she'd let you date."

"Well, I just turned sixteen, so she'll probably let me start dating soon," I say as I turn toward him and try not to look out the side window in case I see someone I know. This way, hopefully, they won't recognize the back of my head.

At that moment I realize how strenuous and difficult it is to tell a lie, and I don't feel happy or good about it.

"I understand, believe me. My mother is just as strict, and she'd rather I didn't date any girls. She's afraid I might find a girl and get married," he says with a faraway look in his eyes as he turns to go up Ninth Street.

I knew he'd go up Ninth Street, the quickest way out of Kolfield, without going through downtown or near my house.

"So your mother is strict too. Then you understand what I'm going through at the moment."

"Yes, I certainly do, so don't worry about anything. Let's just enjoy each other's company tonight and not think about our mothers."

Scrutinizing him, I give his pink shirt a once-over. With the top two buttons open, a silver medal on a chain can be seen hanging from his neck. The shirt is quite a contrast to his black hair and tanned skin. As I study his face while he drives up Ninth Street, it's obvious that he does have a big nose and a thin white scar on his right cheek from his ear to his nose. Other than those two little things, he's really handsome. His lips are full and look like they are waiting to be kissed. *Where in the heck did that thought come from?* I ask myself as I quickly turn my head away.

"By the way, how old are you and where do you work?"

"Actually, I'm twenty-two and I work in an office in Johnstown."

Oh, boy, I'm really in big trouble now. He's a man, not a boy. He has a job, is twenty-two, which makes him six years older than me, and owns his own car even though he still lives with his mother and father.

"Does my age bother you?"

"No, I just never thought you were six years older.

After a silent pause we continue talking about our friends, his job, and high school teachers that we may have had in common. We both relax, and for the next two hours we travel around on the many back roads surrounding Kolfield that lead to Johnstown and to Central City, just talking away like we have known each other for years.

He has seen me many times around town and wanted to meet me but didn't know how to go about it. Finally his friends encouraged him to ask me out. He says he was worried I might reject the idea of going out with him.

During our conversation, I figure I might as well get this one controversial item over with right now, since he may never bother with me again after I tell him.

"You know, Ben, I'm not allowed to date Italians or Catholics."

He didn't say anything at first and then said, "Your sister married an Italian Catholic. Why wouldn't you be allowed to date one?"

Aha, so he does know about my family. I explain how that was different, and it wasn't easy for them at first either.

"My sister Liz married Pep because they're so in love. Actually, my mother and father liked Pep very much after they got to know him."

I explain the entire story to him.

"That doesn't sound too bad then. Why don't your parents like Italian Catholics?"

"I don't know, Ben. Heard a story once that my uncle, Dad's brother, was dating an Italian girl. He was warned by her brothers not to see her anymore. One night after walking her home, my uncle was walking home alone by the railroad tracks. The girl's brothers stabbed him."

Taking a deep breath, I continue, "I don't know how true it is, but I think that's why. Anyway, it's not only Italian Catholics but also any Catholics. They discourage my association with them very much even though almost all of my girlfriends are Catholic."

"Let's hope it doesn't prevent us from seeing each other."

We discuss many things and find we can communicate well with each other. His father used to be our iceman who delivered ice for the iceboxes. He would go door-to-door, lifting the huge chunks of ice out of the truck with tongs and carrying them into the houses.

"I remember your father," I say and gently touch Ben's arm. "He was always so nice. He'd let us have small chunks of ice to chew on, and we'd put them on our faces to cool down when it was hot. Some kids would grab bigger pieces of ice when he went into a house, but he never yelled at any of us."

"Yeah, all of the kids liked him, and he liked them."

After a few minutes he explains, "Dad had a stroke that paralyzed him on one side and is bedridden. Mom takes care of him, but I have to help lift him and change his clothes and sheets."

After a minute of silence, he continues, "I really don't want my mother to know I'm dating you. She frowns upon me dating any girl unless she can choose the girl for me. Right now my mother is trying to fix me up with an Italian girl from a family that are friends of ours, but I'm not interested."

I must have looked a little shocked, since he certainly is old enough to choose what girl he wants to go out with.

"Don't worry. I'm old enough to do what I want to do, and I want to date you. I need you to know I'm not a mama's boy."

So, here we are, actually two liars whose mothers don't want us to date, and we're both the youngest in our families. Why did fate bring us together and for what reason?

We stop at Ripple's Drive-In Restaurant near Johnstown. It's a small indoor/outdoor restaurant and is "the place" where kids who drive hang out. Music drifts out of a speaker from the restaurant. The song playing is "Something's Gotta Give," sung by the McGuire Sisters.

Without getting out of our car, we say our order into a speaker similar to the ones at the drive-in movies that you remove from a pole and hook onto your car.

While sitting there talking, a smiley waitress with a lot of teeth appears and hooks a tray onto the driver's side of the door where the window is open. She sets our food on the tray, and Ben pays the check.

Ripple's is noted for its delicious hamburgers called Big Boys, as they're huge and have sweet-and-sour pickles, onions, tomatoes, lettuce, and a special sauce. Ben and I each devour one along with french fries and a Coke.

"I'm glad you're not bashful about eating in front of a guy."

"No, if I'm hungry, it doesn't bother me."

It's strange how comfortable I feel with him. Maybe I wouldn't have eaten if I had been with someone else.

At nine forty-five he parks on Main Avenue between Sixth and Seventh Streets to let me out. He shuts off the motor and looks at me. Such a desire sweeps through me.

We turn toward each other, and before I know it his arms are around me. We both lean into each other and kiss.

When his lips touch my lips, a ripple of shocks goes through my body. He likes it too, as he holds me closer, as if he is never going to let me go. The kiss is fantastic. I feel like I'm on a roller coaster; it gives me the same feeling in my stomach. The scent of his light, spicy aftershave is so divine, and I love his cheek against mine when the kiss is over.

"When can I see you again?" he murmurs as he continues to keep his arms around me.

I'm elated he wants to see me again but can only give a stupid answer. "I don't know. You can't call me in case my mother answers the phone, and besides, someone might listen in on the party line."

"Okay, I'll catch up with you sometime this week. I know you and your girlfriends usually walk downtown for a soda at the drugstore, as I've seen you on numerous occasions. I wanted to stop and talk to you, but like I said earlier I just didn't have the nerve. If we don't see each other, let's meet again like this next Thursday evening."

"That sounds good to me," I whisper as he gives me another kiss that leaves me breathless and speechless. I love his kisses.

After jumping out of the car and hoping no one is sitting on any of the front porches, I walk home. This is the best place to pick me up or let me out, as there are mostly churches and rectories on this block, but there are still a few houses. Those good old maple trees lining the avenue sure do help though, as they hide a lot.

It's exactly ten o'clock when I walk into the dark house. Thank goodness we never lock our doors or I'd be fumbling for a key that I wouldn't be able to hold onto, as I'm trembling. What if someone called Mom and told her I was with Ben or she was at the corner and saw me get out of his car? With my heart pounding I know I'll just have to take the beating, as the kisses were worth it.

I'm aware she likes to sit in the dark, watching us come down the street or maybe catch us with someone we aren't supposed to be with. After four sisters I know that trick, so I'm not about to allow anyone who I'm not supposed to be with get close to my house.

I'm positive Dad is already in bed, as he gets up early every single morning and, besides, he doesn't believe in sitting in the dark. The ceiling light floods the kitchen as soon as I open the back door. It's inspection time. She'll notice if there's anything wrong with my clothes or a hair is out of place, as she is good at this. Thank goodness I don't wear lipstick.

"I was just getting ready to come looking for you," she says while eyeing me up and down.

"It's ten o'clock now," I announce.

Having heard the cuckoo bird pop out of the clock in the dining room, I can picture the little bird rocking back and forth, singing his hourly cuckoos.

"Don't worry. I know what time it is."

"Good night, Mom," I say, wishing I could talk to her about all of this, but she turns her back toward me and walks over to the sink.

"Good night, Anna."

Chapter 31

The next morning, with sunlight in my eyes and Ben on my mind, a wave of happiness floats through me. Oh, man, he's so nice, and those two goodnight kisses are unforgettable. I can't wait until I can see him again.

It's Sunday morning, and I have to get up and get ready for church. The rule in our house is if we don't go to church on Sunday, we're not allowed to go anywhere else during the week until next Sunday. This excludes choir practice on Wednesday, Youth Fellowship on Sunday, and working at bingo on Friday.

Going to church isn't a problem for me, but I don't enjoy Youth Fellowship and choir practice without Jo. She always brought excitement to my life. I miss her and those "forbidden" giggles.

While lying there, I think about my religion. I believe in God and pray but do not feel anything special while in my church.

Sometimes I'd go with my Catholic girlfriends to their churches. It always seemed they were going to church on weekdays and special holidays. I love to kneel and pray with them, watching them put on their scarves or handkerchiefs to cover their hair and loaning me one to cover my hair.

Beautiful statues are lined against the walls, and I love as they dip their fingers into the holy water bowl upon entering the church. With the drops of water on their fingers, they make a sign of the cross, starting at their forehead.

I can sit in any pew and not worry if a certain family has to sit there. I cannot take communion in their church though.

One time the United Brethren Church was having a revival one evening, and the Youth Fellowship kids all had to attend and sit together. The time came toward the end that the visiting minister said, "If you feel saved and believe Jesus Christ is in your heart, please come forward to the altar."

Full of anxiety and fear, I watched while I moved my legs to the side to allow one kid after another to advance to the front altar. I realized that soon I might be the only one left sitting there.

Silence surrounded the minister's words as he shook hands with them. After a while, all the kids who had been sitting with me were standing in front of the altar, and I was the lone Youth Fellowship member left sitting in the pew. Embarrassment overcame me, and I moved forward to be with the other kids, saying I was saved.

After the service, everyone was patting my back and saying that was so wonderful that I had been saved. The kids were telling their parents how great they felt now that they were saved, but I didn't feel anything.

As I was walking home by myself from the service, as no one else from my family had gone to this revival, I started to cry. I prayed silently to God and asked him why I didn't feel anything. Was something wrong with me? Was it wrong that I joined the other kids when I didn't feel Him calling me?

As soon as I got home I wrote Reverend Billy Graham a letter, asking why I didn't feel anything inside and whether it was wrong for me to go to the altar. I never heard from him.

I realize I'm like my father, as I receive more from praying to God directly than attending the functions in church. It seems there are cliques among the people, and I didn't fit in; at least that's how I felt.

One thing I do know, grabbing my chenille robe, is that I better get dressed and get going or I won't be allowed out this week.

After coming home from church and changing my clothes into something more comfortable, like my navy-blue shorts and blue-and-white—striped blouse, I sit on the front porch. I could go in and play some records but now would prefer to daydream a little about my exciting adventure last night.

Believe it or not, my guilt about telling a white lie to see Ben last evening seems to be diminishing. It seems we have so much in common, especially our domineering mothers.

Deciding not to dwell on the lie anymore, I scratch my leg and Mom suddenly interrupts. "Anna, your father and I are going to Ellie and Bill's house. Do you want to come with us?"

"Nope, Sonya and Bev are supposed to be coming over to see me, and we might walk downtown."

Mom and Dad love to play pinochle, and once or twice a month, on a Sunday afternoon, they go to their friends' house in Johnstown to play cards.

All of us kids used to go with them, as they have been doing this for years. As we got older, we didn't have to go and we were thrilled. Besides, Mom and Dad figured we couldn't get into too much trouble on a Sunday afternoon. Boy, little did they know.

As soon as they left, we'd get out the pans and bowls, anxious to make fudge or potato candy. We'd call our friends, and they'd come over to help. We had a lot of fun making the candy, but the best part was eating it.

A smile spreads across my face as I remember one time Mom and Dad had been gone for only about forty-five minutes before they came back, as they had forgotten something.

Sonya and Bev came over and were helping us. We had just mixed the ingredients for fudge and were ready to cook it. Jo grabbed the pot and shoved it into the oven while the rest of us were hiding the bowls and utensils. The potato candy was already in a pan, and it was shoved under the refrigerator.

When Dad came in he knew right away we were guilty of something by the look on our faces. "Whatever you kids are doing, you better clean it up before we get back here or your mother will really be upset with all of you." He picked up his eyeglasses that he had forgotten and returned to the car, where Mom was patiently waiting.

We pulled the pot of fudge out of the oven and sat it on the stove. Trying to find the dirty utensils was quite a job, and we laughed as we recovered them.

When we pulled the pan out from under the refrigerator, there was a little dust on top. A little dust wasn't going to stop us from eating the candy. Besides, Jo said it wouldn't hurt any of us, as the dust wasn't dirty. So we scraped the fuzz balls off and stuck the potato candy in the refrigerator so we could enjoy it after it set awhile. We ate all of the fudge until we almost got sick from the sweetness of it.

Mom knew we did this, as we used her sugar, cocoa, and oleo, but she never said a word about it. It was probably the lesser of the evils that we could get into.

Those days are probably gone forever, I think as I pick up my book and lay it on the bookcase located to the left of the front door.

After getting my orders and seeing Mom and Dad off for their pinochle game, I grab my book and head out the front door. Sitting on the front porch glider, I try to read *And Then There Were None* by Agatha Christie. It's a good book, but it's difficult to concentrate with Ben on my mind.

Suddenly, Sonya and Bev pop their heads up from the side of the porch. "Boo."

"You didn't scare me."

"We want to hear about last night," Bev says while bouncing up the front porch steps. As usual, Bev looks colorful in her pink Bermuda shorts, pink-striped blouse joined together with a red cinch belt. "Are your mom and dad home?"

"Come on, we want to hear all," says Sonya as she tucks her beige shirt in her brown shorts in the back and then rubs her hands together.

"No, they're not home, but I'd rather go for a walk."

We can't converse freely, since all the neighbors are on their front porches. Our conversations can be heard whether anyone wants to hear them or not. The last thing I need is one of our neighbors mentioning to Mom I'm sneaking around meeting a boy—or, should I say, a man.

We walk downtown to the drugstore for a soda, enjoying the nice sunny day, but first we stop at Sonya's house so she can get her money.

Since none of us has a driver's license, walking downtown is the thing to do on a Sunday afternoon. Usually all the teenagers are out walking or driving their cars around, asking the walkers if they want a ride.

Sonya lives below the railroad tracks on Tenth Street. I've always envied Sonya because her parents are so nice and cheerful. Her mother is standing at the sink, washing the dishes. She's tall and slender with long blonde hair. Sonya looks so much like her.

As she wipes her hands on her apron, she asks, "Anna, would you like some pierogi? I made too many today."

"No, thank you. I'm not hungry."

She bends over to pick up something off the floor when her husband, four inches taller and muscular with black curly hair, comes in and slaps her lightly on her behind.

She straightens up fast and tells him in a sweet but firm voice, "Don't do that in front of the kids."

He just laughs, pulls her close to him, and kisses her on her mouth. She becomes all flustered and says, "Behave yourself."

She says this even though she's smiling the whole time and her blue eyes radiate a genuine happiness.

"Don't worry. It's okay for the kids to see because someday they'll be doing the same thing," he says as he kisses her knuckles.

They look so happy together, and that's why I envy Sonya.

After leaving the house, I tell Sonya she has such nice parents. Then I tell her what happened when she went upstairs to get her money.

She just rolls her eyes and says, "They do that all the time. They're always kissing and hugging each other."

Wow, how nice that is. I can't imagine my mother and father hugging and kissing like that. Of course, I'd never tell anyone that. It is just something we never talked about.

Finally, I tell them all about my secret date last night with Ben—how he was such a gentleman and that we rode around and talked a lot. He never tried to get fresh with me but did kiss me good night. They want to know if he was a good kisser, but since I'm not an expert on kissing, I only say I really liked the kiss and would kiss him again.

While we walk downtown I am hoping to see Ben ride by but not this afternoon, as he has to help his mother with his father. Also, his brother and his family are coming over for dinner. Sonya and Bev don't know his father is bedridden, but they do know he has three older brothers.

We prop ourselves on top of the black leather stools at the soda fountain while we drink a soda and talk to the other kids. After enough slurps bellow up through the straws, we know we're done. Then we begin our leisurely walk back home, talking the whole time.

The blue skies and white clouds are beautiful today as I look up at them. It's such a perfect day, and I enjoy the warmth of the sun on my arms.

Our conversation revolves around school starting soon and the different courses and teachers we are hoping will appear on our schedules.

I abandon my friends at the corner of Tenth Street and Main Avenue. This gives me five blocks to be by myself and think about everything. Glancing down at the sidewalk, I notice a penny. Since it's heads up, I pick it up and stash it in my pocket. Heads up means good luck, and I think I'm in need of some now.

With horns blowing, I wave to some of my friends riding by in the opposite direction. Everybody must be out today.

My thoughts wander back to Ben and that kiss he gave me. I'm always thinking and am glad when I sleep so my mind can rest. When I'm not thinking, I love opening a book and becoming part of the story. I read about big cities and how other people think and live. After living someone else's life, I come back to the reality of my own.

I arrive home and play some records but only listen to them for an hour before I get bored. I open the squeaky screen door and sit on the front porch.

Mabel and Joe are sitting next door on their porch swing. Joe has his arm around Mabel, and they're watching their three girls as they play in the front yard.

Mabel turns to me, smiling, and asks, "Anna, are you looking forward to going back to school?"

"Oh, yes, I love school," I answer back with a bigger smile.

"I'm looking forward to it too, as all my kids will be back in school. Even though I'll miss them, I'll have some free time and they will be learning new things."

The middle daughter, Susan, is dancing with a broom and singing the Tennessee Waltz. I watch as she and the broom dance together over the brick sidewalk and then on the grass. You can see the pride mingled with the smiles on Mabel's and Joe's faces.

They're good parents and love their kids. I know that because I never hear them screaming at their kids or beating their kids. Their voice tones may rise once in a while but nothing like it used to be in my house when we were growing up.

As usual, the Sunday afternoon symphony of food enters my nose, awakening my appetite.

I move to the glider and try again to read my book so I don't think about Ben. It's comforting to sit on the glider and slide back and forth. No matter how hard I try, I can't get Ben out of my mind.

I'm glad there's no Youth Fellowship scheduled tonight, as I really just want to relax and think about my situation some more.

Mom and Dad come home at about seven o'clock, and after talking to them for a while about their afternoon and their pinochle games, I'm ready to go to my bedroom and read.

"Did you do anything this afternoon, Anna?" Mom asks.

"No, absolutely nothing. Sonya and Bev came over and we walked down to Main Line Drugstore for a soda. That's about it. How did you do at pinochle?"

"Tell her, Daisy, how we men won them all," Dad cuts in with a smile on his face.

"I don't think that's quite true, since the two of you cheated a lot. I saw you signaling each other," she says as she jabs her finger into his chest.

"Come on, Daisy, we didn't cheat. Just admit you lost."

"Oh brother, men! They're never wrong. Anna, always remember that men don't always tell the truth, and sometimes they only tell you what you want to hear. If you remember that, you'll never get hurt."

Chapter 32

During the last two weeks before school starts, Ben just happens to ride by when I m walking downtown in the evening with my girlfriends. He always seems to know my schedule, so he must ride around a lot looking for me. Of course he's aware that I'm never available when I walk downtown on Wednesday evenings (as I have choir practice), Friday nights (as I work at bingo), and Sunday evenings (as I have Youth Fellowship).

I light up with happiness upon seeing his gray Pontiac pull up to the curb. There's never the slightest hesitation on my part to get in his car. My girlfriends are good about keeping my secret these past few weeks even though they miss the "good old days" of all of us hanging out together and sharing secrets and stories.

Ben and I share a lot as we ride around and talk. He said since I'm taking driver's education when I go back to school he's going to teach me how to drive.

"Are you serious?"

"Yes. Besides, it will be fun," he says as he winks at me.

He drives out on a back road where there's no traffic, and it's still daylight. He pulls over to the side of the road, and I scoot behind the steering wheel as he gets out and slides in the front seat via the passenger door.

He sits in the middle next to me, and I love the closeness of his body to mine and the smell of his aftershave. I don't know where they come from, but such wonderful sensations go through my body and I wonder how I can concentrate with him so close.

He explains it's very important when I look at the road and while I'm steering that I keep the ornament of the hood lined up with the right side of the road. The ornament is an Indian head that looks like the wind was too strong for him and it stretched his head piece straight back into one smooth line.

I try to do it his way but, personally, I don't agree with him, because while keeping my eyes on the hood ornament I can't look at the signs and everything else while I'm driving. I don't want to discourage him and definitely don't want to hurt his feelings. After all, he is teaching me to drive.

During these couple of lessons, he's right there with his left arm flung around my shoulders and his right hand free to grab the steering wheel if he has to do so. Everything feels so right.

We listen to the radio and sometimes sing along with the music. One of my favorite songs is "How Many Arms Have Held You" by Eddy Arnold. I love to sing along with it and tease Ben by asking him how many arms have held him. He just smiles and refuses to answer.

We enjoy each other's company and see each other several times these last two weeks. Mom doesn't seem suspicious at all, nor does Ben's mother. I still hate this lie, but I don't know what else to do. We love being together.

Finally school starts, and I know I won't be seeing Ben as much since I'm not allowed to go out as much during the week.

On the first day of school I wear my favorite dark-brown skirt that is A-line, and inside the waist is a one-inch rubber lining that keeps my blouse from coming out of my skirt. I love this skirt even though it's too long. I pull it up and fold the waist down about one and a half inches so the entire skirt can be pulled up to be the right length. It twirls a little when I spin around. I never owned a poodle skirt but consider this one as my poodle skirt without a poodle. I wear a tan blouse and a red cinch belt that covers the rubber lining. My penny loafers contain two brand-new shiny pennies.

Entering the double doors with the top halves filled with small glass panes, I bump into Sonya, who tells me Jack is looking for me. I'm anxious to see him again even though he didn't call me once during the summer. She sees someone else and leaves, shouting, "I'll catch up with you later."

First, a morning assembly is held in the auditorium for everyone. Mr. Saxton, our very bald principal, always gives a speech on the first day of school.

On the stage there's a wooden podium with a background of dark-blue velvet curtains decorated with KHS in large white letters in a circle in the middle. Boys and girls are pouring in everywhere, and there's so much chattering going on. I don't see Jack anywhere, but Sonya finds me again and sits next to me.

Jack and I finally find each other in the hall after the morning assembly. Tanned and more muscular, he's so cute with his eyeglasses and a curl from his hair hanging down in the middle of the forehead. His face breaks into a smile when he sees me and says, "I've been trying to find you. How was your summer?"

"It was fun but it went by so fast. I can't believe we're back in school again."

"Sorry I never got to see you this summer or even call you. I worked on the farm, and walking back and forth to work each day made the days long. I was always so tired at the end of the day that I usually ate my supper and then went to bed."

"I figured you were busy, and we did say we wouldn't worry about seeing each other this summer since we lived so far apart. I want you to know that I met a guy a few weeks ago, and we've been dating these past several weeks."

"Do I know him?"

"I don't know. He graduated several years ago. His name is Ben Arno."

"Nope, I don't know him. Does he treat you nice?"

"Oh, yes, and I really do like him. I'm sorry, Jack.

"Not a problem. Just remember if it doesn't work out, let me know and maybe we can try again."

Just then the bell rings to get to our first class. Jack leans over and kisses me on the cheek and says, "If ever I can do anything for you, let me know. We'll always be friends."

I feel so miserable seeing the sadness in his eyes but nod in agreement, knowing that after this year he'll be going to college. Next year I'll still be here, but then I'll be a senior. That sounds good, but right now I'm happy to finally be a junior.

I know Ben is going to be happy. He was concerned that I might want to start dating Jack again when school started. Ben seems to know everything about me, even that Jack took me to the junior/senior prom last spring.

As I walk down the hall to first period, it's good seeing all my friends again and comparing our class schedules. I'm so excited because I'm scheduled for driver's ed the first semester. The kids who are already sixteen go first, and the kids who turn sixteen later will have it the second half. That means I'll be getting my driver's license before Thanksgiving.

Connie and I are happy to see each other in our first period class as we hug and laugh.

"You got your hair cut. It really looks nice," I say as I touch the curly waves in her brown hair.

"Forget the hair. I want to know all about Ben and you. I've been hearing bits and pieces about him from Sonya and Bev, but I want to hear it from you. Did he kiss you yet? Is he a good kisser? Is he good-looking?"

"Whoa, wait a minute. I'll tell you all about it at lunchtime when we have more time, but yes, he kissed me, and yes, he's good-looking. At least I think so." I grab her arm and say, "Come on, let's get our seats by each other in case this teacher doesn't assign them."

The class is Typing II, and the teacher is Mrs. Wilkinson. She's a short woman with reddish hair clipped short and gold-rimmed eyeglasses attached to a gold chain around her neck so she doesn't lose them. She doesn't assign seats and, for this, Connie and I look at each other and smile. At least we can talk once in a while between typing.

The rest of the morning classes whiz by, and before we know it lunchtime arrives. Since we don't have time to walk home and back, we usually bring a brown paper bag lunch or buy something at the school store.

Today we get our usual orange creamsicle and pretzel stick from the school store. We perch ourselves on the black iron railings that line the sidewalks leading to the high school's front doors. A nice breeze is blowing, and the sun feels warm on our backs.

As we balance ourselves on the railings, Connie says, "Okay, now tell me about Ben."

"You really want to know?" I laugh, teasing her.

Punching me in the arm, she says, "Of course, hurry up and tell me."

Chapter 33

Basking in the warm sun, I enjoy telling Connie all about Ben—how we both have to lie to our mothers and how much we enjoy being together.

She already knew about his father and one of his brothers, Mike, who lives in Kolfield. She tells me some of the stories she heard about Mike, including how he is always drunk, has several kids, and isn't married. I'm surprised. Ben didn't seem to be like him at all. I have to remember to ask Ben about Mike.

The rest of the day flies by, and before I know it, I'm walking home. I am really surprised when Ben pulls up about a block away and asks me if I want a ride home. Turning to Sonya and Bev, I ask them if they want a ride home, and we all pile in the car.

After dropping Sonya and Bev off at Main Line Drugstore, Ben and I ride up past Kolfield Park.

"How come you're home and not at work?"

"I took a day off. My mother wanted me to take her somewhere."

"Oh, who stayed with your father?"

"My brother Mike. He's not working right now, so he's available."

I want to ask him about his brother, but I wouldn't like it if he asked me anything about my sisters, so I decide I'll wait until he's ready to tell me.

"Did you talk to that guy that took you to the prom last year?"

"Yes, and I told him I was seeing you. We're still friends but not dating friends."

"That's good, Anna, because I really like you a lot and would rather you didn't date anyone but me."

"Are you asking me to go steady?" I ask, filled with hope.

"Yes, but we can't let my mother find out. I told Mike about you, and he told me not to get too serious, as he can't take care of my father, and I have to be the one that stays at home. My other brothers live in different states, and I know they don't want to be bothered. They each have a wife and kids."

"Does Mike have kids?"

"Yes, four kids, and now his girlfriend is expecting another one. He won't marry her, but he sees her all the time. Sometimes he drinks too much but not on Sundays, as he brings his girlfriend and kids over to the house to see my mom and dad. Mom makes a pot of sauce every Sunday so we can have a spaghetti dinner together."

"Doesn't his girl care that he doesn't marry her?"

"I guess not."

"Gosh, look at the time. I've got to get home. I have to babysit tonight for some people."

"Okay, maybe I'll see you one evening this week."

Ben drops me off on Main Avenue after I gather my books and he kisses my hand. As I'm walking home I wonder why Mike doesn't marry his girlfriend and why his mother doesn't say something about them getting married. After all, if there are already four kids and she's expecting another one, what are they waiting for? Society frowns on unmarried women having kids.

Dismissing my thoughts, I walk fast, as I have to get ready for my babysitting job. Tonight I'm babysitting Amy, and all I know is she's a physically disabled baby. The parents never go out but decided to celebrate their anniversary dinner at Gracino's, a local Italian restaurant. I arrive at their house at about six o'clock, and they show me what to do, which is really nothing except check on Amy once in a while. I'm not allowed to pick her up or even change her diaper.

They present a list of numbers they composed and lay it on the table. For any problems at all, I'm to call immediately.

As I look at Amy lying in her crib, I want to cry but keep my emotions contained. She's hooked up to many things, and she cannot do anything but open and close her eyes. She's deformed but that's the way she was born. The parents tell me they're happy for each day they have her, but I know it must be heartbreaking.

After they leave, I check on her constantly, and once her eyes seem to look right at me, so I say her name softly to her. I sing a lullaby to her, and she closes her eyes. I can't imagine how these parents must feel, knowing she'll never run and play like other children.

The parents are back before eight o'clock, after calling on the phone twice. Upon returning, the mother goes straight to Amy's room to check on her.

The father asks, "Did you have any problems with her? Did she cry at all?"

"No, she was very good, and she didn't cry once. If she had, I'd have called you immediately."

After paying me, he asks, "Do you need a ride home?"

"No, thank you. I can walk."

"We may call you again sometime if we ever decide to go out."

"That would be great. Thank you." I open the door to leave.

Walking home, I can't get Amy out of my mind. These thoughts continue as I crawl into bed. I lie there thinking how she'll never be able to walk or talk or play like other kids and how much love radiates from her parents. I thank God for allowing me to meet Amy.

Tonight I welcome the sound of the train's whistle as the sadness of it mixes with my emotions and allows me to cry myself to sleep.

Chapter 34

Several months fly by and colorful leaves decorate the sidewalks and roads. Ben and I see each other as often as we can. School is great and I'm enjoying every minute of it.

The only sad thing that has happened is Amy, the little girl that I babysat, died. I cried an entire evening, remembering her in the crib and her eyes meeting my eyes. I know she's a real angel now, as she was an angel when she was alive. The viewing and funeral was for family only. Feeling bad for Amy's mother and father, I sent them a sympathy card after writing a few words in it.

Otherwise, my school year is great.

My driver's education class is so much fun. The written test is easy, and I pass it with flying colors. The driving instructor shows me everything about driving, from adjusting the mirror and seat to pushing the actual clutch in with my right foot on the brake. To move, I slowly allow the clutch to come out while stepping on the gas.

What I don't like about it is when I stop on a hill and try to maneuver the clutch and gas without going backward. It scares me because, if I don't stop it in time, I could drift back into another car. Finally, I master it.

The big day comes in November when the state police arrive at the school to give the driver's test. I'm scheduled to take my test right after lunch and am very nervous. The snow is falling, and I hope they won't cancel my driving test because of bad weather.

One of the boys, dubbed our class clown, comes in to say he failed the test. Knowing him, he probably clowned around too much, but hearing that someone actually failed shakes my confidence.

Finally it's my turn. Since I don't have a car, they allow me to use the school's car.

I slide into the front seat, and the state trooper gets into the passenger side. I adjust my mirror and seat, hoping I'm not forgetting anything.

The state trooper is very nice and senses my fear. When he speaks, my fear leaves me.

"Don't be afraid, just relax, and drive the way they taught you to drive," he says, watching me start the engine.

Nodding my head I drive down Sunshine Avenue for a couple of blocks while the snowflakes continue their gentle fall everywhere. The state trooper tells me to do a U-turn in the road. I do it very well, turning my wheels at the right time when I know I will only have to back up once to complete the U-turn.

After getting back to the school, he proceeds to tell me I did everything right, including turning on the directional signals to turn, the parallel parking, management of the clutch with the gas, and, of course, the U-turn.

Yippee! I pass my driving test, and he congratulates me as he signs my form. Happiness floods through me, and I can't wait to tell everyone. Mom and Dad will be pleased, I think.

My parents did promise me I could have the car for the evening on the day I pass my driver's test. Now I'm worried that I might not be allowed to have the car if this snow continues.

It's the middle of November, and our first snowfall is predicted starting around noon and continuing into the evening. Usually our first snowfall is no big deal, so I try not to be concerned.

Arriving home I excitedly tell Mom and Dad that I passed my test. Mom says it might be too slippery for me to drive, but Dad refutes her words by stating the weatherman forecast only light snow and there would be no significant accumulation. He has already put the snow tires on the car, and somehow he knows how much it means for me to be able to take the car out by myself.

My mother finally consents. But since I'm driving the car I have to be home at nine o'clock instead of ten o'clock.

Edna and Reds arrive, stomp their feet on the back porch, and enter with snow clinging to their coats.

"Brrr, it's cold out there," says Reds as he brushes snow from his coat sleeves.

"Hey, there, Anna banana, I heard you passed your driver's test. Did you have to bribe the state trooper, or did he feel sorry for you?"

"No, silly, I'm a good driver, and I practiced a lot in driver's ed," I answer, knowing he's just kidding.

They're going to play pinochle with Mom and Dad tonight, and in a way I'm thankful for that so they can concentrate on the cards and not worry about me.

It's difficult for me to contain my enthusiasm, as I'm finally a driver and not a walker. Also, because I know I'm going to see Ben later.

I already made arrangements in school with Sonya and Bev. We're going to ride around town, as that's the highlight of finally getting your driver's license in Kolfield. You have to let everyone know you have your license. The light snow continues and, as usual, the first snowfall is beautiful, as it's so pure and white.

Sonya and Bev know I'm going to meet Ben, so they made arrangements to meet up with some other kids at Main Line Drugstore later. I drive slowly and carefully and toot the horn when we see any of our friends. There are several kids out, but it's not a good night for walkers.

We drive twice around Kolfield and, after dropping them off, Ben's car appears in my rearview mirror. It's amazing how he automatically appears out of nowhere.

Actually, I'm very happy to park the car, since it's snowing harder and I definitely don't want anything to happen to Mom and Dad's car. After parking on Main Avenue several blocks from home, I climb into Ben's car and we drive slowly down the street.

We stay in town and ride around for a while, but the snow is falling fast and swirling around in front of the headlights, making it hard to see the road. Several inches have accumulated on the ground. I know my parents are going to be worried, and I need to get the car back to them. Finally I tell Ben I have to go home even though it's only eight o'clock.

He slowly navigates his car in back of my car and leans over to me. My stomach feels like there are Mexican jumping beans in it. He kisses me and, wow, how I love his kisses. I really think I could sit there for an hour kissing him. We hate to say good-bye but we must, as I'll feel better after I get the car home.

Getting in my cold car, I wish I could have stayed in Ben's warm car, not only from our kisses but also from the heater. Ben waits until I start the car and follows me to Fifth Street to make sure I'm okay. I take my time driving home these couple of blocks and am very careful.

As I walk in the back door, everyone looks at me. They're sitting in the kitchen having coffee, since they're done playing cards, just waiting to make sure I arrive home safe and sound.

"Reds and I went out looking for you, Anna. We couldn't find you. Where did you go?" asks Dad as he lifts his cup of coffee to his mouth.

With my heart pounding and trying to act nonchalant, I ask, "Just where did you two go?"

"We drove all the way up the Ninth Street hill figuring that was the way you were going to come home. We didn't see you anywhere and were worried with all of the snow coming down."

"I didn't want to come down the Ninth Street hill, as it's too steep and slippery, so I came the long way home. Who won at pinochle tonight?" I ask, hoping to change the subject.

"The men won, of course," Reds answers as he pumps out his chest and thumps on it. "By the way, Anna, why did the chicken cross the road?"

"Oh, Reds, like I don't know the answer," I say, smiling. "Well, got to put my coat and scarf away and get to bed. All of this excitement of driving in the snow has made me tired. Good night, everyone."

"Good night, Anna," they all say in unison except for Reds, who says, "Good night, Anna banana." Reds named me that, but I don't know why—maybe just because it rhymed.

As I'm climbing the stairs to my room, I realize that Mom never said a word, probably because I was home before the required time. I wonder how Dad and Reds couldn't have seen the car. It was parked not too far from here, right on Main Avenue. Maybe Dad and Reds saw the car but decided not to tell Mom and get her upset. Then again, maybe they didn't see it because they weren't looking for a parked car and the snow covered it. Most of the cars are black and gray anyway, and that helps my situation.

I'm more concerned they might notice I didn't use much gas. If they notice, I'll just tell them I put gas in it. At twenty-seven cents a gallon, I could have put a gallon in it because they know I had fifty cents. Yeah, that's what I'll tell them. Boy, this lying is getting more and more difficult. I suppose it's all worth it, but it wears me down trying to keep my stories straight.

That night I thank God for everything and ask him to bless everyone and pray that everyone in this world is as happy as me. I also thank God for Ben. I stretch my feet out, feeling the cold sheets and smelling the freshness of the sheets and blankets. I am one lucky and happy person to have clean sheets, a boyfriend, and my driver's license.

Chapter 35

Ben and I are developing a forbidden seriousness with our kisses and hugs, wanting more but holding back. It seems like what we're not allowed to have, we desire all the more because it's prohibited. The kisses are becoming more intense as we profess our undying love for each other, and our bodies seem to cling to each other. All my friends know we're seeing each other, and we don't know how long it will be before the secret is revealed to our mothers.

Two of my male friends who have gone to school with me since first grade tell me they don't think Ben is good enough for me. I just ignore them, as I feel they just don't know him well enough to say such a thing.

One Saturday evening I'm quite surprised when Ben asks me if I want to meet his father. His mother went to five o'clock mass, and we can go to his house while she's gone.

Ben reminds me, "My mother is very demanding and doesn't want me dating any girls, so we have to be out of the house before she returns."

"By the way, Ben, what's your mother's first name?"

"It's Concetta, and my dad's name is Tony," he replies as he squeezes my hand.

We park in front of the single-family white house decorated with green shutters and green trim. A wooden swing built for two or three people is hanging by chains from the front porch roof. Two metal chairs are situated on the other end of the porch.

We hold hands while we walk up the four steps to the wooden porch and enter the front door of his house. Upon entering the house, I walk into a delicious smell of spaghetti sauce and garlic.

My heart's thumping, and I'm nervous about meeting his father. He takes me straight upstairs and down the hall to his father's room situated in the front of the house, overlooking the street.

Ben introduces me to his bedridden father and, when I see him, all my anxieties vanish.

His father is very tiny and thin, lying in bed with the blanket covering him to the middle of his chest. There's a slight medicinal smell that reminds me of a hospital.

He motions for me with his movable hand to sit in the chair by the side of his bed, near his good side. As I sit down, he reaches out and holds my hand.

One side of his mouth lifts up, as if he is trying to smile, and he tries to talk but I cannot understand him. I look up at Ben, who interprets. "Dad wants you to know he is pleased to meet you."

I look back at Tony and tell him I'm very glad to meet him and that Ben has told me so much about him. I can see how much Ben looks like his father.

Ben says he'll be back in a minute and leaves the room, as he wants to change his shirt. I sit there, holding his Dad's hand and rattling off different things about Ben and me. I tell him I remember when he delivered ice for the kitchen iceboxes and how he would sometimes give us chunks of ice that we could rub on our faces to cool ourselves off on a hot day.

We are there only about twenty minutes when Ben says we have to go before Concetta comes home. I kiss his father lightly on his cheek and tell him good-bye. His father has tears in his eyes, and it seems to be contagious, as tears form in my eyes. Thoughts race through my mind about how he has to lie there day after day and depend on other people to help him.

I wonder if he reminisces about how his life used to be before the stroke. My one hope is Concetta doesn't in any way make him feel like a burden. Ben would never make his father feel that way, as he loves his father very much and would do anything in the world for him.

Hating to leave but knowing it's too dangerous to stay there with Ben's mother coming home, we get ready to leave. Goodness knows what she might say or do from what Ben has told me about her.

"You know, Anna, my father really likes you. I can tell," Ben says as we walk down the stairs.

"I hope so because I like him too. He seems to be such a nice person. Maybe I can visit him again sometime, and maybe he'd like someone to read to him. I'd love to do that."

"I wish you could, Anna, but my mother won't allow it. She just doesn't want anyone around that might be a threat in taking me away from her."

On our next date, Ben tells me his father likes me and even managed some words that Ben interprets as my being pretty, sweet, and friendly. Ben says it made him so proud when his father conveyed that message.

That news is overshadowed by the fact that Ben's mother found out that he brought me to the house.

Ben relates the entire episode to me. A neighbor told Concetta that she had seen Ben take me into her house. Concetta yelled and screamed at Ben that he can't get involved with any girls, as he has to stay at home and help with his father.

At that point I wonder if Ben's father overheard her screaming and, if he did, how that must have made him feel.

Ben notices the expression on my face, grabs my hand, and says, "Don't worry about her. She's just upset but she'll get over it, especially once she meets you and gets to know you."

I have my doubts but I smile at him and squeeze his hand.

I'm still waiting to see Ben's father again but believe that Ben is afraid to take me there, afraid his mother will find out. What a shame! I'd love to be able to read to his father or talk to him about different things. I could sit with him if no one else is available. I'd love to help his mother in any way possible but doubt if she will ever give me that chance.

Ben explains, "Please understand that I'm the only one that can help my mother take care of my father. That's why she becomes hysterical if she thinks I'm serious with a girl."

I reassure Ben, "I do understand so don't worry about it. Somehow it'll all work out, as I'm a true believer in everything is meant to be. We don't always understand when something happens and it may be painful when it happens, but it will all make sense to us later."

If I had allowed my brain to think instead of relying on my heart, I would have paid attention to all of these warning signs. There were so many and, yet, I saw none.

That night as I lie in bed I pray that God will lead me and direct me to do the right things in life. I'm tired of the white lies that I utilize to deceive my mother and father in order to be with Ben. I'm tired of sneaking around, and I miss my freedom of being with my girlfriends.

Tonight I say a special prayer for Ben's father, who is lying in his bed and probably hears the same train whistle as it chugs through Kolfield to the mines. I wish the train could load my white lies instead of the black coal and take them far, far away.

Chapter 36

The months fly by and, before I know it, spring is here. Ben and I are still sneaking around, but it's getting more and more difficult. Everyone knows except Mom and Dad, and I'm not too sure about them. If they know they are probably hoping it will pass or I'll meet someone new.

Jo's been writing me to visit her in New Jersey this summer when school gets out. I wrote back that I'd love to but it would be up to Mom. Mom has no problem with it. That's what makes me think she knows about Ben and me and is trying to separate us.

Right after I tell Ben I'll be visiting my sister in New Jersey in the summer, he surprises me. He tells me everyone at work is talking about *Cinerama Holiday* that is playing in Pittsburgh and wonders if I will be able to go if he buys tickets.

Also, his friend Nick, the wannabe gangster type, wants to go and take Connie, my best friend, with him. I tell him I'd love to and we can work it out somehow, so he buys the tickets.

Then I ask Mom and Dad if I'm allowed to go with Connie and her mother to visit her aunt in Pittsburgh and attend the theater. *Jeepers, another white lie for me.* They have no problem with it. I'm glad Mom doesn't know Connie's mother. This way they can't compare stories.

Connie is allowed to go, and I envy her that she doesn't have to tell a white lie to her mother. I'm thrilled to think of spending an entire Sunday with Ben. That's always his day with his family, as Mike and his girlfriend and kids always come to the house for dinner.

He tells them he bought tickets to see *Cinerama Holiday* in Pittsburgh and tells me they know better than to say anything since he is always there for them.

So with excitement and anticipation, on a sunny but cool Sunday in April, Ben, Nick, Connie, and I drive to Pittsburgh to see *Cinerama Holiday.* Connie and I are excited and try not to show our childish anticipation.

Our arrival in Pittsburgh is two hours before the picture starts, and we're very hungry. After parking, we walk around looking for a restaurant and stumble upon the William Penn Hotel. It's a huge building.

The doorman opens the door for us and directs us to the dining room. We walk into an exquisite area called the Terrace Room. Soft music is playing, and older people sit around candlelit tables. We are debating on whether to turn around and walk out or stay, when a waiter with a towel draped over his arm comes toward us.

"Table for four?" he asks.

We nod our heads and follow him to the table, where he pulls out a chair for me. As I sit in it, he pushes it forward to the table. He proceeds to do the same thing for Connie. I don't dare look at Connie or we will bust out laughing. No one ever did that for us before today.

I glance at my menu and almost become sick. The cheapest meal is imported ham with honey over it for four dollars. Since we don't know how much money our boyfriends have with them, we tell them to order for us.

Immediately Ben and Nick have a caucus.

It might be my imagination, but everyone around us seems to be laughing and staring at us. One man, directly across from our table, is talking about his trip to England, from which he had just returned the day before. Connie and I sit in awe, but our boyfriends aren't paying any attention, as they're trying to figure out what we can afford to eat.

Our waiter is patient and gracious, treating us with courtesy and respect. Needless to say, Ben orders the ham with honey for all of us. The ice water that has already been poured serves as our drinks. The food is delicious, and the treatment makes us feel special and important.

After we're done eating, Ben raises his hand to the waiter and asks for the bill. He seems to know what he's doing, like he's been here before. He's the only one who actually has a full-time job, as the rest of us are still in high school. I'm sure he pays the majority of the total. He's good-hearted like that.

After walking outside and holding Ben's hand, I thank him for the meal. He squeezes my hand as he smiles at me. When our eyes meet, I feel so much love emanating from his big brown eyes and know that this must be true love.

It's a beautiful cool afternoon as we walk toward the theater, with Connie and Nick lagging behind. I feel so proud of Ben and that he's my boyfriend.

The theater is huge and reeks of royalty, with the plush seats, huge screen, and everything trimmed in gold. There aren't enough words to describe *Cinerama Holiday*. It opens with a breathtaking airplane view of the Alps, and then you actually feel like you are skiing and riding a bobsled. You can hear the wind rushing by as you ride the bobsled, or so it seems. It's so realistic.

The day is perfect, but before you know it, it's time to head home. On the ride home, I snuggle next to Ben while he drives. All of the excitement and anticipation has vanished, but we've made some memories. There is so much that I want to see and do outside of Kolfield but still have next year to finish high school before beginning my adventures—at least that's what I thought.

Chapter 37

Finally, my junior year is over. Our last day of school is in May, right after the seniors graduate. My girlfriends and I hug each other with joy on this last day, as we are now officially seniors. What a great feeling knowing that in one year I'll finish high school and do anything or go anywhere I desire.

Mom and Dad just got back after leaving me with Liz and Pep for a week while they drove to New Jersey. They attended Jo's graduation from modeling school in Philadelphia. I'm so proud of her. She was pretty to begin with, and now she must be beautiful, as she has learned so many things from posture and clothes to applying the right makeup. I can't wait to see the new Jo this summer, but first I have an interview for a job.

I already have a part-time job working at the W. T. Grant store located in the middle of town on Main Avenue. Most of the time it's fun working in the office, but when they're short on help I usually work behind the candy counter and love it. When I have cramps, one chocolate crumb on my tongue seems to help ease the pain. Because I work only on Saturdays, I now want a more important job with more hours.

Senator Jordan has a local office in Kolfield and likes to have a high school senior work for him the summer before she graduates and through her senior year. Sometimes he hires them permanently after they graduate or during the summers if they go to college.

My teacher submitted my name with two other names to Senator Jordan for job interviews in his office. I'm excited that my teacher recommended me, as I want to get experience working with him and maybe someday become a lawyer.

The interview develops into a memory that I'll never forget. Wearing my black-and-gray tweed suit with high heels and nylons with seams going up the back of my legs, I'm ready for this interview. I have to be very careful. My concern is I may get a runner in my nylons before the interview, and this is my only pair of nylons. Short white gloves and a small black purse accent my outfit.

When I arrive at the office, the secretary is very nice as I hand her my résumé. After typing and shorthand tests, she tells me to have a seat and Senator Jordan will be with me shortly.

Sitting there ladylike with my hands folded in my lap and clutching my purse, I watch the secretary type all the while hoping my tests are okay.

When Senator Jordan comes out, he gives me one of those big politician grins, shakes my hand, and ushers me into his office.

He's a very large man with little hair and is dressed in a dark-gray suit, white shirt, and red tie. His dark-brown eyes stare right into my eyes when we start talking about Kolfield and school before finally getting down to the job.

"You did excellent in your tests, so I know there's no problem there," he says as his eyes lock onto mine.

I breathe a sigh of relief and hope it isn't within his hearing range.

He continues, "There is one problem though."

I feel myself tense up, not knowing what it is or what I did.

"You're a very pretty girl, Anna. It's just a matter of time before you get a boyfriend, and you'll probably get married as soon as you graduate."

I just stare at him, not knowing what he means. Where on earth did he get such an idea? I'm not going to get married. These thoughts race through my mind.

He sees the puzzlement on my face and explains further.

"I'd invest too much time and effort in training you only to have you leave me," he explains. "Remember, I know you'd make an excellent secretary, but you're just too pretty and I know some man will come and sweep you off your feet in no time at all."

It's difficult for me not to break out in tears, but I manage. I don't hear much after that, but suddenly he stands and extends his hand, which I shake. He says, "If there's anything I can do for you, please call my office."

After the handshake, I thank him for his time while hoping tears won't fill up my eyes and overflow in front of him. In the outer office I manage to thank his secretary and walk out.

While driving home the tears start creeping out of my eyes, and I dab them with my gloves. How crazy all of this is. Everyone tells you how lucky you are that you're so pretty but you can't get a job because you are too pretty? It just doesn't make sense. What a crazy world we live in.

To me this is plain rejection, and it hurts. Now I feel the only good thing in my life is Ben. He never rejects me and is always there for me. We love each other very much, but I'd like to get a job and be on my own before we even think of marriage.

Chapter 38

The next couple of days my family and friends console me about my interview, explaining to me how politicians try to please everyone, which I know is utterly impossible. The one who gets the job is probably someone he owes a favor or to whom the job has already been promised. By telling me that I'm too pretty, he thought he could compliment me and let me down easy.

That's so wrong. I would rather have been told the truth. Later I find out he really did promise the job to someone else, and that's okay, but why put me through all of that? I lost a lot of respect for politicians after that interview.

Since I didn't get the job with Senator Jordan, I have plenty of time to make arrangements to visit Jo in New Jersey. Ben isn't thrilled that I'm going, but he knows I want to see my sister. He tries to talk me out of it, but I'm determined no one is going to keep me away from Jo.

My parents drive me to the train station, and I feel a cloud of doubt and fright hanging over me. I'm scared to be traveling by myself but am excited to finally take a train ride. We say our good-byes, and the conductor tells my parents he'll take good care of me. Settled in my seat I watch the other passengers as they board and position themselves in their seats. I find I learn more things by observing and listening.

The train slowly pulls away from the platform, and my excitement escalates. Not long after our departure an announcement is made that we'll be going around the famous Horseshoe Curve in Altoona. We reach the Horseshoe Curve and suddenly I'm scared. It's just what they say it is, a curve shaped like a horseshoe, and at this point I'm afraid the train will tip over and fall off the tracks.

It's strange how you can see the other part of the train if you look out the window toward the other side of the horseshoe curve. I relax only after we coast around the curve and I can't see any more of the train that I'm riding in.

It's exciting to look out the windows and watch the countryside go whizzing by. I enjoy the rhythm of the train, and the conductor leans over and tells me if I want to sleep, it's okay, as he'll wake me when we reach Philadelphia.

I eventually doze off but not into a deep sleep, as the excitement of seeing Jo again keeps my mind churning. Then another fear jumps out and clings to me. What in the world will I do if Jo isn't there to meet me?

I have to let go of these worries. Whatever will be will be. Mom and Dad would never have put me on the train if they thought Jo wouldn't pick me up—at least, I hope not.

Even though it's a long trip, the time flies by. An announcement is made that we're only a few miles out of Philadelphia, but I already surmised that as the scenery began to change many miles back. Instead of fields and forests, I see tall buildings, factories, and warehouses.

As we pull into the station, I look out the window but don't see Jo. Full of fear, I step out of the train to the platform. Looking around I don't see anyone familiar. There are so many people scurrying about and so much noise. I don't know which direction to go.

Carrying my suitcase I decide to follow the crowd up the escalator. At the top of the escalator I stop and look around. I'm amazed at how big the station is—the marble, the pillars, the train board with the times of incoming and outgoing trains, and a huge counter in the center where you can ask questions or get information.

Suddenly someone grabs me from behind with their hands over my eyes.

"You have three guesses who I am."

Recognizing her voice and with relief, I say, "Queen of England?"

"Wrong. Next guess."

"Elizabeth Taylor?"

"Wrong. Last guess."

"I know it's not First Lady Mamie Eisenhower because she's taking care of the president, since he had surgery a couple of weeks ago. I guess it must be Joan of Arc."

"You're so silly," Jo says as she removes her hands from my eyes and I turn around.

"I'm so glad to see you," I say with such enthusiasm while we hug each other tightly.

"You weren't scared, were you? Come on, Anna, you don't think I'd leave my baby sister all alone in the big city, do you?"

"Of course I wasn't scared, not for a minute. I knew you'd be here, but I never know what you're going to do next, Jo. You know how daring you are."

"Mom and Dad would never forgive me if I didn't meet you. After all, they entrusted you to me."

"I'm a big girl and can take care of myself. Boy, you're looking fantastic, Jo. You're beautiful. Hey, Lily, how are you?" I ask after hearing her laugh at us. I turn and give her a big hug too.

"Doing good."

Lily never was one for a lot of words. She leans her head sideways and back a little when she talks, trying for a tough person image. She and Jo are like night and day but are the best of friends. She has blonde hair, a cute little nose and mouth, and a plain face, as she wears no makeup and is always in jeans.

After we finally find our way out of Philadelphia, I discover that big cities are quite different from the small towns, such as Kolfield. No doubt it's easy to get lost on these streets.

The scenery changes after leaving the city to beautiful trees and flat land. I didn't know land could be so flat with no mountains.

They borrowed a car from one of their friends, and the ride to Glasstown goes very fast as we chatter away with gossip about Kolfield and the inhabitants that they know.

"Bunky came to see me," Jo says.

"Wow, are you back together?"

"No, I can't forgive him for what he did."

"Geez, Jo, it was a mistake, and he told you that."

"I'm sorry but if he does it once, he'll do it again."

"Did he come on the train or bus?"

"Neither, he hitchhiked."

"He hitchhiked the entire way? Well, that alone shows how much he loves you. You're such a stubborn, hardheaded person."

"Hey, I'm enjoying my paychecks, and also I'm dating a couple of other guys."

This whole time Lily never says a word as she's sitting in the passenger side but then pipes up with "Anna, if we're working and you're alone, don't open the door to anyone, okay?"

"Sure, but if you're working, no one will come knocking on the door, as they know you're not there."

"You never know."

"Yeah, Anna, that's a good idea. Do what Lily says," Jo remarks.

The trip goes fast, and before I know it we're in Glasstown, New Jersey.

Chapter 39

Glasstown is an industrial town with a huge glass company situated at one end. Its population is five times larger than Kolfield's. Many of the employees are from other states, as the glass company advertised in many towns, offering the high school seniors good-paying jobs. The plant is open seven days a week, three shifts each day, and employs over three thousand people. This glass company is one of the largest employers in Glasstown.

The houses and lawns along Laurel Street and North Pearl Street are well kept with colorful flowers lining the porches and walks. Swings, gliders, and chairs decorate the porches, where people enjoy sitting while chatting with their friends and relatives.

Jo and Lily work in the corrugated department. Working with the various boxes needed to ship bottles creates a paper dust that they breathe. It also covers them with the dust, but they both agree the paycheck is worth it.

After parking in an empty parking space near the Sunray Drugstore, we load the parking meter with coins. The furnished apartment they rent is located on the second floor above Feinstein's Furniture Store, a few doors away from the drugstore.

After entering a separate door next to Feinstein's Furniture Store entrance, we climb eleven steps to a small landing and then eleven more steps to a landing where their apartment door is located.

Unlocking and opening the door, Jo bows for me to enter, as if royalty. Laughing, I step through the door, and the odor of cigarette smoke hits me. The faded-green furniture is well worn and looks dismal. Marred tables embellished with drink rings stand by each end of it. The living room is quite dark, as it contains no windows.

The kitchen contains a small, red Formica table trimmed with chrome. A matching chair on each end of the table face yellowed white cupboards on the other side of the room surrounding a very used stove. A small noisy refrigerator is situated next to the stove and cupboards. The furnished apartment is okay but is nothing like home.

If you go through the kitchen, you enter Lily's bedroom, but the door is closed and I sense Lily doesn't wish to open it.

Jo has the bedroom in the front of the building, and that's where I plop down my suitcase. The room is large enough for a double bed and two dressers, which have seen better days, and a closet. The wallpaper is brown-and-beige–striped, with one piece beginning to come down by the ceiling in a corner.

Gazing out the front window I'm amazed to be staying smack-dab in the center of town and looking down on people. It's going to be fun. I just know it.

After a few days, I realize what I really hate is going to the bathroom in their apartment, especially after dark, because when you flick the lights on, cockroaches are scurrying every which way to find a dark opening to hide in. I always hike up my pajamas, afraid that one might latch onto the bottom and go back to bed with me. Never do I go barefooted.

Jo forewarned me about these ugly creatures, so I'm thankful for that; otherwise, I might have just gone in without the lights and stepped all over them. Imagining the crunch, crunch, crunch under my feet, I can picture myself screaming while jumping up and down all over the place. Jo already notified the landlord, who's going to send a bug killer to take care of them.

While Jo and Liz work the afternoon shift, three to eleven, at the factory, I stay in the apartment and look out the front window, watching everyone walking in and out of the various stores, shopping. It's exciting, as there are so many different types of people.

Jo warns me again and again that I can't go out after dark, to not answer the door if anyone comes knocking, and definitely keep the shades down on the window after dark.

One night, at a quarter after eleven, there's a knock on the door. I'm expecting Jo and Liz home any minute, but they always use their key. The knocking scares me, and I don't open the door but as instructed ask, "Who is it?"

"I'm looking for Lily. Open the door," a man replies.

"Lily isn't here."

"Open the door anyway. I'll wait for her."

"I'm not supposed to open the door."

"And just who are you?"

"I'm Jo's sister."

"It's okay. Let me in. Hasn't Lily told you about me?"

"No."

With relief I hear Jo and Lily coming up the stairs. All three of them come in, and Jo introduces me to Paul.

"Hey, you've got a pretty sister, Jo."

"I know. Just stay away from her, Paul," she answers as she pushes me into the kitchen.

After a few minutes, Lily comes into the kitchen and says, "We're going for a ride. See you later."

"Bye," we say in unison as we get ready to have a cup of tea.

I don't mind staying at home by myself, as I enjoy being with Jo when she isn't working. On paydays we eat at the Sunray Drugstore, and she usually buys me a new shirt or scarf at Rooney's Department Store.

One day Jo and I are sitting on the couch, and we start talking about Bunky's visit.

"Yes, we were surprised to see him and happy too, but I didn't let him know that. We had to let him stay with us, as he had no place to go."

"That was nice of you. Where did he sleep?"

"Oh, he didn't want to put us out since we were working, so he slept on the couch. He seemed to be okay with that," she says as she traces a square with her finger on the checkered pillow on her lap.

"You don't think you'll ever take him back?"

"Nope. Once a cheat, always a cheat, and I can't go through that again. It's too painful."

"You know he loves you and realizes he made a big mistake making out with that girl."

"So he says, but he had his chance and now it's over. He told me he was going to join the service. I told him I didn't care, end of subject. Now what's going on in your life, and who is this guy you're seeing?"

I know she still cares about Bunky, but she's just being Miss Stubborn who has too much pride.

"Well, his name is Ben Arno and he treats me nice. He has brown eyes and dark hair. Anyway, he's taller than me and slim built, not big and muscular. He tells me all the time he loves me and I love him. We're going steady so we don't date anyone else."

"I don't know, Anna. You're too young to be going steady. You should go out with other guys and enjoy life a little."

"Jo, I'm really happy with him. Just don't tell Mom, okay?"

"You know I won't tell her, but I think you're getting too serious with him. You haven't done anything with him, have you?"

"No, never. Now let's not talk about that kind of stuff," I say as I stand up and move toward the kitchen.

"Where are you going? I didn't mean anything by that, but you do have to be careful. If you do anything, he has to wear a rubber so you don't get pregnant."

"I'm getting a drink of water," I reply as I walk out of the room with my fingers in my ears.

"I'm just telling you for your own sake, don't trust men. They can be deceitful and you never know it until it's too late," she says as she follows me into the kitchen.

"Come on, let's go over to the Five & Dime store and get a soda," she says as she squeezes my arm. Then she hollers, "Hey, Lily, want to go with us?"

Lily comes out of her room and says, "Can't, waiting for a call from Paul."

"Oh, forget him. He's married. You can't sit around waiting for him all day. Come on."

"No, I don't want to miss his call."

As Jo and I are walking down the stairs, I ask Jo who Paul really is besides a guy who wants to see Lily.

"Oh, he's one of our coworkers, and Lily thinks she loves him. He's married and has a really pretty wife but no children. He only wants one thing from Lily and that's sex. She believes everything he tells her. She's going to be hurt by him, but she doesn't seem to care. I've heard that he dates a lot of the other girls working at the glass plant."

"Jeez, doesn't his wife know?"

"Probably, but she's married to him so that's like a safety net for her and him both."

That night as I lie in bed, I think of Lily and Paul and his wife. So many people are going to be hurt by all of this, as Paul would have to divorce his wife to marry Lily or Lily will be hurt if Paul doesn't get a divorce. It seems like Paul is the only one who is going to benefit from any of this unless both women leave him and he really does love one of them. It all makes my head spin.

Boy, now I'm getting homesick, and I really do miss Ben. I received a letter from him today in which he tells me he misses me so much and wants to know when I'm coming home. I'll answer his letter tomorrow but don't know exactly when I'm going home.

Actually I'm beginning to look forward to going home, as I miss my train whistle at night, and oh yes, I do miss Ben. Saying my prayers and drifting into sleep, tonight I hear only the sounds of the cars and trucks on the street outside the open window.

Chapter 40

$\mathcal{J}$ enjoy reading Ben's letter and writing back to him. Last summer I was writing to two Marines that I met at the Kolfield Recreational Park, but they became too serious in their letters, and after meeting Ben I figured if they didn't just want a pen pal, then I wouldn't write anymore.

One of them came to see me when he was home on leave. He looked so handsome in his uniform, but there was no attraction for me. It was different when I went out with Ben, as I felt something right away. So reading and writing these letters are special, as I know I love Ben very much.

One evening Jo and Lily borrow a car and for a treat are going to take me to the Barrel to eat. It's a drive-in restaurant, and I can see where it gets its name. It's shaped like a big barrel, and you pull up and someone comes out and takes your order, similar to Ripple's back home. Jo and Lily worked there as waitresses for a couple of weeks before starting at the glass plant.

After pulling in and giving our orders, a guy of medium height and muscular build with blond hair, thick strands of it lapping over his forehead and almost touching his eyes, comes out of the Barrel. He's wiping his hands on a big white apron covering the front of him, giving me the impression that he must be the cook. He comes over to the car and orders Jo and Lily to get out so he can give them a big hug. Jo introduces him as Bill Shoup to me, and he gives me a big hug. I wonder if he cracked any of my ribs.

"Just call me Shoupy," he says to me. "Everybody else does."

"I can't believe you're still working here," Jo says.

"Hey, I like it, and I only work part-time now. You know I got married and my wife's pregnant."

"Congratulations," Lily and Jo say in unison.

"Yep, she's beautiful too," he says, pulling out his wallet to show some pictures.

They continue to converse while I look around at the cars and the people in them. I feel so out of place, as everyone is a lot older than me. I'm still amazed at seeing a building that looks like a barrel and am sure Jo has some stories about this place.

"I gotta get back in there and cook. Nice to have met you, Anna," he says as he returns to work.

Jo and Lily start telling me stories about when they worked here. The stories are funny, but one is unforgettable to me.

"Yeah, Shoupy is a great guy, but don't piss him off," says Lily.

"No, don't do that. He has quite a temper," Jo chimes in.

"Speaking of which, remember that one time, Jo, when a customer sent his soup back because it had no flavor?"

"I'll never forget that incident."

"What happened?" I ask as I lean forward from the backseat of the car and rest my chin on my folded hands on the top of the front seat.

"Well, the bowl of soup came back, and Shoupy took a bottle and peed in it and then proceeded to pour some of it in the soup. He heated the bowl of soup up and sent it back to the customer with his apologies."

At this point Lily and Jo bust out laughing.

"I don't think that's funny. I wouldn't want anyone doing that to me," I say and lean back in my seat.

Still laughing and having a hard time talking, Jo says, "No, no, the funny part is the customer really liked it and ordered another bowl."

Now they're hysterical with laughter. Their laughter is contagious, and soon we're all laughing.

"It's a good thing you told me after I ate here. Otherwise I never would have touched the food," I say amidst my laughter.

After laughing fits and a short four weeks, I know it's time for me to leave New Jersey. School will be starting in several weeks, and I want to get home to catch up on everything. Several letters came from Sonya, Beverly, and Connie, keeping me up to date on our friends and what everyone's been doing.

Ben wrote me one letter, pleading with me to come home, as he misses me so much. I know it's time for me to go home, as I'm getting homesick for my own bed and the train whistle, all of my friends, and, yes, even Mom and Dad.

Jo and I are both melancholy our last day together, but we understand it's just a matter of time before we see each other again. Soon I'll be back in school—and as a senior, I excitedly think to myself. Jo says she'll try and come home after a three-to-eleven shift, which allows her three days off in a row.

So armed with the knowledge we're going to see each other again in a couple of months, we smile but still cry and hug each other.

After getting on the train, I happily dismiss my sadness, knowing I'm going home and am very elated. Certainly Jo has dismissed hers too. Now she can date again. Knowing Jo, she didn't want to date while I was there and leave me alone.

Three days ago I mailed a letter to Ben, telling him when I was coming home and that we would catch up with each other that following week. In the letter I explained my girlfriends would be coming over to see me as soon as I got home so I could catch up on all the news.

Leaning back, relaxing, and enjoying the train ride, I know deep in my heart there is no place like home.

Chapter 41

The words "time sure does fly" flit through my mind as I sit at my desk, writing to Jo. It doesn't seem possible but I've been home over a month from my New Jersey vacation and have been back in school a week.

Smiling, I remember how happy Ben was to see me. He said he missed me so much and hopes I never have to leave him again, which triggered mixed emotions in me. "Absence makes the heart grow fonder" is an old saying.

That was the night we could not hold back any longer and had sex. It felt so natural with our bodies close to each other, and we seemed to melt into one. We loved touching each other and knew we had a love that would last forever.

He used a rubber, saying there was no need to worry. He was positive I wouldn't get pregnant. His doctor told him it would be difficult for him to get a girl pregnant. It had something to do with when he had mumps growing up. I didn't question it, as he said it wasn't serious.

The thought of getting pregnant scares me even though I love Ben. I have to graduate, as all my sisters did, and if I get pregnant, I wouldn't be allowed to graduate. The school has rules that a pregnant girl cannot attend school anymore.

The time has come to decide what kind of career I really want, since I'm a senior this year. I'm good with typing, shorthand, algebra, and business math, and I want a job where I can use these skills. A lot of businesses will be visiting our school this year, interviewing the seniors, so maybe I'll get an idea from them. College is still in the back of my mind, but it's not the way I'm leaning.

After finishing my letter to Jo, I figure it better get mailed or else lay forgotten on my dresser and become old news. Mom's sitting at the kitchen table, making out her grocery list from the store sales listed in the newspaper. Passing through the kitchen, I tell her I'll be right back after I mail a letter. She nods her head in acknowledgment and keeps writing.

Haste makes waste, and as I practically run down the back porch steps, I forget and slide my hand down the wooden banister, acquiring a splinter. This is an easy one to pull out, which I do immediately before it gets embedded further.

Slowing down and walking through the alley, I kick a few stones forward as I mosey along. Going through this alley reminds me of all the times we walked over to Edna's house with Dad carrying me and Jo hanging on his back until he started complaining that we were getting too big and made us walk.

It reminds me of the times we took our watermelon rinds to our neighbor's cow that he kept in his backyard. I wonder what happened to that cow. One day it just wasn't there anymore. Oh, well, they probably ate it or it died of old age or maybe from eating too many watermelon rinds.

Smiling, I know those were the good old days when Jo and I did fun things together. It's amazing to think we were making memories at the time.

Arriving at Sixth Street, I make a left and go up to Main Avenue, brushing the top of the hedges with my hand as I walk along them. Faint organ music comes from the church across the street as someone is practicing. No one's hanging out at the corner store today, and that makes me a little sad.

After inserting the letter in the green mailbox on the corner, I decide to walk home on Main Avenue and down Fifth Street. It's a quiet day with few cars on the road.

I think about Martha's visit home this past summer.

She was in a good mood the whole time I was around her. I can only think that she's in love. She had been dating one of her colleagues, Brent, who just graduated with some kind of degree in engineering and has been hired to work in South America. He wants her to go with him, and she was seriously thinking about it but would have to give up her last year of college.

In the meantime, there's another guy, Frank, who's interested in her. He's an only child, and his parents are missionaries in Africa. He's going to be a minister like his father, and naturally, everyone is steering Martha toward the minister.

Personally, I'm rooting for Brent, as I know she's really in love with him, since her face lights up when she talks to him on the phone or when she mentions his name. But who am I to tell her anything? She's the one who has to make up her own mind and be true to her heart.

My thoughts are interrupted as I pass in front of Donnie's house and he runs out of the house toward me.

"Anna, wanna play ball?" he asks as he gives me that never-ending smile.

"No, not today, Donnie. Mom said I have to come right home," I tell him, knowing it's a white lie, but I don't want to hurt his feelings.

He shrugs his shoulders but, keeping his smile, says, "Okay."

Doggone it. I feel so sorry for him and, yet, he just keeps smiling away, not a care in the world.

Turning down Fifth Street, I realize that my favorite season is right around the corner, and I'm looking forward to it.

My love for this season includes not only the brightly colored leaves but the ability to shuffle through them after they float down from the trees. Sounds of the band practicing outside school and watching the football players practice for their games are all part of fall. The cool crisp air that we breathe warns us that winter is not far behind.

I sit on the front porch steps for a few minutes, permitting the warm sunshine to penetrate my skin, allowing me to enjoy the warmth. The sunshine makes me feel good. After all, my zodiac sign, Leo, is ruled by the sun.

Next door the neighbor kids are chasing each other around their yard, playing cowboys and Indians. They hoop and holler while patting their mouths with the palms of their hands to break up the sound just like the real Indians did. Their little black-and-white dog, Chipper, is part of the cavalry, yipping and barking while chasing them. I have to chuckle watching them. And to think I used to do things like that.

My thoughts turn to Ben, and I wonder what he's doing, as he doesn't work on weekends. He's probably helping his mother take care of his father. I'd like to see his father again, but Ben says his mother's anger would be overwhelming and she may become ill if he brought me to the house again. He thinks she needs time to accept me.

The phone rings with two short rings, so I know it's for us. I can hear Mom answering it and talking. It must be for her or she would have called me by now.

Oh, well, I better go and figure out what to wear tonight. Ben and I are going to a movie in Johnstown, and then we'll stop at Ripple's for a famous Big Boy hamburger and french fries.

Opening the back screen door, I hear Mom say, "That's wonderful. We'll expect you both then."

Hanging up the phone, she notices me standing there and smiles.

"That was Jo. She's coming home for a visit in a couple of weeks and bringing a friend."

"Jo's coming home? When? What friend is she bringing?"

"Calm down. All I know is it's a man and his name is Nick. That means Jo will be sleeping with you, and Nick will stay in the little room."

"That's great," I say as I run upstairs.

"Supper will be ready in about twenty minutes, so don't go anywhere."

"Okay, okay."

I'm thrilled Jo's coming home, but who's Nick? I never met him while visiting her and not once did she mention his name. He must be somebody new in her life.

I haven't seen Bunky around lately. I wonder if he really did enlist in the service or if he went to college. If he's home, hopefully, he won't see Jo with this Nick or it'll break his heart.

My evening with Ben is enjoyable but the movie, *A Cry in the Night*, is way too scary for me. I like Natalie Wood, but she plays the girl who's kidnapped and I don't like that kind of stuff. She and her boyfriend are parked, and a crazy guy knocks him out and kidnaps her. At one point I'm clutching Ben's hand so hard that he has to laugh at me. I whisper, "No more parking for us."

We don't stop at Ripple's for our Big Boy hamburger, as Ben isn't feeling well and has a cold. At one point when he sneezed into his handkerchief at the movies, I saw a string of snot coming out of his nose before he wiped it away. Suddenly I realized that it didn't turn me off or make me sick; I had only pity because he's sick. That must be real love. If I told anyone that story they'd probably laugh at me.

Lying in bed that night, I wonder if everyone is as happy as me. Now I'm a senior and have to start planning on what I'm going to do after graduation. I'm still telling my white lies, but I'm sure everyone, except Mom and Dad, know Ben and I are together.

Mom still wants me to go to college. That entails spending a weekend with Martha at her college to see if I like it. There are too many decisions to make, and things are changing so fast. Suddenly, the train's whistle reminds me it's on its way to load up with the beautiful black coal. My life seems to revolve around black coal and white lies.

Chapter 42

Colorful October arrives and Jo comes home as she promised, fetching her new friend Nick. He isn't what you'd call movie star good-looking, but he's not ugly either. He's about two inches taller than Jo and has blond hair that hangs over his forehead, almost touching his bright-blue eyes. His nose is wide, or maybe it just looks that way because his mouth is so tiny, like it's lost under his nose. He dresses nicely with khaki pants and a blue pullover sweater, and he is well mannered and polite. I definitely like his brand-new beautiful blue-and-white 1956 Oldsmobile convertible. His favorite color must be blue.

Edna and Reds invite all of us to their house Saturday evening. Liz and Pep and Louis along with new sister, Angela, arrive, adding lasagna to the baked chicken, scalloped potatoes, and various dishes Edna prepared.

Edna set up two card tables in the living room, and we move around with our tally cards, exchanging partners. The evening goes by quickly, playing cards, laughing, and joking around. Nick listens and laughs with us and seems like a nice, friendly guy—but not Jo's type, I think to myself.

Of course Mom likes him, since he's Protestant and not Italian. Everyone seems to like him, and I only wish Ben could be sharing this time with us. It works out well for both of us, as his mother needs him to stay home tonight and that doesn't put any pressure on me to use another white lie to go out with him.

The next morning we all go to church except for Dad, Jo, and Nick. Mom can't force them to go, and I realize how much Jo enjoys this, since Mom can't order her around anymore.

Edna and Liz and families are coming over for dinner. Mom cooks a huge meal that she started long before we went to church, and after eating, we sit at the dining room table, talking about New Jersey, Clear Glass Company, and Kolfield in general.

When Jo and Nick first arrived, I made quite a fuss over Nick's brand-new beautiful convertible. Somehow the subject rolled around to his car again, and Jo, sensing my joy, said, "Nick, why don't you let Anna have your car for an hour or so. She's an excellent driver."

With no hesitation whatsoever, Nick gives me the keys while Jo smiles at me and winks. Nick puts the top down while I'm rounding up my girlfriends on the phone. I gather he loves Jo a lot to relinquish his car just like that, and he doesn't even know for sure if I'm a good or a bad driver.

Everyone gathers around the car while Nick shows me where everything is located. I love the thin white steering wheel and the chrome ring where I can honk the horn. The seats are white and beautiful.

"Thanks a lot, Nick. I'll be very careful."

I pull out slowly, getting used to the power and the sound of the car, while everyone yells, "Be careful."

I pick up Sonya and Bev and, of course, they can't believe it either. They're thrilled to ride with me in this beautiful car that emits such a beautiful rumbling sound when you slow down and downshift it into first gear. Nick showed me how to do that.

We cruise around town and hopefully will see Ben even though I know he's at home with his family. Everyone waves at us, and we stop a few times to talk to our friends. After the third time through town, one of the local policemen stops us, asking to see the car registration. After all, it's an out-of-state car and he's very curious, probably, as to who owns it.

"That muffler is a little too loud," he says and walks around the car, examining it.

We think it sounds great, but you can't talk back to a policeman. We were always taught to answer with a "Yes, sir" or "No, sir." After reading the registration and satisfying his curiosity, he hands me the registration while he removes his cap. He's a young policeman, and I've never seen him before. He smoothes his hair down and, with his forehead crinkled and his eyebrows touching, he says in a very serious voice, "Try and keep the noise down." He places his cap on his head and turns away.

We giggle as we pull out because Nick has configured the car to make some noise that I can't prevent. I parallel park the car on Main Avenue, and we drink a soda in Main Line Drugstore but do so with haste, as we want to spend our limited time riding around in this beautiful car and showing off.

Everyone we see is amazed at such a beautiful car. We're forever pulling over so other friends can touch it and look at it closely. I just wish Ben could share this experience with me.

That night as Jo and I lie in bed together, I whisper, "Jo, you have a nice boyfriend but I still like Bunky better." We can't talk too loud or Nick will hear us in the next room, even with the doors closed.

"Anna, first of all, Nick is not my boyfriend. He's just a guy who offered to bring Lily and me back to Kolfield for a visit. Second, forget Bunky. We're done, and I don't want you to bring his name up anymore."

"I'm glad Nick isn't your boyfriend, because he just doesn't seem your type. And okay, I won't mention Bunky's name anymore no matter what I hear."

"You can mention his name only if you have something important to tell me about him," she whispers as she grabs my arm and gives me an Indian burn.

"Ouch, stop it. That hurts," I say as I push her away.

"Well, that's what I'm going to continue giving you if you don't stop bringing Bunky up."

We laugh and talk some more before falling asleep, just like old times.

Chapter 43

The next morning Jo and Nick have to leave, as they're scheduled to work the graveyard shift, eleven to seven, that night. They need to pick Lily up, as she rode back with them, and the trip takes about five to six hours, so they still have plenty of time for breakfast with Mom and Dad.

I have to leave for school. This is the fifth year I haven't missed a day of school, and I don't want to mess up my attendance record.

We say our good-byes and I give Jo a hug, and then Nick gives me a hug. I thank him again for letting me use his car, and he just smiles, which helps make his little mouth look larger and not like a Cheerio.

"Don't forget to write," Jo says. "I enjoy your letters."

"Okay and drive carefully," I say, waving, and walk out the back door. I know I can't stay a minute longer, as I already have tears in my eyes. Thank goodness it's eighteen blocks to school, so it gives me time to compose myself.

In some ways it's sad knowing that Jo won't be there when I get home, but there are too many exciting things happening at school to spend time dwelling on our farewells, which aren't permanent.

In the meantime, my mother is hounding me to visit my sister Martha at her college for a weekend. She graduates from college this year, and Mom is hoping I'll go to her college. Well, sending me for a weekend with Ms. Martha definitely turned me against going to college.

Martha lives in a large dormitory room with six beds in it. The dormitory seems so cold, not homey at all. There are pink curtains on the windows, and the walls are beige. Family pictures are near the beds, and a big corkboard is hanging by the entrance covered with schedules and messages.

A round table sits in the middle where they can study or write letters, whatever they prefer. And they have the library, dining room, classrooms, and other study rooms located throughout the campus in different buildings.

Of course snooty Martha doesn't want to be bothered with me. I'm sort of left on my own. One consolation is her friends are really nice to me, and I enjoy talking to them.

As we walk around the campus, Martha introduces me to a couple of guys she knows. After the introductions, Martha disappears.

One of the guys she introduces me to, Dale, is very interested in my high school and what I'm going to do when I graduate from college. He's tall with dark curly hair and glasses, reminding me of Jack. His interest seems to focus on my future, as he's going to be working with Christian youth when he graduates in a year. He isn't trying to hit on me, or anything like that, but is just very pleasant and easy to talk to. Before we part, he asks for my address so we can correspond with each other.

Martha takes me to the football game, but she and her friends eventually ditch me. It is exciting listening to the crowd cheer and watching the cheerleaders perform along the sidelines. The band, blasting its music at halftime, makes me homesick for my high school and our football games.

It's no fun watching the game by myself, and so when halftime is over, I walk back to Martha's dormitory. There are very few people wandering around, as mostly everyone is at the football game.

Back in the dormitory I start reading a book. Martha comes in after the game. I think she might have a tiny bit of worry hanging over her about me, but then again, I could be wrong.

"I wondered what happened to you. We looked everywhere for you. How did you get lost?"

"Oh, stop it, Martha. I didn't get lost. You got lost or, better yet, you wanted to lose me."

"Oh, don't be so silly. You're a big girl and you found your way back, didn't you?"

I don't comment because I'm afraid of saying something I'll regret later.

Doris, one of her roommates, comes in, asking, "Okay, you two ready to go and get something to eat?"

Martha grabs her jacket, but I reply, "I'm not hungry, so I think I'll stay here and try and finish this book."

Martha nods her head in approval and smiles with that robot grin and nose in the air as she and Doris head out the door.

I pretend to be asleep when they come back so I don't have to interact with them.

"Anna, you're not asleep, are you?" Martha asks.

She walks over to me, and I don't move. I can play her game too.

"Oh, well, guess we can't tell her how much fun we had tonight, Doris."

Finally, the next day Mom and Dad arrive to take me home.

Naturally, Mom is anxious to hear my opinion about the weekend and asks me how I like the college.

Answering in a very dejected tone, I reply, "I didn't like it and really don't want to go to college."

She shakes her head and only says, "We'll see."

Chapter 44

Being on the yearbook staff is a lot of fun. Our theme is "The Hearts of Kolfield." The white pages are surrounded with black coal and red hearts, making the contrast sharp and interesting.

Also, we're getting ready to perform a two-act play, and since I'm a member of the Thespian Society I'll be helping as much as possible. The senior play will be next and is not only a big event for the seniors but also gives the underclassmen something to look forward to, as only seniors can be in it. I'd like to try out for a part and am looking forward to the tryouts.

A couple of weeks after Jo left for New Jersey, a letter arrives from Jo saying that she and Nick are still dating. Even though she's my sister, I'll never understand her.

Then after I receive Jo's letter, I receive a letter from Nick saying that he really likes me and asking if I would go out with him if he came back to Kolfield. He says he and Jo have broken up.

As soon as I receive the letter, I'm devastated. This is my sister's boyfriend. How can he do this to her? Does he think I'd go out with my sister's boyfriend even if they did break up? He knows I have a boyfriend, because Jo told him all about Ben. He must be some kind of shallow Casanova.

I'm in a quandary and don't know what to do. Should I call Jo and tell her, or should I tell my mother? Maybe I'll just forget it, but I'm afraid Jo will get mad at me if she somehow finds out and might think I encouraged it. So after much deliberation, I give the letter to my mother. She's better at handling these things.

Naturally, she blames me. She glares at me and says, "Did you encourage him in any way or give him some idea that you liked him?"

"What are you, crazy? I don't even think he's cute."

"I'm not accusing you, Anna. I just need to know before I call Jo."

"I'm just as surprised as you are."

"Okay, then I'll call Jo tonight when she gets home from work and see what she says. Don't worry about it anymore." With that she folds the letter and tucks it in her apron pocket.

Why did this have to happen to me? I didn't encourage it. It seems I'm always going on a guilt trip for things I have no control over, and I don't even understand what causes them. I blame myself for everything, even if it isn't my fault.

The next morning Mom is still asleep when I go downstairs. On cold mornings like today it's hard to crawl out from under those warm blankets.

In the kitchen Dad is standing in front of the stove, placing a lid on the pot that contains the oatmeal he just made.

"Dad, do you know if Mom reached Jo last night?" I ask, reaching for a bowl.

"No, she didn't answer, so we went to bed. Don't worry, she'll get hold of her today."

"I hope so. Nick is such a jerk."

"How come she never dates Bunky anymore?"

"Oh, it's a long story, and you really should ask her, Dad."

I finish my oatmeal and leave for school. I love school, where I can learn new things and see my friends and get out of the house.

After school, I don't dawdle on my way home. I'm anxious to hear what Jo says to Mom and hope and pray she isn't mad at me. I smile, thinking how many times I've been told that only dogs get mad while humans get angry, and yet I still say it.

Sitting at the kitchen table, I turn a red apple over and over while Mom talks to the operator. Two freshly baked loaves of bread are sitting on the other end of the table cooling off. Not only do I love the smell of them, but also they look so tempting sitting there. Mom's jelly on a piece of that would be great right now. Instead I bite into the apple.

Mom finally reaches Jo. "Hi, Jo, how's everything going?"

After a pause Mom replies, "No, we're all okay. I just wanted to tell you that Anna received a letter from Nick." She reads the letter to Jo.

After a few moments of silence Mom says, "We just thought you should be aware of it. Is there anything you want us to do?"

"Okay, we'll wait to hear from you. Bye."

Mom turns to us and says, "Jo broke up with Nick but she can't believe that he would have the nerve to write a letter to Anna asking her out. She's quite upset with him and is going to talk to him. As soon as she finds out what this is all about, she'll call us back."

Turning to walk away she stops and says, "She did want me to tell you, Anna, that's it's not your fault and she knows how you worry, so don't give it another thought."

The next day Jo calls, as she confronted Nick with it.

Mom motions me over to listen to the conversation with her.

With our heads touching and our ears sharing the earpiece of the phone, Jo says, "Nick said he didn't mean anything by it because he knew we were breaking up and thought Anna would go out with him. He also said he did it so he could get closer to me—at least that's his story."

"Well, just be careful, because if he's writing Anna a letter asking her out he might be asking other girls out."

"Oh, yes, I'll be careful, Mom. Also, tell Anna I'm not angry with her. She didn't write the letter. I'm angry with Nick."

"Okay, she heard it. She's standing right here listening to me."

"I love you, Jo, and I'm glad you're not mad at me."

"I love you too. Now I have to get to work. Bye."

Mom and I both say in unison, "Bye."

I guess it's a good thing I gave the letter to my mother, as I love Jo too much to see her hurt again.

Jo and Nick continue dating each other, but they aren't a couple exactly. They agree they can date anyone they want to date. Right now they're too busy working to have time for dating. They're working different shifts and getting overtime pay, which they don't mind, as the holidays are coming.

At the beginning of December we're notified via letter that Jo has confirmed her worse fear and she's pregnant. Of course, there's no doubt that Nick is thrilled, as now Jo will have to marry him. I guess sometimes you can learn to love someone, and that's what she feels she has to do, as there's going to be a baby involved now. I'm happy for her but know deep down inside she'll always love Bunky.

Pregnant Jo gets married, and no one really cares except to whisper to each other that she had to get married.

After hearing the news of Jo being pregnant, I lie in bed that night and wonder what life is really all about. Jo went to modeling school and got her own apartment and job, and now she's getting married. I wonder what the future has in store for me.

As soon as I graduate I'll become a free person to make my own decisions and do what I want to do.

Chapter 45

Last Christmas Ben bought me a beautiful pair of rhinestone earrings and a necklace to match. They're green and blue stones surrounded by white stones and, oh, so pretty. Of course, I can't show them to my parents, as Mom would want to know where I got them. So I just keep them hidden in a blue velvet box in my bedroom. Every so often I look at the sparkling beauties and wish I could wear them.

How stupid of me to think I could ever hide anything from Mom.

It's the middle of December, and Christmas is fast approaching. After coming home from school one day I see my rhinestones on the kitchen table. A jolt of fear runs through me as I realize Mom knows. I think I stopped breathing for a few seconds while *What am I going to say? What am I going to say?* runs round and round in my head.

At that moment Mom walks into the kitchen with one hand on her hip and the other pointing to the jewelry and says, "Where did you get those?"

"They're a present."

"Who gave them to you? Was it that Eyetalian man you're seeing? That Arno guy?"

It always makes me cringe when she pronounces "Italian" like that. "Yes," I say with a lot of anger mixed with relief, as I'm upset that she's been snooping in my room but relieved she knows and, darn, she even knows his name.

"You thought I didn't know about him. I try not to interfere, as I keep hoping you'll meet some other boy more your age, someone from our church. You have to stay away from him, do you understand? You're not allowed to see him anymore. He's too old for you."

"You can't make me not see him. I love him and he loves me." I gasp, as I don't know where those words came from. I never meant to say them.

With those words escaping my lips, she slaps me across my face and it stings but also stirs up anger in me. I don't want to argue, as I always hated it when my sisters argued with Mom, but now I can't help it. She just doesn't understand.

I shout, "You can't keep me locked in my room! I'm graduating this year and then what are you going to do?"

She slaps me again, and I run out of the room to my bedroom upstairs but not until after I grab the rhinestone set.

I hear Dad saying, "Daisy, don't hit her. Leave her alone."

"You mind your own damn business. I'll handle this. If she sees him again, I'll beat her with the strap."

I lie across my bed and sob, wondering what I'm going to do. I'm supposed to see Ben tonight, but it looks like I won't be able to get out of the house. I'll tell my girlfriends in school tomorrow that when they see Ben to please explain to him that Mom knows and I won't be coming out for a few days.

I know that next week Mom and Dad are going to New Jersey to visit Jo, and I'm going to stay at my sister Liz's house since they don't want me staying home alone.

At that moment I decide that I can't wait until then. I pack my clothes and call Liz to come and get me. I'm crying hysterically, and she says she'll be right there.

Liz comes over and talks to Mom and Dad while I sit in my room. She comes upstairs and hugs me, saying it's okay and I'm going to stay with her for a while.

When we go downstairs I kiss Dad good-bye but don't say anything to Mom. She stays in the living room so we don't see each other. At that moment I wonder if I'll ever come home again.

I enjoy living with Liz and Pep. They allow Ben to come over and see me and are with us all the time except when we go to the movies. They act like parents are supposed to act, loving and understanding. I adore my nephew and niece, Louis and Angela, and love playing with them. Liz reads to them every night, and we all play games with them. They are such a loving family, and I wonder why our family was never like that.

Ben asked me weeks ago to go with him to his Christmas dinner. With the money I saved from working at bingo and Grant's, I buy a beautiful blue velvet dress at Penn Traffic in Johnstown. It has a square neckline and fits my waist and then flares out. The long sleeves are fitted, tapering down to a point in the middle of the back of my hand. It's just perfect. I finally get to wear the rhinestone set that offsets my dress.

Liz takes pictures of us in front of her Christmas tree as we smile and make more memories.

Upon arriving at the dinner party that is being held at the country club in Johnstown, we check our coats. The Christmas decorations are beautiful. There are green pine branches over the doorways with gold angels floating in the air, as they're tied to the ceiling with invisible wire. A huge Christmas tree is in a corner with red and green balls and gold icicles hanging neatly from every branch. Underneath the tree on a red velvet tree skirt are colorful presents neatly wrapped, flaunting beautiful bows and ribbons.

I've never been to anything like this and again feel out of place, as everyone is married or going to be married and much older.

Ben puts his arm around me and introduces me to everyone, and I know I'll never remember the names. My only hope is I remember all my manners and what silverware to use. I silently thank my mother again for taking the time to teach my sisters and me this stuff.

Everybody is very nice to me, and I do more listening than talking, as we really don't have anything in common. The women talk about their children and their houses, but who wants to hear what happened in social studies or in gym class? Of course, I'm a lot younger than everyone there, but Ben is proud of me and that's what really counts.

Finally, I excuse myself by going to the ladies' room, where I need to freshen my lipstick and take a couple of deep breaths. When I return to the party, everyone is laughing, dancing, and having a good time. I sit down at our empty table, and after a few minutes Ben comes over and sits down beside me.

He takes my hand and kisses it, asking, "Do you want to leave now? I don't dance, and you don't drink, and that's what the rest of the night is going to be, dancing and drinking."

That's the best thing he could have said to me.

"Yes, that's a great idea," I say, squeezing his hand back.

Later, after kissing and hugging me, Ben says, "A lot of the guys asked how old you were. When I said seventeen, they said I was a cradle robber."

"Did that bother you?"

"Heck, no, they're just jealous that my girl is young and beautiful."

"Well, it bothers me. I didn't fit in with them, and we had nothing to talk about. They all stared at me like I was a baby."

"No, you felt that way because they're married with kids and you had nothing in common with them, but someday you will."

Chapter 46

Christmas was always an exciting and colorful time at our house, but it won't be this year, since Mom and Dad are away.

The aroma of raisin-filled cookies baking in the oven along with many other varieties of cookies and breads made the anticipation more exciting than the holiday itself. Mom baked for weeks before Christmas. She loved to make the various cookies and decorate them so colorfully and prettily that you didn't want to eat any of the Santa heads, reindeer, angels, or stockings stuffed with colorful toys. The homemade fudges and cream candies were delicious too.

We were always aware Christmas was coming, but when the wooden platform, two feet high, was set up in the living room and covered with felt, the anticipation heightened.

The next day Dad and Mom would buy or chop down a Christmas tree, bringing it home tied to the top of the car or in Dad's old truck. After adding and or sawing branches off, the tree was placed in a red-and-green metal tree stand that held water to keep the tree fresh. Mom's job was to keep it filled. She didn't trust anyone else to do it for fear of knocking the tree down and disturbing anything under it.

Dad's job was finished when the platform was set up and the tree was on it. The trains were placed on the platform with the tracks situated on the outer edge of the platform circling the tree and village. They chugged through a tunnel and up over a small hill and went backward and forward and could stop anywhere, including at the train station.

Mom loved decorating the tree and creating the village. She had an ice-skating pond on which little skaters were placed. She created little streets that curve and wind up to and past each building. There were black lampposts that lit up and little colorful figures on the sidewalks along with carolers singing under the lamppost.

Actually, two trains chugged around the village. One of the trains was a silver passenger train, and sometimes I'd imagine being a passenger looking out of the train window as I rode through town, listening to the Christmas carols being sung by the carolers and seeing couples holding hands and skating on the pond.

The other train naturally was a coal train. White smoke came out of the engine after a pill was placed in the smokestack. The coal train also carried a log car that stopped at the loading platform, and a little man would appear and unload the logs onto the platform or load them onto the train.

Sometimes I'd pretend that I lived in one of the little houses in the village and was inside decorating or baking cookies. Jo and I played guessing games as we sat on the blue mohair sofa with the pretty white crocheted doilies on the back and arms. We had to be very careful not to wrinkle them, as they were starched and ironed, ready for the holidays.

A special part of Christmas for us was when the Miners Union had a Christmas party for the children. Dad would take us to the VFW hall located in a small village nestled next to Kolfield.

We stood in line to see Santa Claus, and after sitting on his lap, he gave each of us a red net stocking filled with an orange, some walnuts, and a decorated box full of colorful toy candy and chocolate drops. The stocking had a colorful cardboard folder over the top, which was stapled so nothing would fall out.

We were thrilled to go to these Christmas parties, and Dad enjoyed taking all of us, holding my and Jo's hands. Mom always made sure our hair was combed, plated, or curled, and tied neatly with ribbons and bows. Our white high-top shoes were always polished, and we had on pretty dresses that she had ironed.

At Christmas, other holidays, or on my older sisters' birthdays, Mom set the dining room table with a linen tablecloth and napkins. She retrieved her good china dishes and silverware from the china closet and buffet situated in the dining room. The whole family was seated around the large dining room table, feasting on all the good food she'd prepared from scratch. She's the best cook, and there's nothing she can't create, bake, or cook.

Mom insisted on cleaning the table and washing the dishes after these special occasions, as she had this fear, which was not unreasonable, that we might break her good china. I always thought she learned a lesson from the time she and Dad fought. Having broken some of the china dishes, it took her a long time to replace the various expensive pieces.

Maybe next year everyone will be here for Christmas, and it can be like old times again—even if it means I have to sit at the kitchen table with Louis and Angela, as the family is growing but the table isn't.

Christmas isn't the same anymore, with only me living at home with Mom and Dad. This year it's really different, as our house is empty and bare with no colorful decorations or tree.

Chapter 47

All of us knew that on our graduation from high school, Mom and Dad would give us our first wristwatch. It was exciting to watch each of my sisters when they graduated and unwrapped the beautiful wristwatches, placing them on their wrists. Naturally, I can't wait until graduation so I can receive my wristwatch and experience that moment.

I mentioned it to Ben sometime ago but forgot all about it.

On this Christmas Eve of my senior year, he presents me with a present all wrapped up in gold paper with a small green bow on it. I'm left speechless when I open it. It's a beautiful, stylish, gold wristwatch with little diamonds around it. I love it and am overjoyed but feel sad because I know Mom wants to buy me one for graduation.

I thank him but still feel disappointment inside, as that seems to be going against my mother again. Now I have to definitely keep this a secret from Mom, as I don't want to hurt her feelings.

Mom and Dad come home after Christmas, and Mom telephones Liz and Pep and tells them she wants me home. She still doesn't want me seeing Ben, but she feels I should be at home this last part of my senior year. Liz is good about explaining these things and making me believe in myself.

When Liz finishes explaining—giving me reasons, such as I would be better in my own bedroom instead of sleeping in Angela's bedroom on a cot; I would be able to borrow Mom and Dad's car; I would have access to all of my clothes; Mom wants to buy my graduation dress, prom gown, other clothes, and shoes; and, of course, Dad's oatmeal (which made us laugh)—I am convinced. We laugh, and as she hugs me she tells me I am always welcome at her house.

So I go home without a word said between Mom and me, and we try to avoid each other as much as possible.

The wristwatch doesn't stay secret for long, as I have it on for New Year's Eve, since I am all dressed up even though we are just going to the movies. As I am leaving the house I reach for the doorknob to open the door and my coat sleeve moves up my arm a little, and Mom sees it. She grabs my wrist and is very upset.

"Did that damn Eyetalian give that to you?" she yells.

How I hate that word and think, *Here we go again.*

In a very calm voice, I say, "Yes, he gave it to me for Christmas."

"You know we always buy each of you kids a watch for graduation and were going to buy you one. You have to give it back to him."

"I am not giving it back," I say sternly as I walk out the front door to meet Ben and thus avoid an argument.

Maybe she's afraid I might leave home again, because the watch is never talked about after that. Relief comes over me, because she knows and now I can wear it.

We don't speak to each other, and then one day we just start saying words to each other—nothing important, just a question about dinner or something trivial. Ben is never mentioned again, but I continue seeing him.

It's like Ben and I are inseparable. Every chance we have, we're together. My friends want me to do things with them, but Ben always wants to see me. Sometimes I just tell him I want to go somewhere with my friends, but then when I do, I miss him as much as he misses me.

As I lie in bed that night and think of Ben, I think of the one secret love since seventh grade that I always had until I met Ben—the one boy who I cared so much about but with whom I never went on a date.

In junior high, the kids from the other end of Kolfield were friends, and all of us on this end of the town were friends. Then one day something happened, which made me notice a certain boy. The boys from the other end of town had carved their initials into their arms. Word got around and the principal had a fit. He called them all in his office and called their parents.

Parents were pulling up and taking their sons home, with them knowing they were going to get punished somehow.

A few days later Angelo smiled at me, and I asked if I could see his arm. He pulled up his sleeve, and I saw his initials, thin and scabby white lines forming two letters: AG.

"Why would you do something like that?" I asked him.

"Because all of the guys were doing it, and I wanted to do it too."

"Would you do it again?"

"No, I learned a big lesson from it," he said, pulling the sleeve of his shirt down.

From that day on we were good friends and are still good friends. Sometimes I think about how it would've been if we had gone on a date and maybe found out we did like each other. We see each other every day in school, but when we graduate, we'll never see each other again. We act like brother and sister, advising each other about girls he dates and about Ben, whom he dislikes. But still, not knowing, I can't help but wonder.

Chapter 48

The holidays are over, and I suddenly realize that in less than five months I'll be graduating and stepping into the real world.

My best friend, Connie, and I always say we're going to be the best secretaries in town. Our goal is to be secretary to the superintendent of schools. Being a secretary is the greatest thing to us, since we're well prepared, knowing how to type and take shorthand.

We live in a small town that really has nothing to offer in the way of jobs. We've concluded that the most important secretary in town had to be to the superintendent of schools.

Then the most wonderful thing happens. The Central Intelligence Agency (CIA) arrives at our school to recruit seniors for jobs. They're looking for young men and women to come and work for them in Washington, DC, after they graduate.

It sounds thrilling to actually move away to a big city with a guarantee of a job. After an impressive and alluring talk by the CIA representative, I ask for one of their thick applications containing page after page of questions on it.

Moving to Washington, DC, if I get the job, sounds like a solution for my situation. Then Ben would still be close enough to visit me or I could come home for visits.

We're allowed to take the application home, as our parents have to help us with many of the questions, especially concerning relatives. Then they can be mailed back to their office in Washington, DC.

The CIA representatives tell us to be honest when filling out these forms; they have to do background checks on all of us and will know if we lied.

What a job to list all of my uncles, aunts, grandparents, parents, sisters, and their husbands, plus their birthplaces and dates of birth, where they live and work, or date of death.

One of the questions is "Do any members of your family belong to the Klu Klux Klan?"

Years ago I observed a scene from my backyard that I'll never forget. From our yard, you can see the side of a mountain next to us, as we're in a valley near the bottom of another mountain. White figures were circling a big fire in a farmer's field. Even though they were miles away, they looked scary. After asking who they were, my neighbor told me the Klu Klux Klan. What a silly name. It sounds like a tongue twister.

When Mom found out I was watching them, she whisked me into the house and scolded me for looking at them. So that's all I heard about them but knew if they had to wear masks, they must be bad—unless their faces were so ugly they had to hide them or were ashamed of what they were doing.

Also I heard that one of my great uncles was a member of the Klu Klux Klan, so I wrote down his name after I verified it with Dad, who thought I shouldn't put it down. After all, it was my great uncle, not me and not my parents, and they did emphasize that we must tell the truth. Anyway, he died a long time ago.

After a couple of weeks of filling out the application and asking my dad and mom so many questions, I mail the application and forget about it.

So I continue working for the firemen at bingo on Friday evenings in addition to working in the office of W. T. Grant on Saturdays.

Greg is still coming to pick up his mother at bingo and still wanting me to go out with him. He's really a nice guy, but I'm in love with Ben and I'd never cheat on him. I do enjoy chatting with Greg when he comes to take his mother home.

Last week he told me he's dating a girl and wants me to meet her. I told him I'd love to, so he brought her into bingo the following week when he came for his mother.

He introduced Janet to me. She was pleasant, tall, with shoulder-length black hair, brown eyes, and a nose that is long and slender, leading to nicely shaped pink lips. On her chin was a beauty mole underneath a genuine smile. You could tell she loved him, as her eyes sparkled and she hung onto his arm, fearing he might disappear.

I never wanted to date Greg and am happy for him and Janet but feel sad, wondering if this is the end of our friendship.

That night as I walk home, I think about Greg and hope he's as happy with his new girlfriend as I am with Ben. It would've been easy for me to allow Greg to take me home when he offered, as Ben never comes by on Friday nights. Ben tells me it's his night out with his buddies.

They loiter around a gas station on the corner of Main Avenue and Seventeenth Street, where they drink sodas and just plain socialize. I'm sure they talk to all of the girls who walk by, and that makes me a little jealous, but I know Ben loves me and I don't think he'd ever cheat on me. But you never know. Look at what happened with Bunky and Jo.

Then a devastating accident happens several weeks later. Greg is going home one cold night on his motorcycle, and it slips on an icy patch on the road as he goes around a bend, hitting a huge tree head-on. He's killed instantly. The news crushes me with grief, and my tears flow. I can picture him joking around with me, and remorse and guilt fill my heart because I'll never see him again.

Ben doesn't believe I should go and pay my respects to Greg's mother, but I have to go regardless of what he thinks. I'm going whether he likes it or not, and there is nothing he can say to stop me.

There are so many cars at Greg's house, and I end up parking down the street. I walk slowly on the slippery brick sidewalk and creep up the salted wooden steps while holding onto a thin wooden banister.

Opening the screen door, I notice a tear in the screen and wonder if Greg was going to fix that and didn't have time. Arlene always bragged about how handy he was around the house, fixing and patching things.

After knocking on the door, the neighbor, Gladys, opens the door, recognizes me from bingo, and hugs me.

Sadness punches me in my lungs and takes my breath away when entering Greg's house. Hushed whispers hang in the air along with the smell of food brought in by the neighbors. Arlene is sitting in a chair in the living room, clutching a handkerchief. Greg's picture is on the table beside her.

I kneel at her side and tell her how sorry I am. Her eyes are red, and even though she's in pain, she consoles me and says how much Greg always liked me. We hug and, while shedding our tears, talk about Greg. Arlene tells me Janet is in the kitchen.

Walking into the kitchen I see the poor girl's eyes are puffy from crying and her nose is red. I think to myself that could have been me if I had gone out with Greg instead of Ben. I hug her and we both cry.

"What am I going to do without Greg?" she sobs, wiping her nose with a tissue.

Not knowing what to say, I just stand there and squeeze her hand.

"I'll never love anyone again like I love Greg."

"And he loved you too. Never forget that. He was so proud of you when he told me about you and wanted me to meet you."

"I know he thought a lot of you."

"Yes, you could say we were bingo friends," I say, and we both break into a little laugh.

Janet settles down a little, and we share some hot tea and cookies while talking about Greg. It seems to make her feel so much better to talk about him.

In bed that night, my pillow is damp from crying for Greg, his mother, and Janet. Death is so painful for the ones left behind. I'm glad that Greg came into my life even if it was for such a short time. The coal train acknowledges my sadness with a mournful whistle.

Chapter 49

In school the senior class is told there will be no senior play. It seems there were a few problems encountered with some of the boys, and the entire class is punished. The principal says that if everyone starts behaving, he might reconsider. Of course, that never happens.

In March the Kolfield Fire Department asks me to enter the Miss Kolfield contest, which will be held at the theater downtown. They'll sponsor me, and I'll represent them as Miss Kolfield Fire Department. I really don't want to be in a beauty contest, but after a couple of weeks and pressure from my mother, I consent.

Then before you know it, it's time for our spring chorus competition at another school. The girls all have to wear black skirts and white blouses while the boys wear black pants and white shirts.

Not having a decent white blouse to wear, I decide to not go. I do attend school though. Since one of my teachers is at the competition, I sit in study hall during that period and read. The principal is in charge of that study hall period, and when he walks by I ask him to sign my yearbook. He does and tells me to keep up the good work.

That is on Friday, and on Monday the principal is furious. After the morning announcements, he reads a list of names over the intercom. They are to report to his office immediately before first class. My name is one of them.

We all report to the boardroom and sit and stand around the long oval table. He yells at us for not going to the concert competition and skipping a day of school. We are an embarrassment to our school.

He notices me and, pointing at me, yells, "You, Anna. I'm not giving you a five-year perfect attendance award. You just lost it by skipping school on Friday."

Shocked, I say, "I didn't skip school. I was here. Don't you remember? You signed my yearbook in study hall."

"I'll check on that. Everyone that wasn't here on Friday better have a doctor's excuse or they'll be suspended. Now get back to class. I'll deal with each of you individually."

With that, he turns and walks out.

Talking to the other kids, I find out they had all skipped school and went on a picnic somewhere. Whew, am I ever glad I came to school that day! I almost lost my attendance award.

Later that day when the principal calls me into his office, he says, "I checked and you were in school that day. Why didn't you go to the competition?"

"I didn't have a decent white blouse to wear, and I couldn't afford to buy another one."

"All right. You're excused, but if something like that ever happens again, come and talk to me, okay?"

"Yes," I say and walk out of his office, almost ready to cry from relief.

In late April when I come home from school, Mom tells me there's a letter for me on the dining room table. Excitement runs through me as I see it's from the CIA. I tear it open, and the colorful CIA emblem on the letterhead jumps out at me, with the letter informing me that my application has been approved and there's a job waiting for me. As soon as I let them know, they'll make arrangements for me. Immediately I write them back, telling them I accept the job. Now I just wait to hear when I will go and what the job entails.

Then another surprise pops up when Mom tells me Martha and Frank are planning to get married in June. Liz is supposed to be the maid of honor but is unable to do so because she's scheduled for surgery a couple of weeks before that date.

Jo is second choice, but she's pregnant and due around the beginning of July and happy she can't do it. So I'm third choice to be the maid of honor. *Whoopee.* That makes me feel wanted. I really don't want to, but I have no choice, since Mom feels one of her sisters should be in the wedding party.

Martha graduates from college in the beginning of May, my graduation occurs at the end of May, and Martha is getting married in the beginning of June. So much is happening so fast.

Before you know it, my graduation is here and Martha already received her college degree and is busy planning her wedding. I try not to think about the beauty contests and focus on my last days of school. My graduation date is set for the twenty-third of May.

Edna, Reds, Liz, Pep, Louis, and Angela come over the night before graduation. Mom has baked a cake and adorned the top with a girl figurine in a black graduation gown and cap, holding a diploma.

Mom hands me a gift and says, "Since you already have a wristwatch we decided to get you this instead."

It's a small box. I open it and there's a beautiful gold ring with a huge pale-green stone in it.

"It's your birthstone, Anna."

"Thank you. It's beautiful," I say, slipping it on my finger. It's a perfect fit.

After giving Mom and Dad a kiss, I open my other gifts that are mostly money tucked away in pretty cards.

The next night is a gloriously pleasant evening, and I'm so happy.

Graduation is always held in our school auditorium. This year there are 162 of us graduating. What a fantastic feeling when my name is called and I walk to the podium to receive my diploma.

Mom and Dad attend the graduation and afterward hug me and take my gown, cap, and diploma with them, as my girlfriends and I are going out together.

Sonya is driving and we ride around town, tooting the car horns and waving to each other. A bunch of us meet at a diner in Johnstown and sit around talking. Angelo is there, and we talk and laugh about what we're going to do now that we're out of school. Angelo is going to college, and he congratulates me on my job with the CIA. He knows I'll do well there.

Afterward, we all hug each other and go our separate ways. I get into Ben's car. He's waiting outside with a big smile when he sees me. He's happy that I have graduated from school, as now we can be more serious about our lives together. Hopefully, we won't need any more white lies.

Chapter 50

Invitations have been sent out and replies are coming in. Martha is having a fit because she feels the outside of the house has to be painted before her wedding day. Her reasoning is that it will look so much better in the pictures with a coat of fresh paint on it. Actually, it's obvious that she's ashamed of it.

After much discussion and Martha being upset, Dad and Frank decide to paint it.

The landlady supplies them with gray paint and, armed with their brushes, they start with the front porch and work their way toward the back of the house. A tall ladder is needed for the front above the porch roof and the side. Dad unanimously votes for Frank to go up it. After all, "It's Frank's wedding," he says.

They get to the middle of the side but, alas, there's not enough paint to do the entire house, so they have to stop. The wedding is only a few days away, and if the paint is ordered it'll never be here in time.

Martha is not happy about it, but what can she do? She just has to make sure all the pictures are taken in front of the house, including getting into the car. She emphatically tells everyone that no pictures are to be taken facing the side or back of the house. Of course, I think it's pretty funny and wish I could be the one taking the pictures.

Our hats are so big and flimsy, and all of the bridesmaids are wearing them differently. Martha picks on me because, of course, I'm her sister. She pulls my hat down on the sides and then decides it should be down in the front instead. Finally I walk away from her, as none of the other bridesmaids are doing anything about their hats.

Regardless, everything goes fine and Martha marries Frank in a big beautiful wedding on a sunny Saturday in June. It's an afternoon wedding, with a small reception in the church basement following the ceremony.

I think to myself, *All of that fuss and it's over in two hours.* I think of all the painting Dad and Frank did, and for what?

Walking out the side door of the church I see Ben ride by. Supposedly he's curious and is checking on me. He voiced his concern that I might meet another guy at the wedding. He doesn't realize this isn't like a big Italian Catholic wedding, but I wish he could be here with me.

After the wedding, I'm glad to go home and change my clothes, as I have a date with Ben tonight. I'm relieved that all of this is over for now.

The following week I'm notified that I am officially Miss Kolfield, as there's no time to have a local contest. I have to go to Blair County for one contest and to Cambria County for another contest. Since our county has no contest, no one can figure out which one Kolfield should be part of, since this is Kolfield's first year in the beauty pageants.

Since we're located between the two counties, I can choose one or the other or be in both of them. These are preliminaries for the Miss Western Pennsylvania contest. The firemen sponsoring me feel I should be in both of them.

Now this is pressure. What is my talent going to be? Am I even pretty enough for a beauty contest? Then I find out I have to wear a bathing suit and high heels on the stage, and I nearly freak out. How can I walk out there in a bathing suit in front of everyone? I have to have two different evening gowns, as I can't wear the same one in each contest. There's so much to worry about, and I thought with the graduations and wedding over I could relax.

The next week I visit Jo in New Jersey. She's due with her baby around the end of June or beginning of July, and I'm trying to avoid the beauty contests that are coming up.

Mom keeps telephoning me in New Jersey and says the firemen want to know when I'll be back. They have all the dates arranged, and I'm scheduled to have dinner with the judges.

It's a lot of pressure, since I have no talent and don't know what I'm going to do. I find a book of poetry at the library and memorize a poem from it, putting some actions to it. I have no musical talent, no dancing talent, no acrobatic talent, no singing talent, nor am I a magician, so I don't have any choice.

After arriving home, I'm scheduled first for the Cambria County pageant. I have a new gown and bathing suit. The other girls seem so mature and have beautiful gowns and colorful bathing suits. My bathing suit is green-and-white–checked with boy cut legs, and I wear white high heels to go with it. My gown is plain light-blue but elegant.

I'm a nervous wreck. Walking out on the stage in my bathing suit and heels, I recognize the whistling and clapping and yelling of my two brothers-in-law, Pep and Reds. I look to where the sound came from and see my sisters Liz and Edna and my mom and dad. I'm so embarrassed.

Ben told me he couldn't make it, and I was sad in a way but happy that I didn't make a fool of myself in front of him.

When I recite my poem, I realize my mistake as soon as it happens. I mispronounce a word. Instead of saying bugle corp with a silent *p* on the end, I pronounce the *p*. When I pronounce it, the *p* sounds so distinct and hangs in the air as I realize the horror of my mistake. There's a long silence—or at least I think it's long—and my heart is beating faster than a drum in an African mating dance. I don't know how I keep going, but I finish the poem and return backstage, wondering why I allow myself to be made a fool of since I know I have no talent.

Then they have to ask us a question, and they ask me what person I feel has had an influence on my life, not including my family or friends. I want to say God, but they ask for a person and I feel God is a spirit, so I say George Washington, as he's the father of our country and our first president.

The next girl says God, and I'm so upset with myself for not saying God, as He has had the most influence on me. He's the one I talk to every night and always pray to for guidance and direction. They had asked for a person, so I didn't think they meant God.

Needless to say I don't win. I am very embarrassed and had suffered so much in preparation for this, and it all seems so artificial.

The next contest is in Blair County and is in a couple of weeks. At this point, my family knows I need some help.

Mom takes me to Penn Traffic in Johnstown, where she buys me new lipstick, an eyeliner pencil, and face powder. I don't wear makeup, but everyone in the contest did.

My sister Liz is the biggest help to me. Since she loves to write poetry and stories, she sits down with me, and we write a poem together that I can act out and for which I can take all of the credit.

We sit down night after night and write a poem that I'll never forget. It's about a lover who I lose and miss so much. Maybe it's a warning that my life is going to change. The first stanza of the poem is:

We came here not too long ago,
The one I loved, my only beau.
Many dreams we dreamed,
Many plans we had.
Then God took him and now I'm sad.

I practice it over and over, and Liz tells me how I have to hold my hand out, palm up like I'm checking for raindrops. Then I have to run a few feet and pretend to enter a cave. I'm carrying a large basket filled with flowers, like I'm picking them. I have on a pretty blue dress with a large blue hat to match. In fact, it's the bridesmaid dress I wore in Martha's wedding.

First, the contestants have to have dinner one evening with the judges. Two firemen volunteer to drive me to Blair County and wait somewhere so they can bring me home. We sit and eat with judges, who ask us all kinds of questions. My mother is a stickler for manners at the table and taught us many things for which I am now thankful. Also, I read a lot and learned a lot from Emily Post's rules.

I have just taken a bite of food, and the judge asks me a question. My mouth is full, and I slowly raise my pointer finger, as if to say, "Wait a moment." She nods her head, and I know I've the right thing. After I swallow my food, I answer the question. *Thanks, Mom, for always teaching us that we should not talk with our mouth full of food.* It's an interesting evening, but I can't wait until it's all over.

Finally, it's the night of the contest and it's very hectic backstage. They have set up little tables and mirrors for each of the contestants. There are all kinds of women there to help with the makeup, which I normally don't wear but have to that night, and to help you change in and out of your clothes. It's so hectic, even more so changing from gown to bathing suit to my talent dress and back to my gown.

I probably should have worn the plain elegant gown to this one but instead wear a bright-peach frilly one. However, I do wear the same bathing suit.

The girls in this contest are much older than me. They have been in many contests and are not an amateur like me. I'm seventeen, and they range from nineteen to twenty-three.

After getting through the bathing suit judging, it's time for my talent. I go through the poem without a problem, acting it out. I've rehearsed and rehearsed, and it all comes naturally after the first line, when my fear leaves me.

Everyone claps hard and long when the poem is finished. Later one of the mothers comes backstage and tells me that I'm very good and should keep on writing. I thank her.

At this point I know this is going to be my last beauty contest. These beauty contests are not my bag.

Thank goodness it's all over.

That night I thank God for getting me through these beauty contests and for guiding me to my new job in Washington, DC, in September. The train signals me it's time to sleep as it passes through to load up with black coal and carry it far away. Maybe someday I'll be like the black coal, traveling away from the dark mines and white lies.

Chapter 51

$\mathcal{I}$ don't need an alarm clock this morning. The Fourth of July arrives with the bright sun peeking in my window along with a lot of excitement. The neighborhood kids are up and outdoors early this morning, shooting their cap guns. It seems the bangs have no place to go but zoom upward. Naturally they enter through my open window, letting me know the celebrations have begun on this freedom holiday.

Freedom—that's what I have now. I'm all done with school, and I have a job in Washington, DC. What a wonderful feeling! I stretch and know sleep will not return.

Mom and Dad left last week, after the beauty contests, for New Jersey, as Jo's baby is due any day. Last night I spoke with Jo on the phone, and she said she couldn't wait until it was all over and she got her figure back. I can't picture her without a figure.

Two short rings on the telephone startle me, and I jump out of bed and run down the stairs to answer it. It's Mom, acting as my alarm clock. She's calling to remind me it's time to get up and get ready for the parade today. She talks fast, as she and Dad are leaving for the hospital. Jo went to the hospital around 5:00 a.m., when her labor pains started. Mom thought she better call now so I'll be wide-awake when Liz comes over to help me with my gown.

The Fourth of July means I have to be in the parade as Miss Kolfield. I dread it, but it is my obligation. I'd much rather be watching the parade.

True to form, Liz and Pep arrive promptly at 9:00 a.m. with Angela and Louis. Almost one year old, Angela is dressed in a red, white, and blue sunsuit, with her blonde curly hair held back with a red barrette. Louis is dressed as a cowboy with a cap gun in his holster. He's excited and shows me how he shoots it.

Holding my ears I wait for the loud bang, but there's just a click.

"You don't think we'd ride with Louis in the back with a roll of caps in that thing, do you?" says Pep while chuckling.

"Thank goodness. That's all I've been hearing since 7:00 a.m. I woke up to cap guns when the neighbor kids were allowed outside."

After making sure my hair is tied back into a bun with a tiara on my head and my blue gown is in perfect shape, Liz, Pep, and the kids drop me off at the fire hall, where the convertible is waiting.

Liz hugs me and kisses me. Demonstrating a smile and waving, she says, "Remember, smile and wave, smile and wave. We'll be looking for you, and we'll pick you up here after the parade."

Thank goodness it's a beautiful sunny day. The firemen have arranged for me to sit up on the back of a brand-new white Buick convertible while holding a bouquet of red long-stemmed roses. They drive me to the stadium where the parade will start.

The field is full of visiting high school bands, floats, and dignitaries that will be riding in other convertibles. With the bands warming up, the musical sounds mingle with shouts and conversations as they try to line up in the right order.

Senator Jordan is talking to several men and turns, sees me, and gives me a big smile and wave. Smiling, I wave back but know deep down inside he'll never get my vote. My faith in his honesty was shaken when he lied to me. It seems there are white lies everywhere, not only mine.

I listen to the Kolfield High School band warming up and know I'll miss hearing them practice at school this fall.

The parade starts, and my waving and smiling begin. Wearing white elbow-length gloves, I cradle the beautiful flowers in my left arm while waving with my right hand.

The scent of the flowers drifts to my nose, and I hope I don't sneeze. I keep smiling, and after a while the smile freezes on my face and my teeth feel dry. It's not a bad thing to have a smile frozen on my face—as it's better than a frown—but I wonder if my face will ever be the same again. I try to lick my lips but it's almost impossible, so I decide it's just easier to keep the frozen smile.

Seeing my friends and relatives who shout my name, I keep smiling and waving. The spectators' arms are extended outward as they wave their miniature United States flags. Sonya and Bev are screaming my name and waving. I wave back, as now it's automatic.

Louis is shouting while waving his little flag, "Aunt Anna, Aunt Anna!" I give him my frozen smile but also blow him a kiss. Angela is in her dad's arms and looks surprised to see me on top of a car. So far I haven't seen Ben anywhere and figure he must be helping his mother today.

After the parade, Liz and Pep find me and take me home.

"We're all going to have a picnic this afternoon at Edna and Reds', so if you want to come along, just call and we'll pick you up." Liz leans forward as she sits in the back with Angela and Louis so they don't get my gown dirty.

"Okay. I don't know what I'm going to do yet. I may go swimming at the park with my girlfriends. Also, they're having a dance there tonight."

"Just remember we'll come and get you if you need a ride," she says as she slides into the front seat of the car.

It feels good to walk in the house after the parade and wash my face and drink a glass of water, wetting my dry teeth and lips.

Tonight Ben and I are going to see the fireworks at the park, so I'm looking forward to that.

The telephone rings twice.

"Hello."

"Anna, you're an aunt again. Jo has a beautiful baby girl weighing in at six pounds and five ounces."

I let out a little happy scream and say, "That's wonderful. Who does she look like? How's Jo?"

"She's a little tired but she's glad it's all over, and the baby is beautiful just like her mother."

"Well, tell her I love her and can't wait to see my new niece. Do you want me to call anyone to tell them?"

"No, I called Edna and she'll tell Liz. Edna said the parade was great. She tried to get your attention but there was too much noise. By the way, what are you going to do today?"

"I might go swimming, and maybe I'll go with my girlfriends to see the fireworks at the park tonight."

"Well, don't stay out too late, and don't have anyone at the house."

"Don't worry, I won't. When are you coming home?"

"We'll probably be home in a couple of days. I'll let you know."

"Okay, tell Jo and Nick congratulations, and tell Dad I said hi."

"Okay and be good."

"I'm always good. Bye."

Chapter 52

I get ready for the park, putting on my navy-blue Bermuda shorts, light blue tank top, and white knee socks with my penny loafers. I walk downtown and get about four blocks away when Ben stops for me.

After I slide in, he leans over and gives me a kiss, wishing me a happy Fourth of July. The scent from the little tree hanging on his mirror is overwhelming and kind of strong today. He must have just placed it there.

"Sorry I didn't get to see you in the parade today. Had to help my mother," he says as he puts the car into low gear.

"Not a problem. It was just a parade, and I had a frozen smile that just defrosted an hour ago and a tired arm from waving so much."

"I bet you were beautiful. I would have loved to wave to you. Maybe next time."

"There won't be a next time. It's all over for me. I did everything they wanted, and I don't think there's anything else now except to get ready for my job in Washington, DC."

"I don't think you should go to Washington, DC."

"It's a great job and I'm excited about it. You can still visit me, and I'll be home now and then."

Silence surrounds us as we ride up Ninth Street.

"I'll be back later to be with you and see the fireworks."

He lets me off at Kolfield Park, where Sonya and Bev are supposed to meet me.

As usual Sonya and Bev are full of laughs, and we joke around about everything. They brought a blanket that we sit on while we talk about what has been happening since graduation.

"Did you know that Joy is pregnant? She was pregnant when we graduated but no one knew it. She's lucky no one knew or she wouldn't have been allowed to participate in the graduation services," says Bev as she smoothes out the blanket.

With eyes blazing, Sonya replies, "That's not right. Why does the girl always have to go through the bad stuff and the guy gets off scot-free? It's so wrong."

"I think it is too, but we know Joy and Andy really love each other so they'll probably get married. Not all guys would desert a girl. I know Ben would never do that to me. We love each other too much."

"Yeah, I guess you're right. Ben is an exception. We know he loves you," Bev chimes in.

With a very serious face, Sonya decides to put in her two cents. "But always remember the guy can walk away and the girl is left holding the bag, or should I say baby."

"Ben would never do that. He has too much integrity," I say, standing up, ready to move about the park and see what's happening.

We stroll around the park, talking to everyone. Some people are swimming while others are just getting suntans, and the rest are eating at picnic tables. Kids are running around shooting their cap guns, and laughter is everywhere.

I have my Brownie camera with me, so I take a couple of pictures and then ask a Marine in uniform to take a picture of the three of us.

"I certainly will for three beautiful young ladies like you." He smiles, showing a beautiful set of perfect white teeth. He must be about twenty years old and is as handsome as they come. He has olive skin and brown eyes and looks so perfect. *Or is it the uniform?* I wonder.

He takes two pictures of us as the three of us hang on each other, goofing off.

Returning the camera to me, he asks, "You wouldn't be available to go out on a date, would you?"

"I'm sorry but I'm going steady." I can't help but smile. If I wasn't going with Ben I know I'd go out with him, but it's Ben I love.

"Okay, just thought I'd take a chance and ask," he says as he tips his hat and wanders off.

"Wow, I wish he would have asked me out," whimpers Bev.

"Oh, come on. You're too much in love with Zudie. Let's race back to the blanket and eat our sandwiches—that is, if the ants didn't get them," I say and take off, getting a head start.

Before you know it, the afternoon is over and, true to his word, Ben shows up an hour before the fireworks start.

The place is now overflowing with people. Some have chairs, blankets, and cushions to sit on so they can plop down wherever they want. Ben parks where we can stand by the car and watch them.

After the fireworks, we get in the car and I kiss his scarred cheek and tell him, "I want to go home now."

"It's only ten o'clock," he says as he pulls me close to him.

"I know but it's been quite a day and, believe it or not, I'm really tired," I say, trying to stifle a yawn.

"Are you hungry at all? We could go to Ripple's."

"No, I just want to go home to bed."

With that, he smiles and moves his eyebrows up and down. "Can I join you?"

"Gosh, no. I'm so tired and, besides, I'm not allowed to have anyone in the house." I emphasize the second half of the sentence while stroking his cheek.

Slowly he drives me to my house to drop me off, since Mom and Dad aren't home.

"Can I kiss you good night?"

"Of course you can, silly," I say as I slide closer to him.

He gives me one of those tingling kisses, and I hurry up and get out before I change my mind, hearing him groan as I close the door. Throwing him another kiss, I run up the back porch steps.

At this point I don't care if a neighbor sees me. I graduated from high school and will be eighteen in another month, so they can gossip all they want. I didn't let him in the house, and that's all Mom cares about at this point.

It's a strange feeling walking into an empty house, but I'm not afraid, as everyone who has stayed home to watch the fireworks is still outside on their porches, conversing with each other. We never lock our doors, and yet I have no fear.

Getting ready for bed, I sit and look in the mirror. What a day it's been—actually, what a couple of months it's been. I don't think I've ever been this tired before.

I think about Jo and my new niece. I now have two nieces, Angela and Katie, and, of course, my favorite nephew, Louis. I wish Edna and Reds would have a child, but so far, none. They've been married longer than Liz and Pep, and I know they love children. I wonder why they don't have any of their own.

Chapter 53

───

The mailman brings exciting news the next day from the CIA. They have made all of my arrangements, and I'm to report to Washington, DC, on the ninth of September, one week after Labor Day.

Whoever is driving me to Washington, DC, that day—which, of course, will be Mom and Dad—will take me to the YWCA, where they reserved a room for me. The letter states my classification and my pay amount. I'm so thrilled. My prayers are answered, and my life is beginning.

I call Mom and Dad at Jo's, and they're almost as happy as me. They don't want to see me living in a big city by myself, but I know it'll be okay. Dad is really thrilled and proud of me, as he can now say he has a daughter who works for the CIA. I never realized how much this means to him.

July comes quickly, and then it's gone and it's my eighteenth birthday. Since my birthday falls on a Saturday, Ben and I are going to the motorcycle races at the Kolfield Stadium. The noise is tremendous, and before we climb the stands to our seats, he pulls me aside behind the bleachers and hands me a small box. I open it, and a beautiful solitaire diamond engagement ring sparkles up at me.

Surprised, I look at him. He smiles and says, "Will you marry me? I know we can't tell anyone we're engaged, but as long as we both know it, who else should matter?"

I'm speechless and look at the ring again while he continues. "I don't want you going to Washington, DC, to work for the CIA. If you take the job at the insurance company that you were offered, we can be together all the time."

"I don't know, Ben. I'm looking forward to going to Washington, DC. I'd disappoint a lot of people, but Dad would really be disappointed. He wants me to work awhile and see some of the world before getting married and settling down. Besides, your mother would never approve of me."

"Look, if you got pregnant, then no one can stop us from getting married. I don't want to lose you, and if you go away we may never see each other again. I promise you as soon as you're pregnant, we'll get married. My word of honor," he says as he raises his right hand.

Wow! I'm shocked. Sure, I am afraid of going to Washington, DC, by myself, but I am going to do it. Getting pregnant? I don't know. Then again, maybe it's meant to be, since we love each other so much.

I realize this is one of those turns in life's road that helps determine your future. Which way do I go? Of course I'll go the way of love. Isn't that what life is all about? I'm young and still believe in fairy tales. Ben loves me, and now he wants to marry me, and I love him. So how can anything go wrong? We'll be one happy couple, and our parents will understand and love us all the more when we show them how much we love each other.

On the other hand, I'd like to be independent. I want to work in Washington, DC. I want to be my own boss. I want to have my own apartment.

Ben is very convincing. I have absolute trust and faith in this man and love him very much. After a week of debates, I finally agree that this is probably the only way we can get married. So from that day on, we use no protection when we have sex, in hopes that I will get pregnant.

Ben has everything all planned, including that we'll live at his house with his mom and dad, and I can help his mother take care of his dad. I agree to all of this and am willing to do so, since I love him so much.

The main thing that I dislike doing is notifying the CIA that I won't be coming to Washington after all. I really wanted to go and was looking forward to it. It's bad enough that Dad was disappointed when I told him I wasn't leaving and was going to work at the insurance company.

With much sadness, I telephone the CIA, and they're very nice about it. They tell me if I change my mind, they'll still have a job available for me.

Accepting the job at the insurance agency is easy. Mom lets me drive our car the first day of work and tells me to ask if there is anyone I could ride to work with and pay them. The night before my first day, I ask Ben if I can ride back and forth to work with him, as it's on his way. I'd even walk up to Main Avenue and meet him between Fourth and Fifth Streets.

He explains he's already taking another girl as a rider, but I can ride with him with one stipulation. I'm not allowed to tell the other girl that's riding with him we're engaged, let alone dating each other. He says his mother likes her, and she has some sort of crush on him. He's afraid she might go back and tell his mother.

The other girl sits up front, and I sit in the backseat. My feelings are really hurt, and I mention it to Ben when I see him that evening.

"Just remember you're engaged to me, and that's all that matters. We have to keep everything a secret. You know how my mother and brother would react if they found out about us."

He never realizes that I'm following my heart instead of my brain by agreeing to everything he's saying. Sadness hangs over me. This isn't the way it's supposed to be.

We should be shouting to the world that we're engaged and going to be married soon. It doesn't feel right. I should have trusted my gut instinct.

Chapter 54

The people at the insurance company are happy and outgoing. I'm secretary to the general manager, Mr. Calli. He's tall — very tall, well over six feet. His dark hair and brown eyes blend in with his olive complexion. He is probably the best-dressed man I know. He wears suits and colorful ties with his white shirts. A gold-framed picture of his pretty blonde wife and three sons sits on his desk.

One day, after listening to my idea, he gives me permission to initiate it. It's the creation of a weekly newsletter for all of the insurance agents. The agents look forward to reading it, and it becomes a big hit.

Never did I dream that work could be so much fun and, to boot, I receive a paycheck for it. When I go to church on Sunday, I'm able to place my envelope containing five dollars in the collection, exactly 10 percent of my weekly paycheck before taxes.

Glancing out the window, I realize it's already late September and the leaves are turning. It won't be long before we're surrounded by bright colors. Once in a while I miss not going back to school and seeing all of my friends, but I'm an adult now, secretly engaged, and working full-time.

By the first of October the realization hits me that I have missed my period and must be pregnant. When I tell Ben, he's so excited. Now we can get married and no one can stop us. He tells me he would prefer if we go to Maryland to get married. This way we don't have to tell anyone that we're married until they notice I'm pregnant, and then we can say we've been married.

He has such a fear of his older brother and what he's capable of doing. Mike knows that if Ben doesn't stay and help with their father, Mike will have to help.

Ben and I both request a vacation day so we can drive to Maryland to be married. Ben decides to take a week's vacation so it doesn't look suspicious to his mother. We discover that in Maryland we don't have to wait three days and we don't need blood tests, so we can get married immediately.

It is the middle of October, and Mom and Dad have gone away for the week so I don't have to worry about them.

It's such a beautiful autumn day, with the warm sun shining on the car while a cool breeze blows through my hair as we ride with the windows down. On the way, we stop at one of the lookouts on the mountains so we can see the splendor of the colorful trees. It takes my breath away as I look at the different shades of orange, red, and gold, creating a colorful blanket covering the mountainside. No matter how many autumns I have seen, each one is beautiful in its own way. It's more beautiful today, because I know that on the way back when I look at it I'll be Mrs. Arno.

After arriving in Maryland, we ask for directions to the Marriage License Bureau. We take a deep breath, hold hands, and open the glass door to the office. A musty smell of paper and mimeograph ink greets us.

An older woman behind the counter looks up and smiles when we enter. Her gray hair is pulled straight back, and she has a few laugh wrinkles. She looks at us with her glasses down on the end of her nose as we tell her that we would like to get married. Smiling, she explains we need no blood test but do need identification.

We show our driver's licenses. After looking at Ben's, she nods her head in approval, but then she sees my age is only eighteen.

"I'm sorry but do you have a paper signed by your mother and father giving you permission to get married?"

"No, I didn't know I needed one."

"Well, since you're under twenty-one, you have to have your parent's permission. If you give me your phone number, I'll call them."

"My mom and dad are away. No one's home."

"Well, I'm sorry then. We can't issue a marriage license without their consent," she says in a sympathetic voice.

She continues, "I'll give you this form and they can sign it and have it notarized, and if you bring it back, we can issue the license."

One minute I'm standing on top of a beautiful mountain looking at all of the colors, and the next minute I'm so sad that I can't believe I've gone from high to low this fast in one day. Oh, I dread having to tell my parents, but what choice do we have at this point, as they have to sign for me?

I can't help but cry when we get to the car. Ben hugs me, saying, "It's going to be all right, Anna. You'll see. We'll just have to tell your parents and they can sign for a marriage license in our county. We have to have blood tests and will have to wait three days, but that's okay."

"Are you sure it'll be all right?" I sob.

"Yes, it'll be all right. The only thing I'm worried about is my brother finding out about it."

When Mom and Dad arrive home from their trip, I can't tell them. I'm scared. I know it won't be long before I start showing, and then everyone will know I'm pregnant.

Thanksgiving comes and goes, and every night Ben asks me when I'm going to break the news to my parents. I always answer, "Soon."

The first week of December I say to Ben, "You know I have to resign from my job. My clothes are getting tighter, and some I can't even button or zip up."

"I agree with that. Just say in your letter of resignation that you're getting married, and hand it in this week," he says as he kisses my cheek.

Finally, in the second week of December, I timidly approach my parents. "I'm pregnant and Ben wants to marry me, but we need permission from you, since I'm not twenty-one."

Mom's hand flies to her mouth. Dad's face reveals nothing.

"When's he going to marry you?" asks Dad.

"As soon as you sign for me."

"Call him and tell him we want to talk to him."

Of course they're upset, but what can they do? I explain to them we already tried to get married but I need permission from them. There's a lot of crying. Mom asks questions, but Dad keeps unusually quiet.

Ben comes to the house that evening. Dad corners Ben before we can all sit down and discuss this. I don't know what they say, but there are no loud voices, thank goodness.

After discussing my situation, we all agree that one day next week we'll go to the county courthouse and apply for the marriage license. Ben and I need to arrange to take another day off from work. The next day we have our blood tests taken at the hospital.

The following week Ben and I ride with Mom and Dad to the county courthouse, and they sign for their underage daughter. The clerk in the office says the marriage certificate will be ready in three days, and if we don't want to pick it up, they could mail it to us.

I'm relieved that it's finally going to be over and we'll be married. Ben says he doesn't want to tell his mother until after we're married. Again, I agree, knowing how important this is to him.

The next night Ben comes over and we watch TV together. It's so nice not sneaking around and telling white lies. Mom and Dad are pleasant to him, probably because they accept he is going to be their son-in-law. How I wish it could have been like this all along.

I walk with him out to the back porch, where he kisses me good night.

"I'll be over tomorrow night. If you want, maybe we can go to Ripple's and get something to eat."

"Sounds good. I'll be here waiting for you," I say as I touch his cheek and smile, never realizing it would be the last time we touch each other with tranquility and happiness in our hearts.

Chapter 55

The next night I wait for Ben to come over. I wait and wait and wait. The cuckoo clock reminds me at nine o'clock and again at ten o'clock how late it is, making me finally realize he's not showing up. Something must have happened. At ten thirty I go to bed with a heavy heart. I can't imagine what has happened to him, and I can't call his house.

The following evening he shows up.

With tears in his eyes, he says, "Anna, I can't marry you at the county courthouse. My brother Mike found out. He knows someone who works at the courthouse. The person told him we applied for a marriage license, and Mike became very angry and upset. He threatened me that if we get married he'd tell my mother. I don't need that right now. I don't want to upset my father or my mother."

After talking awhile and some crying, Mom and Dad approach us as we're sitting at the kitchen table. They sense something is wrong. Ben explains about his brother finding out and that he doesn't want to upset his mother and father and maybe we could get married some other way.

After some discussion, I say, "Maybe I can go to Jo's house in New Jersey."

"I don't know. She has a new baby now, and it might be too much for her," Mom says as she bites her lip.

"I don't think Jo will mind," says Dad.

"What do you think, Ben?" I ask.

"That sounds like a great idea to me. You go ahead, and I'll take a week's vacation and follow you. That will give us plenty of time to get married."

"Let's call Jo first," says Mom as she gets up to get the phone.

Ben grabs my hand and says, "It's going to be all right."

"Operator, I'd like to make a long-distance call to New Jersey."

After giving the operator the number, Jo answers the phone. She's quite surprised it's Mom and wants to know if there's anything wrong. Mom proceeds to tell her about Ben's brother not wanting him to marry me and explains the situation, including my visiting her.

After Mom gets off the phone she explains, "Jo thinks it's great that you'll be visiting her and is looking forward to seeing you and Ben too. She's going to make a doctor appointment with her doctor, and he'll do the blood tests and an examination to make sure everything is okay with your pregnancy."

"I already handed in my resignation, and I'm training my replacement. I only have one more week to work, so I can go right after that."

"Let's wait until after Christmas to go. We want to see Angela and Louis on Christmas morning," says Mom, with Dad nodding his head in agreement.

"That sounds okay to me," I say as I look at Ben for his opinion.

"That's great. I'll put in for my vacation and come down for New Year's, and we'll be married. I'll tell my mother before I go, and then what can she say?"

"Are you sure you don't want me to go with you to tell your mother?"

"No, it might make matters worse. I'll handle this on my own."

After more discussion, Ben says he has to go but will see me every night before I leave.

True to his word, Ben and I are together every night. Ben is worried about the weather and hopes it doesn't snow. Mom and Dad will drive me to New Jersey the day after Christmas and will sign any necessary papers, allowing me to get married, and then will return home. I'll stay there and wait for Ben.

It'll be a long trip, but it'll give me time to think, and I'm glad that I'll be seeing Jo, Nick, and Katie again. Having only seen Katie once when they visited, I'm excited to see her again. Jo does send pictures of her every other week. I've been so busy with my job and Ben and this pregnancy that I have no time for anything else. I haven't even been able to see my best friends. All my time has been devoted to Ben. But they're away at college or have jobs now and are busy too.

Jo and Nick bought a new house before the baby was born so they'd be settled in and have the baby's room decorated before her arrival. It's a three-bedroom brick home with a finished basement, where they have a bar and TV.

Jo has sent me a lot of pictures, and her house is beautiful. She's a great cook, baker, and decorator. If she wanted to, Jo could probably take cow dung, dry it out, and make it into a beautiful centerpiece. That's how talented she is.

I think back to last Christmas, when I spent it at Liz and Pep's house. At that time I was looking forward to this Christmas, when everyone would be together again. Never did I dream it would be like this—I'd be pregnant and running around, trying to get married.

My thoughts are interrupted by Dad's voice.

Dad always jokes around when we go on a trip, as he loves to travel. We just got the toll ticket at the Bedford exit on the Pennsylvania Turnpike, and he says as we pull out, "Okay, let's get out the baloney sandwiches."

Thinking he's joking, I say, "Oh, Dad, you know we don't have any baloney sandwiches."

"Yeah, I know, but sometimes it seems there's enough baloney floating around we could make our own and then some," he says in a sad tone.

There is nothing I can say, so I'm silent. In my heart I know he still believes that Ben is not going to marry me, but Ben will. After all, he promised me and gave his word of honor.

Chapter 56

After seven hours on the road, lunch, and several bathroom stops, we arrive in Glasstown, New Jersey. It's just dusk and as we pull onto their blacktop driveway, the lamppost goes on and we see Jo coming to the front door with the baby in her arms.

Jo is thrilled to see us. Nick is working the evening shift and won't be home until eleven thirty.

The aroma of roast chicken drifts in from the kitchen when we enter the house. We walk into their living room and, as usual, Jo has done a terrific job decorating their colonial-style home.

Two maple end tables flank a beige print sofa with maple arms. The living room has light-peach walls and lush, brown wall-to-wall carpeting, so I take off my shoes even though Jo protests.

The guest room is where Mom and Dad will sleep, and I have the honor of sleeping on a rollaway bed they set up in Katie's room.

Finally I reach out and take Katie from Jo's arms. She's a beautiful baby girl with blonde hair and blue eyes. Touching her pudgy cheeks makes her smile at me. Sitting in the rocking chair while holding her, I talk to her as she looks at me with those big blue eyes. I know she understands me, since she smiles and gurgles so much while clutching my finger.

Mom takes her from me and tells me to go help Jo set the kitchen table.

After dinner and discussion of Ben and me, Jo and I catch up on Kolfield friends while Mom and Dad watch the news in the living room.

Drying a dish, Jo turns to me, lifts one eyebrow, and says, "I hate to tell you I told you so, but didn't I warn you about using a rubber last summer? Remember?"

"Well, at least I planned mine. You didn't. Where was your rubber, huh?"

A punch in my arm made me say, "Be careful. You don't want to hurt my baby now, do you?"

We laugh and hug each other.

I have an appointment next week with the doctor, and Jo has found out where Mom and Dad need to go to sign the necessary papers for my marriage certificate.

The next morning we complete the task of getting the necessary papers signed and notarized while Nick stays home and watches Katie. Mom and Dad are leaving the next day. Ben won't be here for New Year's, as his vacation was postponed for a week. His boss is home with a broken leg.

I write a letter to Ben, telling him how much I miss him and I'll write more after my doctor appointment.

On the third day I receive a letter from Ben:

December 27, 1957

Hi darling,

I'm sorry I didn't write last night but I couldn't find the address. I hope you have gone to the doctor's office by now. How are you feeling? I'm so worried about you. I miss you terribly.

I haven't told my mother and father yet, but I think I will tomorrow. I told the girls that ride with me that you were on vacation. I think next week I'll tell them that you quit and that we've been married since October 16. I think that was the day we went to Maryland. I just remembered I was on vacation that week and it may sound like a good time because of that.

How are Jo, Nick, and Katie? Tell them I said hello. I can't wait to be down there with you. I'm so sorry I couldn't get my vacation next week. (I love you.)

I've been thinking about going to see my priest before I come down so I can make arrangements to be married by him. I hope you think it's a good idea. If not, let me know.

My mother knows there's something wrong but just doesn't know what it is. I wish you were here to tell her.

Well, I'm at a loss for words now, so I'll close for now. Please keep loving me as much as I love you. I'll see you soon. All my love and kisses are building up till next week when I see you again.

Love forever,

Ben

After refolding the letter and putting it in the envelope, I wish I was home. I don't like the tone of his letter; something bothers me about it, especially the part about his not telling his parents yet. I know I should've been with him when he told his mother, but he was adamant about doing it alone.

I write a short letter back immediately.

Dear Ben,

I was hoping you told your mom and dad, but I know how hard it is. It will be so much easier if you don't delay telling them, as your vacation is going to be here soon.

Jo is taking me to the doctor in a couple of days, and Mom and Dad left for home. They have signed all the necessary papers for our license.

I will write a letter to you tomorrow. I miss you so much. The baby is really beginning to grow now. Wait until you see me.

The baby and I both miss you, and I pray for you every night. If you want to talk to the priest, please go ahead. I will turn Catholic for you, and we will raise our baby Catholic.

Well, I want to get this in the mail, so I have to close now.

Love,

Anna

I don't share the letter with anyone.

A few days later Jo drives me to her doctor's office at one o'clock. The doctor's office is in his huge home that has a swimming pool and tennis court next to it. A separate part of the house is set aside for his examination room and office.

He's a tall, elderly gentleman with white hair and a small white mustache the width of his lips. There's an unusual dime-sized lump protruding from his forehead. Semiretired, he has only a few patients, and they are from families that he has treated over the years. Jo's in-laws happen to be one of the families. That's how Jo is able to have him as her doctor.

The doctor's examination goes well even though I'm embarrassed. The nurse explains the examination and helps me place my bare feet in the stirrups on each side of the table. I endure his examination with my arm over my face. I never had a pelvic examination before and feel awkward. He talks to me in a nice tone while his nurse holds my free hand.

After the examination, he calculates a due date of early May for my baby. He draws my blood for the blood test for our marriage license and says it will be ready in three days. He also informs me that my fiancé can come to his office for a blood test if he doesn't already have one.

When I get back to Jo's I write a letter to Ben about the doctor's examination and my due date and that, so far, everything is fine. I ask if he told his mother and father yet. I tell him how much I miss him and look forward to seeing him next week.

Our letters cross in the mail.

December 29, 1957

Hi darling,

Seven more days and seven more nights and we'll be together again.

Well, I hope you've been to the doctor by now. Did you get your blood test yet? I don't know where to get mine. I have half a notion to get it when I get there.

I've been so lonely since you've gone, and I don't know what to do with myself. How is the baby? And I don't mean Jo and Nick's.

Well, tomorrow is the day when I tell the girls that ride with me that we're married and you've quit your job. Also, I'll probably get a letter from you and then I'll have to tell my mother about us. I almost told her tonight, but I just didn't have the nerve. Oh, how I wish you were here. I guess we'll have to find a place of our own, because my mother said she'd throw me out if I have to get married this way. I hope you understand how it is here at home with my father, sick the way he is.

Honey, if it is at all possible that my mother says we can live here for a while, let's give it a try. Please try to understand, honey, I really love you and want you to be happy more than anything.

I hope you got my other letters. I am sort of doubtful because I couldn't find that piece of paper with the address on it in my wallet, and I forgot to put "c/o Nick Holding" on the envelope. Well, I'm just about out of words.

I saw Paul today and he gave me a receipt to give to Pep for his 1958 dues to the VFW.

I saw Bud this afternoon, and I asked him when he was bringing his baby over to my house for my mother to see it. He said I should take her over to his house. Even though he is my friend, he doesn't feel I am treating you right. He thinks I should stand up to my brother and mother.

I just reread what I just wrote and I realize how much I scratch with a pen. I hope you can read it.

Tell Jo, Nick, and Katie hello for me, and take the best of care of yourself and our baby because I love you both. See you soon. Love and kisses.

Forever,

Ben

Laying the letter on my lap, I realize I don't understand what he's saying. All along we both said we would live with his mother and dad if his mother allowed it. Maybe I'm reading too much into his letters.

I sit down and immediately write him a letter.

My Dearest Ben,

I received your letter today. I love you so much and have always told you I would live with you and your parents, helping as much as I can.

Of course, if your mother doesn't want us living there, there is nothing I can do about that. This would upset me to no end, as I know how much you love your father. You know I would do anything for you.

As I told you in my previous letter I went to the doctor and everything is fine. He drew blood for my blood test, and he will do the same for you when you arrive here if you don't have one. Mom and Dad have already signed the papers and everything is in order.

I can't wait until you arrive and we're married. I'm sure your mother will be okay with everything. She'll realize how much we love each other.

Love and kisses.

Love,

Anna

I address the envelope, lay down the pen, and think about last year when I was visiting here. At that time I was worried about the beauty contest, and now I'm pregnant and worried about Ben. I'd rather be worried about the contest. Maybe it's good we can't predict our future.

Days go by and I don't hear from Ben, by phone or by letter. Liz calls and tells Jo that Ben's mother, Concetta, called her and wants to know what's going on. She asked if it is true that Anna is pregnant. Liz told her I was pregnant and that Ben and I are planning to be married.

Evidently, she started screaming at Liz, and finally Liz calmed her down. Pep is Italian, and Liz did turn Catholic for Pep, so that's probably why Concetta called her. Liz doesn't know anything else that has happened since that conversation.

After hearing that, I wonder why Ben hasn't gotten in touch with me. It's not like him. He told me not to call his house, so naturally I won't. I'm not sure when he's coming anymore, since I haven't heard from him. Finally, I receive a thick letter from Ben.

January 3, 1958

Hi darling,

This is the first chance I got to write. Please don't be angry with me. I've been really busy at work. My boss is off again, and we don't know when he'll be back. He got his cast taken off, and the doctor won't let him come to work. The guy that I fill in for when he's on vacation is off sick. They took him to the hospital yesterday. We're just really piled up with work.

Well, I guess I'll start at the beginning. Your letters arrived on Monday, and my mother opened them. She understood enough to know that you are going to have a baby and that we were going to get married in New Jersey. That's when she called Liz and asked her about it. You know what happened next. When I came home from work, I went in the house and my mother was upstairs with my father. When I got upstairs she started: Why didn't we tell her? Why didn't we do something sooner? Why didn't we tell your mother before this? Why? Why?

My father wouldn't believe it, so when he asked me and I said yes, he started to cry. I felt terrible. I didn't know what to do or say. My mother started asking questions again. My father was only worried that I was going to leave him and no one would take care of him. I reassured him that I wouldn't leave.

First my mother said that I should marry you in church, and now she is dead set against us getting married at all. I am so afraid something is going to happen to her. Oh, honey, I don't know what to do or what to say. My mother said first we could live here at my house, and then she thought it over and said no. She feels that with the baby coming it would be a lot of extra work for her.

Anna, no matter what happens, I'll always love you. In case things turn out that we don't get married, I want you to sue—yes, sue me for support of the baby. Please try to understand that I am not saying this because I don't love you, but that I love you enough to want to help in any way I can.

I have no say at home. Mike and my mother have decided all the plans. It's not the way I want it. What I can figure out is that they want me to stay at home to help out without getting any extra work for themselves.

I guess this is the worst letter I've ever written to you. I haven't told you anything but my troubles. I've been so upset since you've gone that I can't even think straight anymore. I tried to write yesterday and today at work, but I just couldn't get anything down on paper that I wanted to say. I felt very hurt when my mother said I couldn't marry you and that I should just pay you off and support the baby. Darling, I shouldn't tell you but I just laid on the bed while my father was sitting up and I actually cried. I asked you to come home, but the way things look I don't actually think it will do much good. No matter what happens remember this one thing. I love you, and I always will love you, and anything that comes out other than we planned will not be my doing. I just hope that one day very soon we can get all this straightened out.

I think if we told my mother together, everything would have been all right. I really love you, Anna, and nothing can change that.

Please let me hear from you as soon as you can, and mail the letters to

Ben Arno, c/o my work.

Love,

Ben

I'm crying hysterically, and Jo runs to me, asking me what is wrong. I hand her the tear-stained letter while I sob and gasp for breath.

"What am I going to do?" I blubber. "I've given everything up for him, and now I'm carrying his baby and I don't know what to do. He promised me. I believed him that he loved me."

Chapter 57

With red puffy eyes and a tear-stained face, I sit down and write to Ben.

> My dearest Ben,
>
> I became very upset after reading your letter. You seem to be giving up and wanting nothing to do with me even though you say you love me. This is *our* baby, and you are the one who convinced me to have it so we could get married. Now you're saying you don't think we can get married? Why?
>
> Yes, I wish we had told your mother together, but we didn't. You told me you were going to tell your mother. Why didn't you tell her when you said you would? Instead she opened the personal letters I wrote to you and found out that way.
>
> I'm sorry but I'm very upset and can't stop crying. You can't even begin to imagine how I feel. I don't know what to do anymore. Now I wish I hadn't believed your promises.
>
> I'll be home tomorrow, so by the time you get this, I'll already be home if you want to call me and talk.
>
> I will always love you, and I hope you know that.
>
> Love and kisses,
>
> Anna and baby

Afterward Jo tries to convince me to stay, but she sees it's to no avail. She drives me to the bus station the next day, and I ride the Greyhound home with swollen eyes, ready to cry at a moment's notice.

The whole trip home I think about what I'm going to do if Ben doesn't marry me. Where will I live? I can't work until after the baby is born. What am I going to do? I feel trapped and suffocated. It is so difficult to believe that Ben would do this to me. It's like a bad dream and I can't wake up.

Mom and Dad are waiting for me at the bus depot in Bedford, as no one will know me there, even though my coat hides my stomach. I can see my breath when I talk, but the cold doesn't bother me, as I'm still numb from Ben's news.

Mom hugs me while Dad gets my suitcase. When we get home, they tell me Jo already called them and told them everything that happened. Liz had called them about the phone call from Concetta, so they knew there was a problem.

"What am I going to do?" I start crying again while holding my stomach.

All this time I've told them nothing but white lies. Now they can throw me out and say, "I told you so."

But, no, instead Mom hugs me and says, "Anna, don't worry. You can live with us. I'll call Dr. Hansky tomorrow and make an appointment with him. You have to see a doctor. It's not healthy for you or the baby to delay it. You also need a doctor to treat you during your pregnancy and deliver your baby."

Dad agrees and, while brushing his hand through his crew cut, says, "I knew he wasn't going to marry you. I could tell but I didn't want to say anything. Don't worry. This isn't the end of it. That son of a bitch isn't going to get away with this. I'm getting a lawyer. You were underage when he first started going with you."

"No, Dad, you can't do that. He promised to marry me if I got pregnant, and I agreed. You can't sue him."

"The hell I can't. He can't do this to you," he shouts.

"I can't take this anymore," I scream and run upstairs to my bedroom.

I lie on my bed and cry and cry and cry. *What am I going to do? Oh, God, please help me. I'm so sorry for all of the lies I've told.* Now I know I'm being punished.

Chapter 58

Day by day goes by and Ben never calls me. I try calling him on the phone when I know he's home from work. Concetta answers and screams at me to leave him alone, slamming the receiver down. It makes me cry all the more. I've written him several letters to his office, but he doesn't reply to them. *Oh, Ben, why won't you talk to me?*

I receive in the mail the marriage license we applied for at the county courthouse last month. How ironic, and it makes me cry all the more. I'm tired of blood tests and applications. It's ridiculous that I graduate from high school at seventeen but I'm not of legal age until I'm twenty-one. It doesn't make sense.

I wonder when I'll run out of tears, as they seem to be endless.

By now everyone knows I'm pregnant and going to be an unwed mother, as news travels fast in a small town.

Bev and Sonya come over to visit me, since I can't go anywhere with my stomach popped out, lest everyone sees I'm pregnant. They inform me they see Ben riding around town, but he never stops to talk to them. He ignores them. They never see him with a girl, but that doesn't mean anything. He told me he loved me, and yet he won't even talk to me.

I think of Chicken Little when he thought the sky was falling, and I understand how he must have felt because that's the way I feel now. All I do is cry. It's become such a nightmare for me that I want to die. It's a terrible feeling to have been abandoned by Ben, the one who told me how much he loved me, and I was stupid enough to believe him.

Now I can't go anywhere and can't be seen pregnant, since I'm not married. Having to stay in the house all the time except when we go visit my sisters or to the doctor for my checkup makes me feel so isolated from the world.

When someone comes to the door, I have to run upstairs and hide in my bedroom until they leave.

One day a tall man in an overcoat and hat knocks on the front door. Mom tells me to run upstairs quickly. After Mom opens the door I hear him asking for me.

My mother tells him I'm away right now and asks what he wants. He has a list of all of the senior girls who graduated this past year and is selling them pots and pans for their hope chest. I'm listening on the stairs, and sadness fills my heart, as I know I'll never have a hope chest. Actually, I feel like I have no hope for anything.

Another day one of the firemen, Pete, knocks on the front door and hands Mom a small makeup suitcase for me, one of the prizes for being Miss Kolfield. He says to tell me there's something else inside for me. Mom thanks him and brings it upstairs to me. It's a pretty brown-checked square suitcase, and inside are several items, including a hairbrush, perfume, and a gift certificate. I start crying again, remembering how great everything used to be.

How did I ever get in this predicament? It was the white lies. I never should have told them, and I never should have believed Ben.

I know my parents are ashamed of me, but they don't say anything. They love me because they're helping me even after I told them all those white lies to be with Ben. Again, I cry when thinking about it. Everything that has happened doesn't seem real. I try to not dwell on any of it, as I cannot change anything. I'm suffocating in a fog.

Nancy, a friend of the family, brings her two daughters over one evening so I can talk to them. She wants me to make them understand how loving a boy and having sex with them is so wrong.

"Anna, can you come down here a minute? I want you to talk to Julie and Mary about boys."

"No, I'd rather not," I say as I close my bedroom door.

She marches her daughters upstairs to my bedroom and, after opening my door, pushes them to sit down on my bed. She's a tall lady with blonde hair pulled tightly back and held with a barrette. She wears tight-fitting clothes and high heels with a lot of straps. Her blouse is partially open with the top two buttons not buttoned, and you can see the crease between her breasts.

"Tell them how bad it is when you go out with a boy and let him touch you, how wrong it is for boys and girls to touch each other and what can happen to them. Show your stomach so they won't want to look like that. Tell them how the guy just walked away and left you with this whole mess."

With that she walks out of the room and goes back downstairs.

Actually, their mother did all of the talking and I just cried most of the time, so they know I'm sad but they're still young, ten and twelve years old. How could they possibly understand what I'm going through right now?

All I can say through my sobs is "Don't tell any white lies."

They just sit there holding each other's hand and nodding their heads.

"Now go back downstairs and tell your mother you love her."

I want to be left alone and pray to God that He will allow me to die. I read a chapter each night from the Bible, hoping to find comfort there. I'm so lonely and sad. I'm not afraid to die—at least I'd be at peace. But would I go to hell or heaven? I'm full of confusion and tears.

One evening Edna and Reds show up to play cards with Mom and Dad.

After one game and a few hands of the next game, Mom says, "Anna, I want to fix some snacks. Would you come down and take my place until I'm finished?"

I know she just wants me to forget about my pregnancy for a few minutes, and I do. Of course it is the men against the women.

The cards are dealt, and after a few hands Edna and I are winning, but it's a very close game.

"Hurrah!" I shout after getting double pinochle and making it possible for us to win the game.

Dad looks at me with so much anger on his face as he gets up, moves toward me, and slaps me across the face. He slaps me really hard.

"You're no good. Look at you, pregnant like that, and he doesn't want to marry you."

I realize he's hurt, and looking at me pregnant like that is too much for him. I'm hurt too, but there's nothing I can do about it.

Mom comes running in from the kitchen. "Fritz, what's wrong with you? You can't slap her like that."

How ironic—I think as I walk slowly upstairs to my room, crying and holding my hand over the red print on my face—my father hitting me while my mother protects me. Dad and I never talk again until after my baby is born.

Chapter 59

As it gets closer to my due date, everyone starts nagging me about putting my baby up for adoption. Edna and Reds have no children and say they would gladly adopt the baby. I know they'd be wonderful parents, but I don't want to be an aunt to my child.

This child was conceived out of love and is part of Ben and me. I still hope and pray that Ben will come back and marry me.

The preacher of our church, Reverend Miller, is a very small, thin man with glasses and a soft but distinct voice. His fingers are long and white, as if they are never in the sun, a contrast to his darker face. They remind me of sticks of chalk ready to break but somehow always bend when they flip the pages during his Sunday morning sermons. I remember them distinctly—that is, I remember them from when I used to go to church. Now I can't even go to church because of my pregnancy and being unwed.

Reverend Miller and his wife have two small children, and I, on occasion, have babysat for them, so we aren't complete strangers. He appears one afternoon, knocking on the front door. Mom invites him in, and he tells Mom he wants to talk to me.

"Anna, come down here. Reverend Miller is here and wants to talk to you."

I wipe my face with a cold cloth, as I've been crying again, and slowly walk downstairs. I remember the good times of running down the stairs and Dad telling me to slow down. How I wish I could go back to those times and have Dad holler at me for going so fast.

Reverend Miller stands up when I enter the room, and the chalk sticks reach out to shake my hand.

After sitting down, he says, "I'm wondering if you would like to give your baby up for adoption. I know so many people that would love to adopt your baby. The baby would have a good Christian home with a mother and a father and would be loved."

He never asks me how I am doing or how I'm feeling, if I'm saying my prayers or if he can give me communion, since I'm not allowed to go to church. He just zeroes in on letting me know many people he knows who would love to have my baby.

I can only say, "No. This is my baby and I'm keeping it."

"How are you going to manage to take care of a baby and be able to afford the food and milk?"

"I'll manage somehow."

"Well, think about it, and if you change your mind, please call me."

With that he stands up. After saying good-bye to Mom, he walks out the front door onto the porch.

Even though I want to die, it's at this point that I begin thinking about "our" baby—the one that was to bring us together and make us man and wife, the one that we were thrilled to be having, as this baby would allow us to get married. Now this baby will be mine and mine alone, with unconditional love.

Every night my prayers are to have a little girl. If I have a little girl I'll never ask for a little boy—that is, if I ever have any more children. *If I'm to have children of one sex, please, dear Lord, let it be girls and not boys.* I don't want to have a boy and have him realize his father didn't want him. With a little girl I can help her to deal with all of this and let her know I'll always be there for her.

So I pray to God that if He won't allow me to die, then please give me a little girl.

Sonya and Bev still stop by to see me once in a while and tell me when they see Ben riding around. He still doesn't talk to any of my friends or even try to get a message to me. Just a note with "I love you" on it would suffice.

It's times like these that the crying cannot stop. Ben seems to have recovered from it quite well, and here I am in my prison. What have I done that's so wrong that I need to be punished day after day? I still feel that there is nothing wrong or sinful with my loving Ben.

It seems my father can't recover from Ben jilting me and won't let it go. He hires a lawyer and presses charges against Ben. The charges are called fornication and bastardy. Heck, I don't even know what that means.

How can he press legal charges against Ben because we love each other? What is that going to prove? It'll prove that I'm stupid maybe for believing him but nothing else. It's over, done with.

The lawyer explains to Dad that it will go to the grand jury after the baby is born, and they'll make a decision on whether it should go to trial or not.

I beg Dad not to press charges, as I don't want all this controversy, but by now he hates Ben with such a passion for doing this to his daughter. After all, Dad is the one who hears his daughter cry herself to sleep every night.

Then my girlfriends bring word back to me that Ben's brother Mike said the fornication and bastardy charges better get dropped. If they aren't dropped, he'll find a bunch of Ben's friends who will go to court and testify that I had sex with all of them. I can't believe that someone can be so evil and make up such lies. Why isn't Ben stopping him? Where is the man who I loved so much and who promised me we would get married if I got pregnant? I'm beginning to think that he isn't a man after all. He's scared, a coward, and afraid of his brother and mother.

I don't understand why I have to stay hidden and Ben is allowed to come and go in the world as he pleases, why I'm being blamed by his family and they don't even know me, why it's so evil to be pregnant and unwed, why Ben has done no wrong but I have, and why the blame is not shared even though it involved us both.

Chapter 60

I'm due at the beginning of May, one year after graduating from high school with all of my dreams and happiness. I was seventeen when I graduated, but now I'm eighteen, single, and ready to have a baby. All my plans and dreams have turned into sad nightmares. Having loved someone with my whole heart is not good. I promise myself that I'll never let that happen again.

At my eighth-month doctor visit, Dr. Hansky showers me with instructions.

"You and the baby are doing well and are very healthy. You gained a lot of weight, and it's important for your health not to gain any more. It looks like you're going to have a very big baby, so there are some precautions that I'll be taking when the time comes. I don't want you looking on this as a painful experience and then never wanting any more children."

"I doubt I'll ever have any more children."

"You shouldn't say that. You're young and pretty. You'll get married one day and have more children. I can practically guarantee that."

"I don't think I can trust another man," I say with tears in my eyes.

"That will pass after your baby is born. You're just feeling depressed right now."

To change the subject I ask, "How's Lennie doing? You do know I graduated with him? I heard he was going to college. Does he like college?"

"My son just made it through his first year of college, and I warned him that if he didn't stop partying and start studying next year, I was going to cut off his money source. I made him get a job for the summer. He's got to learn the value of money."

"Oh, I'm sure he will. He's a great guy and he gets along with everyone," I say, remembering how Lennie always was a fun person, joking around, laughing, and evidently still doing it. Growing up takes time, but I doubt any of us growing up understand what it's all about at the time.

"I hope he finishes college, but I have my doubts. Now make sure if you have any spotting or bleeding to call me immediately. You might not go to May, as your baby is quite big."

"I hope I have the baby as soon as possible."

On the way home from the doctor, with Dad driving and Mom in the front passenger seat and me in the back, I start crying and wanting to die again. I feel so ugly and fat, and I'm so tired of being pregnant and imprisoned. I clench my fists, hold my breath, and bounce up and down on the backseat, telling Mom I want to die. I'm sick of living this way and, of course, I'm uncomfortable.

This huge bulge protrudes from my stomach, and I still don't know what evil things I did to create such unhappiness. I don't remember what it's like to laugh anymore, and I envy my girlfriends when they come to visit me. They're free and not made to feel ashamed. Ben is enjoying his life, as he can come and go as he pleases.

Mom tries to calm me down, and as soon as I get home I slowly walk upstairs to my cell that has no bars and has sunlight yet it is dark—my bedroom, which only a year ago I loved to be in so much.

Finally, the time comes for the birth of my baby. My pains start early on the first Tuesday in May. My mother comes to my bedroom when she hears my cry.

I stand up to go to the bathroom, and water gushes down my legs all over the floor. I think I've peed myself even though I have no control over it. I'm embarrassed for making such a mess, but Mom is smiling as she wipes it up.

"Don't worry, Anna. It's all right. Your water just broke. It's time for the baby to arrive."

The pain is so intense, and I'm sure it must feel this way if someone should stab a knife in my stomach. Then suddenly there is no pain. What a relief.

Mom and Dad drive me to the hospital a couple of blocks away. Mom takes care of the paperwork while the nurse preps me to deliver the baby. Dad goes home. My parents are going to take care of the hospital bill.

Dr. Hansky is waiting for me with a smile. The nurse puts me in a wheelchair to take me to my room to get ready. The doctor pats my shoulder and tells me everything is going to be all right.

At this point, I really don't know what to expect and am surprised the pains are so sharp even though I have a few minutes between each one.

So here I am with my shattered dreams and hopes, and now I'm having all of this physical pain. *Oh, Lord, just get me through this.*

Every time a pain stabs me, I grab the rails of the bed and clutch them, but I don't scream. I hold it all inside, as I don't want anyone to hear me. I'm so alone and afraid. *Oh, God, please help me.*

After six hours of intense pain, the doctor examines me and says I'm ready. Since this is my first baby and it's going to be a big one, he wants to sedate me very heavily. He repeats what he told me in his office, that he doesn't want me to have such a hard time and that I'll never want any children again, as I have my whole life ahead of me.

As I grow woozy, I hear the doctor talking to me. He's asking me something, but I'm having a difficult time talking. All I know is the time has come, and at this point I don't care about anything. I seem to be floating and then enveloped in a fog.

I do remember the pains and everyone telling me to push and how, as soon as I had the baby, all of the pain stopped. All of that pain and suddenly it's gone. Unbelievable. The doctor is calling my name and telling me I have a little girl with a lot of black hair, weighing ten pounds and three ounces. All I want to do is sleep.

When I do awake and they bring the baby to me, I see so much of Ben in her that I cry. Her one ear is just like his one ear, the top a little different from his other ear. This is supposed to be such a happy time, but I feel so lonely and sad even though I have this beautiful little girl.

The doctor comes in to see me and says that—by law, when I'm under sedation—he has to ask me the name of the father. He says when I answered him, it sounded like "beano," so he guessed that meant Ben Arno.

I said, "It is Ben Arno."

I wonder why they have to ask me that, and I can't understand what kind of law that is. Why aren't they asking the father these questions or pursuing him for answers?

They settle me in a ward with the rest of the new mothers, but then I'm moved to a private room the very next morning. The nurse tells me it's best for me, but I had already heard two of the other nurses on the other shift talking.

One of the mothers complained and doesn't want me with them, as I'm single and they're all married. She didn't want her husband in there when I was. Why? I don't know. I don't even know her.

So, the hospital director, after talking to my mother, felt it was in their best interest to keep peace. They move me to a private room, and Mom agrees to pay the extra charge.

I'm not going to nurse my baby, but the mothers still sit together when it's feeding time. It's difficult sitting with the other mothers and learning how to give the bottle to my baby when they ignore me and talk to each other. I feel like an invisible person.

At one feeding they're all sharing stories about the babies' names and nicknames.

The mother who I think doesn't like me says, while talking to her baby, "You're so cute, Patty Paditski."

I think, *What a cute little nickname.* Not realizing what I'm doing, I can't help but say, "Where did you ever get a cute nickname like that?"

She glares at me as she holds her baby tighter and moves backward in her chair, away from me. "That's her real name. Besides, it's none of your business what I call my baby. You're nothing but a tramp."

I feel like a fool. I didn't know that was her real name, and now I'm being called names. Tears flow as I hand my baby to the nurse and disappear to my room.

After putting the baby back in the nursery, the nurse stops by my room. "Don't let her get to you. She's probably one of those that didn't get caught and is jealous that you're so pretty." She smiles as she fixes my sheets.

"Thank you." That's all I can say, as I'm still choked up.

After that I never voice my opinion again. After requesting permission from the doctor, I'm allowed to feed my baby in my room.

All I can think of is maybe Ben will come and see the baby and me. But he never sends a card or even good wishes through my girlfriends. We have created this beautiful baby and we love each other so much, so why doesn't he attempt to contact me? The pain of having the baby is nothing compared with the pain and hurt I am feeling from all of this rejection.

All my family visits me except for Dad, and, of course, everyone loves the baby. Bev, Connie, and Sonya come and visit me and tell me they saw Ben riding around on a brand-new motorcycle. He's telling everyone he bought it to celebrate the birth of his baby. His mother always forbid him to have a motorcycle, and now it must be okay because he listened to her and didn't marry me.

I name my new baby Sarah Daisy, because I like Sarah and the middle name is after my mother. After all, she did support me through all of this and allowed me to live at home even though I felt like I was in prison.

Before leaving the hospital, I'm given a set of instructions titled "Mother's Instructions," which lists thirteen things for the mother and eight things for the baby. For me: must avoid steps for at least one to two weeks, no heavy lifting or heavy housework, no baths for six weeks, periodic rest at short intervals, etc. For the baby: wash eyes with plain tap water, offer baby water between feedings, soap and water sponge bath until cord is off, avoid drafts, etc.

Dr. Hansky comes in to say good-bye and pats my shoulder. "Everything is going to be all right. You have a beautiful baby, so take good care of her."

"Thank you for everything," I say with tears in my eyes but a smile on my face.

"Remember, don't wear a girdle. Try to hold your stomach in on your own. It'll make your muscles stronger. Make an appointment for your six-week checkup, and the baby should be seen in one week. Take care of yourself, and I'll see you soon." He shakes my hand.

Three days later, after leaving my cell with a huge belly, I return to it with Sarah and a much smaller belly.

Mom has fixed up a white bassinet for the baby in the bedroom by my bed. For the first few nights when Sarah wakes up for a feeding, I get up but Mom gets up and tells me to go back to bed.

"You need your rest," she says.

She warms the bottle and feeds her. She sterilizes the bottles and makes the formula. I begin to feel like the baby is hers and not mine. I know she's trying to help, and for the first couple of nights it's okay, but then I tell her I'll feed Sarah at night.

When I'm half awake and half asleep, feeding Sarah, I wonder why I just don't let Mom do it. She enjoys doing it. Why? I don't know. I can't imagine how she did it with all of us.

Supposedly, it reminds her of the time when she had all of her babies. When she had so much work to do she couldn't enjoy them. Now she can enjoy her grandchildren. I just don't want to be a child anymore and be told what to do. I need some space, some room to breathe, and precious freedom.

We get into a routine, and Sarah is a very good baby. She starts sleeping all night after a few weeks.

After my six-week checkup, I know I have to get a job. And I can't stay in this town where everyone knows I'm an unwed mother.

Also, I'm afraid I'll run into Ben, and I want nothing to do with him. He probably thinks he can do as Mike did, keep getting a girl pregnant and not marry her.

After this past year I realize Ben is a liar and, even though I still love him, I can never trust him again. He hurt me so much, and God is the only one who knows how I feel, as He is the only one I talk to about my true feelings.

Jo wants Sarah and me to live with her in New Jersey. She thinks I can find a job there. She and Nick both agree that I can live with them until I get settled.

Katie, our little firecracker, is now going to be one year old on the Fourth of July.

One day Mom is sitting in the kitchen making out her grocery list.

"Mom, I want to go live with Jo in New Jersey."

Putting down her pencil, she looks at me. "You can't, Anna. Your case will be coming up before the grand jury, and you have to be here for that."

"I can't stay here in this town, Mom. Everyone knows I'm not married, and I don't want to subject Sarah to that. I have to get a job, and Jo will babysit Sarah, as she can use the money."

"Why don't you leave Sarah with me, and after you find a job you can get her."

Leaning on the back of the chair with my hands, I say, "No, Mom, I want to take her with me. I went through all of this pain and heartache so I could keep her. I want her with me."

"What about the court?"

"I can come back for that. You know I love Kolfield, but there's nothing here for me anymore. I don't want to walk down the street and run into Ben. I don't want him ever seeing my baby."

"Let me think about it."

Chapter 61

Chubby with rosy cheeks, Sarah is now two months old. I love her more every day even though my life has changed drastically. After many conversations, Mom realizes there is nothing she can do to keep Sarah and me living with her.

Deep down inside she knows I'm right. I'm convinced of that, and she also knows I want nothing to do with Ben anymore. He has caused me so much suffering, broken his promise to me, and never made an effort to see his child or me to explain why he couldn't marry me.

My only exercise is walking around the house, feeding the baby, washing diapers, and making formula. All my friends are at college, working full-time jobs, married, or have moved away. They're living their lives, and I'm happy for them. That's how I know it's time for me to become more independent.

After many letters back and forth to Jo, she begs me to bring Sarah and live with her. She says there are plenty of jobs and she'll babysit Sarah for a small fee. Later, when I'm able, I can pay some rent. It seems that may be my only way out of this town and away from Ben.

Jo, Nick, and Katie come to visit and take Sarah and me with them back to New Jersey. Since Katie was born and Jo had to quit work, they traded in the new convertible and got an older Oldsmobile station wagon. They are watching their pennies, Jo says.

New Jersey is so different, and I feel alive again. I can go outside and walk around, pushing Sarah in her stroller. I'm finally free—or at least I think so.

I scan the ads in the *Glasstown Evening News* each evening and reply by writing a letter to each company. Every morning I place my replies in the white mailbox at the end of the walk and put up the red flag so the mailman will take them to the post office for me.

The rest of the time Jo and I take our daughters for walks or look through magazines at homes, furniture, and decorations. We learn to make various crafts for the holidays.

Today we decide to visit Minnie, the neighbor next door. Her husband drives a truck for Coca-Cola and delivers cases of Cokes to the stores. He's always busy in the summer, so she welcomes our company since she gets lonely.

Jo and Minnie are complete opposites. No doubt about it.

Minnie wears black-framed glasses and is always pushing them up on her nose. Her hair is straight and cut below her ears, showing her round face. She is short and chubby.

Today she's wearing a pink-checked blouse that hangs out over her green-plaid shorts, making her look heavier than she really is. She's not one for fashion or matching colors, but she is a wonderful person and would do anything for you. Her house looks the same, not coordinated but always smelling like someone has just scrubbed it with a strong detergent.

Minnie has two little girls of school age, and sometimes we pack a lunch and all go to the park, where there's a wading pool and picnic tables.

Today we sit in her backyard and discuss our kids as we watch the older ones baby the little ones.

"You know I got a reply for a job offer, and it really sounds good. The only problem is I need transportation. I've asked most of the neighbors, but no one goes in that direction or they work shift work. I don't know what to do."

"So what you really need is a car," Minnie says as she picks up the ball that rolls by her feet.

"Yeah, I need a car so I can accept this job in town, and I can't accept the job until I definitely have a car. They're giving me a week to decide. The problem is I can't buy a car without a job, and I can't take a job until I have a car. Does that make sense?"

"Well, Mom has a 1950 Ford that she wants to sell, as she has no need for it right now. She's giving up her house in town and moving in with us."

"What does she want for it?"

"She's asking $150, but I bet she'd sell it to you for $100, since you need it and she needs the money right now."

"Well, let me think about it and I'll get back to you," I say, watching her push those darn glasses back up on her nose.

"Okay, just let us know," she says as she coos to Sarah and pinches her little fat cheek.

After we go back to Jo's house, Jo says, "I wish I could give you the money, Anna, but we're really broke right now. With me not working and diapers and baby stuff, insurance, taxes and a mortgage, we're completely broke." Then she gets this bright idea. "How about we visit Martha and

Frank? They live only an hour and a half away. We could go up on Sunday when Nick is off so he can watch Sarah and Katie. We can spend a couple of hours with them and then come home. They always seem to have money. Martha is always buying new clothes, and they seem to want for nothing. Maybe she'll loan you the money."

Jo calls Martha to ask her if it's all right to visit. Martha approves it, but it has to be early afternoon, as she and Frank are busy before and after. So with Nick babysitting both kids, Jo drives me to Martha's house one Sunday afternoon to spend a couple of hours with Martha and Frank. I dread it.

We arrive at their house, ring the doorbell, and Martha greets us.

"Hi, come on in." She gives each of us a brisk hug like we have a contagious disease.

"Frank's over at the church and will be here shortly."

"You have a nice house, Martha," I say while standing and looking around, smelling the pot roast in her oven.

The living room at the front of the house consists of a light-tan couch, a needlepoint of beautiful lilies and purple lilacs hanging behind it on the wall, two dark-brown armchairs, three mahogany tables, an overloaded bookcase, and several crosses on the walls.

"I like that needlepoint picture," Jo says, examining it closer.

"Yes, Mom made that and gave it to me when we moved in here."

"I thought so. She gave me one with geese flying over a pond. I love it, and it fits right in with my decor."

After some small talk, Frank walks in. He's a jovial type. His hair is now short, similar to a crew cut. Being so tall, he leans over and gives each of us a big hug, saying, "It's so good to see both of you. How's everybody doing?"

"Well, I'll get dinner ready," Martha says as she goes into the kitchen.

"Do you need some help, Martha?" I'm thinking maybe it would be a good time to ask to borrow the money.

With her robot smile, she looks back and replies, "No, I can handle it."

Jo gives me a funny look, but I avoid saying anything.

After about ten minutes of conversation and clanking in the kitchen, Martha announces it's time to eat.

We sit down around the table and hold hands so Frank can lead us in prayer. Naturally, Jo sits between Frank and me, and I have to hold Martha's hand. Jo squeezes my hand, as if to say I better ask soon, as we'll be going home.

The table is set nicely with a beige linen tablecloth and napkins to match. The china is white and trimmed in blue flowers. The pot roast looks good. I guess Martha finally learned to cook. Martha and I smile at each other, as if reading each other's thoughts.

After eating, we clean off the table, refusing dessert, as we have to get home. Jo pinches me in the back to ask now.

After hugs and good-byes, Frank goes back to the church and Martha walks us out to our car.

As we stand there talking, I finally get up the nerve and blurt out, "Is there any possibility you can lend me a hundred dollars, Martha? I have a job offer and need a car to go back and forth to work. Jo's next-door neighbor has one for sale. I'll pay you ten dollars a week until it is paid in full. I promise. Please, I need this job." My heart is pounding, and I hate asking for anything, especially from Martha.

She looks at me for a moment and then actually laughs. "Why would I want to lend you a hundred dollars? Anyway, I don't have a hundred dollars to spare for something so frivolous as buying you a car. You'll have to find another way to buy it."

It isn't the refusal but the way she says it that makes me feel like I am begging. She always did have a way of making a person feel inferior to her, but I know deep inside that I'm not. She is the one with a problem.

Jo is more upset than I am and, on our way home, says, "Just wait, Anna, there'll be a day when Martha needs something from us. What goes around comes around." Little did I know that day would come, but it would be years later.

Chapter 62

It seems there's so much rejection in my life. I can't afford to buy that car, so the neighbors sell it to someone else. There's no way I can take a job in town without transportation. Jo is getting a little upset with me because I'm not working. I can understand that, as I have no income. She's supporting Sarah and me.

The next day I receive a letter from Mom. She sends me the summons that I have to appear in court on a certain day. She writes that I have to come back for this court appearance and must bring Sarah with me. I don't want to go, but I have no choice.

Trying to think of the future, I talk to Lily, Jo's best friend, and she offers me a solution. I tell her I'll think about it and get back to her.

Autumn is here, and Sarah and I have no choice but to go back to Kolfield because of the summons. It's difficult arriving back to where I had so many wonderful, happy memories and so many painful, sad memories.

With the leaves changing color and the cool air touching my face, it feels like home. Mom and Dad are happy to see us. They love Sarah, as if she's their own child.

That evening we talk as we sit around the table and laugh at Sarah as she makes funny sounds and funny faces. She's now five months old. Mom and Dad are looking forward to tomorrow so everything can be over with once and for all.

Mom and Dad had put up a crib for Sarah in my room and removed one of the dressers. They think of all of these things.

Exhausted from traveling today, I'm glad to go to bed. As I lie in bed, I realize how much I've missed the clean smell of the sheets, Dad's cigarette smoke, and Mom's Coty powder, and the train's whistle as it takes away more black coal. Naturally, I cry.

The next morning I dress Sarah, and Mom takes her downstairs while I get dressed. I glance around the room and remember the days and nights I sat here, slept here, cried here—all because of a broken promise.

I don't know what to expect in court and will be glad when it's all over.

I think of my conversation with Lily. Jo doesn't know I talked to her, as she's upset with Lily right now. Last week Lily told Jo I should live with her. That really upset Jo even though she's been on my case about getting a job. It's not that I'm not trying.

Anyway, Jo is changing. She found out she's pregnant again, and Katie is only fifteen months old. She and Nick argue a lot, and I'm afraid maybe I'm causing it.

Lily understands what's going on and says I can stay with her in her apartment. Since she lives right in town, I can walk to work. She doesn't know of any babysitters though. Her suggestion is I leave Sarah with my mother and father until I can save some money and get my own place. No matter what and how much it hurts, I have to think of all of these options. *Damn you, Ben!* No, I can't blame him. I was just as guilty, but I've paid for my white lies.

"Anna, it's almost time to go. Bring Sarah's sweater and hat down. It's quite chilly out so early in the morning."

"I'm coming," I say as I walk past the mirror, pausing to look at myself while lifting Sarah's sweater and hat out of the suitcase.

As I walk down the stairs I'm glad that at least I'll get to see Edna and Reds along with Liz and Pep. Of course I can't wait to see Louis and Angela. I know they're all looking forward to seeing Sarah, as Liz called me last evening. She wanted to wish me luck. We'll be together tonight. We're all having supper at Edna and Reds's house.

The ride to the courthouse goes fast, with Sarah asleep in my arms.

Looking out of the car window, I realize how much I do love Kolfield and how beautiful Pennsylvania really is. Seeing the mountains and the colorful hillsides, I'm homesick even though I'm here.

After parking, we walk up the stone steps to the front door of the courthouse. It seems so big and so cold. Naturally, I'm afraid of the unknown.

As we walk in I can smell cigarette and cigar smoke mixed with people smells, such as perfumes and aftershave.

We walk down a long hall with busy people walking by us in both directions. Women's high heels click along with mine. Mom stops and asks a young lady who is walking slower than the others where a certain room is. She points to the stairs and tells us we have to go one floor up and to our right to find a huge room where an information counter is located in the middle.

We walk into the room upstairs, and people are sitting around, as if in a doctor's office. Inquiring at the information counter, we're told to find a seat and sit down until our name is called.

Huge pictures with wide gold frames show past judges. They line the walls with their name and dates engraved on a brass plate underneath. They look stern, and none are smiling. I hope that's not a sign.

Sarah is wearing a little white dress with a collar trimmed in pink, and her natural curly, black hair looks so adorable. I remove her pink sweater and hat and fold them. Mom reaches out her hand and takes the sweater and hat. It's the set that Edna knitted for Sarah.

My green-and-blue–plaid jumper covers a long-sleeve blue jersey. Matching blue nylons adorn my legs, and my high heels make me look taller. I've lost all of the weight I gained while pregnant, and I feel good dressed up.

Mom looks nice in her gray suit and pink blouse, while Dad looks handsome in his white shirt, light-blue tie, and dark-blue suit. Here we are, all dressed up and ready.

All of a sudden, it seems like the whole nightmare is coming back. I'm so afraid to run into Ben. I'm hoping I will but hoping I won't. What do you say to someone who broke your heart into such little pieces?

Sarah starts fussing, and Mom asks, "Do you want me to hold her?"

"No, that's okay. I need to walk anyway."

I walk around, holding Sarah, as she likes the movement. If I stop, she'll cry, as she's bored and really needs a nap.

On one of my trips around the room, a nice-looking man in a dark-gray suit, white shirt, and blue-striped tie approaches me.

"Hi. You have a beautiful baby."

"Thank you."

"I'm a lawyer, and someone told me you're here today because the father never married you and you're a single mother. Is that true?"

Puzzled I say, "Yes, it is. Why?"

"I'm a lawyer, and my wife and I are looking to adopt a baby. We haven't been successful having one of our own. Any chance you'd be interested in giving her up for adoption?"

I balance Sarah on the top of the information counter for a couple of seconds and then shift her to my other arm.

I smile and say, "Sorry but no. I can't give her up for adoption. She's mine."

"Okay, but here's my card in case you change your mind." He pulls a card out of his jacket pocket and hands it to me. "Call me anytime."

"Thank you, but I doubt I'll be calling you." I smile while stuffing the card in my pocket.

I don't see Ben anywhere and wonder where he's hiding. I know he has to appear, but evidently his brother is making sure we don't see each other.

Nervous and not knowing what is going to happen or even why I'm here, I just want to go home. I wonder where home is, as I don't feel like I have one anymore. I feel disgraced and humiliated, and all of this is because at one time I loved someone so much and believed him.

It's time for the grand jury to interview me. My name is called, and I have to take Sarah with me into this huge room with huge windows surrounded by maroon drapes. There are ten or twelve people sitting around a long table in chairs that swivel and can roll back and forth. A gray-haired lady motions me to sit down in an empty chair near the end of the long table. These men and women are looking at Sarah and me, as if they're studying us. I feel so scared and embarrassed to be here.

The gray-haired lady starts by asking, "What is your name, and where do you live?"

"My name is Anna, and right now I live in New Jersey."

I explain my situation of why I'm living in New Jersey. Some of them nod their heads as if they understand.

Then they start asking me all kind of questions about Ben and my relationship with him. How long have I been seeing him? How did we meet? In my own words, is there anything I want to say about him?

I tell them that I love him and he loves me, that we were engaged, and that Ben convinced me the only way we could get married is if I got pregnant. I'm crying hysterically by then. It seems everything that has been held inside of me is released again.

They ask me if I consented to have sex with him, and I said, "Yes, I did. We love each other and were going to be married."

I showed the engagement ring he gave me, the ring that his brother wants back.

Sarah starts crying, since I'm crying, and she senses something is wrong. I try to comfort her but to no avail unless I get up and walk out of the room.

Finally, the gray-haired lady asks, "Is there someone in the waiting room that can hold your baby for you?"

I reply, "My mother."

Someone gets my mother, and I give Sarah to her so I can finish answering the questions.

After Mom leaves the room, I say with tears running down my face, "I don't want any charges pressed against Ben. My father insisted on doing so even though I pleaded with him not to do it. I want no more problems and want to get on with my life. If Ben's brother and his mother hadn't interfered, we would be married."

Wiping my eyes, I continue, "Please, I beg you to just drop the charges against Ben. His brother has already sent me a warning that he would get a group of guys to testify that they had sex with me, and it's not true. I just want to be left alone to raise my daughter."

After what seems like an eternity and more questions, they thank me and tell me to wait outside the room while they make a decision.

Outside I sit down by Mom and Dad, and Sarah puts out her arms and wants on my lap. I hold her and pray silently that this all goes away.

Shortly thereafter, I'm called to go back in. At that time they tell me they're not going to send this to trial. I thank them, as I do not want a trial. I just want to get on with my life.

In addition, I can keep the engagement ring, and Ben has been ordered to pay fifteen dollars per month in quarterly payments. So four times a year I am to receive forty-five dollars. That would be equivalent to fifty cents a day for milk.

At this point I really have no feelings about anything. I just want to find where my home is and who I am.

Chapter 63

Riding home from court I ask, "Dad, what did you prove by doing all of this? I consented to have this baby with Ben."

"Yes, but he promised to marry you, and I want people to know that he's no good. Now everyone knows it, as his name was in the paper with the charges. People should know he doesn't keep his word. He's not a man of honor."

After arriving home, and before we go to Edna and Reds's house, I tell Mom I need to talk to her.

We sit down at the kitchen table covered with a white tablecloth sporting yellow and white daisies. Mom has made us a cup of tea and is filling the sugar bowl. Dad has taken Sarah into the other room while singing to her. She loves his singing and smiles at Dad the whole time. I remember him holding me when I was little and how safe I felt in his arms. What a shame Sarah doesn't have a father.

"Mom, I can't find a job without some kind of transportation. Jo's friend Lily has an apartment in Glasstown, and she says I can live there but I can't take Sarah there. I'd be able to walk to work, but I'd have to find a babysitter and I don't know anyone."

Stirring her tea, she says, "Look, Anna. Just leave Sarah with us. You won't have to worry about her, and we love her so much. Get a job and save some money. Then you can take her with you after you're all settled."

"I hate to do that, but I'd know she'd be safe with you guys. Thanks, Mom," I say, crying while we hug. Dad watches us from the other room with Sarah in his arms.

That evening it feels good to be back with family again. Angela and Louis are growing like weeds. They're so adorable, and I can't stop hugging them. Angela looks so sweet with her curly blonde hair, while Louis acts like a little man with his crew cut and endless questions.

An enjoyable evening with my family goes by so fast. As I watch everyone interact with each other, I realize how much love is in our family. They all stood by me and helped me get through my painful and heartbreaking time. Thinking Mom and Dad didn't love me was a fantasy of my imagination. They showed their love in other ways and were there for me when I needed them the most. I actually feel sorry for Ben, who missed being part of a wonderful, loving family and who will miss the joy of Sarah growing up.

The next day I'm on the bus back to Glasstown by myself after hugging and kissing Sarah good-bye, hating to let her go. Now my mind is racing with so many thoughts. Maybe I should let someone adopt Sarah. What can I offer her? I can't even afford to feed her. The lawyer who was interested in adopting her would probably treat her wonderfully and love her and give her everything she needs, such as clothes and college. What can I give her? I ask myself these questions as the bus moves along the highway and the tears roll slowly down my cheeks.

I'm sitting by the window so no one bothers me and am thankful the seat next to me is empty. Looking out the window and watching the landscape fly by, I wonder if I'll ever be able to trust another man again. I doubt it and close my eyes, knowing there is an open wound inside me that is not yet healed.

Chapter 64

As I run in the rain and try to hold onto my red umbrella, the puddles gush upward and soak my nylons and high heels. Lightning flashes, and the thunder rumbles, reminding me of the storms back home in Kolfield. How I wish I were there. But I'm not, so I grit my teeth and remind myself that I'm back in New Jersey and without my baby.

Finally reaching Lily's apartment, I run up the front porch steps and shake my umbrella before closing it, taking it into the house to the bathroom so it can drain in the bathtub. Lily is working three to eleven, so I have the apartment to myself.

After changing my clothes and grabbing a slice of cheese, I recall how sad it was leaving Sarah behind. It was difficult making these decisions, but now I have to focus on the future.

After my return to Glasstown without Sarah, my sister Jo isn't happy because I have moved in with Lily. She's happy that I can work, as she knows I'll be getting a job and making money. She was counting on making some money from me by babysitting, but she lives too far away and I don't have a car.

After resolving our differences in my moving, it doesn't take me long to get my stuff together. Lily picks me up in her 1955 green Chevrolet.

Lily's apartment isn't the greatest place, but it is a place to sleep.

Situated on the first floor it has one large bedroom, and I have to share Lily's bed with her. The wallpaper is dark and dingy, and I just know there are cockroaches in the bathroom. The kitchen is small and so is the living room. The apartment smells of many cooked meals and old cigarette smoke. It needs a strong wind to blow through it, cleansing the air. It also needs new wallpaper. I'm so thankful that my baby, Sarah, does not have to live here.

When I return from Pennsylvania, I apply for several jobs and accept one with an adjustment bureau. It's a one-man satellite office with the home office located in Atlantic City. The office is small but big enough for my desk and two filing cabinets. My boss, Jay Culbert, has his office in back of mine but is rarely there. His job is to travel around looking at wrecked cars for insurance companies, make offers on them, and notify auto repair shops of these totaled cars. They can then bid on them so they can salvage parts for their shops.

Jay is tall, handsome, and rugged-looking. He is a great guy who is always bragging about his wife, Maggie, and their five children, who range in age from one year to ten years. His desk is covered with pictures of them. I see him only two or three times a week, but we call each other every day so we both know what is happening. Sometimes he comes in at night and leaves dictation tapes for me on my desk.

Not long after starting the job, I become friends with a legal secretary, Peggy, who works across the hall. She's a very tiny, thin, gray-haired lady. Her nose is long, matching her long face, but her huge faded-blue eyes grab attention immediately. She is eloquent and loves telling funny stories and making me laugh. She has worked for many lawyers over the years.

Almost like a lawyer, she's very inquisitive but friendly. After a few weeks and many questions, I confide in her, explaining my circumstances and why I'm living in Glasstown. She's very understanding and wants to help me in any way she can.

Once a month on Fridays we lunch at the Cumberland Hotel. Peggy's generosity is overwhelming, and she insists on paying the check, saying she invited me.

The Cumberland Hotel is where all the lawyers, doctors, and everyone who is anyone dine at lunchtime. Linen tablecloths, cloth napkins, water glasses, and china dishes adorn the tables with a centerpiece in the middle. Once again, I think of Mom and am thankful she taught us manners and what silverware to use when we eat.

A couple of weeks later Peggy wants to introduce me to her boss, Mr. Klemstein. She confesses to me that she told him my story and he'd like to meet me.

A time is set for after five o'clock so it doesn't interfere with my work schedule. She's still working when I walk into her office, and she immediately stops typing and stands, saying, "Follow me. He's in his office." She doesn't believe in wasting any time.

Entering the door, she says, "Mr. Klemstein, this is Anna, the girl who works across the hall. Remember I told you all about her and you wanted to meet her? Well, here she is."

He stands up and walks around his desk, motioning to a chair. "Come in, come in. Don't be bashful. Have a seat."

His salt-and-pepper hair matches his expertly shaved mustache on his upper lip. He has on a three-piece tan suit, white shirt, and gold tie that all blend with his shiny brown wingtip shoes.

I notice the diplomas on the wall behind his desk and a picture of his wife on his desk. Her beauty is stunning. Another picture on the wall shows his three sons and him on a skiing trip.

I sit down, and Peggy sits in the chair beside me so we both face his desk.

After talking for about fifteen minutes about Glasstown and work, he leans toward me and says, "Peggy told me your story, and I sympathize with you. I just want to warn you that you must never tell anyone that you have an illegitimate child. They frown on that."

"But it's the truth," I say, smoothing my skirt over my knees.

"Yes, it's the truth, but you must remember people love to gossip, and that's what will happen if you tell anyone. You're lucky it was Peggy that you told, as she won't tell anyone but me."

"I hate lying. That's what got me into trouble in the past."

"You have to remember that sometimes people can be vicious, and other people just plain love to gossip. It makes them feel important. Don't forget, no one's perfect."

The three of us talk about Ben and my story. I leave out no details. When all done, I stand up to go and he stands and shakes my hand, saying, "Remember, don't tell anyone that you're an unwed mother. It will only bring you more grief."

I nod my head and walk out. As I walk down the stairs to the bottom floor, I can't believe so many people actually dislike or are against unwed mothers.

After that day, Mr. Klemstein always stops and talks to me when he walks down the hall. I know he's headed for the men's room because he's carrying his newspaper and that's the only place past my office.

I know he meant well that day when he talked to me, but I hate lies.

Then disaster strikes!

Chapter 65

⁓⁓⁓

The day after Thanksgiving, Jo and Nick are downtown shopping. The phone rings at Lily's, and it's Nick's sister, Lucy, calling from their farm.

"Anna, do you know how to get hold of Jo and Nick? Mom's babysitting, and Katie's very sick. They're taking her to the hospital now, but we need to find Jo and Nick."

"Jo told me they went shopping downtown."

Lily had just made a cup of coffee and is sipping on it as she walks into the room and sees my face. "What's the matter?"

"It's Nick's sister. They need to find Jo and Nick. Katie's sick."

"Come on, I'll drive you downtown and we'll look for them."

"Lucy, we're going to look for them now. I have to go."

We grab our jackets and rush out the front door. Lily and I jump in the car, praying it will start, and it does. With the windows down, we ride down Laurel Street, slowly searching the faces in the crowd of shoppers. I spot them coming out of Rooney's Department Store.

"Jo, Jo!" I yell.

She turns around and waves at me with a big smile.

Lily stops the car in the middle of the street, and I jump out and run to Jo.

"You both have to get to the hospital right away. Katie's sick. I don't know what's wrong with her."

They run to their parked car a few yards away, and the tires squeal as they drive out of the parking space. I wait for Lily, as she has to ride around the block. Jumping into the car, I tell Lily to hurry, and a few minutes later she drops me off in front of the hospital.

When I open the emergency room door, I see several people waiting but not Jo or Nick. One has a hand injury, and another boy is holding his arm and accompanied by his mother. The smell of medicines and antiseptics hits me, triggering memories, and nausea overcomes me. *No,* I tell myself, *I will not be sick, I will not be sick.* Overcoming it I go to the main desk and ask the nurse where I can find Jo and Nick.

Just then I hear crying and screaming. Nick is holding Jo up, and they're coming out of a room at the end of the hall with the doctor.

"Anna, Katie died. She's gone," Jo screams. "I have to see my baby."

"No, that can't be," I yell as I run and hug her.

Nick says, "You better come to the house, Anna. Jo needs you right now," he says as tears slide down his face. "We're going to see Katie now but will be home soon."

"I'll be there waiting for you." I sob.

At their house, Nick's sobbing mother explains to me, "I was babysitting and getting supper ready. Katie walked into my father's room. She saw a little stool, pulled it over to his dresser, climbed up, and found his red heart pills. When I discovered she wasn't in the kitchen, I went in there and saw that she had taken some pills. I called the doctor who prescribed the pills, and he said even if she took any, they wouldn't hurt her. So we sat down to eat, and suddenly she started throwing up. I called Katie's pediatrician, who told us to get her to the hospital immediately, but it was too late."

As word spreads, the neighbors arrive with sympathy and food. I call Mom and Dad to tell them. They call back later, saying they're all coming down the next day.

I try to console Jo, but all she keeps saying is "I told them if Katie ever got sick, call our pediatrician. Why didn't she do that immediately? Why wasn't someone watching Katie? Why did we go shopping? Why, Anna, why?"

After getting her calmed down, I talk to Nick. He's quiet but you can tell he's upset, especially since it happened at his mother's house and it was his grandfather's pills.

With all the people and details to attend to, the time goes by fast and it's time for the funeral. It's heartbreaking to see such a little casket lined in pink with a beautiful little girl lying in it. I still can't believe this has happened.

All my sisters and Mom and Dad are crying. My tears won't stop, even when I think all my tears have been shed.

Jo passes out at the funeral and screams when they lower Katie into the ground. Nick holds her tightly. All of us are sobbing when we return to the cars.

After everyone has gone home, Jo tells me while starting to cry again, "You know the last time I saw Katie alive was when we walked in the hospital. They were running down the hall, carrying her, and her long blonde hair was hanging down. I'll never forget that scene."

There's nothing I can do but hug her and cry with her. I don't know what I would do if I lost Sarah like that.

Two weeks later Jo goes blind. She can't see anything, and the doctor says it's hysterical blindness and will eventually go away. It lasts for a few days, but everything seems to have gone wrong for her. She's pregnant and doesn't know if she can handle it.

We all miss Katie so much, remembering how she liked to hold her little nightgown up while dancing and clapping her chubby hands when we clapped. She was only sixteen months old but so smart and advanced for her age. We try to take one day at a time, and I pray for Jo.

Another Christmas comes and goes. My memories of the good holidays while growing up help me get through all of this—the good old days when I couldn't wait to grow up. But now I realize that growing up brings a lot of responsibilities.

Chapter 66

It's January, and the adjustment bureau that I work for informs me they're going out of business. I've only been working several months, and now it seems like I'm never going to be able to get ahead and bring Sarah to live with me.

When Mr. Klemstein finds out I'm going to be out of a job, he informs he knows the owner of a company where he can get me a job. It's Silky Soft's, a manufacturer of high-quality lingerie, nightgowns, and robes for women.

He explains that he'll tell the manager my story, but I must never tell anyone else. On the application I have to check that I'm single (which technically I am) and have no children, which is another white lie.

I want to put down that I have a child, but he says I can't do that, as it'll only create problems for me.

I get the job immediately after applying, and I start working right away. Of course, I have Mr. Klemstein to thank for the speed in getting me this position. Working in the sales department keeps me busy, and I enjoy it very much. In addition, they have a small retail store for employees where there are fabulous prices on negligees. Hopefully, someday I'll be able to afford to buy these beautiful items for Mom and my sisters for their birthdays.

I keep to myself and try not to get too friendly with anyone.

Sharon, the office matchmaker, always talks to me and we become friends. After knowing her for two months, I tell her about Sarah and how I am trying to save money to bring her to live with me. She doesn't condemn me but listens to my story and can only say, "Damn men."

On a busy Thursday morning, a good-looking salesman with blond hair combed in a nice wave appears for his quarterly meeting. A smile lights up his face like sunshine, making his green eyes sparkle. I have never met him, but he does give me a nice smile when passing my desk.

Sharon says his name is Van. Knowing Sharon is my friend, Van asks her to introduce me to him. After the introduction, he asks me out. I really don't want to go out with anyone but tell him I'll think about it.

But Sharon won't leave me alone and convinces me later that I need to get out. At the time, I'm not aware that Joan, another girl in the office, has a crush on Van.

Finally at the end of the day, after his meeting, Van arrives at the front of my desk. "Well, did you think about it? Will you go out with me?"

"Okay, I'll go out with you."

"We'll go see the Globetrotters in Atlantic City. How about this Saturday night?"

"All right, what time?"

"How about six o'clock? What's your address?"

"Here's my sister's address. That's where I live."

I certainly don't want him picking me up at Lily's apartment. This way Jo and Nick will be home and I won't have to ask him in afterward.

Saturday night arrives, and precisely at six o'clock he picks me up at Jo's house. Lily had dropped me off there earlier for the weekend.

Jo is still sad but quite impressed with Van. I doubt if she'll ever be happy again and hope this new baby will help her.

Van is driving a brand-new Buick, and he opens the car door for me. It smells so good as I step into the passenger side. It's a musky smell and must be his aftershave. After he's sure I'm completely in, he closes the door and walks around the car to the driver's side, slides in, and smiles at me.

As we drive to Atlantic City, which is about an hour and a half away, we talk about Silky Soft's and the lingerie they manufacture.

Arriving in Atlantic City, he finds a parking lot close to where the Globetrotters are playing. When we walk to the ticket window, he says to the man in back of the glass window, "Two, please."

"I'm sorry but we're all sold out."

Van looks at me with a dejected look on his face.

"I must apologize. I should've gotten these tickets two days ago, and now they're sold out."

"That's okay. I'll see them another time."

"Is there anything else you'd like to do? We can go to the Five Hundred Club."

"I've never been there but okay." I've never been there and don't even know what it is.

We walk in the club and it's quite dark, but cigarette smoke floats around the dim lights. The waitress asks if we want a table, and Van says, "Are you hungry? Do you want something to eat?"

"No, thank you. I ate at home."

"Okay, then, let's sit at the bar." He turns to the waitress and says, "We'll just sit at the bar, if that's okay."

"That's fine," she says.

"I'll have a Coke," I say while looking around, since I've never been in a club before. There are a lot of tables with lit candles and a big bar surrounding a small stage. In the far corner an older man is playing love songs on the piano. I really don't need that.

"Make that two," Van says. "I'm driving."

I ordered a Coke because I don't drink and, besides, I'm underage.

After about an hour, two Cokes, and a lot of love songs, I don't feel comfortable with the whole bar scene and finally ask, "Would it be all right if we go home now?"

"Sure, not a problem. Is there somewhere else you'd like to go?"

"Not really, I don't know anything about Atlantic City."

He holds my hand while we walk to his car, and again he opens my door for me. He's so mannerly and treats me so nicely.

On our drive back to my sister's, our conversation is about various topics, from sisters and brothers to language accents from different parts of the country. We enjoy our conversation, but before we know it we arrive at my sister's house.

The front house light and the lamppost are on, and the neatly trimmed bushes along the walk look so pretty. Even with her mourning, Jo keeps busy and still has the best-looking house on the block.

After pulling onto the blacktop driveway, we sit in the car for a few minutes talking. As I place my hand on the door handle to get out of the car, he touches my arm and says, "May I kiss you?"

I nod yes, and he leans over and kisses me on the lips. It's a nice kiss but doesn't make me tingle.

"May I see you again? This time I'll take you somewhere really nice."

"Sure, just let me know when," I say as he gets out to open the door for me.

After he opens my door, I stand up and he kisses me again and says, "I'll call you or see you at work next week. We'll plan something."

"Okay, and thanks for a nice evening."

"No," he says, "thank you."

As I open the front door, I think, *Okay, so no drums are beating or bells ringing but still he's very nice.* Besides, I don't think I can trust another man after what Ben did to me.

My sister is waiting for me in her housecoat and nightgown, curled up in a chair. I kick off my high heels and flop on the couch.

"How are you doing, Jo?"

Sadly Jo says, "Okay, Anna, it doesn't get any easier, and I miss Katie so much."

"I know," I say softly. "I miss her too."

Trying to change the subject, Jo says, "Now tell me all about your date. Did you have fun? He's a good-looking guy."

"Well, first of all, we didn't get to see the Globetrotters, as they were sold out of tickets. We did go to the Five Hundred Club, but it's just a bar, and you know how I dislike bars. Besides, I'm not twenty-one yet."

She smiles. "It seems everyone goes to bars. The Five Hundred Club is supposed to be a really nice club. Didn't they ask for your ID?"

"No, I'm glad they didn't. Anyway, I ordered a soda, since I don't like to drink. Van knows I'm not twenty-one, but he says I could have a drink if I wanted one. I told him I'd prefer soda, and he didn't push the issue."

"Are you going to see him again?"

"He said he wants to see me again and will give me a call, but you know how that goes. He did say he'd see me at work on Monday, since he'll be in town all next week for meetings."

Chapter 67

Monday arrives with the need for raincoats and umbrellas. I'm looking forward to seeing if Van looks any different since we went out. I'm hoping I'll have more feelings for him when I see him again.

After drying off and sticking my purse in my desk drawer, I sit down at my desk. I wish I could have a picture of Sarah on my desk, but she's my secret. A coworker, Joan, looks over at me and gives me a dirty look. She doesn't speak to me and walks away when I move forward to her desk. I have no idea why she's upset with me.

Later that morning Van walks by my desk so he can say hi to me. He gives me a big smile and says, "I'll call you this evening. I'm going into my meeting now but doubt I'll be out before you leave."

"Okay," I say and return his smile.

After a hectic day at work, I go home and wait by the telephone for his call. It never comes. The next day I see him, but he doesn't say anything to me and avoids me. He's talking to Joan and she looks very happy.

Now it's lunchtime and I smell stuffed peppers coming from the cafeteria. I think I'll just settle for something light today, as my stomach is in turmoil as I wonder why Van isn't talking to me.

I sit down at a table with a bowl of chicken noodle soup, not looking at anyone.

Sharon comes in and sits in the seat next to me. She whispers to me, "Oh, Anna, I'm so sorry. Believe me, I never would have said anything if I knew how mean Joan really is."

"What are you talking about?" I ask while folding my napkin on my lap and picking up my spoon.

"I told Joan that you have a child and were never married and how important it is for you to save your money so you can have your baby with you. I didn't know she'd tell Van. Please forgive me."

I freeze. The pain shoots through my body. *Not again.* I hurt so badly inside but say, "Don't worry about it, Sharon. Van doesn't mean anything to me. Besides, it's the truth. Now sit down and eat your lunch."

I never hear from Van again, but he does start dating Joan and continues to do so.

It hurts me so much to think people believe that having an illegitimate child is one of the most horrible and sinful things. I suppose this so-called sin will always be my albatross, hanging from my neck for all to see and condemn me. Never can I change that.

As I go to sleep that night, I wonder if any of this will go away. So many questions run through my mind. Can I ever love another man again, or am I branded for life? Will there ever be another man who loves me?

For someone to love me, he will have to accept me as I am and love my daughter. As I lie there, I pray for the future but wish I could be back in my bed in Kolfield, listening to the train whistle one more time before my innocence disappeared with Ben.

Chapter 68

$\mathcal{It}$ is the beginning of March, and Sarah will be one year old in May. Saving money is not as easy as I thought—with rent, my lunches (which I can't give up, as I don't eat any supper), and the bus to get to and from work. When the days get longer, I'll walk, but now it gets dark so early. I feel safer taking the bus.

I'm at the point where I don't know how I'm going to save enough money to bring my baby to live with me. When she lives with me, I'll have to pay a babysitter and buy food and clothes for her. The fifty cents a day I receive from Ben goes right to the milk bill, as Mom and Dad pay for everything else for her. I know Liz and Edna buy clothes for Sarah too.

I've been looking for and finally find an apartment, as I feel I'm hindering Lily's lifestyle. It's on the third floor and has a kitchen and a living room. All I need to buy is a sofa bed, and I'll be all set. It'll be perfect.

Mr. Bloomberg, an attorney, owns it. He and his family live downstairs, where he also has his offices. He wants me to help him a few Saturday mornings in his office, and that will help with the rent. He'd also like me to babysit in the evenings when he and his wife go out. I'm so happy. Now it won't be long before I can have Sarah with me.

Mom and Dad love Sarah so much, and she loves them. I go back to visit at least once a month or every six weeks, but it's difficult to go back and forth and save money. Mom and I write a lot of letters, and she sends me pictures. I know Sarah's getting the best care. It's better than leaving her with strangers in a strange town. Besides, I can't afford to pay a babysitter and work too.

I smile as I recall when Jason, a friend of Jo's, became a good friend of mine and brought Sarah and me home to visit my family for a couple of days. He's from Pittsburgh, so he was coming this way anyway—or so he said.

This last time I went home, it was by bus, and we were having a family get-together. Curious Louis looked up at me and innocently asked, "Aunt Anna, where's Jason?"

I have to admit Jason was handsome, charming, and had a great personality. He lost his hand in a machine while working one day and wore an artificial hand, shaped like a fist and made of wood. The hand had no movement, so it was obvious it wasn't real even though it was painted the color of skin. If he didn't wear the hand, then he'd have to wear a hook. He felt most people feared a hook, so he preferred the artificial hand.

We always play pinochle when my family gets together, and that time was no exception. The problem was Jason couldn't hold the cards with one hand and play them too. So Pep and Reds thought about it and came up with a solution. They got a wax paper box and set it in front of him so he could place his cards in the closed box sticking up.

It worked perfectly, but naturally Louis said to Jason, "How come you have a funny hand? It doesn't look real. What's wrong with it?"

Liz jumped up and grabbed Louis, saying, "Don't you have to wash your hands, Louis? They're awfully dirty."

Jason and I just smiled at each other, since I knew that remark didn't bother him. He knew Louis was being curious. Afterward he explained all about his hand to Louis. Yes, Jason was a very nice man and was a true friend.

Looking at Louis, I told him, "Jason couldn't come. He had a doctor appointment."

He thought about it for a minute and then said, "For his hand?"

"Yes, Louis, for his hand."

"Are they going to give him a new one?"

"No, honey, they just have to check it every so often," I said as I squeezed him and started kissing him all over his face.

"Stop, stop," he managed to blurt out, as he was hysterical with laughter.

Chapter 69

Fridays are paydays. On my lunch hour, I walk from Silky Soft's down Broad Street and across the bridge to the bank, where I cash my check.

A new girl just started working with me a couple of weeks ago. Suzanne Winner is a redhead who's energetic, always laughing, and has a very positive personality. She has a cute turned-up nose and freckles galore. Suzanne is married but her husband, Rod, seems like a very quiet person and quite opposite from her.

We became good friends and, when she asks about my personal life, I tell her the truth. I'm sick of white lies.

It's the first Friday in April, and Suzanne wants to walk to the bank with me. As we walk downtown, Suzanne, with her long red hair moving about in the breeze, says, "You know, Anna, you need to get out and have some fun. You just can't work, work, and work."

"I have no interest in going out and, besides, I can't afford it."

"Come out with me tonight. I've been invited to a private party, and I can bring you as my guest. We'll have a lot of fun."

"No, really, I don't want to."

"Do you think the guy who jilted you is sitting at home pining over you? Hell, no, he isn't. Come on out with me."

After a little more coaxing, I accept her invitation.

At seven o'clock she picks me up in her sister's car, and we drive to a house on the main street. She parks and says, "Come on, let's go in."

I have my doubts, but she reassures me. I know I won't know anyone.

As we climb the porch stairs, the front door opens and a thin man, slightly balding, in a nice white shirt with no tie says, "Come on in. You're at the right place. May I take your jackets?"

"That's okay. I'll just keep mine," I reply, clutching the front of it.

Suzanne takes off her jacket and hands it to him. He winks at me and leaves us to wander around. The smell of liquor and cigarette smoke is everywhere. Men and women are standing around, talking with drinks in their hands.

This must be a man's house by the looks of the furnishings. The walls are bare, but the floor is covered with a large Oriental carpet. There's a black couch, chair, and TV—no desk, no pictures. It's livable but sparsely furnished.

Watching the women drag on their cigarettes makes me wish I could smoke, but I don't know how and I can't stand the smoke in my mouth. Jo smokes, so maybe I'll get her to teach me how to do it.

After a while one of the men in white shirts comes over and introduces himself. "Hi, I'm Jim. I don't believe I ever met you before. Are you new around here?"

Suzanne laughs and says, "You have to get a better line than that, Jim."

"Hey, Suzanne, I didn't see you standing there. I was so enthralled by this young lady that I only had eyes for her."

"That's okay. Since it's Anna, I'll forgive you."

I stare at him and realize he's a nice-looking man but too old for me. He must be in his early forties.

"Aha, so your name's Anna," he says, holding out his hand for me to shake it.

I shake his hand and say, "I'm glad to meet you, and, yes, my name is Anna."

"What would you like to drink?"

"Pepsi, if you don't mind."

"Don't you want a beer or a mixed drink?"

"No, a soda is fine."

He leaves to get me a soda, and I notice that Suzanne has disappeared. *Where in the heck did she go?*

When I look at everyone, they seem to be much older than me. A couple of the women smile at me and I smile back.

Walking over to one of the women, I ask, "Could you please tell me where the ladies' room is?"

She points up the stairs. "First door on the right."

"Thank you." I turn to go up the stairs, and Jim is behind me with my glass of soda.

"Here's your soda," he says, smiling.

"Thank you, but could you hold onto it for a minute? I want to use the ladies' room."

He nods, and I can feel his eyes watching me as I climb the stairs.

When I walk in the door, it opens up to a large room that is connected to a bathroom. Evidently, this used to be a bedroom but now has a sofa and chairs and a mirror in it.

There are three women sitting around, and they start asking me questions about where I live and where I work. I suppose they can tell I'm new at this and ask the strangest thing.

"Can you say f-u-c-k?"

I'm shocked but say, "I don't say that word, as it's swearing."

"No, it isn't," says a lady with wavy gray hair and red-rimmed glasses. She has a nice figure, but she looks older, likes she's in her late thirties.

"In fact, before you can leave this room, you have to say that word, as it's the password to get out of this room."

They start chanting, "Fuck, fuck, fuck."

I can't believe they're acting like this. These are grown women. How weird!

Just then, Suzanne walks in the door and says, "Leave her alone. Fuck! That's for her. Are you happy now? Come on, Anna, Jim is asking about you." She grabs my arm and pulls me out the door.

Going down the steps, I say, "They're crazy, Suzanne. They act like children."

"Don't pay any mind to them. They've had one too many drinks."

Jim is waiting at the bottom of the stairs with my soda. He hands it to me, and I take a big gulp and want to spit it out, but the only place would be in Jim's face. I should've, but I'm too polite. It burns all the way down.

"Whoa, that's liquor. I want a soda, not a mixed drink," I say, handing it back to Jim.

"Sorry, must have gotten it mixed up."

With that he leans over and kisses me on my mouth. It's disgusting, and these people are disgusting. Just then a telephone rings, and one of the other guys answers it and says, "Jim, your wife wants you on the phone."

I'm horrified. This Jim is married and at a party, trying to make out with other women. *Oh, my God, I have to get out of here.*

"Suzanne, I've got to go home. I'm sorry. I can walk. You can stay."

"No way, Anna. I brought you, and I'm leaving with you. Come on while I get my coat."

On the way home she tells me a couple of them are married, and a few of them have been seeing each other for years. The place is paid for by all of the men, sort of like a club.

"Who was the gray-haired lady with the red-rimmed glasses?"

"Oh, that was Isabelle. She's been trying to trap this one guy for years. The only way she's going to get him is to get pregnant."

"That doesn't mean he'll marry her."

"He's Italian, and they're believers in marrying a girl they made pregnant."

I just smile and think about how we stereotype people and it's not always true. I know that for a fact. Ben didn't marry me.

"Suzanne, if I had known Jim was married, I never would have even talked to him. Imagine his wife calling there. Where do you think he told her he was?"

"He's a doctor so I'm sure he can make up pretty good excuses. She has to stay home, as they have four sons."

"Wow, are there any men that can be trusted?"

"I don't know. I haven't met one yet. That's why I do what I want to do. You have to learn to do the same."

Chapter 70

The following Friday during our walk to the bank, Suzanne starts on me again.

"Come on. Let's go out tonight. It'll be different, I promise."

"I don't think so."

Her red hair is in a bun today, and she looks beautiful in her tan blouse and dark-brown skirt and matching high heels. My hair is pulled back in a ponytail, and I'm wearing a black skirt with a green blouse and black high heels. We're quite a pair, walking down the street.

"Seriously, we will truly have fun, and if you don't, I'll bring you home."

I really don't care if I go or not, but she insists that she take me to the Line, as it's called. The Line is situated on the Glasstown Pike and consists of several bars within approximately a couple of miles. One of them is called the Hamilton Bar, and we can start there. Since her husband is working tonight, he doesn't care if she goes out or not.

"I don't know. Even though it's payday, I don't have a lot of money, and neither do you."

"Heck, I'll borrow my sister's car. We won't need much money, as we can sip on one drink the whole evening. Come on, Anna, you need to have some fun."

"I never go to bars. I was always taught they aren't a place where a nice girl hangs out. I'm really not a drinker."

"Who cares what people think? They don't pay your bills or feed you, do they?"

"You're right, I guess. Sometimes I just feel inferior."

Knowing my story, she says, "Come on, Anna. You can't live your life like this forever. Don't you think Ben is having a good time and dating?"

"Yes, I guess."

She finally convinces me to go with her. I have to admit she does make me laugh.

She picks me up in her sister's 1954 Buick. We stop at a gas station, where we buy fifty cents' worth of gas, and we laugh. The man pumping the gas smiles and asks, "Where are you good-looking girls headed tonight?"

"We're starting at the Hamilton Bar," Suzanne says with a wink.

"Maybe I'll stop around when I get done here."

"Okay, we'll be looking for you."

With that she steps on the gas and says, "Hamilton Bar, here we come. Anna, you're going to have a good time tonight. I know it."

Upon entering the bar, I have a hard time adjusting my eyes to the darkness. After I can focus, I see a huge bar shaped like a horseshoe occupying most of the room. Next to it is a small dance floor with tables and chairs surrounding the sides. The place is really packed with people. Beer and cigarette smoke odors caress us and surround us, as if we have walked into a light fog.

We sit at the bar even though I feel it's not right for women to do this. But we have no choice, as there are no available tables and chairs.

I don't even drink beer, but we each order one, since it's the cheapest. The draft beers cost ten cents each, and as we sip them we know one beer will last us all evening. I moisten my lips on the glass and pretend to drink, but it's difficult for me, since I can't stand the taste or smell of beer.

While sitting there, Suzanne fills me in on who's who. It seems she knows everybody. Then she points out a good-looking guy whose name is Mickey. She says she'll always love him even though he's single and she's married.

In fact, she tells me a short version of the story of how she was with him the night before she got married. I can't believe that she was with another guy the night before she was going to take her wedding vows. Then Mickey comes over and whispers something in her ear. She laughs and introduces him to me. Mickey is a little taller than Suzanne and has dark hair and brown eyes—Italian, of course. His hair is combed straight back with every hair in place.

They start talking and whispering to each other. So they can have some privacy, I turn and look around. I happen to glance across the bar and see a tall, dark, handsome man. He's leaning with his left hand against the wall with a bosomy woman facing him. She has a drink in her hand and is laughing. I don't know why, but I can't stop staring. Something about him fascinates me.

All of a sudden, he turns and looks at me. Our eyes lock, and I have the strangest tingling sensation flow through my body. My face must be beet red, as I feel hot. I feel so attracted to him. We keep staring at each other until the girl tugs his shirtsleeve.

Finally I turn my head as Suzanne touches my shoulder to ask me a question. Mickey has disappeared.

I don't know what she's saying, but instead I ask, "Don't point, but do you see that handsome guy leaning against the wall on the other side of the bar? Do you know him or his name?"

She replies, "Yep, that's Johnny Morella. Why, do you like him?"

"I think he's really attractive."

"Look, Mickey is taking me home, so why don't I ask him to find out if Johnny can take you home. We can all ride together. Mickey can bring me back later for my car. Come on, we'll go get something to eat."

After a few seconds, and after Suzanne's eyes plead with me (as she really wants to see Mickey), I agree, but not without some reservation. Oh, sure, I would love to have Johnny take me home, but after he finds out I have a child, I'll probably never see him again anyway, so what do I have to lose?

Suzanne waves to Mickey, who comes right over. Placing her hand on his shoulder she asks, "Mickey, honey, do you think you could ask Johnny if he'd like to take Anna home?"

Mickey reaches up and grabs her wrist, pulling her hand to his lips. After kissing her hand, he says, "Sure, I'll find out and be right back."

As he walks away, I watch Suzanne's eyes following him. They do make a nice couple.

"Thanks for doing this for me. I want you to know Mickey and I will always love each other, no matter what."

I want to ask why she married Rod, but this isn't the time or place.

Deep down inside I really do want Johnny to take me home, but I would hate to be rejected again. My thoughts are spinning around. He's so handsome, and the way we looked at each other took my breath away. I always felt I could never love anyone but Ben. When Ben hurt me though, I felt empty inside and thought I wasn't capable of ever loving anyone again.

I wonder if there's any possibility that someone as handsome as Johnny could actually be interested in me.

Mickey comes back within ten minutes and says, "Johnny is already taking another girl home, but his brother, Sam, would love to take you home."

I look around and think to myself, *Who in the heck is Sam, and where did that name come from?* He is probably some goofy-looking guy who really has something wrong with him. I reach for my folded sweater on my lap. I knew the way Johnny and I looked at each other was too good to be true. I have to stop believing in fairy tales and that's there's no such thing as love at first sight.

Why in the world would I ever think somebody could be interested in me? I just went through being rejected big time, a year of really sad memories, and complete and total rejection by practically everyone. For me to believe there is someone out there for me who will love me for me and also love my daughter, I must be crazy.

My thoughts race through my mind, but I am interrupted when Suzanne says, "Hi, Sam, how are you doing?"

When I turn around and see Sam, I've never been so thrilled in all my life. He's the guy Suzanne said was Johnny. Suzanne had gotten the brother's names mixed up. Thank goodness Johnny was already taking a girl home or I'd never have had the chance to go home with Sam, the one who makes me believe in myself again and that there is love at first sight.

Sam and I look at each other and smile. "I don't have a car, so we'll have to ride with Suzanne and Mickey."

"That's okay with me."

Sam puts his arm around me, and we walk through the crowd of people by the bar. We walk past the bosomy girl who is a wee bit tipsy, and she grabs Sam by the arm and says with a slur, "Don't forget to give me a call sometime." He just nods and smiles as we continue out the door into the parking lot.

What nerve she has, saying that to him when he's with me. My goodness, am I jealous? But then I realize I don't own him and really don't know him. I know for a fact that half the time when people are drinking, they don't remember the next day what they said or did. Maybe she'll forget.

I recall drinking one time at Jo's house. It was peach brandy, and she said, "Go ahead, it won't hurt you. Just try a little bit in a glass."

I drank that glass and loved it. It tasted so sweet, and I love sweet things. I kept on drinking it, and before I knew it, nausea overcame me. I ran to her bathroom and kept throwing up. I was sick, and the next day my head was pounding.

Jo and I laugh about it to this day, but I learned a big lesson and will never touch peach brandy ever again.

Sam takes my hand as we walk to the car.

He's wearing a brown suede jacket, and I love the smell of his aftershave. He sits by one door, and I sit by the opposite door in the backseat. Mickey is driving with Suzanne in the front. I think she's there, even though the front seat looks as if only one person is driving the car. They can't get any closer.

Since Suzanne and Mickey really shouldn't be seen together, and because none of us is starving (except me, maybe, for love), we won't stop at the drive-in restaurant. Mickey drives us over a dirt road to a deserted area and parks the car. I think, *Oh, great, now what am I going to do?* I don't ever want to be hurt again.

Suzanne and Mike disappear or seem to melt into the front seat. Sam asks me if I want to sit beside him. We both slide over and meet in the middle, and it feels so right to be with him. He kisses me and I love it. I can't believe that I love his kisses. This is better than kissing Ben.

He says, "You know I've seen you walk downtown on your lunch hour. I saw your long beautiful ponytail just moving back and forth as you walked, just like in the song 'Chantilly Lace.' I hit the horn a couple of times, but you never looked."

"I guess if I heard a horn, I probably thought it was for someone else."

"Next time you should look and wave," he says with a smile and gives me another kiss. I love his kisses.

It is kind of awkward and a little embarrassing for us, with Suzanne and Mickey doing a disappearing act in the front seat. Finally they come up for air.

"Suzanne, don't you think we better leave?"

"Yeah, I'm ready," she says, laughing.

On the way home Sam asks, "Do you want to go to a drive-in movie with me tomorrow evening?"

"I'd love to." It's thrilling to be able to say yes without white lies.

"I'll ask to borrow my mother's car or brother's car, since I don't have one. When I was drafted, I gave my mother my car. I just came home from Germany a few days ago and don't have the heart to ask for the car back."

"So you were in the army?"

"For two long years."

Sam walks me to my door and asks for my phone number, saying he'll call me the next day. The evening ends with a tingling, wonderful kiss that seems to flow through my body. Sleeping Beauty must have felt like this when awakened from her deep sleep.

Chapter 71

Sam telephones me early the next day. "I borrowed a car, and I'll pick you up at your apartment. Is seven o'clock okay?"

"I'm looking forward to it. See you at seven."

I look out the window and, since it's such a beautiful sunny Saturday, decide to walk downtown. The air is fresh, and I enjoy the walk. I notice Peggy sitting on her second-floor balcony as I walk down Commerce Street.

"Hi, Peggy."

"Hey, Anna. Where are you going?"

"Just downtown for a walk, since it's such a beautiful day."

"Do you have time for a cup of tea?"

Knowing how lonely she must be, I reply, "Sure, I'll be right up."

Climbing the many stairs to her apartment, I realize this isn't the greatest place to live, especially for a woman of the world like Peggy.

Knocking on her door, I hear her shuffling around inside—probably straightening up, like we all do when someone visits us.

Opening the door, I'm surprised to see an old man with white hair and a cane sitting in a kitchen chair. He's smoking a cigarette and must be a chain smoker, as the apartment is so smoky.

"Anna, I want you to meet Dan."

"Hi."

In a gruff voice, he replies, "Nice to meet you."

The teakettle starts whistling, and Peggy turns the gas off.

After pouring our tea, she says, "Let's sit outside on the balcony."

She leads me outside, and we sit down. She says, "Sorry I never told you about Dan. He lives with me, but we're not married. We figure we can save money that way."

I don't judge anyone, as I never liked to be judged, so I say, "There's nothing wrong with that."

She pats my hand and sips her tea. It's amazing how many people have secrets.

"How do you like your new job and apartment?"

"I love it. My apartment's perfect for me and so sunny and clean. Now I can really save money to get Sarah."

"Always remember what Mr. Klemstein told you. Don't tell anyone your secret."

"I've found that out, but I'm tired of telling white lies."

After leaving Peggy's, I finish my walk and return home, looking forward to that evening.

The evening is perfect for a drive-in movie. Sam knocks on my door promptly at seven o'clock. When I open the door, my stomach does a flip-flop. I invite him in, and he looks around and says, "You have a nice little apartment here."

"Yes, it's something I can afford right now."

"Where in the heck do you sleep?"

Gee, does he think that I'm going to have sex with him? I hope not. I turn away and say, "Well, my couch opens up into a bed at night."

"I just wondered, as I only see a kitchen and living room."

"The only thing is I can't cook anything here. I do have a coffeepot."

"Well, you know you can hard-boil eggs in that if you want to."

"Thanks for the idea. I'll try it tomorrow."

Since the stairway is narrow, he leads the way down to the outside entrance.

Holding the car door open for me, he says, "You know you can sit beside me if you want to."

I chuckle and slide over.

Sitting close to him makes me aware of his entire body. He's so handsome and mannerly.

It doesn't take long to arrive at the drive-in. After pulling the speaker inside the car and hanging it on a partly opened window, he puts his arm around me and squeezes me. Just before intermission, he asks, "What would you like to eat? I'm a little hungry."

"Well, a piece of pizza, box of popcorn, and a soda."

He starts laughing and says, "You're my kind of girl. I'm glad you like to eat. Let's go before intermission so we miss the crowds."

We walk together down to the refreshment stand, laughing and holding hands. It seems we're so right for each other. All I can think is he's my tall, dark, handsome Italian guy.

Back in the car and after eating our food, we watch the intermission advertisements on the screen. An advertisement comes on about an engagement ring, and he says, "There's something I have to tell you, Anna."

At the same time I'm thinking about telling him about Sarah.

He takes my hand and says, "I'm married."

I stop breathing. I think I'm dreaming. Maybe I don't quite understand him. I pull my hand away and say, "You're married and you're out with me?"

He says, "Please, listen to me. Let me explain."

I know he has just gotten out of the army and has only been home a couple of days, but saying he's married makes everything blurry after that. My thoughts consist of how stupid I am to believe in love at first sight and now to find out he's married.

Oh, my God, it's starting over again. I'm allowing myself to get into a situation where I'm going to be hurt. The sound of his voice is sad, and I hear him through the fog and my confusion.

"We were only married a week and went on our honeymoon. Immediately after the honeymoon I was shipped to Germany. Dorothy cheated on me as soon as I left town. She even wrote me a Dear John letter, asking for a divorce. I couldn't divorce her, as long as I was in the army. I talked to the chaplain and higher-ranking officers, but everyone said I had to wait until I got back to the United States. The first day back, I went to see the priest who married us. Father told me to forgive her and forget and get on with the marriage. I told him I could never forgive her for the two years of suffering she put me through. I told him if that was the way the Catholic Church was, I wanted nothing to do with it. I wanted to know why I couldn't get an annulment, but Father said I should stay in the marriage."

After realizing what Sam is saying, I begin to listen more to him. He explains how the past two years were pure hell for him and there was nothing he could do. She continues to receive his paychecks and spends them as fast as she receives them and also runs up bills in their names.

I feel so sorry for him. It seems he was hurt like I was.

"As we talk, right now, a detective is watching her so I can have grounds for a divorce."

"A detective is following her?" I ask in amazement.

"Yes, if you have a detective's report and pictures of her cheating, then I have grounds for divorce. I already hired a lawyer, and he gave me the detective's name and phone number. So you see, it's just a matter of time before I'm free."

He kisses my hand and smiles at me. I know then it is my turn.

"There's something I have to tell you. I have a daughter who's almost a year old, and I've never been married."

"That's wonderful, what's her name? When can I see her? Is she as beautiful as you?"

I'm amazed that he doesn't look down on me for being an unwed mother.

"Her name is Sarah, and she lives with my mother and father in Pennsylvania. I want to bring her here to be with me, but I haven't been able to save enough money, as I'd have to pay a babysitter."

"Well, that will be easy enough. I'll help you."

"But you hardly know me."

"I feel like I've known you all my life. When I looked over that bar last night and your eyes met mine, I felt we were meant for each other."

"I felt the same way, but I didn't want to say it, thinking you'd laugh at me."

"I'd never laugh at you, but I would laugh with you, if you let me."

Do I trust him, or is he another Ben? My hesitation leads him to say, "I would never be like the guy that got you pregnant. He's a shallow coward not to marry you and love your baby."

We kiss each other, and I know I really do love him, but, still, can I trust him?

Chapter 72

$\mathcal{I}$ buy some eggs and boil them in the coffeepot, and it works. Now I can have hard-boiled eggs to eat. I tell Sam it worked, as he calls me every evening and always tells me he loves me.

When the electric company calls Sam about a job opening, he tells them he wants to think about it for a day or two. He wants to go back to work at the glass plant, where he was working before he was drafted. Going back there will preserve his seniority and credit his time already worked.

The very next day he is called back to work at the glass plant and is happy that now he can help me financially. His mother packs him a lunch every day even though he would rather eat in the cafeteria. She makes him a sandwich that he eats at break time, and a plum and Tastykake that he always saves for me.

The days are happier for me, knowing that I'll be seeing Sam each day. The detective has no problem catching Dorothy committing adultery in the backseat of a car and gives Sam all the information.

Sam turns the detective's report and pictures into the attorney, and his divorce is granted immediately on grounds of infidelity, but there is a waiting period before the divorce is actually final.

After paying the detective, the lawyer has agreed that his fee of twelve hundred dollars can be paid in installments, for which we are thankful.

"Okay, now it's time for me to meet Sarah, and it's time for you to think about bringing her home," Sam says one evening when we are walking downtown.

"Okay, let me call my mom and dad and tell them. I want them to be prepared. I also want them to know that I'll be bringing her back with me soon."

Mom and Dad aren't too happy about giving Sarah back to me, but I've told them all along I was going to come back for her.

The days are getting warmer as summer is fast approaching. Sam has three days off coming up, and they fall on a weekend, which is great for both of us. This way I only need to take one vacation day from work and he misses no time.

Sam picks me up at my apartment bright and early the day of our trip. He's wearing a short-sleeve shirt with tiny red and white checks covering a white T-shirt. The shirts are tucked into nicely pressed khaki pants. He looks so nice and is so handsome. He always looks like he stepped out of a men's fashion magazine.

I have beige slacks and a green top, and all my hair is pulled straight back into a nice ponytail.

Driving back to Kolfield I wonder how Sam and Sarah will react to each other. I'll be watching both of them closely. The trip goes fast, and going through the tunnels on the turnpike and up and down mountains is fascinating to Sam, as New Jersey is so flat.

Sarah's first birthday was several weeks ago, and I feel bad I wasn't there for her. Around noon, we pull into Edna and Reds's driveway, as everyone is supposed to be there for a picnic this afternoon.

Liz limps toward me, as her ankle is hurting her. She hugs me first, and then Edna comes over, wiping her hands on her apron. I introduce Sam to everyone, including Mom and Dad, and everyone shakes hands.

Suddenly Louis and Angela see me and come running over, leaving Sarah standing by herself, holding onto the hammock. They hug me tightly, and Sarah finally sees me.

"Mama," Sarah cries out, reaching her arms outward toward me.

I run to her, swooping her up and hugging her.

"Oh, Sarah, Mommy misses you so much."

She's wearing a pink shirt with hearts on it and little red corduroy pants. Sam walks over to my side, and Sarah reaches her arms out for him to hold her. He takes her from my arms, and she gives him a big kiss. It's love at first sight for Sarah too.

It's good to be back home among family again. As I look around and watch everyone, I realize what a great family I have. Sam and Sarah adore each other and are constantly together.

"Come on, everyone, it's time to eat," Liz hollers as she motions for me to sit by her.

After the picnic, we go back to my old home, and I dread going back into that house. I'm quite surprised that it doesn't upset me like it used to, even though the sad memories are still there.

We discuss everything with Mom and Dad, telling them that as soon as I find a larger apartment, I'll be taking Sarah back with me. Mom isn't too happy, as she's so attached to her, and Dad loves her so much also. I don't want to hold them back any longer, as they should be enjoying their retirement, not starting over with a baby.

"So you just got out of the army, Anna tells me," says Dad. "Do you carry a draft card or something?"

"Yes, I do." Sam reaches into his pocket and pulls out his wallet, takes out the card, and hands it to Dad.

"Hmm, according to this card, you're married."

I smile and think, *That's my Dad, always checking things out.*

"Yes, I was, but I got a divorce. She cheated on me the whole time I was overseas. There wasn't anything I could do about it either until I came home."

"Well, I can understand how you feel. My first wife did the same thing to me."

Now they have not only me but also this in common. It seems then that Dad and Sam really bonded.

We take Sarah with us everywhere we go for the next couple of days. After visiting the coal mines and the Ship Hotel located on the side of a mountain, Sam and I have to return to New Jersey, since we have to go back to work.

Kissing and hugging all around, we leave, with everyone knowing we'll be back for Sarah soon. Everyone seems satisfied.

We start apartment hunting the very next day. After looking at apartments, we find one on the street near the high school. It's a large apartment on the second floor and has a huge bedroom, living room, and kitchen with high ceilings. The bedroom is big enough to have a crib in it too.

Since I don't have any furniture, as the places I rented were furnished except for the sofa bed I bought, Sam and I venture downtown to Feinstein's Furniture Store. Mr. Feinstein has white hair, in contrast to his darker skin, and wears wire-framed glasses that rest on his large nose. He's quite a salesperson and works with his customers. Naturally, he's always ready and willing to help everyone buy furniture from him with easy payment plans. We buy a beautiful four-piece cherry bedroom set and will make weekly payments.

The landlord finds an old kitchen table and chairs that were left there and tells us we can have them for our kitchen. He also supplies us with a stove and refrigerator.

I had already bought the sleeper couch and a chair, so we are all set.

It's an exciting time for me, fixing up our apartment and knowing we're bringing Sarah home to be part of our family.

In one week, the apartment is ready and I move into it. Sam is still living with his mother, two sisters, and two brothers. He's waiting for the divorce to become final so we can be married.

The following week I call Mom and tell her we're coming to get Sarah. She isn't happy, but she knows it's for the best.

When we arrive back in Kolfield, she tries to talk me into letting Sarah stay with them.

"You know, Mom, I said I'd be back to get her when I could afford it. I really do appreciate everything you've done for me, but it's time I take her, as she's my daughter."

"She's right, Daisy. Let her go," Dad says, even though he's going to miss her too.

Eventually Mom gives in and packs Sarah's clothes. We already have a crib that a friend of Sam's mother gave us. Mom hands me the last bill from the milkman. Sam takes it from me and, without a word, reaches into his pocket and pays her.

This time leaving Kolfield, I only feel happiness. An entire year has gone by, but now I'm ready to be the mother and wife I always wanted to be.

Chapter 73

Silky Soft's is closing down their business, and I have to find another job. I search ads in the newspaper, hoping to find any kind of job because I can't afford not to work.

Sam tells me every day to not worry because he'll take care of me, but I can't be like that.

One evening Sam comes up to the apartment after I have just bathed Sarah. She's running around in her pajamas and runs into his arms as soon as he opens the door. He hugs and kisses her but he looks hurt, angry, and sad.

"What's wrong?"

"I just had a fight with my brother."

"Over what? What happened?"

"I asked Mom for the car, and it was okay with her. Then Johnny came home and asked, 'Where are you going, out again to visit that whore?'"

"You mean me?" I ask, pointing to my chest.

"Yes, and I became so angry I wanted to pick up the rifle and shoot him for calling you a whore. I told him he doesn't know you so why would he call you that. He said that you have an illegitimate child so you must be a whore. When I punched him, he told me to get out and never come back."

I see the hurt in his eyes, just as I see the love for me in them too. He was defending me to his brother, something Ben never did.

"Oh, no, Sam. It's terrible that you and your brother are fighting. I'm the cause of it."

"No, you're not, Anna. I love you so much, and he can't call you that."

I start crying, knowing this brand on me will never go away. Sam puts down Sarah and hugs me. I hate crying in front of Sarah and immediately dry my eyes.

"Now, what?"

"I'm going to look for a room tomorrow and move out."

"No, Sam, move in with me."

"I don't want anyone to say anything more about you, even though we're going to get married as soon as my divorce is final anyway."

"Oh, Sam, move in with me. I don't care about people anymore. I feel like we should be together anyway."

After ten minutes of bantering back and forth, he finally gives in. "Okay, but only if you're sure. I'll call my mom later tonight and tell her I'll be over tomorrow when my brother isn't home so I can pick up my clothes and personal things."

"I only hope you and your brother can become friends again. I really feel bad because I'm the cause of it."

"You're not the cause of it, so don't blame yourself."

But deep down inside I know I'm the cause, but that's the way it is and I can't change it.

Sam officially moves in the next day, and since he works shift work, he babysits while I apply for a couple of jobs.

I hope I can find something soon, as I can't expect Sam to support both Sarah and me.

Three days later, the Cola Bottling Company calls me to ask if I would come in to take some tests and be interviewed. I fill out my application, and naturally I have to check I'm single, but I don't list any dependents. This is what Mr. Klemstein had told me to do—not tell anyone that I'm an unwed mother so they don't hold it against me.

After my interview and tests, the supervisor, Nanette, talks to me and says the job is mine if I want it. She explains the pay and the benefits and how great a company it is to work for. The person I'm replacing is pregnant and won't be coming back. I accept the job.

Sam picks me up from work every day, as his mother gave him his car back and she only borrows it when she needs to have her hair done or needs to go grocery shopping. He picks Sarah up from the babysitter for me, and she sits in the front seat, blabbering away.

The job is great, and I handle a lot of money when the men come in after delivering cases of soda, balancing out each day.

After one week, at the end of the day on Friday, Nanette says she would like to talk to me before I leave. I know I haven't done anything wrong, as everything balanced out and she's praised me all week for the great job I was doing.

After closing her office door, she says, "I'm sorry but we have to let you go. The company that bonds our employees will not bond you because you lied on your application. You did not list that you had a child."

"I didn't realize that it mattered. If I said I was married and listed my child, that would have been a lie. If I told the truth and listed I was single and had a child, you wouldn't have hired me. Isn't that right?"

"Unfortunately, that's correct. That's the way it is. Since the bonding company won't bond you, we have to let you go. I'm really sorry about all of this and wish I could change it but I can't. You were doing a fabulous job, and everyone liked you. I'm really sorry."

I pick up my purse and, with tears in my eyes, I walk out to where Sam and Sarah are waiting for me.

As I slide in the car, Sam asks, "What's the matter, babe? Why are you crying?"

"Please just drive away and I'll tell you."

As he drives away I wipe my eyes and tell him what just happened. I've never seen him get as angry as he does then.

"Well, that's it. My divorce is final next week, and we're getting married that day. It's terrible the way people treat you. They don't know what a wonderful, smart, caring person you really are. They can all go to hell."

After crying on and off most of the evening, I finally realize that I'm so sick of having to lie about my life. Now I dislike Ben more than anything in the world. He walks around with no cares in the world and sends through the court a quarterly payment amounting to fifteen dollars per month. I never thought I could dislike anyone this much, but now I do and hope God can forgive me.

I still need Mom and Dad's permission to get married, since I'm not twenty-one. When I call, they say they'll be there in two days. They're anxious to see Sarah, and this gives them the excuse.

After they arrive, we drive down to Maryland and Mom and Dad sign the necessary papers. There's still a three-day waiting period even though we don't have to have blood tests.

Mom and Dad tell us about the new house they are building on the lot next to Edna and Reds. This has always been their dream, and finally it's coming true. It will be a three-bedroom ranch with a living room, dining area, kitchen, and even a garage. They've been saving their money, and since I didn't go to college, they can now build their house and afford a mortgage. So everything does work out in the long run. I'm happy and excited for them.

The next day they leave, as they are meeting with the contractor. They want to start building as soon as possible.

The following week I borrow a dress from Sam's sister, Marie. She offers to babysit and comes to our apartment while we go to Elkton, Maryland, to get married. Jo and Nick are going to stand up for us. We really can't afford to get married, but Sam is adamant about it.

Jo finds a babysitter for their new baby girl, and she and Nick drive us down in their car. We have seven dollars in cash on us. After picking up our license at the Clerk of Courts, we ride around, searching for a minister to marry us. The clerk gave us several names and addresses, and we finally choose Reverend Wallins.

We choose him because we like his name, Reverend E. Z. Wallins. That sounds like an honest name, so we park the car and climb the wooden steps to the front porch. Looking left and right, we notice a door with his name engraved on a brass plate on the front of it.

Not knowing what to expect, we open the door and walk into a large room with several couples sitting there, waiting to be married. The smell of flowers fills the room. Jo and Nick sit down while Sam and I register with the lady sitting in back of a medium-size oak desk. We give her our license.

After sitting down, I glance at everyone. There are three couples here, and every one of the girls is pregnant. It seems odd that I'm sitting here to be married and not pregnant. I feel my flat stomach and think I'm dreaming. I can sympathize with them and, yet, am happy for them that they're getting married. Now they won't be branded as unwed mothers with illegitimate children. All of us women smile at each other as our faces glow with happiness.

Two more couples come in after us, and after the ones ahead of us are married, we're called in to the reverend's office. He's an elderly white-haired man with a pleasant round face that lights up when he smiles, and he has a big stomach. He'd make a good Santa Claus if he grew a beard.

He shakes Sam's hand and then Nick's hand and gives me a big hug. Jo backs off, as she doesn't want to be hugged by him, and her expression almost makes me giggle.

In a few minutes, we're married. Just like that! How fast and easy! He fills out the marriage certificate and gives us a special one enclosed in a pretty blue folder. The cost is seven dollars—five dollars to marry us and an extra two dollars for his special marriage certificate.

Seven dollars is all we have, and we're supposed to have lunch afterward. Sam gives him five dollars and says we can't afford the two dollars right now for the special marriage certificate.

"Is there any possibility we can send you the other two dollars later and you can send us that pretty marriage certificate then?" I ask.

He says, "Certainly, but take the certificate with you. I trust you. Here's my card with my address. Congratulations and good luck." He rushes us out the door so he can marry the next couple.

I'm so giddy, and I love Sam so much. I keep touching my wedding band and looking at his wedding band. We couldn't afford matching ones, so we settled for mine with a design while his is plain. I didn't even want a wedding band, but he insisted on it, opening a charge account at the local jewelry shop.

We get in the car and stop at a diner on the way home. Since we only have two dollars, we figure we can each have a hamburger, and we'll share one order of fries and each can have water. This is our wedding dinner.

Sam is supposed to go to work that night on the eleven-to-seven shift. He tells me he has to, as we need the money, but I explain that this is our wedding night. Somehow we'll get over the shortage of money, but we'll always remember our wedding night.

With that, he grabs me, kisses me, and finally agrees.

"I love you more than all the people on this earth that ever have been and ever will be."

"And I love you more than that."

"You know now that we're married, I want to adopt Sarah."

"Really? That would be wonderful, but right now I want you to know how much I love you."

Epilogue

"*Mommy,* look at me." It's a small voice coming from a beautiful curly-haired girl sitting in the middle of a green wading pool decorated with fish. She picks up her pink bucket with water in it and pours it on her chest that is covered by her red bathing suit.

"I see, honey," I reply, smiling while folding her towel. Sitting down on a lawn chair by the small wading pool, we set up for Sarah in our backyard. I realize how fortunate I am.

Sarah is now two years old and is spoiled by Sam's family and mine. Even though I know she's only two, she acts like she's going on twenty as she struts around with sunglasses and a white straw hat covering her curls. She loves to wear pretty clothes, and sometimes we call her a "movie star" because of how she acts. You can't help but love her, as she's beautiful and knows how to win you over.

Sam wants to adopt Sarah before she starts school, but we have to save some money, as lawyers are expensive and we're still paying for his divorce. We've been trying, but I haven't been able to get pregnant.

We're looking for another apartment, because the house we're renting now has been sold. Mom and Dad are coming down to visit, and this will give us more time to look for another apartment.

My mother-in-law, Grace, is fantastic, and I love her very much. She has jet-black hair and wears it pulled straight back into a bun with every hair always in place. She is a kind person and visits me once a week in the evenings, and we sit and have tea, talking about everything. She loves Sarah very much. On Sundays we meet at her house with the rest of the family for her fabulous spaghetti sauce and the best and biggest meatballs ever made. She's very loving, and I'm thankful to have her as my mother-in-law.

I try not to look back on my past, but sometimes it just pops up. Sam's so different from Ben that I know now the Lord works in mysterious ways. Sam and I love each other so much, and we're so happy. At the time I met Ben, I know I was foolish for telling lies and believing in a complete stranger. But it was at a time in my life when I was growing up and wanting to make my own decisions. Everyone has to go through being an adolescent, and sometimes it's more difficult for some people than others, and some never grow up, but we all learn from our mistakes.

Watching Sarah in the water makes me aware of how much I love her and Sam. I don't think of anyone but Sam as her father, because he loves her so much. Happiness floods through me as I look upward and thank God.

What I don't know yet is my secret, conceived out of white lies, lurks in the darkness and, when I least expect it, jumps out to remind me of the time I lived among black coal and white lies. Once branded, always branded.